www.MinotaurBooks.com

The premier website
for the best in crime fiction.

Log on and learn more about:

The Labyrinth: Sign up for this monthly news-
letter and get your crime fiction fix. Commentary, author
Q&A, hot new titles, and giveaways.

MomentsInCrime: It's no mystery what our
authors are thinking. Each week, a new author blogs about
their upcoming projects, special events, and more. Log on
today to talk to your favorite authors.

www.MomentsInCrime.com

GetCozy: The ultimate cozy connection. Find your
favorite cozy mystery, grab a reading group guide, sign
up for monthly giveaways, and more.

www.GetCozyOnline.com

MINOTAUR
BOOKS

Other Mysteries from Joan Hess

The Merry Wives of Maggody

An Arly Hanks Mystery

JOAN HESS

St. Martin's Paperbacks

This is a work of fiction. All of the characters, organizations and events portrayed in this novel are either products of the author's imagination or are used fictitiously.

THE MERRY WIVES OF MAGGODY

Copyright © 2009 by Joan Hess.

For information address St. Martin's Press, 175 Fifth Avenue, New York, NY 10010.

ISBN: 978-0-312-36564-6

Printed in the United States of America

Minotaur hardcover edition / January 2010
St. Martin's Paperbacks edition / February 2011

St. Martin's Paperbacks are published by St. Martin's Press, 175 Fifth Avenue, New York, NY 10010.

10 9 8 7 6 5 4 3 2 1

One

Still water may run deep, but the rapids will leave you bruised and battered in Maggody, Arkansas (pop. 755). That is, if the locals don't get you first. Some of them are devious, some are stupid, and some are merely annoying. My mother falls into that last category.

I kept my eyes on the far bank of Boone Creek as she approached the hickory tree. "I came here for the solitude," I muttered.

"I reckon you can come here for whatever reason tickles your fancy," Ruby Bee said as she plopped down beside me. She does not plop with grace, being a short and sturdy sort with a deceptively benign face. Her blond hair is sensibly short; anyone who mentions the gray roots is liable to regret it long after the chickens have come home to roost in a condo. "Being that I heard tell you've been sitting out here for nigh onto four hours, I thought I'd have myself a nice lunch while I checked up on you. You can have some or not." She opened a picnic basket and started pulling out plastic containers. "Lemme see now, I got fried chicken, pimento cheese sandwiches, dill pickles, potato salad, and a couple of chunks of fudge cake. How 'bout some lemonade, Arly? I made it just the way you like it."

"No thank you."

"Suit yourself, Miss Sulky Pants." She kept shooting sly

glances at me while she munched on a drumstick. "You intending to sit here the rest of the day?"

"Maybe. Is there a reason why that's any of your business?"

"Can't think of one. Dahlia's looking for you, but it's on account of Jim Bob won't let her park in the handicap space at the SuperSaver Buy 4 Less."

I couldn't stop myself from wincing. "She's not handicapped."

"She claims she is, what with the twins and baby Daisy. Not that having a baby should qualify somebody for a handicap sticker. Having babies is normal. If people didn't have babies, well—there wouldn't be any people to not have babies, if you follow me. Sure, it's a chore those first couple of years, but it ain't that hard as long as you got family nearby to help you. I've been there."

"I know you have," I said, relenting enough to pat her on the knee. I relented a little more and poured myself a cup of lemonade. "That's one of the things I've been thinking about. If you don't mind, I'd really prefer to be alone. I'll come over to the bar and grill for supper. Okay?"

Ruby Bee does not respond well to subtlety. "You talked to Jack?"

"Yes, I have. Go away, please."

"What did he say?"

I felt like a hapless hiker being stalked by a mountain lion (although the hiker would have had a better chance than I). "Jack called a couple of days ago to tell me about a fantastic opportunity to join a National Geographic Society team headed for the Brazilian rain forest. Their photographer broke an ankle, so Jack's going to be in charge of filming. He won't be able to get in touch with anyone for six weeks, maybe longer."

"And you let him go?" gasped Ruby Bee.

"I didn't *let* him do anything. He didn't call to get my permission, just to let me know where he'll be and why I won't hear from him." I threw a hickory nut into the water and waited for it to surface. It did not oblige. I wondered if piranhas were feasting on it.

Ruby Bee wasn't interested in nature. "What did you say to that?"

"I told him to watch out for headhunters."

"But not a word about your . . . condition? Are you as plumb loco as Dimson Buchanon?"

I raised my eyebrows. "Is that what we call it these days? A condition?"

"Yes, missy," she said as she picked up the picnic basket, "we call it a condition. We also call it a predicament. You can't spend the next seven months sitting here like a wart on a widow's chin, you know."

"Sitting here's a lot more amusing than peeing on strips of plastic. I have enough of those to build a model of the Eiffel Tower. Run along and let me decide what I'm going to do about this so-called condition."

For a moment I thought she was going to whack me with the picnic basket. She managed to get herself under control, then said, "You ain't thinking about . . . ?"

"I am thinking about all of my options. If I have to climb all the way to the top of Cotter's Ridge to get some privacy, I will—even if it means I'll end up covered with chiggers and ticks." Or tiggers and chicks, if you prefer.

I watched her stomp back toward the highway, smiling when I noticed that she'd left the containers of fried chicken and fudge cake next to the tree. For the record, Jack is a charming man with a lopsided, contagious grin. His hair is shaggy, and whenever he runs his fingers through it, I melt. His favorite attire, except in certain adult situations, is denim. He makes divine blueberry muffins and shares the Sunday newspaper. Neither of us can solve a sudoku puzzle, but we make a helluva team tackling crossword puzzles. Most importantly, he was the sperm donor.

It takes two to tangle.

* * *

Dahlia Buchanon grunted as she tried to lift the double stroller onto the porch. It was heavy to begin with, but even more burdensome with bulgy diaper bags hanging from the handle and boxes of juice in the back pocket. Kevin kept telling her to leave it on the lawn, but she didn't trust that filthy ol' fool Raz not to steal it from under her nose. She was pretty sure he'd stolen her panties off the line a few weeks back.

Kevvie Junior and Rosemarie were racing around the yard, yapping like wolf pups. Her precious Daisy was snoozing in the playpen, although it was a wonder how she could do it with all the commotion. Dahlia wheezed sadly as she remembered what it was like before she'd had the twins, and then Daisy. She and Kevin had used to sit on the porch swing and spoon, or even sneak off to do the sort of things that Brother Verber railed about from the pulpit every Sunday morning. Back then, she'd been Kevin's love goddess, his honey bunny, his beloved for all eternity. These days she was a short order cook, a janitor, a nurse's aide, and a full-time employee at a launderette.

She almost squealed when a male voice right behind her said, "You want some help, pretty lady?"

It sure weren't Raz, she realized as she reeled around to gape at the man. He was tall like Kevin, but his hair was slick like a televangelist's and he was dressed right nice in trousers and a short-sleeved shirt with a tiny logo. He had a funny little mustache that could have been drawn with a crayon. He looked to be a few years older than Kevin, but there was something familiar about him. She squinted more closely at him. "Do I know you?"

"You sure do, Dahlia O'Neill. Well, Mrs. Kevin Buchanon now, ain't it?"

"Mebbe," she said suspiciously.

Chuckling, he picked up the stroller and set it on the porch. "Got a couple of wild ones, I see," he said, gesturing at Kevvie Junior and Rosemarie. "Me and their daddy were little hell-raisers, too. Many's the time we'd get into mischief, and his ma would tan our behinds with a switch. Kevin would blubber for hours like the devil hisself was pinching him."

She chewed on this for a while. "You're kin, ain't you?"

"I'm Bonaparte Buchanon, Kevin's third cousin. His great-grandpa and mine were brothers. There was bad blood between them, and my family ended up outside of Neosho. In Missouri."

"I know where Neosho is."

"You ask Kevin about his cousin Bony, and how I used to yank down his pants in the co-op in Starley City. Uncle Earl got so fed up that he stopped taking us with him on Saturday mornings."

Dahlia didn't much like his smarmy grin. "Kevin'd kick your butt if you tried that now. You best be on your way, Bonaparte Buchanon. I got to fix supper." She looked over his shoulder. "Kevvie Junior, don't make me come over there! Don't think for a second that I can't see what you're aimin' to do to that poor cat. Rosemarie, I don't know who taught you to tie a noose, but you untie it right this minute or I'll paddle your behind until you can't sit down for a month of Sundays!"

"I see you got your hands full," Bony said. "I was hoping to visit with Kevin, but I'll go on to Uncle Earl and Aunt Eileen's house. When Kevin gets home, you tell him that I said he was a lucky guy to land a prize like you, Dahlia. You still have that sexy, full-figured body I remember from all those years ago, when you used to charge me a nickel to touch your titties out in the barn."

He left her standing on the porch, her mouth slack and her multiple chins quivering. She was still staring as he went out the gate and ambled down the road like he thought he owned it.

Mrs. Jim Bob (a.k.a. Barbara Ann Buchanon Buchanon) banged her gavel on the dinette table. "We need to get down to business. The first Maggody Charity Golf Tournament begins a week from Saturday. The Almighty Lord is in charge of the weather, but everything else is up to us."

"Amen," rumbled Brother Verber, eying the plate of lemon squares. They were mighty tasty, all tangy and crunchy. He realized the ladies were watching him. "May the Almighty Lord smile down on us in our humble endeavor to bring aid and comfort to the wretched golf widows all across this fine country of ours."

"It's downright tragic," Mrs. Jim Bob added. "My second cousin's sister-in-law told her that she saw some of these golf widows on *Dr. Phil*. They're alone all the time and have nobody to rely on but each other. Most of them don't even have jobs so they can support their children. They're all thin as rails from malnutrition. Just thinking about how they bravely sit at home breaks my heart." She plucked a tissue out of her purse and dabbed her nose. "It'll mean so much to them to know we care."

The members of the Missionary Society nodded their heads, but they'd all heard it so many times that no one was moved to sniffle. Brother Verber took the opportunity to sidle closer to the plate of lemon squares.

Mrs. Jim Bob had never gotten closer to a golf tournament than on the TV, but she'd done research and was confident that she could organize one. After all, she'd overseen countless church potlucks, rummage sales, and Christmas pageants, and they always went without a hitch. The golfers on TV were respectable and polite.

She opened her notebook. "Green committee?"

Eileen Buchanon shrugged. "Earl's been mowing the fairways in Raz's back pasture every other day, and it's coming along. He plugged Bermuda on what'll be the greens. They'd look better if Raz's mule hadn't trampled all over them after that rain the other day. We got two ponds for water hazards, three if you count that boggy bottom next to Boone Creek. There ain't much Earl can do about the poison ivy, though. The golfers better stay in the fairways."

"Hardly *our* problem."

"I'll have Earl take the posthole digger and plant tin cans on the greens," Eileen continued. "Edwina Spitz is sewing the red flags to attach to the iron poles we found behind the old Esso station. They may not stand up real straight, but they'll do."

Edwina awoke with a jerk. When everybody looked at her, she said, "I agree."

"Very good." Mrs. Jim Bob ticked off the first item. "Hospitality?"

"I've arranged to borrow a revival tent from the Hickory Hollow Evangelical Lutheran Church," Elsie McMay said smugly. "Folding chairs and tables, too. Millicent's gonna have Jeremiah and some of the boys fetch everything on Friday. The SuperSaver's providing paper plates, napkins, and plastic forks. Saturday night we can use the buffet pans from the Elks Club in Farberville. We can just provide doughnuts and coffee on Sunday morning."

"What about the rest of the time?" asked Brother Verber. Despite himself, he leaned toward the glistening lemon squares like the Tower of Pisa. "I hope we're aiming to feed the golfers better than that. After all, man doth not live by bread alone. The Israelites would still be living in Egypt if they hadn't been promised a land flowing with milk and honey."

Mrs. Jim Bob ticked off the second item. "This is for charity. We'll serve sandwiches at noon Saturday, a nice supper later, and doughnuts on Sunday morning. I'm quite sure the Almighty Lord will forgive us for missing church, since it's for a worthy cause. The golf widows will fall to their knees in gratitude that anybody truly cares about them."

"Hallelujah!" Brother Verber said with such piety that tears glistened in his eyes and droplets of sweat dotted his bald head. He clasped his hands. "You're a saint, Mrs. Jim Bob—and the Almighty knows it as well as the rest of us do. Hallelujah!"

"Let's hear from the publicity committee," she said.

Lottie Estes pulled out several sheets of paper, then settled her bifocals firmly in place and cleared her throat. "I sent press announcements to all the area newspapers, but there hasn't been much of a response. A few of them said they'd run it in their community calendar column. The public golf courses promised to pin the flyers on their bulletin boards. Some smirky man from the Farberville Country Club called to find out if this was a real tournament, and I told him in no uncertain terms that it most assuredly was and that I didn't appreciate his attitude one bit. None of the area television stations seem interested."

"Well, they will be," said Mrs. Jim Bob, "when they hear about our prize for the first hole-in-one. Yesterday I went to visit with Phil Proodle." She paused while they gaped at her. "As you all know, he owns the biggest boat dealership in Stump County. After some persuading, he agreed to put up a bass boat that retails for more than forty thousand dollars."

Joyce Lambertino looked as if she'd discovered a sea serpent in the inflatable pool in her backyard. "Phil Proodle's all the time on TV, doing those crazy commercials. Do you recollect the one where he rode an elephant in the lot? I'd never seen anything like that in all my born days."

"Wearing nothing but two skimpy towels, one wrapped around his head and the other around his privates," Millicent McIlhaney added in a scandalized voice.

Mrs. Jim Bob frowned. "That is neither here nor there. What's important is that we get all the publicity we can. This prize is for the first hole-in-one. Not that anyone will actually win it, mind you. Our golf course isn't like those fancy ones you see on TV. There'll be more golf balls in the ponds than beetles in a sack of corn meal. I made it clear to Mr. Proodle that a charitable gesture would get him better publicity than hovering over the lot in a hot air balloon or dressing up like a cowboy and chasing heifers between the boats. He finally came around to my way of thinking."

"A forty-thousand-dollar boat," Joyce said. "Larry Joe's gonna turn pea green. His old rowboat sank last year, and he moaned about it for a solid month."

"He must beware the deadly sin of greed," Brother Verber said. "The river that carries the righteous to heaven is strewn with temptations like fancy boats. The ark was good enough for Noah, even though it was mighty crowded. And don't forget about baby Moses. He came drifting along in a basket made of reeds."

Mrs. Jim Bob was beginning to get irritated by his interruptions. His agenda was saving lost souls, but hers was more pressing. She'd read about charity golf tournaments in the newspaper. It'd seemed like an easy way to prove that Maggody was a town filled with generous Christians willing to do the Lord's work on behalf of the less fortunate. The fact that Maggody lacked a golf course had not stopped her. A quick visit to a public course had provided her with an idea how to fit eighteen holes in Raz's forty acres. She'd given Earl no choice but to help her design the course and then plow up the neglected pasture. When it was time for volunteers, the members of the Missionary Society had stepped forward, although some of them had needed a shove in the back. The one thing she didn't need was a running commentary from the pulpit. "Lottie, you need to send out new press releases immediately. Mention the trophies but emphasize the boat. Now we come to registration."

Darla Jean McIlhaney squirmed as everybody looked at her. Right offhand, she could think of a hundred other places she'd rather be. A slum in India, the dark side of the moon, the dentist's chair, even the front pew of the Voice of the Almighty Lord Assembly Hall, which was within spittin' distance of the pulpit—literally. Her mother had volunteered her because Darla Jean was good with her computer and could use it to keep track of the names and addresses of those who'd signed up. It hadn't been much of a chore. "Uh, as of this morning, seventeen people have sent in their checks for a hundred dollars. There may be more in the next week."

"There'll be at least one more," Eileen said. "Do y'all remember Bonaparte Buchanon, that little hellion that visited here summers? He managed to stay out of prison and took up playing golf. He showed up on my doorstep yesterday. He's a member of the PGA, and swears he earns his living from playing in golf tournaments."

"The PGA? Is that one of those cable channels?" Eula Lemoy asked. When she was staying at her cousin's house, she'd stumbled upon a show with naked people seated on couches and chairs, discussing politics. She'd watched it for most of an hour, unable to believe her eyes.

"The Professional Golfers Association, for pity's sake!" said Mrs. Jim Bob. "Haven't you paid any attention to what we've been talking about for the last three months? I swear, living in that trailer park must not be any better than living in a cave up on Cotter's Ridge like Diesel Buchanon."

Lottie nodded. "I'll put that in the new press release, too. Having a real live professional golfer should help attract more players, along with the bass boat."

"Hallelujah," Brother Verber intoned. He needed to run along home and work on his sermon, but he figured they'd take a break for refreshments pretty soon. He hadn't had a chance to sample Eula's caramel-pecan coffee cake.

By the following day, there was only one topic being discussed in Ruby Bee's Bar & Grill, and it wasn't the weather.

"One helluva fine boat," said Jim Bob Buchanon, mayor of Maggody and owner of Jim Bob's SuperSaver Buy 4 Less. He had the Buchanon look about him—beetlish brow, yellowish eyes, and a curled upper lip. His boot camp haircut accentuated his lumpy skull. He was wilier than most of the clan, however, which is why he reigned over the town like a schoolyard bully. "I'd lick the dew off a bull's balls for a Ranger Z21."

Jeremiah McIlhaney refilled his glass from the pitcher. "With an Evinrude E-TEC, a hydro jack plate—"

"Trolling motor with lift assist," cut in Larry Joe Lambertino, getting misty as he pictured himself out in the middle of Greezy Lake, a beer in one hand and a rod in the other. Joyce would be at home with the kids, getting ready to fry up the fish and a batch of hush puppies. Larry Joe loved Joyce's hush puppies.

"It's a fuckin' shame that some outsider's gonna walk away with it," Jim Bob said. "If any of us was to win it, we could all own shares and take turns using it."

"The problem being," said Roy Stiver, proprietor of Stiver's Antiques: New and Used, "is that none of us can play golf. How are we supposed to win this helluva fine boat?"

Big Dick MacNamara poked him. "Didn't you used to play golf down in Florida?"

"I couldn't play worth a damn, even after a couple of lessons, so I sold my clubs and took up duplicate bridge. The ladies fought over the privilege of playing with me, since I was the only fellow in the club without a catheter bag. I had more homemade pies and cakes than I could eat in a lifetime, and dinner invitations every night. Sometimes, breakfast was included." He leaned back and grinned. "Beat the hell out of trying to whack a golf ball on a hot afternoon."

They stared morosely at the empty pitcher.

From behind the bar, Ruby Bee tried not to laugh at their hangdog faces. "Look at those ol' boys feeling sorry for themselves on account of that expensive boat. It's a darn shame the tournament's not about shooting a mess of squirrels."

"As if you care," Estelle Oppers said as she plucked a pretzel out of the basket. She glanced at her reflection in the fly-specked mirror and absently patted her towering beehive of red hair adorned with spit curls and plastic cherry blossoms. It wouldn't do for the owner of Estelle's Hair Fantasies to be spotted with anything short of a perfectly styled hairdo, as well as thick mascara, orange eye shadow, and an undeniably bold slash of crimson lipstick. "You heard anything new from Arly?"

"Not in the last five minutes since you asked. I'm hoping she'll show up for supper tonight." Ruby Bee went into the kitchen and blotted her eyes on the hem of her apron. She couldn't for the life of her guess what Arly was likely to do, what with her lying low like a groundhog in a cabbage patch. After a stern lecture to herself, she checked on the brisket simmering in the oven, stirred the pot of ham and beans, and went back out the back door. The sign for the Flamingo Motel out behind the bar looked worse for the wear. Another neon letter had flickered out, and now it merely advertised the existence of a VCAY. It sounded like an ointment for psoriasis.

Beyond the gravel parking lot, where many a surly sumbitch had found himself sprawled on his rear end after mouthing off inside, the stoplight seemed stuck on green. The tourists had no reason to stop or even slow down as they headed toward the artificial paradise of Branson, home to has-been celebrities and theme park employees with bright, unfocused eyes. Raz rattled by in his muddy pickup, his pedigreed sow Marjorie riding in the passenger's side. Ruddy Cranshaw's Nash Rambler was trailed by puffs of black smoke. Mrs. Jim Bob drove by in her pink Cadillac, her expression merciless. Ruby Bee wondered if she was hunting Jim Bob, who had a reputation for dalliances at the Pot O' Gold trailer park.

She was about to go inside when a long, sleek black car adorned with blinding chrome rolled by with the majesty of an ocean liner. The windows were tinted, hiding the occupants from view. "Omigod," she whispered. Her knees threatened to buckle. She leaned against the concrete block exterior of the bar and willed herself not to crumple into the weeds. Maybe it was just a trick her mind was playing, she told herself. Or more likely, a similar make and model. It wasn't like there was just one Imperial Crown made forty-odd years ago, and surely a goodly number of them were black.

Nearly ten minutes passed before she made it into the kitchen, splashed water on her face, and went out to the bar. Estelle stared at her. "You're pale as a baby's bottom," she said. "Did you see a mouse?"

"More like a rat," Ruby Bee said as she poured herself a shot of bourbon from the bottle she kept stashed in a cabinet below the cash register.

Tommy Ridner guffawed as his opponent's ball splashed into the creek that ran along the edge of the Farberville Country Club's seventeenth fairway. "You lose this one, you're down a hundred bucks. What say we double up so you have a slim chance to get your money back?"

"Screw you." The man teed up again and sent a second ball into the creek. "I give up. Cash or check?"

"Hey, no hard feelings," Tommy said grandly. "I know you're good for it—you always are. Let's go back to the clubhouse and have a couple of drinks. You seen Dennis Gilbert around today? I want to ask him about some idiot tournament over in Maggody."

"There's a golf course there?"

"So they claim." Tommy stuck his driver in his bag on the back of the cart, then took the driver's seat and grimaced. One of these days he was going to need a bigger cart if his gut continued to grow. Golf was the only sport that did not discriminate against red-faced, sweaty, overweight white guys who smoked cigars and kept flasks in their back pockets. Tommy was in his early forties, with the same blond crewcut and freckles he'd had in college, but his knees creaked when he stood up. He saw a chiropractor twice a week. Pain pills comprised one of his basic food groups. His internist had given up lecturing him about a myriad of health risks, as had his ex-wife, who'd dumped him for a banker with capped teeth and a cloned mansion in a gated community.

"How was Cabo San Lucas?" the loser asked.

"Those corporate boys know how to travel." Tommy veered around a sprinkler head. The club rules forbade driving carts off the paved paths, but it was a helluva lot more fun to careen up the fairways. "Private jet, fantastic house on the beach, servants, and a bartender named Paco who mixed a mean margarita. We played three of the championship courses, but I had to bow out after we went deep-sea fishing. I got into a tussle with a two-hundred-pound sailfish and threw out my back. Luckily, Paco knew somebody who knew somebody who worked in a *farmacia*. I ended up with enough Dilaudid to put half the world out of its misery." He pulled out a plastic pill case and tapped several tablets into his palm. "Want one?"

"Thanks, but I'll stick with martinis."

Tommy downed the tablets as they drove to the clubhouse. He stowed his cleated shoes in his locker and went to the bar. As he'd hoped, Dennis was sitting at one of the round tables. Regrettably, his wife, Amanda, was seated next to him, filing her talons. She wasn't unattractive, but her incessant bitching and expression of total boredom did much to cancel the appeal of her abundant auburn hair and shapely figure. Dennis, in contrast, had the bland good looks of an anchorman for the local TV station, which he was. Brown hair, brown eyes, perfect teeth, and apparently without any opinions whatsoever. Amanda, better known in the locker room as D'Amanda, had enough for both of them, and was apt to spout off after a few drinks.

"How's it going?" Tommy said as he joined them. He leered at Amanda, but she ignored him.

She was, as far as Dennis knew, the only woman at the country club who was unimpressed by Tommy's sloppy charm. The only woman since high school, even. Dennis had always been a gentleman, but he'd been trampled by the women chasing after his best friend, who wore baggy clothes and usually reeked of alcohol. By the time Dennis had ventured to first base with a girl, Tommy had already scored a home run. The hottest girl in college had declined Dennis's invitation to a coffeehouse and squealed when Tommy invited her to a keg party. If Dennis made a birdie, Tommy made an eagle. But now Dennis had Amanda, the love of his life. He smiled when she turned away from Tommy.

Tommy gave up on her. "Hey, Dennis, what have you heard about this golf tournament in Maggody?"

"I was informed that it's a benefit for golf widows."

"Golf widows? You gotta be kidding."

"I'm afraid not. I assumed it was total nonsense until the station received a second press release. It seems that the little town of Maggody has lured in a PGA player. Name's Bonaparte Buchanon. I'd never heard of him, but I checked the list and he's down near the bottom."

"I'm a golf widow," Amanda said, "and grateful for it. I don't know what I'd do if you hung around the house all weekend." She went across the barroom to sit with some of her women friends.

"I've heard of him," Tommy admitted. "He makes the cut every now and then, but he's a real ass-kicker if he wins any money. Buys everybody endless rounds of drinks, makes all manner of crude remarks about the winners, and tries to pinch the butts of all the women under seventy, whether or not their husbands are standing there. He's banned from half the courses in the country."

"Sounds like he should be." Dennis gestured to the waitress. "What's more interesting is the hole-in-one prize."

"A three-legged mule? A portable outhouse? Dinner for two at the local greasy spoon?"

"A Ranger Z21, twenty-one feet, all the gadgetry." Dennis ordered a gin and tonic, then glanced at him. "Want a drink?"

Tommy whistled. "You're fuckin' making that up. How does that crappy little podunk come up with a prize like that? Yeah, maybe clubs like Southern Hills or Diamante can afford to give away new cars or vacation packages, but not . . ." He looked up at the waitress, who was thinking about her unpaid utility bills. "Gimme a Johnnie Walker on the rocks, sweetie. Make it a double and I'll take you on a boat ride."

"Sure, Mr. Ridner," she said with a warm smile. After several drinks, he was known to be a big tipper. Mr. Gilbert and his wife were lucky if they got served.

"Of course, you have to *make* a hole-in-one," Dennis pointed out.

"You think the course is seventy-five hundred yards like Augusta? I can probably chip in from the tee. I've won the club championship seven out of the last ten years, for gawd's sake, and the state tournament three times. I can handle what's likely to be a miniature golf course."

"I'm sure you can handle it, buddy." But not Amanda, Dennis thought smugly as he went over to Amanda's table and helped her scoot back her chair. She was untouchable. Nobody paid any attention to their bickering as they left.

Tommy realized he'd been stiffed for the bill.

Kale Wasson was lying on his bed, swaddled in bliss from the pot he'd smoked. The speakers positioned around his room blared raucous music. Sunlight danced across his face. All the scene needed was a naked girl nestled against him, her hands gently arousing him as her tongue slipped into his ear. Rachel, the blonde in his chem lab, with her pouty lips and beads of sweat glistening on her forehead. Or a brunette like Maria Teresa, who swaggered into homeroom every day and had once smiled at him in the hall. Maybe both of them, kneeling on either side of him, their breasts brushing against him. Kale's face flushed as he imagined their animal growls, their hot breath—

"Are you sick, honey?" his mother said as she opened his door. "You've been here all afternoon. What's that smell?"

"Incense. I'm meditating."

Kathleen sighed. "Wouldn't you be better off practicing your chip shots in the backyard? The tournament is in less than two weeks, and you need to focus on it."

"Why? It's not rated. What's the prize? A twenty-dollar gift card for Wal-Mart? I've got better things to do than waste my weekend at some two-bit tournament with a bunch of pathetic losers who've never broken par."

She came into the room, opened a window, and began to pick up his dirty clothes. "Not all pathetic losers. They've snagged a PGA player and a couple of people you know. Would you please turn down that awful music? I don't know how you can stand it in here." She gave him a moment to comply, then did it herself. "Besides, you need the practice for the PGA Junior Tournament. If you want to get a golf scholarship for college, you're going to have to get your name mentioned in the media."

"What PGA player?"

"I don't remember the name. I do know that Tommy Ridner and Natalie Hotz are on the list, along with some golfers from Little Rock, Dallas, and Memphis. The prize for a hole-in-one is an expensive fishing boat. If you win it, we can sell it and get enough for you to go to more tournaments. As it is, I can barely pay the rent."

"You want me to blow my amateur status?"

Kathleen Wasson carried the bundle of clothes to the doorway. "We'll cross that bridge when we get to it. It's not too late to play a few holes at the public course. You wouldn't want to lose to Natalie, would you?"

Kyle did want to lose to Natalie. He wanted to lose his virginity to her in the moonlight, on a soft blanket, with birds singing from the treetops. He rolled over and recast his fantasy.

Natalie was losing to Janna Coulter, who was thudding around the apartment in a worn gray sweatsuit. She reminded Natalie of a rogue elephant in search of a village to devastate. "I don't want to go running today, okay? I must have run like fifty miles this week. I want to go out to the pool, drink a soda, and read a magazine that's about clothes, not about friggin' golf."

"Stop sniveling," Janna said. "We've been over this so many times that I'm about to throw up. Right now you have the potential to burst into the LPGA after a win at the U.S. Women's Amateur. That means endorsements, which translate to millions of dollars. You're young, beautiful, and one of the best female golfers in the state. The media will fawn all over you, as long as you maintain your reputation as an innocent young lady. Those college kids by the pool have cell phones with cameras. One photo of you swilling beer and your reputation will sink to the deep end of the pool and get stuck in the drain."

"Don't treat me like a child. I am so sick of being ordered around by a middle-aged ex-army sergeant with the body of a bag of turnips! You may be twenty-five years older than me, but you're not my mother."

Janna's grin was malicious. "Why don't you give her a call? I'm sure she'd let you move back into that squalid tract house with your snotty-nosed brothers and sisters. If you're lucky, you can join your old high school friends yanking intestines out of chickens at the poultry plant. Get yourself knocked up, marry the illiterate jerk, and raise snotty-nosed brats of your own. Go out to dinner once a week at a chain cafeteria."

"Maybe I will," Natalie said, but her voice was unsteady and she was unable to hold Janna's stare. The bitch was right, she reminded herself. Four years earlier Janna had spotted her at a public golf course, realized her potential, and assured her that wealth and glory were awaiting her—if she agreed to allow Janna to manage her career. Natalie hadn't suspected that Janna intended to manage her life as well, from vitamins at six in the morning until mandatory bedtime at ten o'clock.

"No, you'll do three miles at the track, then work out at the gym. I'll take you to the tanning salon in the morning. The tournament starts in less than two weeks. Even though it's inconsequential, it may get some publicity. I want your name and photograph in at least one newspaper twice a month."

"Does the *Farberville Morning News* count?"

"If it leads to a mention in *Sports Illustrated* or *Golf Digest*, it counts."

I counted to ten, took a deep breath, and walked across the scuffed dance floor to the bar. Estelle was perched on her customary stool at the end nearest the ladies' room, a glass of sherry within reach. She nodded warily at me. Ruby Bee bustled up and said, "About time you showed your face, missy. Barbecued brisket or chicken-fried steak with cream gravy?"

"A cheeseburger and fries," I said.

"That ain't healthy."

"But a chicken-fried steak, mashed potatoes, gravy, corn, fried okra, and buttered rolls are? Don't bother answering. I'll have a Caesar salad with grilled shrimp, low-fat dressing on the side, and a cup of herbal tea."

"Then you better skedaddle back to Manhattan and hook up with that slimy ex-husband of yours," said Ruby Bee. "He can take you out to supper at those places that serve you two spears of asparagus and a peppercorn for fifty dollars."

Estelle shook her finger at me. "Ruby Bee and I were there, if you recall. I was madder'n a wet hen when I had to pay more than fifteen dollars for a bagel and coffee. Imagine calling that breakfast! It's no wonder those people on the sidewalk look like zombies heading back to their cemeteries."

"A cheeseburger and fries," I repeated.

Ruby Bee rolled her eyes, then went into the kitchen. To my relief, Roy Stiver, my landlord, who graciously allows me to live in a seedy efficiency apartment above his antique shop, sat down next to me. He's one of the few literates in town, as well as large enough to block Estelle's stare. "What do you think about this golf tournament?" he asked me.

"I'm doing my best not to think about it. From what I heard last week, there won't be any problem with traffic or crowd control. If a handful of fools want to smack balls around Raz's pasture, they're welcome to have at it."

"Curious that Raz agreed to it. He's a cantankerous old fart."

"Our illustrious mayor sent me to persuade him. The deal was that I'd overlook the still I found in a clearing not too far from Robin Buchanon's old shack if Raz agreed to this so-called golf course on his property. I was as pissed off about it as he was, but I wasn't in the mood to get fired."

"I suppose not," Roy said, shaking his head. "Now Jim Bob's in a particularly foul mood on account of the hole-in-one prize. Larry Joe's niece swore Jim Bob tried to run her down out past the old New Age hardware store. When he had a flat at the foot of his driveway, he cussed so loudly I could hear him from my porch. He damn near bit Idalupino's head off the other day because she was chewing gum at the checkout. All the employees are skirting around him like field mice."

"Because of a recycled trophy from a bowling tournament?"

"No, that's for the winner." He went on to describe the boat in quite a bit more detail than I thought was necessary. "Jim Bob's got a scheme, naturally. Don't go telling anybody, but he's been scrounging around flea markets and pawn shops, buying secondhand golf clubs. We're supposed to meet up at my place later tonight to watch videos about how to play. I used to play a little bit, so I'm the coach. Every afternoon until the tournament, we're gonna haul ass to a driving range in Starley City and practice until dark. Jim Bob says the putting and all that doesn't matter, as long as ever'body can whack the ball a goodly distance. Seems goofy to me, but you never know. One of 'em might get lucky."

"Or one of 'em might get struck by lightning," I said.

"The odds are about equal," Roy acknowledged with a grin.

Normally, Maggody is a hotbed of activity only from sunrise to sunset. Most of the residents eat supper at six o'clock, then settle in to watch television until they fall asleep on their sofas or in bulky faux leather recliners. Some stay awake long enough to watch the local news and get the weather forecast for the following day; others succumb to snoring during their favorite shows. The teenagers make furtive phone calls to each other or venture onto Internet chat rooms until someone yells at them to turn off the damn fool music and go to bed. Dogs howl. Raccoons root through garbage cans. Pink-eyed opossums waddle out of their burrows in search of a tasty meal of roadkill, often chancing upon the remains of their dearly beloveds.

On this particular night, however, a goodly number of the husbands and bachelors of Maggody were squeezed into the backroom of Roy Stiver's antiques shop. They were staring intently as a middle-aged man on a television screen stressed the importance of keeping one's head down and focusing on the follow-through.

Unbeknownst to them (not that any of them would have been interested), a goodly number of the Maggody women were involved in a complex network of telephone calls. Messages were relayed according to the unspoken pecking order. Determination was expressed, doubts suppressed, details debated. Age, arthritis, and allergies were analyzed. Like a spider's web, each strand secured another. Long before the polecats could catch the scent, the web enveloped the town in a gossamer plot.

Two

Bony watched the waitress's ample butt as she stalked away from the table. "There's just something about big, bold women. I'd sure like to see her wearing nothing but two fried eggs and a slice of ham."

"As you told her so elegantly," said Frederick Cartier. He took a sip of tepid coffee. "It's an Oedipus complex, obviously. You had an unhealthy attraction to your mother. Your futile lust is an act of defiance aimed at your father because he had conjugal dominance."

"He was a mechanic, fercrissake."

"Let's return to the topic of this golf tournament in Maggody. What else did you learn?" He leaned forward, his expression intent. His silver hair and sharp nose gave him the look of a merciless judge preparing to sentence a felon to life imprisonment without the possibility of parole.

Bony was intimidated by the piercing scrutiny. Trying not to slither under the table, he said, "They've got about fifty entries as of yesterday. The course is a bad joke. I ruined a good pair of shoes when I stepped in a meadow muffin. Besides poison ivy in the rough, there's some fine-looking marijuana. I'm going to take a plastic bag with me next time I'm out there."

"That would not be wise," Frederick said, hoping no one

in the adjoining booths was listening. "Did you go into any of the local mercantiles?"

Bony's brow wrinkled. He still wasn't used to Frederick's fancy words, even though they'd spent seventeen hours together driving from Las Vegas. And he sure as hell didn't have any idea why Frederick was so damn determined to go to Maggody. It hadn't changed since Bony was forced to spend his summers there. It had never been a quaint little town with ivy-coated cottages. The locals weren't charmingly eccentric; they were surly, ornery, and opinionated. Godliness was a lot more important than cleanliness, if you took in the tobacco stains on the barbershop floor, the litter along the roads, the misspelled graffiti spray-painted on abandoned storefronts, and the acrid stench of fertilizer. He shuddered as he remembered the endless hours of Brother Verber's sermons on eternal damnation. As far as he'd been concerned, the Voice of the Almighty Lord Assembly Hall was a sight worse than Satan's fiery furnace.

But Frederick somehow knew about the upcoming golf tournament, and he had a car and a wallet filled with platinum credit cards. Bony, broke as usual, needed to get out of Vegas before certain people caught up with him. They'd left the casino through a service door and were in New Mexico before the sun rose, and in Farberville late that night. A couple of days to case the situation, and here they were, eating grits in a grimy café, with Li'l Abner in one booth and the Dukes of Hazzard in another.

"No, but I heard something funny while I was having supper at my kinfolks' place," Bony said. "Uncle Earl was carrying on about how no outsider was going to walk away with the bass boat. At first I thought he was talking about a load of buckshot, but we went out on the porch to drink beer and he told me the men in Maggody are secretly trying to learn how to play golf. Not one of them knows a bogie from a booger."

"Good for Uncle Earl," Frederick said.

"That's not the half of it. When I went in the kitchen to thank Aunt Eileen for the meal, she told me that the wives are secretly planning to learn, too. She asked me if I'd give them lessons on the sly. I hemmed and hawed until she told me they'd pay me by the hour. What the hell, I thought. It won't be as though any of them will ever be able to hit the backside of a barn, much less a decent drive."

"Which ladies?"

"I didn't ask." Bony wadded up his paper napkin and tossed it on the table. "I'm supposed to buy used clubs and meet up with them behind a church in Bugscuffle."

"And your means of transportation?"

"I was kinda hoping I could use your car. I'll be back before noon."

"Oh, I think not," Frederick said, "but rather than disappoint the ladies, I'll take you there and watch from a discreet distance. Perhaps I'll pick up some pointers."

"You said you didn't play golf."

"I've played a few rounds over the years, but I'm not in your league. I take an interest in the sport. As I told you in Vegas, I recognized your name when I found out that you were doing commentary during the televised tournament. I felt quite honored to meet you in person. It was unfortunate that you imbibed to excess and attempted to engage in a sexual liaison between the rows of slot machines. How could you possibly have known that the young lady was the casino owner's special friend?"

"Or that she could scream so loud the sprinklers came on," Bony said, smirking as he recalled what he could of the ensuing chaos. "I gotta make a few calls to track down some golf clubs for the ladies. I'll meet you at the car in half an hour." He ogled the waitress as he sauntered out of the café. Her gesture did not imply he would be welcome in the future.

Frederick ordered another cup of coffee, then flipped

through the local newspaper, although his thoughts wandered along a path that took him well into the past. The age when he'd only just begun to cross that bridge over troubled water. Maybe that's what he'd find in Maggody.

Bony was already in the car when Frederick went outside. They drove to several pawn shops, where satisfactory prices were agreed upon for mismatched sets of rusty irons and bent drivers. They arrived at the church in Bugscuffle in due course. Cars were parked in the rutted lot, including a garish pink Cadillac, a station wagon, and a boxy little car with a license plate that had expired a decade earlier.

More than a dozen ladies were standing near a corner of the building. While Bony hauled golf clubs out of the trunk, Frederick scanned their faces. None of them was remotely familiar. He exhaled as he joined them. "I'm Frederick Cartier," he said with a slight bow, "and you must be the contingent from Maggody. What an attractive group, if I may be so bold as to remark. Each and every one of you, in your own special way."

The only one who failed to simper was a thin-lipped woman in a prim white blouse and a navy skirt. Her hair looked as though it could withstand shrapnel. "Let's get the show on the road," she said. "I'm meeting my decorator this afternoon, and I don't have time to shilly-shally. Bonaparte, did you think to buy golf balls?"

"Yes, ma'am," Bony said. "They're scruffy because they were fished out of the water at the Farberville Country Club, but they'll suit us just fine. Let's go around back and get started."

As they trooped along, the rest of the ladies introduced themselves to Frederick. He made a point of noting their names, a talent he had perfected over the years. Their spokeswoman was Mrs. Jim Bob, the mayor's wife, he was told in a reverent whisper. They were an unremarkable mixture of old, young, married, widowed, and spinsters. Only a few of them were remotely attractive: Joyce Lambertino, who had a slim figure and a bouncy ponytail; perky Crystal Whitby, who kept peeking at him in an unsettling way; and Bopeep Buchanon, who'd clearly lost her sheep by the time she was fourteen.

The older women sat down at a picnic table and took out various knitting and needlework projects. Under Bony's supervision, the rest chose woods and fiddled with their grips, adjusted their stances, and began to topple balls off spindly tees. Those who made contact, anyway. An occasional misfire ricocheted off the church wall, eliciting squeals from the sewing circle. Cora Cranshaw's backswing knocked Audley Riley's straw hat off. Eileen Buchanon managed to hit herself in the back of the head. As the hour progressed, Bony looked more and more harried.

Frederick sat on another weathered picnic table and watched, debating which ones might be inclined to offer him coffee, cookies, and, most importantly, gossip. He did not flinch when an errant drive shattered a church window.

Phil Proodle threw down the red cape. "Cut! Somebody go fetch that goddamn bull so we can finish shooting before my pants split." He took out a handkerchief and wiped his neck, mindful of his makeup and the black wig combed into a pompadour. The glue that held on the sideburns was itchy. It wasn't all that hot, but after spending two hours in the parking lot, he was sweatier than a preacher in a whorehouse. This was the sixth time the bull had ignored the matador's provocative cape and headed for the rows of party barges. The fence would contain him, but then everybody had to twiddle their thumbs until he was coaxed into camera range. So he could do it again.

"Doesn't one of the steak houses have a plastic bull out in front?" asked a salesman, who'd given up hope that Proodle would be gored.

Phil's eyes narrowed to slits. "Ain't you ever heard of authenticity, boy? If Phil Proodle says he's gonna grab the bull by the horns and lower prices, then that's what he's gonna do. And now you're saying I should grab a *plastic* bull by the horns? Do you think I want to be the laughingstock of the county? We ain't selling canoes here. Come to think of it, you ain't selling much of anything, are you? Maybe you ought to be washing dishes at that steak house."

The salesman scuttled away. Phil was leery of sitting down, since he was stuffed into a rented costume that was squeezing his internal organs like a sausage casing. He went into the office to suck in the cool air.

"I got a phone message for you, Phil," his secretary said. "I wrote it down, but it doesn't make any sense."

He snatched the note off her desk and went to get a soda in the break room. As he read the message, he almost tripped over a rack of brochures. Despite his secretary's primitive handwriting, he was able to determine that a certain customer was out of prison and wanted a certain boat back. There was no mention of the missed payments that had allowed Phil to repossess it as soon as the drug-dealing creep had been sent south to enjoy free room and board, courtesy of the Department of Corrections. The charge had been aggravated assault, the prison sentence a double-digit number of months. But how long ago had it been? Could there have been a parole or early release?

Phil berated himself for having been bullied into loaning the boat to that damn fool golf tournament. If he'd only been able to stop and think, he would have been able to negotiate a cheaper boat. Hell, he was a master salesman who could sell bikinis to Eskimos and sleeping bags to Bantus. But the woman who'd assailed him was a fearsome wind devil that'd swept away his plaintive protests like scraps of paper along a highway. She'd jabbed him with her finger until he was backed into a corner, literally. He'd had to explain the bruises to his wife, who was still suspicious. At that moment, the boat was in Maggody, displayed in a supermarket parking lot. Having been assured that he could fetch it the day after the tournament, he'd conceded that the publicity was worth it. A lot of the losers might come sniffing around for a deal. But the publicity was not worth a dislocated jaw and broken kneecaps. And that was just for starters.

One of the guys from the ad agency came inside to tell Phil that the bull had been coerced into position and they were ready to try again. Phil followed him to the parking lot and growled at the bull, which gazed back without interest.

The shoot continued.

"You gonna be full up out back?" asked Estelle as she squirted ketchup on a grilled cheese sandwich.

Ruby Bee nodded. "It didn't look good until the boat got everybody fired up. I must have had twenty or thirty calls in the last week. I wondered if I should keep a unit open for Arnold Palmer, but he seems to be skipping this tournament. I've got two women in number three, next to my double unit, a boy and his mother in number four—"

"Which one's the golfer?"

"I didn't ask. In number five, there'll be some man who sounded drunk when he called. A married couple in six, two men from Hot Springs in seven, and a couple from Tulsa in eight. Bony Buchanon's staying with Earl and Eileen. Mrs. Jim Bob has a houseguest, but I didn't hear who it was. Did Joyce tell you anything when she was having her hair trimmed?"

"Just that her third cousin over in Jeeber is gettin' a divorce. She got caught canoodling with her husband's nephew. He ain't but fifteen."

"Lord amercy, what's wrong with young people these days?" Instead of demanding the lurid details, Ruby Bee went into the kitchen to peel potatoes.

Estelle was feeling miffed when footsteps thudded across the dance floor behind her. She knew from the way the glasses behind the bar clinked that it was Dahlia, all three-hundred-plus pounds of her. Dahlia was usually as placid as a dairy cow, but when she was riled, she was more dangerous than a herd of buffalos.

The stool squealed as she sat down. "Estelle, I got to ask you something," she began wheezily, "and I got to be quick on account of the younguns. Eileen's minding 'em, but she sez there's another meeting at Mrs. Jim Bob's house in half an hour. You know how snippety Mrs. Jim Bob can be if everybody don't jump when she snaps her fingers. Last week I was at the supermarket, and she had the nerve to tell me Kevvie Junior and Rosemarie should be spanked on account of them beating on each other with celery. If she so much as lays a finger on—"

"Ask me what?" Estelle said. "If it's a beauty question, I happen to be the best cosmetologist in town." She held up her hand to display her fingernail polish. "This is Prussian Empire. It's on sale for two dollars and twenty-nine cents, plus tax. Should I set aside a bottle for you?"

"No, that ain't it. It's about Kevin. I need an older woman's advice, but I can't ask Eileen."

"Oh." Estelle checked her reflection in the mirror and assured herself she didn't look a day over thirty-five, if you squinted hard. "You better ask Ruby Bee. She'll be out of the kitchen directly."

"It's just that he's actin' strange these days. He doesn't come home for lunch, and swears he's working late every night. Yesterday I called to tell him about Daisy's diaper rash, and Idalupino said he'd gone off with Jim Bob about four o'clock, same as he's been doing for more than a week. You got to admit that don't make any sense. Even though they're both Buchanons, Jim Bob ain't the sort to pal around with the hired help." She took a napkin from the silver dispenser and blew her nose. "It was nearly nine when Kevin got home. When I asked him where he'd been, he just scratched his head and went to make hisself a sandwich. He din't even say anything when I threw one of Kevvie Junior's trucks at him."

She was snuffling so loudly that Estelle was embarrassed. Ignoring the crude comments from the truckers in a back booth, she put a quarter in the jukebox and randomly punched a button. To her dismay, Hank Williams began to complain about somebody's cheatin' heart. Her only hope was that Dahlia was too upset to notice the lyrics.

Dahlia was not. "Do you think Kevin's seeing another woman?" she demanded as Estelle resumed her perch.

"Of course not, honey. It could be a lot of things."

"Like what?"

Estelle racked her brain. "Well, Kevin could have gotten himself a second job, like at a convenience store. He's trying to make some extra money so he can buy you something special for your birthday."

"My birthday was two months ago, and he gave me a set of measuring cups and a box of chocolates. And if he had another job, why would he go off with Jim Bob?" Dahlia armed herself with more napkins.

It was a poser. Estelle thought some more, then said, "Jim Bob and Kevin could be fetching beer at a store in Farberville for the golf tournament. Mrs. Jim Bob must have harangued some poor soul into giving her a discount. She wouldn't want anybody to know that she made the deal because she's all the time carrying on about the sin of drinking alcohol. Even Brother Verber preaches about it, although everybody knows he drinks wine like tap water. Arly once found him stumbling along the banks of Boone Creek. He claimed he was searching for teenagers in the act of fornication, but Arly said he was so snockered he could barely see straight."

"Kevin would tell me if that's all he was doing."

"Not if Jim Bob threatened to fire him," Estelle said triumphantly, almost believing her cockamamie story. "You don't want Kevin to get fired, do you?"

Dahlia pondered this for a minute. "I reckon not."

"You'd better go pick up your children. Everything will

be back to normal once the golf tournament's over. All you have to do is hold your tongue 'til then." Estelle watched Dahlia leave, then reached under the bar and found her private stash of sherry. The more she thought about her story, the sillier it seemed. Dahlia had bought it, but she was far from the sharpest cheddar in the dairy aisle. Estelle drummed her fingers while she waited for Ruby Bee to emerge from the kitchen. There had to be something going on. Idalupino was too lazy to come up with a lie about Jim Bob and Kevin leaving together each afternoon.

It deserved looking into.

There were half a dozen cars parked in the mayoral mansion driveway, so I was mildly surprised when no one responded to the doorbell. Not stunned or flabbergasted, mind you. If Mizzoner wanted me to wait indefinitely on the front porch, I was amenable. The wicker settee looked inviting. I could see myself snoozing, my feet propped on a footstool and my head nestled on a throw cushion. It beat running a speed trap out by the charred remains of the Esso station, which led to unpleasant exchanges with motorists who'd failed to notice the faded speed limit sign behind a clump of tall weeds. The town council, presided over by Hizzoner the Moron, was conscientious about its coffers. So conscientious that I had to plead for new wiper blades for the sole cop car. The water stain on the ceiling of the PD continued to spread. My computer relied on energy produced by caged squirrels on an exercise wheel. Periodically, I requested a raise, resulting in a round of hearty laughter.

I could wait, or I could go by the Dairee Dee-Lishus to get a cherry limeade and run my speed trap by the low-water bridge out past Estelle's Hair Fantasies and the defunct rehab center. Since hardly anybody used the road, I'd be undisturbed unless Raz tried to run a load of moonshine to the next county. It would be a first during daylight hours.

I was contemplating my options when the front door

opened. Perkin's eldest, burdened with a dripping mop and a bucket of gray water, goggled at me as if I had fairies perched on my shoulder.

"Whatcha want?" she said.

"I'll assume you're not asking about my personal goals in life. Mrs. Jim Bob left a message that she feels the need to warn me about potential parking problems during the golf tournament. As the underpaid and underappreciated chief of police, I am here to pretend to share her concern. To be honest, I don't much care if they all park in a pond."

Perkin's eldest was clearly bewildered. "She's out back. I guess you can come on in."

I went inside the house. There was no sound of cackling from Mrs. Jim Bob's coven. I was about to continue on to the kitchen when the reigning witch loomed in the doorway.

"I thought I heard a car pull up," she said as if accusing me of a heinous crime. "I expected you to come by earlier."

"Okay," I said, "but if I try again, you'll have to reset your watch."

Her eyes flickered. "You need to use more starch when you iron your uniform. The town council expects a degree of professionalism. Wait in the living room, and keep your feet off the furniture."

I did my best to look truly penitent, but I doubt I fooled her. "Would you prefer me to wait in the laundry room? Perkin's eldest can give me some tips on crispy creases."

"If I weren't a good Christian woman, I'd tell you exactly where to wait. Go along to the living room. I'll join you when I have time."

"Lucky me." I did as instructed, and kept my feet off the furniture while I flipped through decorating magazines. Perkin's eldest wandered through with a feather duster to redistribute the dust. I heard car doors slam and engines start. I could have wondered what was going on, but I was too busy mentally redoing Ruby Bee's barroom in French provincial.

"Good afternoon," said a male voice that was much too friendly to be that of our illustrious mayor.

I looked up at the tall silver-haired man with a high fore-head, penetrating eyes, and a smile that was oddly familiar. He was likely to be in his late fifties and wore white trousers (with crispy creases), a baby blue turtleneck, and a navy blazer with a discreet emblem. He looked as if he'd been transported from the bar in a yacht club.

"Ahoy," I said.

"May I join you? I gather you're Arly Hanks, chief of police."

"That's what my badge claims, but it came in a cereal box," I said, wondering what on earth he was doing in Mrs. Jim Bob's house. Boone Creek could not accommodate yachts; at best, it was suitable for johnboats and canoes. During dry spells, it hardly qualified as a trickle. "And you?"

"Frederick Cartier. Bonaparte Buchanon's an old friend, so I decided to accompany him to your golf tournament."

"It's not *my* golf tournament, by any means. I'm just here to aid and abet Mrs. Jim Bob in her quest to save the starving golf widows of America."

His lips twitched. "Such an admirable quest. Is Arly short for Ariel, from *The Tempest*?"

I nodded. It was easier than explaining that I was named after a photograph of the bar and grill taken from an air-plane. Ruby Bee had been smitten with the word but weak on the spelling. "Are you named after a wristwatch?"

"How old are you, Arly?"

"Old enough to ignore irrelevant questions. Do you know what Mrs. Jim Bob is doing? I don't have time to sit here and twiddle my thumbs while crime runs rampant in my town. Someone could be shoplifting a candy bar as we speak."

"I believe the dear lady is making herself presentable. She, some of her friends, and I have been in the backyard. Al-though the temperature is moderate, the sun is quite fierce."

"Doing what?"

Frederick shook his head. "A gentleman never betrays a lady's secret."

"I guess I'll run along, then." I closed the magazine and stood up. "Tell the dear lady that she can call me when she has time." ·

"I wish you wouldn't. I'd really like to get to know you, Arly. I've rarely encountered a distaff police chief. You must have some fascinating stories. Please stay and entertain me until Mrs. Jim Bob appears. Would you like a drink? I have a bottle of very fine scotch in my bedroom."

"You're staying *here*?" I said, stunned.

"It wasn't my intention. Bonaparte and I were at a motel in Farberville. When his aunt invited him to stay with them, Mrs. Jim Bob insisted that I stay here."

"Why?"

"I intended to inquire about a vacancy at a local motel. She seemed to think it was more . . . ah, seemly for me to accept her hospitality. I've offered to assist her with the tournament. Bonaparte and I will be leaving Sunday after the final round. Now, about that drink?"

I admit I was curious. "I'd prefer ice water."

"How gauche of me to suggest alcohol when you're on duty. I'll be right back."

I fanned through a magazine featuring Tuscan kitchen decor until he returned with two glasses of water. "So you and Bonaparte Buchanon are old friends?" I asked. I had a vague recollection of Bony, as he was called. He'd been snide, mean, and arrogant when out of range of adults. We all figured he'd end up as an underling in the Redneck Mafia, assuming he wasn't doing forty years in a federal pen.

Frederick fiddled with his glass and coaster for a long moment. "Well, we're hardly war buddies. I've always gotten a kick out of keeping track of the lesser-known PGA players. Some of them soar to the top of the list, while others fade into obscurity. Bonaparte may do quite well once he settles down." He crossed his legs and studied me. "Do you have any siblings, Arly?"

"None that are up-and-coming PGA stars," I said. "So you follow these players from tournament to tournament in hopes of discovering the next Tiger Woods?"

"Merely a select few, and it can be very exciting at times. I can afford my harmless hobby. Why shouldn't I?"

"So you're retired?"

"I still dabble here and there. What's your secret vice? Horseshoes? Redecorating?"

I closed the magazine in front of me. I was on the verge of making a tart remark about personal questions, but instead I leaned back. I was badgered with questions whenever I wasn't holed up in my apartment. Ruby Bee and Estelle had lapsed into a relentless campaign of "what are you going to do?" The rest of the town wanted to know who vandalized their mailboxes or stole their dawgs or tumped their trash cans. No one had ever asked me if I had a secret vice.

"Imagining myself anywhere but here," I said. "Contrary to what you've read, you can go home again—but that doesn't mean you should."

"Where would you go?"

"Running away isn't going to solve any problems." I briefly imagined myself fighting my way through the Amazon jungle, wielding a machete. If I were attacked by a jaguar, my problems would be solved. Stumbling into Jack's campsite, on the other hand, would be disastrous. "Tell Mrs. Jim Bob that she can call me. I'll be at the police department until six. After that, I won't."

"Would you like to have dinner with me?" he asked. "We can go to Farberville or wherever else you like."

I stared at him, perplexed. I can tell when a guy is hitting on me, and he wasn't. The only explanation I could come up with was that he was desperate for sane company. I wasn't in the mood to rescue him. "No, I don't think so. Besides, I'm sure Mrs. Jim Bob will expect you to dine with her this evening. She rarely has a chance to pull out her silver, china, and linen napkins. Jim Bob's more of a paper plate and plastic fork sort of guy. You wouldn't want to disappoint her, would you?"

I hurried out the front door and drove to the police department. The front room served as my office, the back room as a habitat for mice and spiders. The yellow and white gingham curtains that Ruby Bee had forced on me hung dispiritedly over the dusty windows. The red light on the answering machine was flashing angrily. I was surprised when the recorded voice was that of Harvey Dorfer, the Stump County sheriff, instead of Ruby Bee, who called at least three times a day.

I dialed his number and, after the customary battle with LaBelle, the gossipy dispatcher, was put through to the inner sanctum. "Whatever happened, Harve," I began, "was not in my jurisdiction. We are a peaceful, law-abiding community. The only way we can remain so is for me to stay within the city limits, ever alert to the potential peril of bank robbers, horse thieves, cattle rustlers, and international terrorists. There are rumors that Ginalola Buchanon is stockpiling water balloons and beef jerky in the event we're invaded by papists."

"You're a real pain in the ass, Arly," Harve said amiably. "Hold on a sec." I listened to the familiar scritch as he lit a match to fire up one of his noxious cigars. "All right now," he continued, "what's all this about a golf tournament out your way?"

"There's a golf tournament out my way."

"No kidding. I hear tell there's a prize—a Ranger Z21."

"I hear tell that, too," I said. "It's chained to a light pole in front of Jim Bob's SuperSaver Buy 4 Less as we speak. I guess it's the one, anyway. It looks like a cross between a boat and a NASCAR vehicle. Or maybe NASA. I always get those two mixed up."

"Did I mention you're a real pain in the ass? Who all is playing in this tournament?"

"I have no idea, Harve. Mrs. Jim Bob seems to expect quite a crowd."

"Real golfers, or duffers like me?"

"All I know is that there's one PGA player and some people from out of town. Ruby Bee and Estelle aren't involved, and neither am I. Anything else?"

"Sure is a fine boat . . ."

"It sure is. If that's all, I see a misdemeanor in the making. Hedge Hooper is walking toward the barbershop with a wad of chaw in his cheek. We don't take kindly to spittle in Maggody. I'll most likely bring him over to your lockup until the arraignment. Good luck in the golf tournament, Harve."

I could hear him sputtering as I hung up. Harve's a good ol' boy who could easily play the role of a hick sheriff in a movie. Big belly, red ears, close-set eyes, and hands like paws. A few years ago he'd taken to wearing his hat to hide his spreading bald spot. I learned a while back that he's not as stupid as he appears to be. Although he's been the sheriff for more than thirty years, I keep hoping he won't retire as long as I'm around. I'd hate to have to break in a new man.

My chair squeaked as I leaned back and put my feet on the desk. The water stains on the ceiling were distressingly familiar, along with the cobwebs from decades past. Cars and pickup trucks drove by the PD. Birds chirped. A fly buzzed lethargically as it searched for a landing pad. The sounds were pleasantly ordinary, the lullaby of small rural towns. It was naptime.

Estelle parked alongside the county road. The driveway to the back parking area of the SuperSaver was hidden behind scrub pines and brush, but she could see if anybody drove in or out. Idalupino had told Dahlia that Jim Bob and Kevin left at four o'clock, and it was nearly that time. Estelle was aware that one or the other of them might recognize her car, but there wasn't much she could do about that. She'd covered her hair with a scarf and was wearing sunglasses with rhinestone frames. She glanced in the rearview mirror. The disguise was downright becoming, she thought, like an alluring spy in an old movie. When she tried a come-hither smile, she noticed a smudge of lipstick on a front tooth. She scratched it off with a fingernail now painted Cherry Wine Cooler to further her disguise.

She ducked when a car turned at the highway. It would have been a sight more fun if Ruby Bee had come along, since the two of them were a team when it came to investigating suspicious behavior. It may not have always worked out real well, as Arly kept pointing out in a peevish tone of voice. However, Ruby Bee wasn't herself these days, most likely on account of fretting about Arly's condition. In fact, she'd taken to standing at the back door of the kitchen, her hands clutched and her face stony.

The car must have turned around and come back. Estelle took a peek in the mirror as it rolled to a stop behind hers. As soon as she saw who it was, she got out, picked her way along the weedy shoulder, and rapped on the window.

Dahlia reluctantly lowered it. "What?"

Estelle peered at the backseat. Kevvie Junior and Rosemarie were in bulky car seats, with Daisy in a smaller one between them. Daisy was wailing because Kevvie Junior was gnawing on her arm. Rosemarie was styling her hair with the contents of a peanut butter and jelly sandwich. "Just what do you reckon you're doing out here?" she asked Dahlia.

Dahlia twisted back far enough to thump Kevvie Junior's head, then turned to glower at Estelle. "Is this your private property? It's a county road. I've got as much right to park here as you do."

"You may have the right, but you must have been in the basement when God was passing out brains," Estelle countered. "You run along home and let me take care of this. What sort of detective has three kids in the backseat?"

"I don't know what you think you are, all gussied up like a striptease dancer, but you sure ain't no detective. This is about my husband, not yours. Why don't you run along home yourself and paint your toenails?"

Estelle put her hands on her hips, but Dahlia ignored her. She tried another tactic. "How about you go on and I solemnly swear to tell you what I find out? This could be the day Kevin goes straight home. If you're not there, he'll be worried sick."

Dahlia realized there was something wrong with that, but she couldn't quite figure out what. After sucking on her lower lip for a moment, she said, "Maybe we should join forces. You wanna use your car or mine?"

Now Kevvie Junior was bawling because of the thump, and Daisy was wailing because she was being ignored. Rosemarie scowled as she applied peanut butter eye shadow. If they'd been adults, they would have been ankle deep in juice cartons, cookie wrappers, mutilated tabloids, bald Barbie dolls, and washrags that reeked of sour milk and other unpleasant things. Crumbs were sprinkled on the top of the dashboard like laundry powder.

"I'll get my purse," Estelle said hastily.

In his office inside the SuperSaver, Jim Bob erased all evidence of the porn site on his computer, then shut it down. It was tempting to page Kevin over the loudspeaker, but the last time he did, the idiot was spraying produce. Eula Lemoy had not appreciated a full-frontal dousing while she was sniffing melons. Not to say that she didn't deserve it, since Jim Bob had seen her plenty of times eating grapes as she pushed around a shopping cart.

He went out to the front, stared at the checkout girls just to make 'em twittery, then looked at the helluva fine boat and trailer chained to the pole out in the parking lot. His mouth watered. It was so damn sleek and sexy. It was aged whiskey on a summer night, a fine cigar, a voluptuous woman in a naughty black negligee. He felt his privates beginning to throb.

"Hey, Jim Bob," Kevin said as he shuffled up in a dingy apron, "you want I should stack the canned peaches? I'm beginnin' to get the hang of it."

"Hell, no. The last time you tried, you nearly killed one of those Lambertino brats. The last thing I need is a goddamn lawsuit. Go put your apron in your locker. We got to get going in a minute."

If Kevin had possessed a forelock, he would have tugged it. "Golly, Jim Bob, I was thinking maybe I ain't cut out for golf. No matter how hard I try, I cain't even hit the ball half the time. You ought to get somebody else."

"Like who, you dumb shit? Toadsuck Buchanon, even though he's blind on account of drinking a bad batch of 'shine? Diesel? He'd take it right kindly if I barged into his cave up on Cotter's Ridge and asked him if he wanted to play golf, so kindly that he'd rip off my ears and toss 'em in his skillet. His brother Petrol, who's shacked up with Dahlia's granny? Just who'd you have in mind, boy?"

Kevin's mouth went slack, as it always did when he was confronted with a direct question. "I dunno, Jim Bob. What about those ol' boys at the garage over in Hasty? Some of 'em are so gosh darn big they could whack a ball clean over the top of a mountain."

"The boat stays in Maggody," Jim Bob said tightly. "That's why I paid your damn registration fee out of your next month's wages. Get your sorry ass out to the loading dock in five minutes." He held up his hand, fingers splayed. "You can count, can't you?"

"Yeah—I mean, I guess so." Kevin nearly ran into a rack of tabloids as he hurried toward the back of the store.

"The boat stays in Maggody," Jim Bob repeated under his breath. "Whatever it takes, the boat stays in Maggody."

Three

Darla Jean McIlhaney sat on a concrete picnic table in front of the Dairee Dee-Lishus, batting at flies on a dried soda spill. Heather Riley and Billy Dick MacNamara, her two bestest friends, pulled up in Billy Dick's ancient pickup. The surly Mexican fellow who owned the place glowered at them, then slammed the window and disappeared, but not before they heard him cussing.

"Why's he got a tamale up his ass?" asked Billy Dick.

"My fault. I asked him if he'd tape up a flyer about the golf tournament. He wadded it up and threw it at me. I guess that meant no."

Heather giggled. "No way, José. Why do you care about this silly tournament, anyway? Bunch of grown men in really bad clothes, molesting innocent golf balls. Once they get it to fall in a cup, they pick it up and do the same thing all over again. Give me a break!"

"Feel free to run over to Mrs. Jim Bob's house and give her your opinion," Darla Jean said. "She'll most likely give you a pair of gloves and order you to pull up all the poison ivy in the pasture. You better wear jeans and boots. Copperheads are fierce this time of year."

"I'd sooner face a copperhead than Raz. Waylon and I was up by Robin Buchanon's old shack a couple of days back. Raz came out of the bushes like a rabid coon and began screeching at us to get our asses off the ridge. You'd have thought we was trespassing on his private property!"

"What *were* y'all doing?"

"We weren't doing nothing but looking for wild strawberries. My ma wants to make jam." She launched into a highly fanciful story about the hardships that accompanied the search, tossing in descriptive passages about mud, hornets, thorns, concealed tree stumps, and other perils. She had just reached the part about the rumble they'd heard from inside a cave when she realized nobody was listening except the Mexican fellow, who'd come outside to wash the window.

"You seen the bass boat?" Billy Dick sighed dreamily as he thought about the fiberglass hull and the Evinrude E-TEC. "Those things are so damn fast. The seats are upholstered with real leather. Built-in coolers for beer. I can see myself drifting in the middle of some lake, listening to music and smoking weed. Y'all can come, too, if you wear thong bikinis and open beers for me."

"Your wet dream, my worst nightmare," Heather said, swishing her long blond hair for emphasis. "Don't you agree, Darla Jean? Please don't tell me you'd go out on a boat with this pimply pervert."

Darla Jean's limp brown hair never swished, but at least she didn't have crooked teeth like Heather. "Only if the lake freezes in July. Want to hear something hysterical? The tournament registration was really slow until Mrs. Jim Bob made her big announcement about the boat. It picked up after that and grew to nearly sixty. This morning a bunch of the local men signed up. Mr. Lambertino came by and gave me a thick envelope filled with their fees and registration forms. He made me promise not to tell a soul. An hour later, Mrs. Lambertino brought me another envelope with the local women's fees and registration forms. She made me promise not to tell, too. I almost wet my pants trying not to laugh."

"So who's registered?" asked Heather.

"They're almost all married couples, which makes it even funnier. My ma and pa, as well as yours. Yours, too, Billy Dick. Jim Bob and Mrs. Jim Bob. The Lambertinos, obviously. Earl and Eileen Buchanon, Tam and Crystal Whitby, Ruddy and Cora Cranshaw . . ." She took a slurp of cherry limeade while she thought. "Kevin, but not Dahlia . . . oh, and Bopeep Buchanon and her new boyfriend, Luke Smithers."

Heather licked her lips. "He is so hot."

"Have you ever seen him without his shirt on?"

"I'd die on the spot."

"I almost did." Darla Jean imagined Luke in a leather kilt and strapped sandals instead of the grubby jeans and sneakers he was wearing while he tinkered with her father's tractor. "I thought I was in the Coliseum, watching the gladiators parade around court. He looked like Russell Crowe."

"I am so totally horny I could pass out," Heather said. "Call an ambulance."

"His abs are so tight you can see the muscles."

"My pa's never set foot on a golf course," said Billy Dick, ignoring their girlie histrionics. "He doesn't have any golf clubs stashed away in a closet or the garage, and he refuses to watch it on TV. The only game my ma can play is canasta."

Darla Jean came back to earth and flinched at a yellow jacket crawling toward the spill. "Same here. I'd be surprised if any of 'em know how to play. You know, my ma's been acting kinda odd lately. She says she's going shopping, but she never comes back with anything. My pa's been late for supper every night. His excuses are lame. I guess they're pretty serious, though. I've got to go to Farberville in the morning to deposit another four thousand dollars in the tournament account. It's not going to be a secret very long."

"Thank gawd Miss Estes didn't sign up," Heather said. "Can you see her trying to hit a golf ball? She'd be more likely to teach her home ec classes how to turn 'em into a tasty and nutritious casserole. She'd write the recipe on the blackboard and say, 'Now sprinkle the top with one cup of crushed potato chips and bake for forty-five minutes, girls.' "

"Serve with a green salad," Darla Jean added in a high-pitched, nasal voice.

"Are you serious?" Billy Dick said, mystified. "Golf balls?"

The girls laughed so loudly that the Mexican fellow threw a bucket of gray water at them. Somehow, that made it even funnier.

Within an hour, the ugly truth began to spread through town, and by suppertime the tension in some households was thicker than corn syrup. The Lambertino children didn't know what to make of their ma and pa, who weren't speaking to each other. Darla Jean hid out in her bedroom because her ma and pa *were* speaking to each other (but not at all nicely). Bony was disappointed when he realized there would be no bountiful supper served at Uncle Earl and Aunt Eileen's house. He made himself a sandwich and sat on the front porch. Frederick Cartier eased his car out of the garage, where Mrs. Jim Bob had insisted he park it, and drove to Farberville to track down an old buddy that he'd met at the Hot Springs racetrack decades earlier.

Kevin Buchanon was home alone. Dahlia, the younguns, and the car were gone. When he'd called his parents' house, his very own ma had said she didn't know where they were and slammed down the phone so hard his ear still ached. He went to the refrigerator and rooted around until he found the leftover meatloaf. It seemed kind of wrong to heat it up, so he ate it cold.

After a convoluted argument that made no sense, Crystal and Tam Whitby had retreated to different rooms in their house in the treeless subdivision out past the high school. Crystal spent the rest of the evening on the phone with her mother in Lead Hill. Her mother agreed that Tam was a self-centered bully, and cheerfully pointed out that she warned Crystal back in high school not to go to the prom with him.

Bopeep Buchanon loomed over Luke, reminding him who had a job and who lounged around on his lazy butt and drank beer all day. When she came at him with a potato peeler, he hightailed it out of the trailer at the Pot O' Gold. In the trailer next to it, Eula Lemoy smiled as she watched him leave. He was passably handsome, but he was responsible for the whiskey bottles and beer cans cluttering the grass. Eula hoped he was gone for good. Since most of Bopeep's boyfriends lasted only a few weeks, it was likely.

"Just what in hell's name are you gonna do with a bass boat?" demanded Ruddy Cranshaw as he slammed his fist on the arm of the recliner. "It ain't like you can bait a hook without getting weepy." Cora grabbed the remote and sprinted for the garbage disposal.

Audley Riley hurled a can of tuna fish across the kitchen. "If I win this boat, you'll never set foot on it! I'll sell it on eBay in a split second, and use the money to remodel the kitchen." The can bounced off the refrigerator door, leaving a noticeable dent. "And get new appliances," she added darkly as she reached for a can of chicken noodle soup. Rip deflected it with a skillet, thinking he might make a better badminton player than a golfer.

Big Dick MacNamara sat in his truck, using a rag to mop the blood running out of his nose. Lucille's left jab was nothing more than a fluke, he consoled himself. He didn't know why she'd turned crazy when he'd said she could barely walk across a room without tripping on her own shoelaces. He'd been trying to be helpful, that's all.

Earl Buchanon pointed out to his wife that she couldn't operate an electric can opener, much less an Evinrude E-TEC. Eileen suggested what he could do with an Evinrude E-TEC. It was highly colorful but anatomically impossible. The conversation went downhill after that.

Roy Stiver, who was blessedly unwed, searched through his kitchen cabinets. After the first two phone calls of desperation, he'd put the fillet back in the refrigerator and was now wondering if he could make Hamburger Helper with canned sardines for his exiled guests. The phone rang again.

Over in Farberville, things were calmer. Tommy Ridner finished a steak sandwich in the bar at the country club, then ordered another drink. In spite of the real estate slump that was playing holy hell with his income, he was feeling good. Two under par that afternoon had been worth three hundred dollars, most of which he was in the process of spending on rounds of drinks for the members at other tables. He was thinking about his brilliant chip shot at the twelfth green when Dennis and Amanda Gilbert joined him.

Tommy beckoned the waitress. "Put their drinks on my tab, honey," he said grandly.

Amanda ordered a brandy and soda. "Are we celebrating something? I saw Natalie Hotz on the eighteenth green. Did she finally give you the time of day? You're so tedious when you drool from a distance."

"We bumped into each other on the first tee," Tommy said. "Someone in her foursome was late, so she let us go ahead of them. I don't think either of us asked about the time. She's playing in the tournament this weekend." He winked at Dennis. "Maybe one of these days she'll thaw just a tiny bit."

Dennis laughed. "You believe winning this crappy tournament is going to break the ice? She's encased in a glacier. You'd need a blowtorch and fifty years to get to her." He squeezed Amanda's hand. "Not all women are hot for you, Tommy boy."

"I can vouch for that." Amanda withdrew her hand to pick up her drink. "You'd better keep your voices down. The glacier's sitting at a table near the door, and the temperature just dropped fifteen degrees."

"I don't give a shit who wins the tournament," Tommy continued loudly. "The bass boat's a whole 'nother story. The sun in my eyes, the wind in my hair, the rod in my hand.

I'm thinking I'll rent a slip at the Prairie Gulch marina. Takes about thirty minutes to drive up there, but the fishing's good. Lots of college chicks hang out on the weekends. I'm sure some of them would be up for a boat ride to a secluded cove."

"You're such a pig." Amanda took out her compact and inspected her face as if she might have contracted trichinosis from breathing the same air.

"Why are you so sure you'll win the boat?" asked Dennis. "A hole-in-one isn't all that common, you know. You've made what—eight in the last twenty-five years? I've never made one, and I've probably played fifteen hundred rounds. That works out to"—he paused to calculate—"twenty-seven thousand holes. I guess I'm due one, since the odds are one in twenty to thirty thousand."

"You wanna make a little bet?" Tommy said.

"No, he does not." Amanda deftly clicked the compact closed and dropped it in her purse. "You're both being ridiculous. If you've got money to throw away, why don't you donate it to the famished golf widows? They can use it for prosciutto and white asparagus."

Tommy chuckled. "Don't be a wimp, Dennis. What's the harm in a friendly bet, especially when the odds are in your favor? Tell you what—if I don't make a hole-in-one, I'll pay you a thousand dollars. If I do . . ." He thought about it for a moment. "If I do, I get a night of hot, steamy sex with your wife."

"How dare you!" she said, her face turning redder than her hair. "You really are a pig, Tommy Ridner. I'm not chattel to be bartered, like some biblical slave. Furthermore, I wouldn't sleep with you if you paid me a million dollars. Dennis would never agree to such a vile bet. I ought to slap your face!"

"A thousand dollars," Dennis murmured. "Hardly seems worth it."

"Dennis!" Amanda shrieked.

"Okay, good buddy," Tommy said, "let's make it five thousand."

Her head swiveled. "You bastard!"

"Calm down, dear. Everyone's staring." Dennis lowered his eyes while he considered. "How about ten?"

"Seventy-five hundred," Tommy said, winking at Amanda.

She knocked over her chair as she stood up. "I cannot believe either of you! I am leaving—alone! Dennis, find your own way home. Better yet, find your own way to a motel or sleep on a sofa in his filthy sty. And don't bother to call me. I'm going to my yoga class tonight, and tomorrow I have aerobics, a hair appointment, and a lunch date with Chantry. If you so much as step foot in the house while I'm gone, I'll have you arrested for trespassing! Do I make myself clear?" She stormed out of the bar with the subtlety of an Abrams tank flattening the countryside.

Her audience of two dozen or so, including the waitress and the bartender, stared in awe. After a moment, they pretended they hadn't been listening and resumed their quiet conversations. Amanda was not known for moderation in alcohol or gentility.

Tommy waited until she was gone. "She didn't sound pleased."

"No, she didn't," Dennis said.

They ordered another round of drinks.

Kale Wasson sat in front of the TV, watching a game show and laughing at the contestants' stupidity. "Mom, I need another soda," he said as the show went into commercial. He pushed his stringy hair out of his eyes and leaned back on the sofa. Another boring night at home with his mother. He used to have friends, he thought morosely. Golf had ruined his life. Golf had given him zits and thick yellow toenails. Golf had made his eyelid twitch when he encountered Natalie Hotz. If he was a quarterback or a varsity basketball player, he could be hanging out at a party, maybe feeling up some freshman cheerleader. Drinking beer and driving around half the night. Skinny-dipping at the lake. Getting laid.

In the kitchen, Kathleen hung up the shirt she'd finished ironing. When she went into the living room, Kale did not look up. She put down an unopened can and picked up his dinner plate. "Don't forget there's ice cream."

"Yeah, vanilla," he said. "How many times have I told you that I don't like vanilla ice cream? You know, you should be a contestant on one of these brainless games. All you'd have to do is jump around and squeal."

"Vanilla used to be your favorite."

Kale grimaced. "I used to ride a tricycle. So what?"

"I'll try to remember to get a different kind next time. I'm going to pack now. If you want to take any books or CDs, you'll have to put them in yourself. I can't keep track of your favorites."

He began to flip through the channels. "I don't see why we have to go a day early and stay in this podunk. I'm not about to hunt for an outhouse in the middle of the night. Why can't we just stay here and commute every day? It's all of two hours from here, fercrissake." Not that Tibia, Arkansas, was any great metropolis, he reminded himself glumly. If it had a superhero, he'd wear a brown cape and be named the Daring Defecator.

"We could," Kathleen said with great innocence, "but I thought you'd be pleased to have a little extra time with Natalie. She's such a nice girl, isn't she? That manager of hers is something else. A tyrant of the worst kind. She didn't so much as nod at me at the tournament in Little Rock. I don't know why Natalie allows herself to be treated that way."

"Natalie'll be there tomorrow?"

"I'm sure she wants to get in a practice round. For once, we can afford an extra night at the motel. It's very inexpensive."

"Does it have electricity?"

Kathleen smiled at her beloved son. "Of course it does."

She returned to the kitchen and picked up the iron. The only way they would continue to have electricity at home was if Kale won the bass boat. They could surely get at least thirty thousand dollars for it. And if she had to dangle that snippety blonde to persuade him to play a practice round, so be it.

Natalie voiced the same objections that Kyle had, but timidly. "I don't see why we can't drive out there and play a practice round, then come back for the night."

"So you can go out to the pool and get all cozy with that architecture student?" Janna said. "Don't think I didn't see you out there yesterday, crawling all over him. You told me you intended to swim laps, but your hair wasn't even damp when you got back. Did you make a date with him? There's no point in lying; I'm not stupid. I heard that you and Tommy Ridner had a cozy chat at the club yesterday. Did you and he make plans to sneak out behind a barn? You're behaving like a bitch in heat. You told me you'd do anything to make it big in the LPGA. Have you changed your mind?"

"Of course not. I just don't see why I can't have a little fun, too."

Janna took a deep breath while she calculated the most effective response. Dealing with Natalie was harder than breaking in new recruits. It required a careful balance of empathy and authority. "I understand that, Natalie. You're not even twenty yet, but you have to make sacrifices now if you want success and happiness in the future. In a few years, you'll be established, wealthy. There'll be time for fun. To get there, you have to focus on your goal. Sex is a distraction. When you're putting for a birdie, your mind can't wander off."

"How would you know sex is a distraction?"

"Because I've seen casualties in Central America and Iraq. Good soldiers who got careless and didn't adhere to procedure, for no other reason than worrying about their families or their lovers. The suicide rate in the military is higher than the comparable rate of civilians. Stress causes distraction, leading to self-destruction."

"I meant you personally."

"You're pushing your luck," Janna said. "Now pack your suitcase. We'll leave tomorrow after my class at the gym."

I was relieved when the yachtsman did not drop by the PD to reiterate his dinner invitation. There was something almost creepy about him. He hadn't really told me anything about himself, except that he was a friend of Bony Buchanon's. It seemed improbable. I didn't bother to lock the door of the PD as I headed down the road to Ruby Bee's. If one of the locals wanted to break in, he was welcome to it. My gun was secured in a metal cabinet, and my box with three bullets was at the back of a desk drawer. Nothing else was worth spit.

Ruby Bee gave me a frantic look as I came across the dance floor. She'd been acting odd for a few days, too distracted to bombard me with questions about my immediate future. Since that had been the norm for the last several weeks, its absence was disturbing. Almost, anyway.

"What's up?" I hopped on a stool and looked at the chalkboard with the list of daily specials. Chicken 'n' dumplings. Fried okra. Cherry cobbler. Some days I felt like I was eating not for two but for a prenatal football team.

"Estelle's gone missing," she said.

"Gone missing where?"

Ruby Bee glared at me. "If I knew where she was, then she wouldn't be missing, would she? What do you aim to do?"

"Decide between the cobbler and the red velvet cake," I said, frowning at the menu. "Maybe I'll wait and see." I gave her my attention. "What's the deal with Estelle?"

"Look for yourself, missy. She's not here. I called her house, but she didn't answer. Then Boyle Buchanon came in and said how he saw her car parked alongside the road that goes to Seeping Springs and peters out at the old Ferncliff place. Nobody's lived there for nigh onto thirty years. I don't understand why she'd abandon her car there."

"In Seeping Springs or at the Ferncliff place?"

Ruby Bee threw her dish towel in the sink. "No, alongside the road that goes to those places."

I admit I was confused. "How far down the road, then?"

"Fifty yards, maybe."

"So you think she hitched a ride to Seeping Springs and on to the Ferncliff place?" I asked, even more confused. "If she had a reason to go out there, why wouldn't she drive herself?"

"The way I see it," Ruby Bee said, ignoring a holler from a back booth for a fresh pitcher of beer, "is that Estelle had her own reasons for going there. Maybe she was tracking down some old woman's formula for making hair dyes out of bark and berries. Anyway, her car broke down. She decided to walk, but along the way somebody stopped and offered her a ride. A lunatic or a pervert, but she didn't know that when she got in his car. Now he's holding her prisoner and doing all manner of lewd things to her person. You got to rescue her, Arly."

"How long has she been missing?"

"Well, she usually comes in around four, unless she has a late appointment. I called her house at five. It's after six, and I ain't seen hide nor hair of her. If she was giving someone a perm, she would have answered the phone."

"You saw her earlier today?" I asked.

Ruby Bee must have seen the skepticism all over my face, but she charged ahead. "She was here at lunchtime."

"Did she mention this expedition to the backwoods?"

"Of course not." She turned her back on me and adjusted a neon beer sign that was marginally out of alignment. After she'd stalled long enough to concoct a story, she faced me. "Estelle is very closed-mouth when she's on the trail of an important discovery. One of these days she'll find a miracle formula that will make her millions of dollars—if her competitors don't find it first. Cosmetology is a bloodthirsty competition. Lip gloss can sink ships."

"Think of all these cosmetologists slinking through the woods, dressed in camo smocks, carrying M-16 scissors, perm grenades, and curling irons."

Ruby Bee put her hands on her hips. "If you reckon on having chicken 'n' dumplings anytime soon, you'd best go out and investigate Estelle's car for signs of a struggle."

"I thought her car broke down and she was kidnapped while walking to Seeping Springs," I said.

"Then go see why her car broke down," she countered. "When you have some answers, you can have cobbler *and* cake."

"I'm not a mechanic."

"No, you're a chief of police whose duty is to investigate crimes. Run along and do your job."

I realized that I wouldn't get so much as a dimple of a dumpling until I complied. There was a streak in Ruby Bee that rivaled a stone wall. The best I'd ever done was chip away at it, with minimal effect. I left the bar and grill, went over to the PD to get my car, and drove down the road alongside the SuperSaver parking lot. There was a crowd gathered around the bass boat, reverently gazing at it as if it were an artifact out of the Bible. One of the men was furtively wiping his eyes. When a child reached out to touch it, adult faces recoiled in horror.

Estelle's station wagon was parked as purported by Boyle Buchanon. He wasn't the most reliable of witnesses, in that he came by the PD every few months to report a close encounter with polar bears. I frowned as I noted that it was facing Maggody's main road, not Seeping Springs. I continued until I found a place to turn around, then came back and parked behind the station wagon. If it had broken down on her way back from Seeping Springs, she could have easily walked, even in her four-inch heels, to the SuperSaver to call for a tow truck.

I got out of my car and inspected hers for overt damage.

The doors were locked, and the key was not in the ignition. Wherever she'd gone, she'd taken her purse. I drove to the SuperSaver and went to the nearest checkout line.

Idalupino Buchanon nodded at me. "Hey, Arly, how's it going?"

"Did Estelle Oppers come in here this afternoon?"

"Not that I recollect. I always notice her 'cause she looks like she's got a japonica bush on her head. Business has been good on account of the boat out there. People come in to buy something so they have an excuse to stop and goggle at the boat. It's the first time some of the husbands have ever been in here. Mostly they let their wives do the shopping."

"A fascinating insight into tribal behavior. Are you sure you didn't see her? Could you have been on break?"

"Jim Bob don't like us taking breaks, but when you gotta go, you gotta go. Cinatra and me cover for each other." She raised her voice. "Cinatra, you seen Estelle today?"

Cinatra Buchanon glanced up from a tabloid. "Can't say I did."

"She would have needed to make a phone call," I persisted. "Any chance she might have dropped by for a minute and then left?"

"One of us would have seen her," Idalupino said stubbornly. "The pay phone's right there. Jim Bob don't let anyone use the phone in his office. He's afraid he might get caught looking at porn on his computer. He always keeps the door locked except when he's in there slobbering over nekkid girls. He left about four."

"Thanks," I said. It was getting peculiar, and Ruby Bee did have a right to be concerned. Estelle had disappeared sometime during the afternoon, abandoning her car on a county road. I drove to her house, took the key from under a flowerpot and looked in all the rooms, then went back to the bar and grill. All I'd learned was that Estelle had a fondness for romance paperbacks and peppermints.

There were some new faces in the booths and on stools. Ruby Bee was dashing all over the place, slamming down blue plate specials, hamburgers, and pitchers of beer. Hizzoner Jim Bob, Larry Joe Lambertino, Jeremiah McIlhany, and Ruddy Cranshaw were seated in a booth, arguing and jabbing their fingers at each other. Bopeep's boyfriend, whose name I'd never heard (and hoped I never did), was clearly drunker than a skunk. Bony Buchanon leaned over the jukebox, his lips moving as he read the list of selections. An older couple, dressed for a more civilized affair, moved together on the tiny dance floor. From the way they kept stepping on each other's feet, I could tell they were unnerved by the ambience. They stumbled into each other when Hairless Buchanon wandered by with an indignant chicken under his arm.

"Well?" Ruby Bee snapped as she caught my arm.

"I don't know," I said over the din. "Her car's still there, and she's not home. She wasn't on her way to Seeping Springs, though. She may have been on her way back. It's premature to issue an APB." I glanced around. "Big crowd tonight."

"It's on account of this fool golf tournament. Some of the folks from out of state checked in this afternoon, even though the tournament doesn't start until Saturday morning. They said they wanted to get in a practice round, but it seems late in the game to start practicing. You either know how to play or you don't. Not that *that's* stopping anybody. You heard who all has signed up?"

Since she was going to tell me anyway, I obligingly said, "Who?"

"Nigh onto twenty folks from Maggody, that's who. It's causing a real flapadoodle. All matter of husbands and wives didn't bother to tell each other. The women have been taking lessons on the sly, and so have the men. It came out when registration officially closed this afternoon. There's liable to be bloodshed in several households." She tilted her head. "See Jim Bob and his cronies over there? I can't tell if they're angrier at their wives for fooling them or for booting them out on their butts."

I grinned. "That ought to liven things up this weekend. I thought my only headache was the parking problem. Now about the chicken 'n' dumplings . . . ?"

Ruby Bee shrugged. "As long as you promise to get your fanny in action and find Estelle in the morning. I won't be able to sleep a wink until I know she's safe."

I gave her a halfhearted salute and found a vacant stool.

It was eight o'clock when the semblance of a meeting began in Roy Stiver's back room. It was stuffy and crowded, and the best Roy could offer was saltine crackers and grape jelly. Most of the participants were jittery, unsure where they'd be sleeping that night, or maybe the next few weeks.

"What it's called is a tontine," Jim Bob began. "I called this fellow I know who used to be a lawyer afore he went to prison. He drew up the papers. Once everybody signs it, I'll take it to him and he'll have it notarized. If one of us wins the bass boat, it becomes the property of the tontine. We'll each get thirty-six and a half days per year to use it. We'll figure out how to divide it up later. Thing is, if someone moves out of Stump County or dies, his share stays in the tontine. The last man standing gets the boat outright."

"Sounds dangerous," Roy observed.

"Whattaya mean?" asked Kevin.

Jim Bob narrowed his eyes. "All you have to do is sign the paper, dumb-ass. You can write your name, can't you?"

"Sure, Jim Bob, but why is it dangerous?"

"It's dangerous because if you don't sign it, I'm gonna rip out your eyeballs and feed them to Raz's sow. Here's a pen, boy. See this dotted line?"

"What about Luke?" Larry Joe said. "He ain't been in Maggody but a couple of weeks. He can hit a decent drive, mebbe further than any of the rest of us, but he ain't what you'd call a resident. Bopeep's had a string of boyfriends over the last five years. You can ask anyone." He realized he was staring at Jim Bob and edged behind Roy.

"Yeah," Luke finally said as he lit a cigarette, "but I get the rules. I'll take my turn using the boat as long as I'm here. After that, it'll belong to the nine of you."

Everybody shuffled forward.

At eight o'clock sharp, Mrs. Jim Bob banged her gavel on the dinette table. The committee chairwomen, as well as their recruits, were jammed in the kitchen, all jabbering like a flock of grackles. Indignation was running high among the wives present. Most of their remarks included phrases like "Can you believe he had the nerve to . . . ?" and "Who does he think he is to forbid me to . . . ?" Joyce Lambertino was reduced to stuttery rage. Millicent McIlhaney had tears in her eyes. Cora Cranshaw's face was getting splotchier by the minute, her hands flapping so wildly that Bopeep and Audley were dodging like boxers to avoid a stray punch. Brother Verber was doing his level best to hide in a corner, within reach of the pound cake but out of range should violence arise. Darla Jean decided the scene was worse than the high school girls' restroom on junior prom night.

"Order!" Mrs. Jim Bob shrieked, pounding the gavel with such fury that it sounded like a jackhammer. "This meeting is called to order!"

The room quieted down, although most of the wives were replaying the recent arguments in their minds.

"Darla Jean," Mrs. Jim Bob said briskly, "announce the final figure."

"Eighty-two, which comes out to eight thousand and two hundred dollars. I deposited the checks at the bank in Farberville, like you said to, and I have the registration forms here." Darla Jean wished this would be the end of her participation, but she knew Mrs. Jim Bob. She put the envelope on the table. "I wrote down all the names on a list. It's in there, too."

"Very well. I have a bag of pin-on plastic name tags. Write each name on one and arrange them in alphabetical order in a shoe box. You'll have a table in the tent for participants to sign in and pick up their information sheets."

"Mind your handwriting, Darla Jean," said Miss Estes. "It tends to look like chicken scratches. Also, pay attention to the proper spelling of each name."

"Yes, ma'am."

Mrs. Jim Bob moved on. "Elsie, is the hospitality committee ready?"

Elsie blushed as everyone looked at her. "We sure are. The tent will be up by noon tomorrow. The tables and chairs are stored in Earl's barn. It would have been handier to put them in Raz's, but he was right rude about it. I suspect he's got a few cases of his filthy moonshine hidden in there."

Brother Verber realized this was his cue to assert himself as the spiritual leader of his flock. His hands entwined over his heart, he stepped forward and intoned, " 'Know ye not that the unrighteous shall not inherit the kingdom of God? Be not deceived; neither fornicators, nor idolaters, nor adulterers, nor effeminate, nor abusers of themselves with mankind, nor thieves, nor covetous, nor drunkards, nor revilers, nor extortioners, shall inherit the kingdom of God.' First Corinthians, book six, verses nine and ten, for those who might want to study this passage."

Mrs. Jim Bob paused to regather her thoughts. "Is Raz causing any problems with the green committee, Eileen?"

She shook her head. "No, he's still letting Earl mow the pasture, and he agreed to keep his mule penned up until the tournament's done with. Earl's gonna mow a final time in the morning. For all I care, he can mow hisself right into Boone Creek! Why on God's green earth does he have the right to tell me that I don't have any business playing in this—"

"Thank you, Eileen," Mrs. Jim Bob cut in before everybody got all prickly again. "What about the food, Elsie?"

"Muck Haskell over in Hasty is smoking briskets and

chicken wings for us. He's my second cousin-in-law once removed, so he's doing it at cost. I have two big pans of scalloped
potatoes in my freezer. Crystal will pick up buns, bread, and
doughnuts from the day-old shop tomorrow afternoon. Lucille's making three gallons of her pecan cranberry slaw,
and Millicent will fix baked beans. I've lined up a half a
dozen sheet cakes." Elsie, being one of the top quilters in the
county, prided herself on the details. "The high school girls
will make sandwiches and cookies for lunch."

"I volunteered my home ec classes," Lottie added, unwilling to let Elsie take all the credit. "They been properly
trained to handle food in a hygienic fashion."

Darla Jean made a note to bring a sack lunch.

Mrs. Jim Bob nodded. "I had a talk with Mr. Cartier and
Bonaparte about the scheduling. We have twenty and a half
foursomes. Each will have a designated tee time that I'll
put on a poster board. In order to get everybody around the
course, half of the foursomes will start on the back nine.
There'll be a ten-minute interval, and it's vitally important
that we enforce this. Bonaparte said this was cutting it close.
I told him that folks who couldn't play at a brisk pace had no
business entering this tournament in the first place. A high
school boy will monitor each hole. We can't have someone
claiming a hole-in-one without official verification. Mr.
Cartier's going to meet with them Saturday morning to tell
them the rules. Other boys will be there in case someone
wants a caddy."

"Is Mr. Cartier here tonight?" asked Bopeep, her eyes
glittering like a hawk perched on a fence post.

"No, he is not. He is a very thoughtful houseguest, and
assumed I might be too busy to prepare yet another elegant
meal. When I told him about this meeting, he asked me to
pass along his warmest regards and hopes for our success
this weekend."

"He dropped by my house for coffee yesterday morning,"
Cora said. "We had a lovely chat."

"I served him lunch on Tuesday," Elsie said, sneering. "He was smitten with my chicken salad with almonds. He said it was the best chicken salad he'd ever had."

Millicent was having none of that. "Well, he certainly enjoyed my cherry cheesecake yesterday afternoon. We must have sat on the patio and talked for more than an hour. He even kissed my hand before he left."

"You never said one word about it!" Joyce said. "Any of you."

Elsie smiled modestly. "Mr. Cartier was concerned about my reputation. He is, after all, a bachelor. The two of us, unchaperoned, in my home . . ."

"And I'm a married woman," Millicent added. "Mr. Cartier suggested discretion."

Mrs. Jim Bob forced herself to loosen her grip on the gavel before she behaved rashly. "I'm sure Mr. Cartier was motivated by his Christian conscience. He'll be too busy for that sort of gadding about tomorrow. He most kindly offered to handle the beverage purchases. We'll have coffee, tea, and sodas during the day. He and Bonaparte both insisted that we serve alcoholic beverages in the evening. I protested, naturally, but it seems to be customary at golf tournaments. Mr. Cartier understood my reluctance and promised to buy the minimum we can get away with. I gave him a blank check from the account so he can negotiate with distributors in Farberville."

"Does he need anyone to help him?" Joyce persisted. "I'll be happy to go with him." Several other volunteers raised their hands.

Mrs. Jim Bob crossed her arms. "Those of you who will be playing this weekend need to spend every minute of your spare time practicing. Those of you who backed out because of arthritis, rheumatism, back ailments, and so forth can use your time more wisely by helping make sure the tournament runs smoothly. Just because Mr. Cartier is handsome and charming does not excuse unseemly thoughts concerning his personage. We are all ladies." Her lips were tight as she waited for her words to sink in. "In the morning Bonaparte will be here at ten for our last lesson. He thinks that we should learn how to putt. I have no idea why, since the boat will be awarded for a hole-in-one. Putting can't be that hard."

"I'm gonna beat Earl's score if I have to wrap a golf club around his neck," Eileen said. "If I don't win the boat, at least I'll have some satisfaction."

Cora stuck out her chin. "I feel the same way. Ruddy's gonna have to eat his words before he eats one bite of my meatloaf."

"Rip's gonna be eating crow," said Audley, "and I hope he chokes on it. I won't be able to save him, since I'm nothing but a feeble-minded housewife who belongs in the kitchen. I made a quiche for supper. It's been so long it's a miracle I could remember how to do it."

"I ate a box of chocolate-covered cherries for supper," Crystal said proudly.

Brother Verber lunged for the pound cake.

Four

I was gazing numbly at a late-night talk show when my phone rang. All manner of bizarre images raced through my mind as I grabbed the receiver. Had the host heard me yawn? Was the call coming from a pay phone in a Brazilian hospital?

"What?" I demanded.

"Estelle's back," Ruby Bee said calmly. "I thought you might want to know."

I waited until my adrenaline simmered down. "Back from where? Is she okay?"

"You'll have to ask her yourself. She's sputtering like a wet hen and I can't make heads or tails of what she's saying. I still got some cake."

I yanked on a pair of jeans, switched off the TV, and went to the bar and grill. Only one truck was in the parking lot, and as I walked across the road, two men climbed in it and drove away. If I'd been a diligent law enforcement agent, I would have chased them down and issued tickets for public drunkenness and DWI. I was more interested in hearing Estelle's story.

She was sitting on a stool but had run out of sputters. A bottle of sherry was within her reach. She didn't so much as glance at me when I sat down on the adjoining stool. Her hair had held its shape for the most part, but frizzly curls strayed down her neck and covered her forehead. Her face and bare arms were covered with smears of dirt and red welts. Her blue blouse was missing a button and decorated with muddy polka dots.

Ruby Bee put a slice of cake and a glass of milk in front of me. "She makes a smidgeon of sense every once in a while," she whispered, "but I ain't sure what all happened."

"I heard that!" Estelle snapped. "You know how much I hate it when folks talk about me behind my back."

"I'm standing right here in front of you," Ruby Bee said. "Unless, of course, you got your head swiveled all the way around."

Estelle snorted. "Maybe I do. That'd be the perfect ending to the day." She refilled her glass. "It was my own damn fault, so feel free to make fun of me. Make sure everybody in town hears about it. My clients will take to going to Casa de Coiffure over in Hasty. When my savings run out, I can move to an old folks' home and make birdhouses out of Popsicle sticks."

I kept my fork out of her reach. "What did you do to deserve such a fate? Hold up a bank? Run down a bunch of schoolchildren?"

"Dahlia had a flat tire."

Ruby Bee frowned. "Dahlia had a flat tire, so you're moving to an old folks' home to make birdhouses?"

"Likely so. It'll be hard to get used to oatmeal, fish sticks, and canned peaches."

"Explain, okay?" I said, my patience disappearing as fast as the chocolate cake.

Estelle sucked in a breath and said, "Dahlia was worried about Kevin. He's been coming home late and acting all mysterious. I told her I was going to follow him and Jim Bob when they left the SuperSaver yesterday afternoon. She insisted on going, too. The children were in their car seats, so we took her car."

"The husbands have been practicing for the golf tournament," Ruby Bee said. "They were talking about it earlier.

They've all been going to a sort of driving place. I swear on my granny's grave that I didn't know about it until they came in for supper."

"I don't care if they was sneaking off to take tango lessons. They left at four in Jim Bob's truck. Dahlia wanted to drive right on the back bumper, but I explained to her that we had to keep back so they wouldn't see us. We were doing fine until she noticed that we were about to run out of gas. She pulled over at a convenience store and pumped a couple of gallons. Once we got back on the road, they were nowhere to be seen. Dahlia wasn't going to have that, so she put the medal to the petal, or whatever they say, 'til we were going too fast for my liking. The twins loved it. They were screaming and banging on Daisy. I was feared my eardrums were gonna explode."

"Did they?" I asked.

"I don't have to put up with your attitude, young lady. Just hush up and I'll go on." She waited until I meekly nodded. "Well, after a few miles, Dahlia swore she saw Jim Bob's truck turn onto a narrow road. I didn't see it myself, since I was twisted around to tell the twins what I'd do to 'em if they kept throwing Tinkertoys at the back of my head. So there we were, going down this road that was getting bumpier by the minute. After ten miles, it petered out at a wood bridge that had collapsed decades ago. Dahlia ran over some rusty nails when she turned around. I got out to check, and there was the tire, limp as a rubber band. It took twenty minutes to unload the trunk, what with the stroller and fishing gear and boxes of junk. We finally found the spare tire, which turned out to be flat as well. I seriously considered knocking her upside the head with it."

Ruby Bee's eyes were wide. "I don't blame you."

Mine were drooping. "You're all in the middle of nowhere. There's no sign of Jim Bob's truck. The vultures are circling."

"And somebody needed a fresh diaper," Estelle continued grimly. "The last house we drove by was a good five or six miles back. If I hadn't been wearing my new blue heels, I would have walked. Dahlia kept getting madder and madder, blaming the whole thing on Kevin. She was huffing and puffing so fiercely that the cows in the pasture moved away. I took the twins down to the creek and let 'em chase minnows. We had to see to personal business in the woods. When it started getting dark, we sat in the car and ate peanut butter crackers and drank apple juice."

"But then you were rescued," prompted Ruby Bee.

"Do I look like I'm sitting in Dahlia's front seat with cracker crumbs all over my lap? Dahlia and the children finally fell asleep. The snoring and snuffling was bad enough, but then it turned out that Dahlia must have been fixing beans for supper every night for the last month. It got so thick I had to go sit on the hood of the car. The mosquitoes were all over me, and the weeds kept rustling like something was out there."

I finished my milk and stood up. "I assume that instead of being attacked by a mountain lion, somebody came along, took the spare to be patched, and changed the tire for you."

"A very nice old coot," Estelle said, annoyed that her saga had been cut short. "He wouldn't take a dime for helping us."

"A good Samaritan," Ruby Bee said.

Case closed, I told myself as I left.

At nine o'clock the next morning I was drinking a small carton of milk and munching a store-bought cinnamon roll when Kevin Buchanon skittered into the PD. "Hey, Kevin," I said, forcing myself to smile. He was not a sight for sore eyes, especially on an empty stomach. "You want something?"

"It's Dahlia and the younguns," he said as he collapsed into the uncomfortable chair I found at a landfill. It does a good job keeping long-winded visitors from overstaying their welcome (which is five minutes, max). "They din't come home until nigh on eleven last night, and they looked like they'd been rolling in dirt. The twins have bug bites all over. Dahlia must have got into a chigger patch. Her ankles are all swollen up and red. She hasn't said one word to me. I begged and pleaded, but all she does is snuffle."

I put down the cinnamon roll. "That pissed, huh?"

He scratched his head. "I wish I knowed why. We all had breakfast yesterday morning. I told Dahlia I had to work late again. She got awful het up, like a widow woman with a spider in her hair. I left afore she could throw something at me. I called long about lunchtime to find out if she'd calmed down, but nobody answered. I figured she must've taken the younguns outside afore she put 'em down for naps, but—"

"Moving right along . . ."

"Anyways," he said with a gulp, "they weren't anywhere to be found when I got home a little after seven. I called my ma, but she said she hadn't heard from Dahlia since early in the afternoon. I had to go . . . someplace at eight. I figgered they'd be safe at home by the time I got back." He deflated in the chair as tears zigzagged down his acne-scarred cheeks. "You got to make Dahlia tell me what happened and why she won't talk to me."

"That's not in my job description, Kevin. Where did you go last night?" I doubted it had any significance, but I was curious. Potlucks and prayer meetings are reserved for Wednesdays, and the county extension club on alternate Mondays. Maggody once had a chamber of commerce for about a week. Kiwanis and Rotarians have yet to organize, and nobody seems eager to prance around in a bedsheet. Kevin was not among the poker players who gathered at Roy's apartment at the back of the antiques store several times a week. If nothing else, he couldn't afford it. I could hear them from my apartment, and I knew they weren't gambling with pennies and nickels.

"Out," Kevin squeaked, his Adam's apple bobbing like a dried leaf in a stretch of rapids. "Nowhere important, just out."

"Why have you been working late?"

"Not all that late. I been gittin' home long about eight. It ain't like I'm draggin' in at midnight with lipstick on my collar. Dahlia wants me home to help with baths and bedtime. Three kids is a mighty big handful, you know. Dahlia runs the washing machine all day, hangs laundry on the clothesline, fixes meals, tries to keep the house clean, along with changing diapers and—"

I interrupted before he listed all of her domestic complaints, which might take another twenty-four hours. "*Why* have you been working late?"

"I cain't tell you."

"Why not?" I knew the answer, but decided to bait him as punishment for the melodrama of the previous afternoon and evening. "And where did you go last night?"

He hung his head. "Jim Bob said he'd fire me if I told anyone."

"If Jim Bob's engaged in criminal behavior, you have to tell me. Otherwise, you're an accessory." To what, I had no clue. Jim Bob wasn't smart enough to commit an elaborate felony. Raz Buchanon wasn't likely to take on a partner in his moonshine operation. And Jim Bob certainly wouldn't have bullied Kevin into accompanying him to a daily dalliance in a motel.

"It ain't criminal!" Kevin protested. "It's called a tan-tin or a tom-tom or somethin' like that."

I raised my eyebrows. "Are you sure it's not a tutu? Have you boys been taking ballet lessons? I'd sell my soul for a photograph of Jim Bob in the midst of a *grand jeté*. Why, we may have to take to calling him Jim Baryshnikov Buchanon."

"A tutu like what Perkin's eldest wore to church last month? No, it ain't anything like that." Kevin came over to the desk and leaned forward. "You got to make her tell me, Arly."

I rocked back to avoid a view of his molars. "I'll do everything I can. Why don't you go talk to your ma?"

He pondered this for a minute. "Okay, I'll go over to Ma's and see if she has any ideas."

I tossed the cinnamon roll in the wastebasket.

Brother Verber sat forward, his elbows on his knees and a glass of sacramental wine handy, as he stared at the video playing on his TV. Who would have dreamed that golf widows were young, voluptuous, and very naughty while their husbands were at the golf course? Apparently, they were so distraught that they did housework buck naked, found comfort in fornication with plumbers and electricians, battled loneliness and depression by engaging in perverted pleasures with UPS delivery men—and still had supper on the table when their hubbies got home. Their courage and selfless dedication was inspiring, he thought mistily.

He hit the rewind button, determined to watch the video another time or two so he could figure out how best to prepare himself to chase ol' Satan off golf courses and protect poor golf widows from further degradation. He could see himself thundering down a fairway, brandishing a golf club above his head, his eyes blazing with the fury of a soldier in the army of the Almighty Lord. Since he had a diploma from the seminary, he'd surely be a colonel, if not a general. Why, he could get some medals and ribbons at a flea market and pin 'em on his chest like General Patton.

The opening credits were reappearing on the screen when he heard a series of staccato raps on the trailer door. The sound was familiar. Panicked, he turned off the TV, stuck the glass of wine behind the couch, kicked the cassette box under it, and made sure his bathrobe was tightly belted before he opened the rectory door.

"Why, good morning, Sister Barbara. What a delightful—"

"I need to talk to you." Mrs. Jim Bob brushed past him and sat down on an armchair. "I have to go home shortly to make refreshments for after the golf lesson." She looked at the bare coffee table. "I hope I'm not interrupting you in the middle of writing your Sunday sermon."

"You are always welcome, Sister Barbara. No, I wasn't writing my sermon. It was more like I was contemplating the wisdom of the Good Book for how to best shoo sinners back to the path of virtue. Temptation of the most bewildering kind is all around us." He glanced at the remote control, then willed himself not to allow certain images to cloud his mind. "I shouldn't burden you with my fears of the impending Apocalypse, when the Four Horsemen bring forth the end of the world and all that can be heard is the wail of sinners as they're sucked into the fiery furnace. Would you like a cup of tea? I was just fixin' to put the kettle on. I'm afraid I don't have any cookies or cake, but I can make you a real tasty cheese and pickle sandwich."

"No, thank you," she said. She glanced at the corner of a box sticking out from under the couch, but she couldn't make it out. She was reaching for it when Brother Verber plopped down.

"You feel the need to bare your soul?" He beamed at her as his heel nudged the box into the netherworld of dust bunnies and wine bottle caps. "I hope you're not troubled, but I'm here for you if you want to pray over whatever has caused that tiny wrinkle to mar your forehead."

"I'm not here out of vanity, Brother Verber, but out of the need for spiritual guidance. During what some might call a disagreement yesterday with Jim Bob, I recalled a snippet from my wedding vows all those many years ago. You know, the love, honor, and obey part. Is it really a sin for a wife to disobey her husband?"

"It's a matter of interpretation, Sister Barbara," he said cautiously. "Ephesians, chapter five, verse twenty-two, says, 'Wives, submit yourselves unto your own husbands, as unto the Lord. For the husband is the head of the wife, even as Christ is the head of the church.' Then again, we *are* talking about Jim Bob."

Her eyes grew beadier. "I'd as soon submit to a blind dentist. Anyway, he lied about taking golf lessons long before I did. If he's the head of the church, I'd rather be a pagan and make pot roast out of missionaries."

"Ah, the golf tournament." Brother Verber belched softly as he searched his biblical knowledge for an escape clause. "First Peter, chapter three, verse one, says, 'Likewise, ye wives be in subjection to your own husbands.' It goes on after that, but it gets kind of muddled. However, it doesn't say anything about golf. Not one single word. Maybe it was left out intentionally."

"Maybe." Mrs. Jim Bob took a lace-trimmed hankie out of her purse and began to twist it. "Does the Bible say anything about husbands being in subjection to their own wives? That would help, since we'd cancel out each other. I told Jim Bob in no uncertain words that he has no business playing in the tournament out of nothing more than greed. All he and the other men want is the bass boat. He's never said one word about helping golf widows."

Brother Verber winced. It was more than likely that Jim Bob *had* helped more than one golf widow, he thought, but not in a way he wanted to bring up for discussion. "You have a good point, Sister Barbara, a very good point. It's like one spouse voting Democrat and the other Republican. No harm, no foul. The fact that you're motivated by charity tilts in your favor. Shall we pray for the Almighty Lord to keep you out of the rough and on that fairway to heavenly bliss?" He grabbed her hand and squeezed it. It was as smooth and supple as a fish fillet, he thought. Her fingernails glistened like pearls. The simple gold ring around her fourth finger represented a blessing from the Almighty Lord. He was so touched by her saintly presence that he felt a warm glow in his privates. "Come sit here on the sofa next to me so I can comfort you. I can't tell you how much I admire all the time and work you've put into this tournament. You must be exhausted, Sister Barbara. Why don't you take off your shoes and let me massage your feet?"

"I appreciate the offer, but I'm in a hurry, Brother Verber."

"All these sacrifices will be recorded in St. Peter's ledger book. When you get to heaven, you'll be upgraded to a celestial suite."

"I'm not sure making butterscotch brownies qualifies as a sacrifice."

He wasn't either, but he plowed ahead. "You're making them for the betterment of the tournament, which is all about Christian generosity. It's like"—he fumbled for a moment—"when Jesus fed the multitude with loaves and fishes. You're doing the same thing with butterscotch brownies and iced tea." He moistened his lips with the tip of his tongue. "Would you like me to drop by after the lesson and say grace?"

"I don't believe that's necessary, Brother Verber," Mrs. Jim Bob said, unwilling to make enough brownies to feed even a minor multitude. She pulled her hand free and stood up. "You can plan to say grace Saturday evening before we serve the barbecue, and on Sunday afternoon when we present the trophies. Oh, there is something else you can do this afternoon. The trophies are at a sports store in Farberville. I had the bowlers replaced with loving cups and the plaques engraved with the name of the tournament and the date. Pick them up and hang on to them until the ceremony. If the store demands payment immediately, the committee will pay you back." She scribbled the name of the store on the back of an old grocery list and gave it to him.

He waited until he heard her car drive off, and then another minute just to be on the safe side, before he retrieved his glass of wine and picked up the remote control.

Roy Stiver was sitting in a Louis XIV Barcalounger outside his store, dressed in overalls and a splintery straw hat, waiting for unwary tourists to wander into his lair. He hollered at me, so I walked across the road.

"You heard what all's going on?" he asked me.

"I don't know if I've heard *all* of it, but I've heard enough."

He took out a corncob pipe and began to fiddle with it. "What do you think of this tontine crap?"

I sat down on a battle-scarred pew. "I haven't heard about that. It has to do with the bass boat, I suppose."

"It's based on the very feeble assumption that one of them will actually make a hole-in-one. Jim Bob's idea, naturally. He had some lawyer draw up the document, but I'm not sure that it's legal on account of providing the members with too much incentive to bump each other off. You ever read *The Wrong Box* by Robert Louis Stevenson? A tontine may work as a plot in mystery novels, but even then it's far-fetched."

I realized that Kevin had been groping for the word when he was at the PD. A tutu was a lot more amusing. "The usual suspects?"

"Pretty much. Jim Bob, Larry Joe, Jeremiah, Earl, Big Dick, Ruddy, Rip, Tam, Kevin—that makes nine. Lemme think. Yeah, and Bopeep's current boyfriend, a guy named Luke Smithers. You know anything about him?"

"He drinks a lot of beer at Ruby Bee's. Other than that, I haven't had any reason to waste time speculating about him. Bopeep's had more boyfriends than my apartment has roaches. Should I keep an eye on him?"

Roy finally had his pipe smoldering to his satisfaction. "No, not that I know of. He seems kind of shiftless, but so do a lot of other people in this neck of the woods. If he were dumber and uglier, he'd make a fine Buchanon."

"Harsh words, Roy."

"You recall ol' Bangcock Buchanon? He decided that squirrels were Russian spies, so he got a box of dynamite and blew himself to kingdom come."

Kevin's tom-tom was nothing more than a silly, illegal

document. My dream was shattered; Hizzoner was not a closet ballerina.

As soon as he could, Bony called an end to the final golf lesson. Most of his students were a menace to themselves, as well as anyone within fifty feet—and that was with a putter. He declined to stay for tea and brownies, and after unhappily agreeing to return for lunch, he hustled down the driveway to have a stiff drink before Aunt Eileen showed up.

The ladies retired to Mrs. Jim Bob's sunroom to fortify themselves for the following day's challenge. Once they were all settled and cheerfully clucking among themselves, Audley Riley held up a hand. "I'd like to say something." Since she rarely opened her mouth, the room fell silent. "Our husbands have come up with this nonsense about a tontine. Earlier this morning I called my nephew Bryce down in Little Rock on account of him being a lawyer. He told me that a tontine is where everybody signs an agreement that the prize belongs to the group. In the end, the last person alive gets it. Bryce says it's not legal."

"Then why should we care?" asked Eileen.

"Damn craziness," Bopeep said. She realized that she'd stepped over the line, and quickly added, "Darn craziness, I meant to say. The men are acting like a bunch of grubby little boys that build a clubhouse in the woods with a sign that says 'No girls allowed.' As if any girl with common sense would want to join."

Mrs. Jim Bob ignored the snickering as she thought it over. "It is craziness, I agree, but it bothers me. It's like each one of us has to beat all ten of them. The odds don't seem equal. If someone like Jeremiah wins, for instance, then all of our husbands benefit. That doesn't sit right with me."

"You got a point," Joyce said. "The very idea of Larry Joe getting a share of the boat even if he hits every ball in the rough . . ."

"It's just not right," Millicent said firmly. "We should do something. Can we have them arrested, Audley?"

"Bryce didn't seem to think so. He said that it was unenforceable, that's all. The winner gets the boat, and the losers can sue 'til the cows come home, but they can't win in court. Being from Little Rock, Bryce doesn't understand how things are enforced around here."

"I can't see any of them backing out," Eileen said, then paused. "Except for Luke. It's not like he has any ties to Maggody." She looked at Bopeep. "Unless, of course, you two are aiming to tie the knot sometime in the future. I mean, this could be the guy for you. I never meant to imply that y'all are . . ."

"Living in sin? No, we're just living in a double-wide for the time being." Bopeep popped her gum to express her disdain. "I couldn't care less if he gets a load of buckshot in his backside or strung up from a sycamore tree. Besides, he doesn't have a car. No way he could take off with the boat."

"So you think he might take off?" asked Joyce.

"Probably afore too long. He's waiting for a disability check from the army. Something about a foot injury, but he moves real fine. It's not like I'd bring home a cripple."

This prompted Crystal to talk about her bigamist cousin, which led to Cora's demented grandmother, which was drowned out by Lucille's complaints about her years of slavery when Big Dick's mother was alive. The stories grew downright gruesome as the pitcher of iced tea and plates of brownies were passed from martyr to martyr.

Mrs. Jim Bob came to a decision, although she wasn't sure how it would be received. She tapped a teaspoon on the sugar bowl. "We all agree that this ten-against-one is unfair. We have to take action. I propose that we sign a paper that says if any one of us wins the boat, then she'll donate it to the town to pay for a park. We can build it next to the Voice of the Almighty Lord Assembly Hall, with swings and sand boxes and picnic tables. A memorial park, I think, dedicated to deceased golf widows. The donor can have her own name on a brass plaque."

Eyes flickered and lower lips were nibbled as they pondered her words. Finally, Eileen said, "I was thinking of selling the boat and using the money for myself."

"The Almighty Lord does not look kindly on displays of greed and self-indulgence," Mrs. Jim Bob countered coldly. "He blesses gestures of Christian generosity and humility. Besides, you get your name on the plaque. Your grandchildren and their grandchildren will have a reminder of your contribution to the community."

"Do we have to donate all of it?" asked Crystal, who had already talked to a used car salesman in Starley City.

"How about ten percent?" Millicent suggested. "That's what the Bible says to tithe."

Brother Verber, who'd materialized toward the end of the lesson, perked up at the mention of the Assembly Hall. He swallowed a mouthful of brownie and said, "The fourteenth chapter of Deuteronomy instructs us to tithe corn, wine, oil, and firstlings of your herds and of your flocks. With inflation shooting up these days, it'd come to at least twenty percent, or even twenty-five."

Mrs. Jim Bob knew she was on thin ice. "I'll amend my proposal to fifty percent. Think of the shame of having your name on a park with cheap swing sets and rickety picnic tables. You'd be embarrassed to hold up your head when you drove by it. Why, you might even be sued if some poor child got hurt. As for the chances of eternal damnation . . . I shudder to think about it." She faked a small shudder. "Do I hear a second on the proposal?"

"Second," Joyce said in a sulky voice.

"All in favor?"

No one dared vote against the proposal. Mrs. Jim Bob rewarded them with a tight smile. "I'll write out our agreement and everybody can sign it before they leave."

"And may the Almighty be watching over you," Brother

Verber said. "As we're told in Psalm Seventy-two, verse seven, 'In his days the righteous will flourish; prosperity will abound 'til the moon is no more.' And if you Christian servants aren't righteous, well, nobody is. Hallelujah!" He tried to look humble, but he couldn't stop thinking how well his mail-order seminary had done by providing a verse for any situation. Marriages, funerals, confessions of the wickedest sins—yes, he was well armed.

"Amen," said Mrs. Jim Bob.

Ruby Bee was in a tizzy. Not only had the guests with motel reservations shown up, but all kinds of other folks in town for the golf tournament were clamoring for lunch, along with the regulars and a few truckers. Some were happy with the blue plate special (fried catfish, hush puppies, green tomato relish, beans, and slaw); others demanded salads with dressing on the side or dainty sandwiches on silly-sounding bread. The jukebox was blaring, and everybody was yelling at her like they thought she was deaf as a post. It was worse than the county fair midway on a Saturday night.

She went on into the kitchen to start a batch of hamburger patties. She was too busy breading catfish fillets to notice the black 1966 Imperial Crown Coupe glide by as the stoplight turned green.

Five

A couple of dozen golfers milled around under the tent. A decrepit barn, long since weathered into gray, tilted ominously. Rolls of chicken wire and rusty car parts were scattered in the mud. The nearby sty produced an acrid stench. Many of the ladies held tissues to their noses and rumbled with displeasure. Expressions ranged from shocked to appalled.

Tommy Ridner found Dennis and Amanda. "You been out on the course yet?" he asked as he joined them. Emanating lethal radiation waves, Amanda turned her back on him and walked away.

"Trying to get up my courage," Dennis said. "Somebody reported spotting a rogue sow, if there is such a thing. Others swear they saw copperheads in the rough and water moccasins in the ponds."

Tommy handed him a flask. "C'mon, let's play a round. I want to know if I should be using a wood or a wedge off the tees."

"I'm not in the mood to step on a snake."

"The real reason is that you're terrified of Amanda, aren't you?" He retrieved the flask and took a swallow. "Don't be a wuss, Dennis. Just go tell her you're going to play. She can go hide out in that crappy motel and read her magazines. That's assuming she doesn't want to hang around"—he glanced at the barn—"the clubhouse and have martinis."

"Why would I be terrified of Amanda? She's devoted to me, in case you haven't noticed. You've been trying to get her into bed since you were my best man. I admire your perseverance, but one of these days you'll have to admit defeat." He put his arm around Tommy's shoulders and grinned at him. "As they say, two's company and three's a crowd. But we'll always be friends, right?"

"I'm surprised she's letting you play at all. She seemed like she was really pissed off the other day."

"Just a little spat when I got home," Dennis said lightly. "She loves to come to tournaments with me, since we have the evenings to dine, dance, and enjoy ourselves in a romantic suite. The facilities here are substandard, to put it kindly. The only way I could placate her was to promise to use my winnings from the bet to take her on a Mediterranean cruise."

"You're not taking this bet seriously, are you?" Tommy said. "It was the booze talking. The bass boat's the real prize."

Dennis was offended by the idea that a boat was more valuable than his wife's amorous company. "We made the bet, Tommy, and you're not backing out of it. Amanda wants to sunbathe on a Greek island." He gestured at the rutted pasture. "In case you haven't noticed, this is the course. The fairways are the stubby weeds, the rough is the waist-high weeds. The greens are probably covered with dandelions. You can walk across the algae and scum in the ponds, if the alligators don't drag you under."

"It'll be a challenge," Tommy admitted. He pulled off his baseball cap and wiped his forehead with the back of his hand. "Hey, there's Natalie and her boot camp lesbian. Let's get up a foursome. I'll take Janna as a partner and you can have the princess. Match play, twenty bucks a hole between you and me."

"Tempting, but I don't believe the Coulter woman plays anymore, and Amanda will have a fit if she sees me hanging around Natalie. I think I'd better walk the course, then take

Amanda out for a leisurely stroll. I must remember to take along a blanket. We might find a grassy clearing alongside the creek."

"Hard to imagine her wading with the crawdads." Tommy punched Dennis on the arm, then assessed the crowd for potential gamblers. Quite a few people had left, he noted, but they weren't out on the course. He was sure that at least half the field would fail to show up at their appointed tee times the next morning. Those who remained didn't offer much of a threat. Dennis would be too distracted by the possibility of snakes to focus on his game. He'd checked out Bonaparte Buchanon (of PGA infamy) and decided to offer him a few stiff Bloody Marys before the first round. This would not be hard, since Tommy's trunk contained a well-stocked bar, with a variety of liquor, plastic cups, jars of olives, a customized ice cooler, corkscrews, swizzle sticks, and cocktail napkins. It was his version of tailgating, a Southern tradition at which he excelled. He doubted he could serve anything other than a Virgin Mary, the alcohol-free version, to Natalie. Her personal gargoyle would see to that. The best he could do was to keep harping on the abundance of bugs and spiders.

He winced when he saw Kale Wasson and his pasty-skinned mother walking toward the tent. Kale was a punk, but he could hit the ball and had trophies to prove it. His mother was a leech, adept at finding ways to insinuate herself into every conversation and steering the topic to her wonderful, handsome, talented, intelligent son. After all, what could be more fascinating than a pimply, grungy, rude, seventeen-year-old smart-ass?

Other than those, Tommy recognized a few duffers from the Farberville club, and a couple of guys he'd played against at a Hot Springs tournament. Three boys from the Farber College golf team were already drunk. One of them tried to move in on Natalie, but Janna cut him off and sent him slinking back to his friends.

Tommy approached them. "Hey, wanna play a round? Ten bucks a hole?"

They regarded him with arrogant contempt. One of them said, "Sure, old man, but I'd better warn you we're pretty damn good. Can you afford it?"

"Maybe I'll pick up some pointers," Tommy said modestly.

Mrs. Jim Bob had insisted that Bonaparte return for lunch. They ate chicken salad sandwiches and the last of the butterscotch brownies on the patio while Perkin's eldest cleaned up the kitchen and mopped the floor. The sky was clear, the sunshine pleasant. Robins and sparrows hopped about on the lawn, amiably avoiding each other.

She refilled his glass from a pitcher of iced tea and added a sprig of mint from her garden. "So when did you decide you wanted to be a professional golfer?" she asked him. Not that she cared, but it seemed like the polite thing to say.

"It was blind luck, Mrs. Jim Bob. I started caddying at a golf course in Springfield to pick up some extra money. The worst thing about it was watching these rich people in their fancy clothes, using the priciest clubs, taking private lessons from the pro, strutting around like they invented the game. Then they'd proceed to hit their balls in the water hazards or the woods. I took to thinking I could play better than that. When there wasn't no one around, I'd borrow a driver and hit some balls off the practice tee. Turns out I have a real knack for the game."

"How nice for you," Mrs. Jim Bob said. "When did you and Frederick meet?"

Bony had a feeling the truth wouldn't sit well. "Oh, some time back. I was in Vegas, doing commentary on golf tournaments on TV. The customers seem to really cotton to the idea of a real professional analyzing every shot for them."

"Frederick was a customer in this . . . establishment?"

"It's, uh, kind of a place where sports fans hang out. There's always something going on somewhere in the world—horse racing, soccer, tennis, even cricket. Now there's a sport I can't figure out." He took a swallow of tea, wishing it was bourbon and Coke. "You see, you got these men in white shorts, and they stand by what's called a wicket, and—"

"Is Frederick a gambler? I would be very disappointed if he were. He's such a gentleman. I can't recall when I've seen such clean fingernails on a man. Jim Bob comes home looking like he clawed his way up the driveway. He most likely thinks a manicure is what doctors do in veterans' hospitals."

Bony puzzled over this for a moment. "Oh, yeah, I get it. Aunt Eileen warned me that you have a sly sense of humor."

"Did she?" Mrs. Jim Bob's eyed narrowed.

"Anyway," he said, scampering to higher ground, "Frederick and I got to talking one evening. He was real interested in Maggody, for some crazy reason. I told him it wasn't no more than a wide patch in the road, but he wanted to know all about the folks who live here and what they do. You'd have thought he was going to write a book about this place. Damned if I know why anybody'd bother to read it."

"Maggody has a long and rich history," she said automatically, still distracted by the very idea of Eileen Buchanon having the nerve to call her sly. It was clearly a case of envy. She took a breath and exhaled vigorously to cleanse her mind of unkind thoughts. "Has Frederick mentioned anything about his personal life? Is he a widower or a bachelor?"

"He's never mentioned a Mrs. Cartier. For some reason I get the impression he's from Mississippi or Alabama, but he wouldn't say when I flat-out asked him."

"What about his profession?"

"Beats me," Bony said. "He's smart, and dresses in expensive clothes. Could be he's a lawyer or a banker. He seemed to know a lot of the big spenders in Vegas. He doesn't ever have to call his office or anything like that."

"And he's interested in Maggody." Mrs. Jim Bob watched the birds as she thought this over. She was so engrossed in speculation that she failed to notice when Bony slipped inside the house, or Perkin's eldest's screech seconds later.

On Saturday I ambled into Ruby Bee's for a late breakfast (in other places, it might be called brunch, but I doubted the proprietress would appreciate being enlightened). Estelle sat on her stool, while Ruby Bee tidied up behind the bar. Their conversation stopped when they saw me.

"Good morning," I said. "I'm sure you'll both be delighted to hear that Maggody's first charity golf tournament is under way. Parking wasn't a problem, since a lot of people who'd registered either failed to show up or took a look and got back in their cars. It could have something to do with Marjorie watching them from the porch swing. Did you know that sows can grind their teeth?"

"They can not," Ruby Bee said.

I sat down on a stool. "Maybe I was hearing Raz grind coffee beans in his kitchen. How about a plate of biscuits, gravy, and sausage?"

"Do I look like a short order cook? I don't know why you think you can waltz in here like a duchess and bark orders at me. If I didn't know better, I'd think you was raised in a barn."

"Living in Manhattan," Estelle said, waggling her finger. "Those Yankee manners must have rubbed off on you."

Ruby Bee dried her hands on her apron. "I'll rustle up something for you to eat, but it's only because of your condition. Anything that Mexican sells at the Dairee Dee-Lishus is liable to give you heartburn."

Yeah, or heartache. I gazed at a neon beer sign until Ruby Bee reappeared with a heaping plate of all that I'd requested, as well as scrambled eggs and hash browns. It would definitely hold me until lunch.

"What all's going on at Raz's pasture?" Ruby Bee asked as she started filling salt shakers.

"Mrs. Jim Bob seems to have everything under control.

The tent's up, and there are tables and chairs. Once she realized no one else was going to show up, she made a new sign with tee times. None of the wives are playing with the local men. Since the two groups aren't speaking to each other, it's probably a good idea. A bunch of the teenagers are standing around. One of the players offered them beer, but Mrs. Jim Bob overheard him and started squawking like a Canada goose with a feather up its ass."

"I can guess who offered them beer," Ruby Bee said in a tight voice. "There's a man staying out back who caused all manner of trouble last night. He and some of the others got stinkin' drunk here, then went to his room and partied 'til three in the morning. I'm surprised you couldn't hear 'em."

"Not just out-of-towners," Estelle contributed. "Plenty of locals like Jim Bob, Jeremiah, Earl, and Larry Joe were having themselves a fine time, too. They got crabby when Bony showed up, since he was giving golf lessons to their wives, but he weaseled himself into their favor after he swore none of the women could hit the ball more than ten feet." She rolled her eyes. "Not in the direction they were aiming, anyway. Bony was saying how he takes cover whenever Mrs. Jim Bob tees up. The other day she hit three balls on the roof of some church, and they're still in the gutter."

"All them golfers deserve to be in a gutter," Ruby Bee said. "They'd go down the drain and I wouldn't have to put up with them a day longer."

"You should have called me," I said to her.

"I didn't want to mess with it. Yesterday was a bad dream from dawn 'til I fell in bed. Estelle missing, people checking in all afternoon, an overflow crowd at lunchtime and suppertime, lots of complaining about the golf course—as if it had anything to do with me—and two groups checking out and demanding a refund, even though I had to clean their rooms again. Oh, you'll never guess who showed up at about six o'clock. I was so flabbergasted that I nearly dropped a tray in the middle of the dance floor."

"I myself choked on a peanut," said Estelle, making it clear that Ruby Bee wasn't the only one with a fragile nature, "and was gasping for air. Bopeep's boyfriend had to pound me on the back."

"Tiger Woods?" I said.

"No, I seem to think his name is Luke something."

"The person who came in last night," I said, spearing another bite of sausage.

"Tiger Woods?" Ruby Bee's brow crinkled. "Is he any relation to Woodrow Woods that lives out the dirt road past where Hiram's barn burned?"

"I doubt it. So who came in?"

"Phil Proodle," Ruby Bee said grandly. "My eyeballs liked to pop out of my head when I recognized him, and my heart was fluttering."

I poised my fork above my plate. "Of all the beer joints in all the towns in all the world he walks into mine . . ."

"What's that supposed to mean?" she snapped.

"Who's Phil Proodle?"

Estelle stared at me. "You don't know who he is? Why, he has a big boat store and is always advertising on TV. He did one where he was a superhero in a cape and mask, dangling from a crane. He must have been forty feet above his lot. It was so windy that he was flipping and flopping every which way."

"It sounds silly, but I held my breath every time it came on," added Ruby Bee. "It had to do with how he was gonna save Stump County from high prices, I think."

"Oh, yeah, he donated the bass boat," I said, resuming my attack on the biscuits and gravy. "His name's on a tournament on the bulletin board at the Suds of Fun."

"According to Elsie McMay's second cousin's sister-in-law in Starley City, poor ol' Phil didn't have a chance once Mrs. Jim Bob showed up," Estelle said. "After she finished her spiel, he was practically on his knees begging her to take the boat. You'd think a celebrity like him could stand up to her."

Ruby Bee sniffed. "From the way she carries on, you'd think she redecorated the Garden of Eden to suit her fancy." She snatched my plate from under my nose. "You keep eating like that, you'll end up looking like a blimp."

I was almost finished, so I didn't bother to argue. "What did the renowned Phil Proodle want last night? Applause for his generosity?"

"I ain't sure," Ruby Bee said. "He asked if I had any rooms available, which I did. After he got settled in, he came back in here and started buying pitchers like they cost a nickel apiece. He ran a tab over three hundred dollars. The thing is, when nobody was watching him he'd get a pissy look on his face, like he wanted to beat 'em senseless with a crowbar. Then he'd be all smiling and wishing 'em luck."

"Maybe he was assessing his competition," I suggested.

"Not according to Millicent," Estelle said. "She came by early this morning for a trim. Darla Jean kept track of everybody who registered to play. Millicent took a peek at the list Thursday and didn't see his name. She was sure she would have noticed, since he's so famous."

"Then he's a spectator," I said. "If anybody wins the boat, he'll present the key and get his picture in the paper. If you'll excuse me, ladies, I have to go arrest someone. I'm behind on my monthly quota."

"Most everybody's at the golf tournament," Estelle said. "Even the geezers from the barbershop and the pool hall. Who're you planning to arrest?"

"I'll work on it." I walked down the road to the PD, flipped through the mail, and leaned back in my chair. Under different circumstances, I would have taken off the rest of the weekend and driven to Springfield to see Jack. I was crazy about him, and he seemed to reciprocate. We shared a somewhat odd sense of humor, we could talk endlessly, we were more than compatible between the sheets (and in a sleeping bag, alongside a creek, on the rug in front of the fireplace, and once, quite recklessly, in a canoe). He had custody of his two children, but they were happy to see me when I visited—or did a fine job of pretending they were. As soon as I told him I was pregnant, he would be cleaning out half of his closet and pricing cribs online. Marriage was a given. Springfield was only a two-hour drive, so Ruby Bee and Estelle could show up with crocheted booties and embroidered bibs whenever they liked.

"So what the hell's the problem?" I said aloud, thoroughly frustrated with myself. A spider building its web in the corner of a window failed to weave any insights. Out back a blue jay scolded an interloper. A pickup drove by. Sunlight illuminated the motionless dust in the air. Where were the felons when you needed them?

I wiggled around in the chair until my butt was aligned with the saggy seat, leaned all the way back, and closed my eyes. I was envisioning myself rowing up the Amazon, piranhas darting at the surface, giant snakes slithering into the muddy water, fiercely colored birds watching me from thick branches above me, when I fell asleep.

When the phone rang, I nearly fell out of the chair. It took me a moment to realize that I was no longer chatting with Tarzan. I grabbed the receiver. "Yeah?"

"Mercy me, Arly, you sound like a rusty transmission. This is LaBelle. I got to speak to Sheriff Dorfer. I don't suppose he's there, is he?"

I blinked. "No."

"Are you sure?"

"He's not cowering under my desk or sitting across from me, smoking one of his cigars and flicking ashes on the floor. He could be in the back room, but there's not much to do in there. I'll look if you want me to."

"There's no call to get snippety," LaBelle said.

"Does that mean you do want me to look or you don't want me to look?" I raised my voice. "Harve? You back there? Sorry I'm out of coffee. I've cut back on office amenities because I'm saving up for another bullet."

"This ain't funny," LaBelle said huffily. "You just go rustle him up and tell him to call me. Lemme give you my home phone number. I don't know when we'll be able to go back in the building, so there's no use him calling that number."

"What happened?"

"About two hours ago most of the inmates were in the lounge, watching TV. Deputy Murtle had to leave for a minute to . . . well, to see a man about a horse. Soon as he was gone, the scumbags set the couch on fire. The alarm went off. Nasty black smoke was pouring down all the halls. My eyes were streaming so bad I could barely call nine-one-one. We had no choice but to evacuate the building."

"Was anybody hurt?" I asked.

LaBelle harrumphed. "No, but three of 'em escaped in the confusion. It being Saturday afternoon, only Deputy Murtle and Sergeant Beluga were on duty. I was there on account of needing overtime pay. The fire engines showed up, as well as ambulances, municipal police cars, the local TV station van, and reporters. Lights were flashing, everybody was hollering. One of the firefighters accidentally turned the hose on Deputy Murtle and flattened him against the fence like a bug on a windshield. The paramedics insisted on treating me and some others for smoke inhalation. Keeping the inmates together was worse than trying to herd squirrels."

"You still can't get back in the building?"

"Would I be trying to call Harve if all the inmates were in their cells and it was business as usual? The fire chief sez we can't do anything until they inspect for damage. There's water and foam all over the walls and floors, and it smells to high heavens. Right now we've got the inmates stashed over at the city jail. The ones we got left, anyway. Harve is gonna have a fit, but there ain't much anybody can do."

"What about the three inmates who escaped?" I asked. "I don't suppose they were locked up for unpaid parking tickets."

"Two of 'em were involved in a brawl at the Dew Drop Inn last night. Ugly sumbitches, with oily hair and tattoos.

The third one was picked up for a parole violation. He's headed back to the state pen on Monday."

"What was he in for?"

"How should I know? I ain't their guidance counselor, for pity's sake. The deputies take 'em in and out the door at the back. I just process the paperwork when I'm not too busy making coffee or fetching doughnuts for Sheriff Dorfer. If he doesn't stop gulping down those jelly rolls, he's gonna bust out of his britches one of these days."

"Hold that thought, LaBelle," I said. "I assume you called here because Harve's playing in the golf tournament."

"Mrs. Dorfer ain't pleased about it. She had plans for the two of them to drive to Caligula to visit her niece's family."

"Give me your cell phone number and I'll hunt down Harve."

I checked the time and realized I'd napped for more than an hour. If there'd been any stickups at the Dairee Dee-Lishus or antiwar demonstrations at the Pot O' Gold, I'd missed them. However, the town appeared peaceful as I drove toward the road that led to Raz's place. The bass boat was chained to the sign in the SuperSaver parking lot, but no pilgrims were gazing rapturously at it.

Parking did not present a problem. Many of the cars and trucks that'd been here earlier in the day were gone. As I got out of my car, Raz came out on his porch.

"You tell them goddamn trespassers to stay the hell away from my barn!" he yelled at me. His scraggly beard, never a pleasant sight, was sprinkled with crumbs. Flies and gnats hovered around his head. His overalls had the look of stone-washed denim, but his were undoubtedly stone-washed in a creek (if they'd ever been washed, that is). "Iff'n one of them steps foot in it, I'm gonna blow 'em to smithereens! I ain't fooling, neither. I got my shotgun right by the door."

"Is there something in the barn you don't want anyone to see?" I asked.

He spat tobacco juice in my direction. "No, there ain't,

and iff'n there is, it ain't any of their damn business." He pointed a grimy finger at me. "Ain't none of yers, for that matter. They been comin' and goin' all day long, squealing at each other, tromping on my vegetable patch like cross-eyed heifers. Marjorie was so discombobbled that she had to take a seltzer tablet. I ain't gonna have them assholes in my barn!"

He was hopping with fury. As much as I wanted to linger and see if he exploded, I went around his shack to a good-sized open tent. Darla Jean sat at a card table covered with tidy piles of papers and shoe boxes. Heather Riley and a few other high school girls stood behind a table laden with plates of plastic-wrapped sandwiches, cookies, and pitchers of tea and lemonade. Supervising them were the members of the Missionary Society who'd avoided the rigors of golf lessons. Lottie was poking sandwiches to make sure they were tightly wrapped, while Eula counted cups. The ne'er-do-wells from the barbershop were stuffing their faces and surreptitiously passing a jar of Raz's premium hooch.

One long table was occupied by disgruntled wives. Millicent gave me a bleak smile. Lucille was dabbing her eyes with a tissue while Eileen blew her nose in a napkin. Crystal examined a plastic fork as though she were wondering if it might lend itself to hara-kiri. None of them appeared to have an appetite. What energy they had left was being expended on glares aimed at a table in a far corner.

There was no joy at the table commandeered by the partners in the tontine, either. Jim Bob's flask was being passed in plain sight. Roy, Big Dick, Ruddy, and Tam sat like cheap concrete statues, moving only when the flask was stuck under their noses. Kevin's hands were clasped on the table, as if he were praying to be struck by a meteorite.

In that I was a trained investigator, I cleverly deduced that none of them had made a hole-in-one. I glanced at unfamiliar people eating sandwiches or studying a poster while they spoke in low voices. There were a lot of red faces,

sweat-stained shirts, and muddy shoes in the group. Harve
was not among them. Out in the pasture behind swaths of
scruffy pines and skeletal oaks, I caught glimpses of moving figures.

Mrs. Jim Bob was seated at a table at the front of the tent.
Across from her was Frederick Cartier, who was nodding
sympathetically as she spoke. Her lips were almost invisible,
and her eyes lacked their usual flicker of resolution to shove
piety down the throats of anyone within a mile or two.

I went over to them. "Is everything going well?"

"Why wouldn't it be?" Mrs. Jim Bob said tartly. "We're
right on schedule. I'm disappointed that we didn't have more
players, but their fees are nonrefundable. After we've paid
expenses, we'll be able to donate roughly seventy-five hundred dollars to the golf widows. It's not much, I know, but
I'd like to think they'll be grateful all the same."

Frederick patted her hand. "I'm sure they will be very
grateful." He stood up. "Would you like to join us, Arly? May
I bring you a cup of lemonade and a cookie?"

"No chocolate chips for me. I'm on duty. Mrs. Jim Bob,
do you know if the sheriff's on the course?"

"A sheriff?" Frederick abruptly sat down. "Why on earth
would you be in need of a sheriff?"

"Not just any sheriff. I need to speak to Stump County's
one and only sheriff, Harvey Dorfer."

Mrs. Jim Bob looked at her clipboard. "He's on the back
nine somewhere. Everybody should be done within the next
hour. There's no reason for you to dawdle. As you said, you're
on duty. I can assure you there's nothing of an illegal nature
taking place here."

"How about offering alcohol to minors?"

"That has been dealt with and will not happen again.
When Sheriff Dorfer turns in his scorecard, I'll tell him that
you're looking for him."

"I'm afraid it can't wait," I said with a sigh. The fairway
in front of us was not a lush green carpet that had been un-

furled on a gentle slope. It looked more like a bed of nails that a yogi might walk on to demonstrate his power of concentration. In some areas, the mower's blades had scraped down to bare rock. Grasshoppers whirred aimlessly. Raucous cowbirds had taken possession of a dead tree. The course looked as inviting as a Siberian summer camp.

"Please permit me to escort you," Frederick said as he took my elbow. "I've walked around the course, and I know some shortcuts. Truly, I insist. Mrs. Jim Bob, if you'll kindly excuse us, we must find a sheriff. I do hope it's not harder than finding a needle in a haystack—or should I say a hayseed in a haystack?" He steered me out of the tent.

"You needn't bother," I said.

"This is for my sake, not yours. Why these people believe they can learn how to play golf in a week is baffling. I do think someone needs to test the water."

I finally yanked my arm out of his grip. As we walked down the fairway, I said, "From what I could see from the tent, the players are toward the back of the pasture. Where are these promised shortcuts?"

"Up ahead," Frederick said. "Tell me what it was like to grow up in Maggody."

I was considering my reply when a golf ball bounced off a tree less than a yard away. I dropped to the ground. "Where'd that come from?"

"Over that way," Frederick said as he squatted next to me.

I crawled over rocks and roots and peered out from behind a stump. Joyce was hacking furiously at the weeds with a golf club. "Pay attention, Audley," she shouted between hacks. "You darn near hit me."

Audley was in the middle of the fairway. She'd already set another golf ball on a clump and was winding up. She took a mighty swing, then looked up, shielding her eyes with her hand. "Fore!" she yelled, failing to notice the golf ball had rolled between her feet. "Anybody see it?"

A boy in a Farber College T-shirt crept up behind her and

grabbed the ball. Audley almost jumped out of her skin when he touched her shoulder. "Great shot," he said. "It could be on the green, or even in the cup. What a shame it was your sixth shot instead of your drive." He took a couple of steps and bent down to surreptitiously place Audley's ball in a divot. "Mrs. Lambertino, here's your ball."

"Thank you," Joyce said as she picked her way through the brambles. "I must have stepped right over it. Which club should I use?"

"I don't think it matters, ma'am."

Frederick and I waited until they'd moved on, then emerged. "That was close," I said, not adding that I'd almost wet my pants. I had not done well at the police academy when we were training to deal with snipers. We'd almost reached the far side when a ball flew over my head. We hightailed it behind a tree.

"Hush up!" Audley screeched. "He told me to pitch it, so I pitched it. I just happen to have a good arm. If I'd been born a boy, I'd have played for the New York Yankees." There was a moment of silence. "If that's what he meant, he should have said so!"

"This is getting scary," I said. I glanced at Frederick, who looked a little pale himself. We made it through the next thicket without encountering snakes or hornets and came out in a wide swath of weeds. Twenty feet away was a green pond, ringed with cattails and withered stalks. Rings of ripples came from fish, turtles, or alligators; I had no desire to find out which.

I stopped to let Frederick recalculate our route. Before he could so much as point, a ball splashed down in the middle of the pond. A nanosecond later a voice yelled a string of profanities that would make Raz blush (momentarily, at least).

"Jeremiah McIlhaney," I said for Frederick's benefit.

Said player and Luke came up to the far edge of the pond. Jeremiah's arms were crossed, his expression worthy of a horror movie. "Gimme another ball," he said to Luke.

"Just drop a ball on the green. You can start at four and add your putts."

"Four as in four balls in this goddamn pond? I'm going to hit a ball across it or kill myself trying. Now gimme one."

Larry Joe pushed his way out of the woods. "You won't have to kill yourself, asshole. I'll do it for you if you waste one more ball. Bopeep's on our tail, and she ain't waiting for anything. She damn near hit me a minute ago."

"On her drive?" asked Luke.

"No, on my head, moron. Jeremiah, the way I see it is you have two choices. One involves swimmin' and one with walkin' away right now."

Jeremiah's hand tightened around the grip. He took a step toward Larry Joe, which saved him from a golf ball that bounced where'd he been, then plopped into the pond. "What the hell," he said as he threw the club in after it. "Somebody's gonna have to gimme a ball, though." They retreated into the woods.

Frederick and I went around the pond and resumed walking, although I peeked over my shoulder every few steps to make sure no foursome was bearing down on us.

"That's what it was like growing up in Maggody," I said, answering his earlier question. "What about you? Are you from a small town?"

"I wasn't from anywhere until I was twelve. My family moved around a lot." He turned right, and we picked our way through waist-deep pot to another fairway. I wasn't sure which way to go, but Frederick took off as if he were following a map.

I was brushing thistles off my jeans as I caught up with him. "And then?"

His steps faltered. "I went to a small college, got bored, and set off to conquer the world. Didn't we all?"

"Sure we did." We came around a clump of oak trees. There was a small group of golfers approaching an irregular patch that was vaguely green. Toward the center, a rod stuck up at a perilous angle, a piece of red cloth attached near the top. I recognized Harve's potbelly and quickened my pace.

Abruptly one of the men let out a whoop that must have rattled windows in Seeping Springs. He squatted by the base of the flagpole, then sprang up and began to dance in a circle around it. "I told ya so! I told ya so!" he howled, thumping his chest. "I am the greatest!" He careened into another player, and they fell in a tangle of arms and legs. "I am the goddamn greatest in the world!"

"It seems," Frederick said, "the gentleman has made a hole-in-one."

I joined Harve, who was observing the scene with a sour look. "I need to talk to you."

"I ain't in the mood to talk just now."

"There's a problem at the jail," I said as I watched the two golfers on the green struggle to get up. The gloater had a crewcut and was dressed in wrinkled shorts and a T-shirt that did not quite cover his girth; his beaming face was reddened from a sunburn and long-term overindulgence in alcohol. I wasn't surprised when he pulled out a silver flask from his golf bag and insisted that everyone join him. The other man was tall and trim, with dark hair and standard country club attire (except for the streaks of dirt from the impromptu wrestling match). He had an angular jaw with a prominent chin, a straight nose, and an even tan. He was not beaming.

"There's always a friggin' problem at the jail," Harve said. He dug a cigar and a matchbook out of his shirt pocket. "Take two aspirin and call me Monday morning. Better yet, call the quorum court and tell 'em to up my budget. LaBelle's gettin' tired of buying toilet paper for the ladies' room out of her own paycheck."

The remaining member of the foursome was Bony. His lip was curled in the classic Buchanon sneer. I recognized him from a long time ago, though back then his hair had been shaved to low stubble. Now it had peaks and valleys and was well lubricated. He dragged Frederick aside and began to hiss at him. Frederick's face was emotionless, his response inaudible.

"It's more serious than the price of toilet paper," I said to Harve.

"The hell it is." He went to the green and scooped up a ball from nowhere near the hole. Ignoring the ongoing ruckus from the winner, he returned and said, "Ain't much point in finishing the round." The cigar clenched between his teeth, he hefted his golf bag onto his shoulder. "Talk to me while we walk back to my car. Better yet, keep your mouth shut until I'm at Ruby Bee's with a cold beer on the table in front of me, and Waylon Jennings convincing me that I don't mind."

"You quitting?" shouted the pudgy man. "Don't take it so hard, buddy boy. Drinks are on me after the round. How about a bourbon and branch water? Isn't that the drink of choice out here in the booger woods?"

Harve's reply does not bear repeating. As we walked along the fairway toward the tent, I told him what LaBelle had told me. His face began to mottle with fury, and by the time we emerged near the barn, he looked like he was on the verge of a stroke. He opened the trunk of his car and dumped the golf bag. "I'll let you know if we have reason to suspect any of the escapees are heading this way." He said a few more things that again don't bear repeating, slammed his car door, and departed in a most unfriendly cloud of dust.

The players under the tent stared at me. It was likely they'd heard the uproar from whichever hole I'd been at. The optimists may have been hoping that a copperhead was involved, but the more pragmatic looked discouraged, if not suicidal. I decided not to be the bearer of ill tidings, since they'd hear soon enough. I drove back to the main road, made sure Harve's car was not in Ruby Bee's parking lot, then stopped at the PD. After I'd called LaBelle to assure her that Harve was on his way, I decided to go into Farberville, rent a couple of old movies, pick up a pizza, and hide out in my apartment until the final putt was sunk. I wondered if Block-buster might have a DVD of *Cannibal Women in the Avo-cado Jungle of Death*. Avocado, Amazon. Close enough.

Six

My wake-up call coincided with the first glint of dawn. I rolled out of bed, stumbled around until I found the phone, and snapped, "What?"

"Arly?"

"What?" I repeated. My clock read 5:10, which was way too early to stand on sticky linoleum in bare feet and make conversation.

"This is Albina Buchanon. My aunt and me decided to go to Chigger Bush to visit my grandma, who's ailin' something awful. She fell downstairs a few months back and broke her hip. She's always had a sweet tooth for peppermint schnapps. She must go through a pint of it a day, starting with her cup of tea in the morning and never letting up 'til she goes to bed. I disremember how many times the fire department's had to rescue her off her roof. This time—"

"Get to the point, Albina."

There was a moment of silence. "There ain't no reason to get all huffy. I was jest givin' you the background. Anyways, we were driving past the SuperSaver when I saw somebody in the bass boat. You know about the bass boat, doncha?"

"Yes, I know about the bass boat. Why are you calling me?"

"The man's dead as a doornail, that's why. His head is all bloody, and his eyes are blank. Excuse me for waking you up, Chief of Police Hanks. You kin go back to bed. He sure as hell ain't going anywhere soon." She hung up.

I put down the receiver and rubbed my eyes as I looked out the window. Maggody was not yet stirring, although it was likely that some kitchen lights were on and percolators were burping. I pulled on dirty jeans, moccasins, and a T-shirt. My hair was a mess, so I gathered it into a ponytail and secured it with a rubber band. I paused long enough to grab a handful of crackers, then went down the outside stairs. The glint of dawn was likely to be the only glint of the day, I thought as I noticed gray clouds looming across the top of Cotter's Ridge. The air was gelatinous with humidity.

After a brief debate, I went across the street to the PD to get the car and drove to the SuperSaver parking lot. Albina and her aunt must have continued on their mission of mercy. There were no cars in the lot. There was, however, someone in the boat. I approached cautiously, aware of the queasiness in my stomach. I'd had a few bouts of morning sickness, and I suspected another was eminent unless Albina had been making a prank call.

The man's body was slumped behind the steering wheel, if that's what it was called. The back of his head was an unholy mess of bloody flesh and bone splinters. Flies were already crawling on the wound. I went around the boat and climbed in to get a better look at his face. Although blood had trickled across it, I recognized him as the golfer who'd made a hole-in-one the previous afternoon.

Now someone had made a hole-in-him.

I scrambled out of the boat just in time to avoid contaminating the scene. Once I felt steadier, I went back to my car and leaned against the hood. I didn't have a cell phone because reception was sporadic and unreliable. The radio in my car could connect me to the sheriff's office, but no one was there because of the previous day's evacuation. The laws of physics being rigid, there was no way to remain at the scene and go call for backup. At least I couldn't come up with one at 5:20 A.M.

I took a roll of yellow tape out of my trunk and began to rope off the boat as best I could, using light poles and a freestanding sign that advertised a two-for-the-price-of-one canned corn special. I was gazing glumly at my effort when I spotted a pickup truck coming up the road. I ran out to the edge and waved my arms. To my regret, Marjorie had her head out the passenger's window and was regarding me with malevolence. Raz pulled over and rolled down his window.

"Whattaya want?" he demanded. "Me and Marjorie ain't got time to stop and pass the time listenin' to yer whining. I ain't a mechanic, but iff'n I was, I still wouldn't waste my time fiddlin' with yer car. Call somebody what cares."

I bit my lip until I could trust myself. "There's been, uh, an accident. I need you to wait here while I make a call at the PD. As soon as I'm back, you and Marjorie can be on your way."

"An accident?" He cackled until tobacco juice dribbled out of his mouth like molasses. "You talkin' about that feller in the boat behind you? Did he accidentally bash himself on the back of his head?"

"Okay," I said, "not an accident. Will you please stay here and keep people away for ten minutes?"

"Ain't on my schedule. Marjorie has a hankerin' for fresh croissants, so we's headin' for Farberville afore the storm hits. Only got one windshield wiper, and it don't work. Mebbe when we git back, I can do you a favor—iff'n you aim to pay me back one of these days."

"By not mentioning whatever you have stashed in your barn?"

"There ain't nuthin' in my barn, and don't you fergit it! Anyone who so much as spits on the door is gonna be right sorry for a long time to come."

This does not happen on TV cop shows. I had no idea what time the SuperSaver opened on Sunday mornings, or even if it opened before churches loosed their properly chastised sinners for the day. Mrs. Jim Bob was a big fan of blue laws, no matter how archaic they were. I couldn't twiddle my thumbs and watch the flies attack until Raz's pickup rattled back to town.

"Listen up, Raz," I said as firmly as I could despite my queasiness. "If you refuse to cooperate, you're going right to the top of my shit list. You have immunity for that still near Robin's shack, but that's all. When I have a minute, I'll call the ATF and the DEA. I might call the FBI, since you're involved in interstate trafficking. The SPCA may decide to take away Marjorie. The RCMP will come riding across the pasture, accompanied by a SWAT team. Not only will they seize the contents of your barn, they'll wreck your house while they search for contraband. They'll drain your hot tub and dump out your bags of gourmet coffee beans. Could be they'll stumble over the still themselves, or find a cave filled with jars of moonshine."

His eyes slitted. "I reckon I can wait for five minutes, but that's it. Git yer scrawny butt in action and go make yer damn fool call afore I change my mind!"

I obliged, although my butt was far from scrawny.

Harve was less than thrilled when he finally answered his phone. I skipped the pleasantries and told him what had happened. I'm sure he would have responded with a string of obscenities that would have curled my ears had not Mrs. Dorfer been snoring nearby, her face slathered with cold cream and her hair protected by a shower cap. Harve finally grunted a promise to round up his deputies and the medical examiner.

I returned to the SuperSaver parking lot and sent Raz and Marjorie on their quest for fresh croissants in Farberville. As he drove away, I realized I should have begged him to bring me one. Or two. I walked around the perimeter of the yellow tape. The dusty asphalt was scuffed with prints from shoes, bare feet, sneakers, and boots. The boat was covered with smudged fingerprints. Litter included cigarette butts, Popsicle sticks, candy wrappers, aluminum cans, a flattened orange, and a three-wheeled toy car. None of it looked significant.

During the next hour, cars filled with gawkers slowed down or attempted to stop. Perkin peered through a mud-splattered windshield. Falutin Buchanon's brood screamed at me from the back of his pickup; Jeremiah McIlhaney managed not to rear-end them by scant inches. Raz honked at me as he and Marjorie returned from their bakery run. I officiously waved them off as I would gnats. I had less luck when Estelle and Ruby Bee drove up in Estelle's car. Oblivious to my orders to leave, they walked up to the boat and stared at the body.

"Mercy me," Ruby Bee said, her face pale. She clutched a button on her dress to ward off any lingering malevolence. "You see who that is, Estelle?"

Estelle nodded. "No doubt about it. I figured he was in for a hangover this morning, but this is a sight worse. He was a buffoon, but I kinda liked him."

"Because he said you looked like a Greek goddess."

"Because he was a nice fellow. I ain't a pushover for compliments, as you well know. People have been commenting on my bone structure since I was in pigtails and petticoats." Estelle lowered one shoulder and gave us her version of a sultry smile. "When I was a cocktail singer in Little Rock, one of my regulars called me Aphrodite. She was the goddess of love and beauty."

Ruby Bee snickered. "This fellow here was so drunk that he couldn't tell a hound dog from a nanny goat. I have to admit he wasn't the worst drunk to set foot in the bar and grill, though. Do you recollect when Botocks Buchanon knocked out her boyfriend on the dance floor? She wasn't but a hundred pounds, soaking wet. She was still threatening to whack off his pecker with a dull ax when I managed to throw her out. I limped for a week afterward."

102 *Joan Hess*

"Excuse me for interrupting," I said, "but do you know his name?"

"Tommy Ridner." Ruby Bee blotted the corner of her eye with a tissue, as if the victim were a family member. "He checked into the Flamingo on Friday afternoon. I've got his home address and credit card information at the bar. Did somebody kill him?"

Estelle snorted and said, "You don't think he bashed himself on the back of the head, do you? He'd have to be a contortionist to pull that off, and he sure wasn't one. He dropped his wallet last night and had a real hard time bending over to pick it up. I was surprised nobody kicked his fanny."

"Maybe he fell," Ruby Bee said, retreating as she noticed the flies. "Somebody heaved him into the boat, and he bled to death."

"Somebody with a bulldozer," Estelle countered.

"So maybe it took two men. He ain't the size of a hippopotamus, for pity's sake."

"Since when are you an expert on hippopotamuses?"

Ruby Bee crossed her arms. "For your information, the word is 'hippopotami.'"

My head began to throb. "Please go find the information about Mr. Ridner. The sheriff's team should be here any minute." I stuffed another cracker in my mouth. If Ruby Bee and Estelle caught me in a bout of morning sickness, I'd be inundated with advice and herbal remedies. "Did Ridner come in his own car?"

"I reckon so. I don't exactly assign parking spots in front of each unit." Ruby Bee took another look at the body. "I'd say he's more the size of a sea lion."

"You saying he weighs a ton?" Estelle said skeptically.

"A small sea lion," said Ruby Bee, who'd never been closer to a sea lion than she had an African lion. In her world, "lion" was a participle.

They were still bickering as they drove away. I sat back down in my car. The thumpety-thump in my head was almost drowned out by the gurgles in my stomach. My eye-balls were grainy, and my mouth felt as if I'd been chewing straw. Across the road a few children were hunting golf balls with the same gleeful enthusiasm reserved for Easter eggs. More cars drove by at a turtlish speed, and traffic was back-ing up beyond the stoplight. Apparently Maggody offered more excitement than Branson.

I was ready to hide under the boat when cars from the sheriff's department finally appeared, along with McBeen, the medical examiner. He is not easy to deal with under the midday sun. At 7:00 A.M., he'd have the disposition of a bel-ligerent sea lion and the snarl of an African one. I dearly hoped no one pointed out to him that his socks didn't match.

Harve looked at the body, then stepped back to let his men examine the scene. "You didn't tell me the victim was the sumbitch that made a hole-in-one," he said. "If I'd known, I would have gone back to bed."

"I never knew you were such a sore loser. It's only a boat, fercrissake."

"No, it's a Ranger Z21 with an Evinrude, hydro jack plate, and a trolling motor. It retails for forty-two thousand dollars. It's got the grace of an acrobat and the horsepower of a professional wrassler." His jowls trembled as he sighed, and his eyes were teary. He took a handkerchief out of his back pocket and blew his nose. I would have given him a hug if I wasn't so fond of the arrangement of my facial fea-tures. "Yesterday I hit four greens," he continued sadly. "I was sure I was going to get one to roll in. I could feel it in my bones, same as like my great-aunt could predict rain be-cause of her sciatica. But then you show up and that sumbitch makes a hole-in-one. I don't like coincidences."

"It wasn't any of my doing, but go ahead and kill the messenger if it makes you feel better," I said. "Or just keep puffing on that cigar. The secondhand smoke'll get me sooner or later."

Harve's expression turned surly. "Don't push your luck. I

didn't get to bed but four hours ago. I'll tell you one thing—
Murtle is gonna be on the night shift until he hobbles away
with a pension check. Damn moron should have known better than to turn his back on those pissants. They'd set their
own grandmas on fire for the fun of it."

"You need a better class of inmates. In the future, only arrest embezzlers and stodgy judges caught in motel rooms with
their pants around their ankles and fifteen-year-old cheerlead-
ers in the bed. Lawyers, on the other hand, might set their
grandmothers on fire and then sue for mental anguish."

"I don't need any crap from you, little lady. The three
escapees are still free, and the Farberville police chief ain't
happy about housing the rest of the inmates. How in the hell
am I supposed to coordinate a manhunt when I don't have an
office? No desk, no telephone, and half my deputies gone
fishin'. When I set up a command post in the dining room,
Mrs. Dorfer threatened to go visit her mother for a month.
I ain't partial to cold pizza for breakfast and canned ravioli
for supper."

I tried to dredge up some sympathy, but it wasn't in me.
"I'm going by Ruby Bee's to pick up info on the victim,
decorate his motel room door with yellow tape, and then go
to the PD to write up a report."

"You ain't going anywhere 'til I say so."

"Watch me."

"What you *are* going to do is get a statement from every
last soul in town, including the golfers, the parolees at the
trailer park, the tournament organizers, and all those shifty
Buchanon mutants that lurk around town."

"Like Mrs. Jim Bob?" I asked sweetly. "She falls into
several of those categories."

McBeen joined us before Harve could respond. "Chief of
Police Hanks, I should have known you were involved when
my phone rang at an ungodly hour. This town has to be the
most toxic landfill in the state. You ought to open a funeral
home."

He had a point. When I first moved back to Maggody, I complained that nothing ever happened. That was, of course, before we were invaded by silver aliens, militiamen, tabloid reporters, Civil War reenactors, celebrity drug addicts, and other barbarian hordes. These days, we should put up a warning sign at the city limits. Kevin could stand beside the road to hand out disclaimers and bulletproof vests.

"Cause of death?" Harve asked.

"Multiple fractures of the skull, for starters." McBeen sneered at me as if I were responsible for the primitive attack. "I don't know the time of death, but I'd estimate five to seven hours ago."

"Yo, Sheriff Dorfer," one of the deputies called, "I think I found the weapon."

Harve and I went over to the boat. "There's a golf club wedged down here between the body and the side panel," the deputy continued. "You'll see it better after they move the body. There's blood on the, uh, handle."

"What did I do to deserve this?" Harve muttered. "A golf club has three parts: grip, shaft, and head. If this is too complicated for you, just remember the grip is what you grip. The shaft is what you're gonna get if you screw up, and the head is like that useless thing sitting on your shoulders, except it's not filled with feathers and lint like yours."

Other deputies peered at what was presumably the weapon. All of them could have rattled off the names of the most minute parts of a rifle or a fishing rod. They could build a deer stand with their eyes closed. They could gut a squirrel with one hand. And they probably knew as much about golf as they did about opera and haute cuisine.

I'd had enough of the crime scene. I left Harve cussing at me in the parking lot and went to Ruby Bee's. There were a few cars and pickups out front. I sat down on a barstool next to Estelle, who was sipping coffee. Ruby Bee came out of the kitchen with plates in each hand, glanced at me, and then headed for the booths.

"What were you two doing out so early this morning?" I asked Estelle.

"Ol' Fatback Buchanon stopped by my house to see if I wanted to buy fresh eggs. After I finished bawling him out on account of the hour, he told me that he saw you in front of the SuperSaver. I called Ruby Bee to inquire what you were doing, and she was as bumfuzzled as Fatback. Do you remember him? He has six fingers on his right hand, and his pinkie twitches like a caterpillar on a hot griddle."

"No." I lifted off the glass dome of a pie stand and took out a warm cinnamon roll. "Tommy Ridner was here last night, right?"

"He most certainly was, along with a swarm of folks. Most of them were pie-eyed when they came in from the golf tournament supper. Well, maybe not the ladies so much. Ridner made a hole-in-one yesterday, and he was crowing like a banty rooster. Not everybody was as smitten as he was. Around eleven he went out to his unit and came back with a golf club and balls. He had this idea how they should have a contest to see who could hit the stoplight."

I closed my eyes. "And?"

"You'd think Jim Bob would know better, but he slammed a twenty-dollar bill on the table and said he was ready. He wasn't the only one, I might add. Earl wanted to make it fifty dollars. Larry Joe and Luke said they were in. That pretty girl with ash blond hair said she'd show all of 'em who was the best. This got Bony all riled up—he wanted everybody to put in a hundred dollars."

"I didn't hear anything," I said.

"Ruby Bee put a stop to it. She gave 'em a lecture about disturbing the peace and destroying city property, and then threatened to close right then and there if anyone so much as stepped out the door with a golf club. They backed down after that."

The hell they did, I thought, remembering the children

who were scavenging for golf balls in the weeds across from the SuperSaver. The golf balls had not fallen from the sky or mystically appeared with the morning dew.

A thickset woman with peppery cropped hair, flat features, and the broad shoulders of a swimmer leaned against the bar. Her sweatpants and blue work shirt were utilitarian and far from flattering. I could easily picture her as a bouncer at a biker chick bar. "Hello!" she shouted. "Does anybody work here?"

Ruby Bee bustled around the far end of the bar. "I do, and it ain't my fault if you woke up with your knickers in a knot. What do you want?"

"Coffee," the woman said in a more subdued voice. "Black." She pulled a napkin out of the dispenser and blotted her nose. I remembered that I'd seen her the day before, sitting alone at a table and muffling sneezes with a tissue.

I resumed trying to envision the previous evening. Tommy Ridner had been celebrating, as to be expected. The other players in the tournament (I hesitated to refer to them as golfers) had been annoyed, also to be expected. Beer had flowed like Boone Creek in the spring. When Ruby Bee's closed at midnight, the party had continued. I needed to know who slunk off to bed and who stayed up late enough to kill Tommy Ridner.

Still at the far end of the bar, Ruby Bee said, "Arly! Ms. Coulter here says she went by the PD and it was locked."

"The door isn't locked. It sticks when it's humid."

Estelle jabbed me with her elbow. "Go see what the lady wants. She looks mean enough to be a killer. Maybe she wants to confess."

I finished the cinnamon roll, wiped my fingers on a napkin, then took a stool next to Ms. Coulter. "I'm the entirety of the local police department. I'd show you my badge, but I don't have it with me at the moment. Is there something I can do for you?"

The woman held out a hand. "I'm Janna Coulter, Natalie Hotz's manager. Your name is . . . ?"

"Arly Hanks." I held out my hand as well, and tried not to wince when she clamped it. "Why are you looking for me, Ms. Coulter?"

"Call me Janna. You do know who Natalie Hotz is, don't you?" She grimaced when I shook my head. "Well, you should. She's the upcoming LPGA star. She's won the state tournament for three years and will go pro this fall."

"Impressive," I murmured, unimpressed. "I don't moonlight as a sportswriter, so if there's nothing else I can do for you, I guess we're done."

Janna grabbed my arm. "I want to report an assault."

I felt a tingle of fear for whoever had tried it. "Who assaulted you?"

"Don't be ridiculous. Natalie's the victim. I insisted that she sleep late this morning, so she can concentrate on her second round today. Every media opportunity counts, even"—she rolled her eyes—"in a place like this."

"Who assaulted her?"

Her shoulders sagged. "I don't know, and she was too upset to tell me. It happened last night. After dinner, she insisted that we join the others in the bar to congratulate Tommy Ridner. I saw no point in it, but I reluctantly agreed. It was dreadful, of course, and we didn't stay long."

"Where did you go?" I asked.

"Back to our room, of course. I was already in bed when Natalie discovered that she'd left her wallet in the bar. I took an antihistamine and started reading, but I dozed off and didn't wake up until Natalie crept into the room. Her clothes were dirty and her hair was a mess. When I asked, she started sobbing and admitted that she'd been attacked in the parking lot. That's all I could get out of her."

"What time did Natalie come back to the room?"

Janna hesitated. "I don't know. I guess I knocked my

alarm clock off the bedside table when I turned off the reading light. If she hadn't tripped on a suitcase, I might have slept through it. Whoever committed this vicious crime deserves to be punished. I've invested four years in coaching Natalie and fine-tuning her reputation. A few small companies have offered her endorsement fees, but I'm holding out for the real deal. This could ruin everything." She paused, her forehead creased with deep lines. "Or maybe we can play the sympathy card. Natalie could be the spokeswoman for victims of sexual abuse. The media might see it as an act of courage for her to go public with the story."

"Before Natalie makes a deal with Oprah, she'll have to file a complaint in person," I said. "I'll be in and out of the PD all day. Tell her to come by and talk to me. I can't do anything until I have details."

Janna bristled. "If she's up to it. We'll leave as soon as she collects her trophy. This town is a madhouse. Yesterday I saw a woman at the supermarket try to shoplift a frozen turkey. It slid out from between her legs while she was waiting in the checkout lane. We won't stay here one second longer than necessary. I'll have Natalie available for you at my Farberville apartment later this week."

"No, I'm afraid not. I'm going to require all participants in the tournament to stay in town until I interview them and take statements." I gestured for Ruby Bee to meet me by the cash register. I could hear Janna muttering behind me as I said, "I need the names and the unit numbers of everyone who's staying here. After I've spoken to them, I'll come back here and get the information about the victim. If Harve shows up, let him know where I am."

Ruby Bee opened a notebook. "That woman and the girl are in three. A woman named Kathleen Wasson and her son are in four. Tommy was in five, and a married couple, Dennis and Amanda Gilbert, are in six. Seven's empty. Phil Proodle's in eight. I haven't seen any of them except her this morning.

I heard somebody say that today's round starts at ten o'clock. It'll be a wonder if anybody bothers to show up, what with the bass boat taken."

"No, it isn't," Estelle said, whose hearing is comparable to a submarine's sonar.

"Yes, it is," I said. "I was there when Ridner made the hole-in-one. So were Harve, Bony, Frederick, and another player. A high school kid with a bandana tied around his arm initialed the scorecard."

"That was before Tommy heard about the fine print." She made us wait while she took a sip of coffee. "Fatback told me about it. Mrs. Jim Bob announced that he wouldn't win officially until this afternoon, when the awards are given out. Winners must be present and so forth. He wasn't upset about it, mind you. He might have felt differently if he'd known he was gonna get murdered."

"What?" Janna said, so startled that her coffee splattered on the shiny black surface of the bar. "Murdered? Tommy Ridner?"

"Shit," I said under my breath as I headed out to the units behind the bar and grill. If everyone knew that eliminating Tommy Ridner from the second round would put the boat back up on the block, then I had more suspects than a golf ball has dimples.

Okay, not that many.

I knocked on the door of number four. A woman in a bathrobe identified herself as Mrs. Kathleen Wasson. I assumed the inert form under a blanket on one of the twin beds was her son. I was surprised when she merely nodded at my request and closed the door. There was no reason to disturb the upcoming LPGA star, since Janna Coulter had already been advised. A battered white Mercedes was parked in front of number five, and next to it a slinky, well-pampered Jaguar. The former was more likely to have been Tommy's, I thought. I festooned his door with yellow tape and continued on to number six.

The woman who opened the door was less than amiable. Her red silk robe coordinated nicely with her bloodshot eyes. She was armed with a blow dryer. "What do you want?" she demanded. "We won't be checking out until this afternoon, so you'll have to wait to clean the room. My husband will leave a tip on the bedside table, but it won't be much. I wouldn't ask my worst enemy to sleep on that horrid bed. The mattress must be filled with corncobs or whatever it is you people use."

"I'm Chief of Police Arly Hanks." I edged back in case she had a sudden impulse to attack me with a blast of hot air. She looked like the sort to judge people by the color of their badge, and mine was tin, not platinum. "There's been an incident, and we're asking everyone not to leave town until we have a statement." We, as in me.

"Don't be ridiculous," she said. "Dennis and I are going to a cocktail party at six. As soon as he finishes today, we're driving back to Farberville. I have no idea what this incident may be, but Dennis and I are not involved in your little local squabbles."

"Who is it?" asked a man as he came out of the bathroom.

I recognized him as one of the foursome that had included Tommy Ridner. He was now wearing a pale yellow shirt and perfectly fitted white trousers. When he smiled at me, only his lips moved, as if the rest of his face were anaesthetized. His gaze was unfocused, suggesting the effects of the alcohol from the previous night had not completely worn off. He'd managed to shave without doing himself any harm, which I supposed was a good sign. "I'm Arly Hanks, chief of police," I said. "You must be Dennis Gilbert."

His wife went into the bathroom and slammed the door. He did not so much as flinch. "You told my wife there's been an incident. May I inquire into its nature?"

There was no reason not to tell him, so I did.

He squinted at me. "You must have made a mistake with the identification. Are you sure it was Tommy? If the face was covered with blood, couldn't it have been somebody with a similar build? It was dark."

"The Stump County sheriff was in your foursome yesterday, and it wasn't dark when he got here this morning. Two other witnesses identified him. There's no doubt that the victim was Tommy Ridner."

"Poor old Tommy." Dennis leaned against the doorjamb and shook his head. "I can't believe it. We met when we were ten, maybe eleven. I was a meek overachiever, and he was sent to the principal's office at least once a day. Talk about an odd couple. In high school, I was the vice president of the student council and he was a varsity football player. He was the ultimate charmer. He could be loud and boorish, especially when he'd had too much to drink. That, I'm sorry to say, happened way too often, even back in our college days. He had a golf scholarship but was kicked off the team in his junior year for inappropriate behavior. He had a good heart, though, and the charisma of an aw-shucks politician, so he had a large following of the ladies who lunch. They seem to be drawn to bad boys."

"What about next of kin?"

Dennis blinked several times as he thought. "Divorced, no children, no siblings, parents passed away about ten years ago. I don't know if he had family elsewhere. He never mentioned any uncles, aunts, or cousins. His grandparents could be alive. Do you want me to go to his house and look for an address book?"

"I'll let you know later," I said. "In the meantime, I'm asking everyone involved with the tournament to remain in town until I get statements. I understand that you and your wife have an engagement later this afternoon, so I won't delay you any longer than necessary."

He looked over his shoulder. "That would be wise, Chief Hanks."

That left only Phil Proodle, reigning daredevil of Stump County. His expression as he opened his door would have alarmed any potential boat buyer. He had bushy eyebrows, a pear-shaped body, and an orangish tan that undoubtedly washed away in the shower. His ink black toupee was slightly askew. I couldn't begin to imagine him in tights and a cape—which isn't to imply I wished I could. The only thing he looked capable of saving was time.

"I don't need any fresh towels," he said peevishly. "I've arranged for a late checkout time. Run along and annoy someone else."

He started to close the door, but my foot was in the way. "Mr. Proodle," I said, pushing against the door until he stepped back, "I'm not the maid. I'm the chief of police, and I need to have a word with you."

"About the stoplight? I can assure you that no one was able to hit it squarely. It was a very poor idea, and I made it clear that I wanted no part of it. Eventually I did agree to officiate, and for that, I apologize. If there are any damages, send me the bill."

"You do know that gambling is illegal in Arkansas."

"If money was involved, I have no knowledge of it. It was just a friendly little competition."

I decided to let him sweat until someone else brought him up to date. "I need to take your statement before you leave town. The PD is about a block down on your left."

"After the tournament?"

I hadn't really thought about that. I couldn't think of any reason not to keep my potential suspects occupied for several hours. It was Mrs. Jim Bob's decision to proceed or cancel it, and I wasn't in the mood to tangle with her. She would have to be told as soon as possible, though.

I was not a happy caddy as I went through the bar to collect the registration information from Ruby Bee, and then to my car. I scribbled a note to Harve and taped it to the PD door, then drove to the mayoral mansion on Finger Lane.

Jim Bob answered the door. His complexion was gray, and his eyeballs were embedded in his skull like chips of yellow-flecked granite. He licked his lips several times before he was able to croak, "Whatta you want?"

I reminded myself that he was the boss and I was a city employee. "There's a problem. I'll be happy to stand on the porch and fill you in, but it's up to you. You may not want someone driving by to see that you sleep in teddy bear boxers. I myself think they're precious."

He yanked me inside. "What problem?"

I shied away from his breath, which could have dropped a polecat at twenty yards. "Tommy Ridner was killed sometime after midnight. His body was discovered about dawn."

"No shit?" he gasped.

"No shit." I did not gasp.

"God, I need some coffee."

He staggered to the kitchen. Aware that Mrs. Jim Bob was likely to be there, I followed reluctantly. I was relieved to find only Frederick sitting at the dinette. He stood up as Jim Bob veered toward the coffeepot.

"Arly," he said, "what a charming surprise. Would you like a cup of tea?"

"She ain't a guest." Jim Bob flopped down at the table and took a slurp of coffee. "So what the hell happened?" he asked me.

"I don't know. He was slumped in the boat, his head battered in." I looked at Frederick, who'd frozen. "Tommy Ridner, one of the golfers. Sheriff Dorfer and the medical examiner are at the scene. The weapon seems to be a golf club, more precisely a driver."

"Good heavens," Frederick said softly.

Jim Bob scratched his head. "So he was murdered? Is that what you're saying?"

"It wasn't suicide, and I don't see how it could have been an accident. I'm going to have to get preliminary statements from everybody. Then it'll be the sheriff's case. I need to know what Mrs. Jim Bob wants to do about the tournament.

If she cancels it, we may have to put up roadblocks to prevent people from sneaking away."

"What this means," Jim Bob said as he banged down his coffee cup, "is the boat ain't been won after all." A grin spread across his face, and his eyeballs emerged far enough to flicker with greed. "Another eighteen holes left. I was starting to get a feel for it yesterday. Luke did pretty good, along with Larry Joe and Jeremiah. Kevin surprised us all. Who'da thought an asshole like him could drive a ball? When he was a kid, he couldn't even ride a bicycle. We used to call him Scabby."

"It's rather coldhearted to continue with the tournament," said Frederick.

Jim Bob toppled his chair as he stood up. "Ridner was a true golfer, and he'd want us to finish. Maybe we can dedicate it to him or something. I got to shower and make some calls. Mrs. Jim Bob's over at the golf course, getting ready for today's round. Get on over there and tell her what happened, Arly."

"I'm on my way," I said unenthusiastically as he dashed out of the room without so much as a *petit jeté* of joy. "I hope she sees it the same way," I continued to Frederick. "If she cancels the tournament, I might have a rebellion on my hands. Make that a full-scale revolution."

"Would you like me to go with you? She might be less inclined to pitch a fit in front of me. She doesn't seem to be . . . well, fond of you. Do you have a history with her?"

"Nothing that keeps me awake at night. She's convinced I'm already on my way to hell in a handbasket. Yeah, you can come along if you want to. I need to stop by Earl and Eileen's house to have a word with Bony."

"Bonaparte turned in the lowest score yesterday," Frederick commented as he took his cup and saucer to the sink. "He's determined to win the tournament to prove that he's not washed up yet. I'm not so sure. And of course he can't allow himself to lose to the blond girl. That would be the ultimate insult to his manhood."

We walked toward the front door. "It's not about the boat?" I asked.

"Winning the boat would be nice."

"Nice? Half the married couples in this town aren't speaking to each other because of the boat. It's likely that Tommy Ridner was murdered because of the boat. Most of them would use a stronger word than 'nice.'"

Frederick opened my car door and smiled at me.

It wasn't worth the effort to be rude. As we drove down the driveway, I said, "Where's your car, by the way?"

"It's a classic. Even Jim Bob was impressed. Mrs. Jim Bob insisted that I park it in the garage. I haven't had much reason to drive it in town, and it might as well be protected from bird droppings for the time being. It has more than two hundred thousand miles on it, but it rarely complains or causes me grief. Very few people can say that about a relationship."

"True," I said, wondering if Jack and I could go that distance. Neither of us was high-maintenance, but everybody needs occasional tune-ups. And Jack certainly knew how to rotate my tires. I realized I was blushing as I parked behind Earl's pickup. "I'll just be a minute."

Eileen answered the door. "Good morning, Arly," she said. "Won't you come in and have a cup of coffee? Is that Mr. Cartier in your car? I can make a batch of biscuits to go with my homemade strawberry jam. It won't take a minute. How about bacon and eggs, or an omelet?"

"Thanks, but I'm in a hurry," I said. I gave her a brief explanation of the situation and asked her to tell Bony not to leave town. She was still gaping when I got back in the car. "If you're in the mood for breakfast, Eileen will be delighted to fix it for you."

"I think not. You need to speak to Mrs. Jim Bob as soon as possible, and I want to be hovering nearby should you require support. Today's round is scheduled to start at ten o'clock. That's in a little more than an hour, unless the storm comes in. I don't think she'll be popular if she cancels it."

"She's more likely to be lynched. If the mob decides to string her up from a rafter in Raz's barn, then he'll come out blazing. A lot of the good ol' boys around here keep hunting rifles and shotguns in their trucks." I took one hand off the steering wheel to rub my eyes. If ever I needed caffeine, this was the time. Regrettably, it was off my list for the next seven months. All I had to look forward to when I woke up was morning sickness and the inevitable questions from Ruby Bee and Estelle about my future.

I could hear Mrs. Jim Bob's voice as I parked behind her pink Cadillac. Elsie McMay hurried past us, a cylindrical coffeemaker in one arm and a tower of foam cups in the other. Millicent, clutching poster boards and markers, skittered toward the tent. Darla Jean followed her with several shoe boxes. Sleepy high school girls taped white paper on the long tables. I gathered from what I could hear that there was a crisis involving doughnuts and certain volunteers who would never be offered membership in the Missionary Society.

"Well?" Mrs. Jim Bob was snapping at Crystal Whitby, who was shrinking into the ground. "What do you expect me to do about it now? Stop sniveling and take responsibility. Don't be surprised if your name is mentioned next week from the pulpit of the Voice of the Almighty Lord."

I nudged Crystal out of the line of fire. "I need to talk to you, Mrs. Jim Bob. There's a problem."

"There are a passel of problems! Look at the sky. The last thing I need is a storm. How will it look if somebody gets hit by lightning? What's more, last night I spent hours making a poster with today's tee times, but I have no idea how many foursomes we'll have. Complaints, criticism, whining— these golfers are worse than the Sunday school kindergarten class." She turned away and shouted, "Darla Jean! Stop gossiping and make yourself useful. Elsie needs help with the coffeemaker. Eula, cover the doughnuts with napkins before the flies carry them off."

I took a breath and said, "Mrs. Jim Bob, there was a death last night."

She spun around as if I'd pinched her butt. "Whose? Please don't tell me it was someone involved with the tournament. After all I've done to make it run smoothly, I'm not in the mood to watch it crumble. I can't remember when I last had a decent night's sleep. I have a list of lists. I can't trust anyone to handle even the tiniest assignment, so I have assumed the burden of doing everything myself."

"One of the golfers."

"No doubt while driving home drunk. I did what I could to control the consumption of alcohol, but some of the people refused to listen to me. I was against serving it, but I allowed other people to override my decision." She gave Frederick a piercing look. "The Bible warns us against the evils of alcohol. It leads to fornication and degradation. It's a cobblestone on the road to eternal damnation."

"I believe Bonaparte is the one who told you that it's customary," Frederick said, although he stayed well out of her reach. "I merely confirmed it."

"The death wasn't caused by a drunken driver," I said. "It was a different kind of driver. Tommy Ridner was beaten to death sometime after midnight. His body was discovered early this morning in the bass boat. I guess you didn't notice the sheriff's department vehicles in the SuperSaver parking lot on your way here."

She clamped her lips together and stared at me. "Is this another one of your nasty jokes?" she finally said. "If it is, you can consider yourself fired as of right now, Chief Hanks. If Jim Bob doesn't back me up, he'll find himself sleeping in the utility room 'til Boone Creek freezes over."

"Did I mention he's a suspect—and you as well?"

Seven

"Kale, honey," Kathleen Wasson said as she tiptoed into the motel room, "I brought you a sausage biscuit and a glass of milk. You have less than an hour before the second round. You need to shower, get dressed, and eat before we go."

A voice from under the blanket said something that Kathleen pretended not to understand. "You have to get up now," she went on brightly. "You're only two shots off the lead, you know. It's a wonderful opportunity for you to beat that sleazy PGA player. The state newspaper might mention it in the sports section. I must make sure to send them a photograph. I'm very disappointed that they don't have anyone here to cover the tournament. You must be, too."

"Heartbroken. Where're my clothes?"

She opened the closed door. "I brought my travel iron in case your trousers got wrinkled in the suitcase. Where's your lucky blue shirt, the one you wore at the state junior tournament last summer? I could have sworn I packed it."

Shrugging, Kale went into the bathroom. Kathleen sat on the bed, her hands folded in her lap, and waited while he showered. When he reappeared, she said, "I heard the most unsettling news this morning. Tommy Ridner was murdered late last night."

She finally caught Kale's attention. He dropped the shirt and turned around to stare at her. "You're kidding, right?"

"I would never joke about such a thing. His body was found in the bass boat. That explains why the police officer came earlier and asked that we not leave town until we made statements. I didn't want to disturb you."

"A cop came here?" Kale's fingers fumbled as he tried to buckle his belt. He gave up and sat down on the bed across from his mother. "What'd the cop say? Did he want to talk to me?"

"*She* didn't say anything other than everyone has to make a statement before leaving town. It's not as though either of us has anything to tell her. I'm sorry about Tommy Ridner, of course. He was uncouth, but he did spend a lot of time conducting golf classes for underprivileged children and signing autographs at the celebrity events to raise money. I must find out if he was married so that I can write a condolence note to his wife. Do you know, dear?"

Kale shook his head. "Are you sure this cop didn't ask about me?"

"Why would she?" Kathleen said. "It happened after midnight. You were in bed, fast asleep, at ten o'clock."

"Yeah, I guess I was."

"Unless some idiot gets lucky today," Phil Proodle said into the telephone receiver, "the boat will be at my lot tomorrow afternoon. You need to make the back payments in cash. After that, it's yours." He listened for a moment. "No, it has to be cash. Until then, the boat stays on the lot. Don't try anything funny after dark. The fence is topped with barb wire and the two guard dogs are vicious."

While he dressed, he calculated how much cash he had in various bank accounts. How much could a modest house on a beach in Mexico or the Caribbean cost? He could exist on bananas and mangos, as long as liquor was cheap. His passport was valid. Eventually he could open a small boatyard and keep expanding it until he could afford a mansion and a sexy young mistress. Or better yet, no one would make a

blasted hole-in-one and he'd be done with the boat mess on
Monday.

Phil was feeling much better as he headed for Ruby Bee's
Bar & Grill for a breakfast of eggs, grits, biscuits, and ham
with redeye gravy. The only dark cloud on his horizon was
the one settling over Maggody.

"A shame about Tommy," Amanda said as she put down the
mascara brush before she poked her eye out. Her hand would
be steadier after she'd had coffee, she thought as she regarded
her face in the mirror. Her eyelids were puffy, and her hair
was frizzled by the high humidity. At the moment she
looked more haggard than some of the frumpy old biddies at
the golf tournament.

Dennis put his wallet in his back pocket. "At least he was
feeling no pain. I didn't think he could stagger that far without falling on his face. I'm going to miss him." He smiled as
he remembered some of Tommy's more outrageous mo-
ments. No one could believe they were such close friends, he
in his expensive, tailored clothes and Tommy in shorts and
dirty T-shirts. His soft-spoken voice, drowned out by Tommy's guffaws. His composure versus Tommy's unrestrained
passion. He couldn't count the number of times he'd bailed
Tommy out of jail because of some crazy prank. "I guess we
ought to head for the golf course, although I don't want to
play golf today—or ever again. It won't be the same."

Amanda was not known for her sentimentality. "Thank
gawd we won't have to listen to Tommy chortle any more
about his damn hole-in-one. He was so obnoxious about it
last night that I was ready to scream. Someone else must not
have had my self-control." She dabbed some liquid makeup
under her eyes to hide the dark crescents. Her hair was hope-
less. "Are you going to make the funeral arrangements? It
might be nice to have the reception afterward at the club.
Tommy practically lived there."

"Aren't you curious who killed Tommy?"

She pulled on a white tank top that emphasized her tan. "Of course I am. Tommy was your best friend. I said it was a shame, didn't I? Do you think these shorts are too risqué for the locals? Maybe they all dress like Quakers on Sundays and ride around in buggies."

"The shorts are fine. We only have thirty minutes. There'll be coffee and doughnuts at the tent."

"What I think," Amanda said as they went out to the Jaguar, "is that Tommy must have been killed by one of these peculiar people who live here. Remember the guy with the live chicken? Did you see that man who lives in the shack next to the course? I saw him walking into the woods with an enormous, hideous, drooling pig on a leash. And while you were on the course yesterday, this creepy man with more fingers than teeth came over to me and asked if I wanted to 'waller' with him. I was so overwhelmed with revulsion that I gagged."

Dennis put on his sunglasses, then buckled his seat belt and adjusted the rearview mirror. "It makes sense that the killer is one of the locals. Tommy was waving money around. He had one of the caddies go buy him some cigars at the grocery store, then tipped him twenty dollars. After his coup de grace on thirteen, he sent the observer to fetch a bottle of champagne and cups from his trunk. The kid got twenty dollars, too." He braked at the edge of the road to let an RV drive by. "He gave the checkout girl a ten-dollar tip when we stopped at the grocery store to buy tonic water and limes. Once the word got out, any one of them or their friends could have done it." Despite the total lack of vehicles in either direction, he put on the blinker. "Money is a powerful motive."

Amanda twisted the rearview mirror so she could apply lipstick. "You'd think Tommy had better sense than that, but he never did. Last week one of the attendants found him taking a shower in the ladies' locker room. He claimed he was looking for a partner for the mixed scramble, but Lissie

Barquette said he was so drunk she and the attendant had to literally drag him out and put his clothes on him."

"May he rest in peace."

"I hope the golf course in heaven has a nineteenth hole." She dropped the lipstick tube into her purse. "Not that it'll matter to Tommy."

"If you won't tell me, you have to tell Chief Hanks," Janna said grimly as she turned up the road to the golf course.

"Yeah," Natalie said.

Janna sighed and switched tactics. "You were too upset to talk about it last night, and I understand that. I've seen the same thing with soldiers after a deadly encounter with the enemy. The worst thing you can do is bottle it up. Post-traumatic stress syndrome is a very real disorder."

"What's my tee time?"

"I hope this doesn't have anything to do with Tommy Ridner's death. Is he the one who . . . ?"

"Don't be ridiculous. Did you clean my clubs last night?"

"They were so covered with muck that I ended up using a hose at the back of the motel. Kathleen Wasson was doing the same thing. She's so dull that I'd rather converse with a rock. All she could talk about was her son's lucky blue shirt and how sure she was that she'd packed it. If I had that punk at boot camp, I'd slap that smirk off his face so hard his head would spin. Their kind don't belong on a golf course."

"Do I?"

"I'm beginning to wonder," Janna said.

Bony graciously allowed Aunt Eileen to drive him to the tournament site. He'd asked for a glass of orange juice and, when her back was turned, had spiked it with vodka. Since he was a little fuzzy about what all had happened the previous night, he didn't know if he was drinking the hair of a pit bull or a chihuahua. The one thing he remembered vividly was that smug asshole Ridner strutting around the barroom, crowing about the goddamn bass boat. Anyone could have lucked out and made a hole-in-one, he thought darkly. All of the holes would be par threes at a real course. The so-called ladies' tees were halfway down the so-called fairways. At least the blond chick had the decency to play from the men's tees. Now it was a brand-new game, and he was confident he'd walk away with the trophy and the boat. Whatever had happened in the previous twelve hours was history, but it would be nice to know exactly what *had*.

"I think it's my left elbow," Eileen said as she whipped around a tractor that was barely moving. "I don't know how much to bend it on my backswing. Halfway through my swing, I second-guess myself."

"Hmmm," said Bony. He had a vague picture of whacking balls in the middle of the road, although he couldn't recall why it seemed like a fine idea.

"Earl hit three balls into the middle of the boggy bottom," Eileen continued more cheerfully. "I was hoping he'd jump in to fetch them and be attacked by giant leeches. Can you imagine the gall of him saying that I belonged at home, cooking and cleaning! If golf is such a manly game, why do they have the LPGA? Is that supposed to be like the PTA? You don't hear about Michelle Wie organizing a bake sale for the boys." She turned so abruptly that half of Bony's drink splashed onto his trousers. "I'm going to make the first hole-in-one today, and Earl can throw his clubs in the pond along with his balls." She veered toward a squirrel, but it scampered into the woods.

"That's the attitude. You have to think positive." There was something about the stoplight. An argument about whether it had to be green. That only made sense if they were driving. Bony took a gulp of orange juice. But if they were driving, where did they go?

Eileen smiled as she imagined herself accepting the key

for the fancy bass boat. Earl's face would crumble like a
dried mud daubers' nest. He could beg all he liked, but she
was gonna sell the boat, turn over the hefty tithe, and spend
the rest of the money exactly as she chose. Not one penny of
it would go for a bucket of bait.

Brother Verber hadn't given much thought to his sermon,
even though the blessed hour would be upon him pretty darn
quick. 'Course there wouldn't be enough worshippers at the
service to get up a game of canasta—not that he condoned
playing cards on Sunday. The majority of the congregation
was involved in the golf tournament, either playing or vol-
unteering. The rest probably knew about the murder in the
bass boat, or would shortly, since the grapevine missed only
the most remote households. He'd heard it from Chikeeta
Buchanon when she stopped by to get the key to clean the
Assembly Hall before the morning service. She'd heard it
from her ex-brother-in-law, who was sleeping with her niece.
He'd heard it from his fishing buddies, and so on. Everybody
else who could drive, walk, or crawl would be drawn to the
golf course in hopes of more violence.

He was itching to follow them. Before the first person
teed off, he could offer a prayer for the deceased, and then a
homily about the sin of envy. "Thou shalt not covet thy
neighbor's house, thou shalt not covet thy neighbor's wife,
nor his slaves, nor his ox, nor his ass, nor anything that is thy
neighbor's, including his bass boat," he intoned solemnly.
"For the Almighty Lord will smite you with a bolt of lightning afore you reach the first green!"

It had a nice ring to it, he decided, but he was gonna have
to stretch it out into a thirty-minute sermon for whatever
church members showed up. He sat down on the couch to
wait for further inspiration, idly looking at the three trophies lined up on the coffee table. He'd never won a trophy.
The best he'd ever done in a competition was a second-place

ribbon for Bible drill in Sunday school. He had a certificate
for perfect attendance in high school and a diploma from
the seminary. But never a trophy, not even an itsy-bitsy one.

He went to the kitchen and buttered a square of cold cornbread, slathered it with raspberry jam, and took a bottle of
sacramental wine out of the refrigerator. When he sat back
down, he realized that he'd forgotten to get a glass. He looked
at the largest trophy, a plastic loving cup atop a fake marble
base.

" 'Therefore God give thee of the dew of heaven, and the
fatness of the earth, and plenty of cornbread and wine.' "
He filled the cup and picked up the base with trembling
hands. "And the winner is Willard Verber for his outstanding leadership in the Lord Almighty's war against Satan
hisself!" After the riotous applause died down, he drank the
contents.

By nine forty-five, a diminished number of golfers had arrived at the tent. The vast majority were locals, since most of
the visitors had left as soon as Tommy made the hole-in-one.
Mrs. Jim Bob admitted she hadn't mentioned the rule until
after supper because she was too busy overseeing the buffet
line and reprimanding those who'd imbibed to excess. I had
my doubts. After all, the fewer the eaters, the more bountiful the leftovers. I wasn't surprised as other locals drifted in,
some of them with coolers, blankets, and folding chairs.
Mothers smeared bug repellent on their children's bare arms.
Men slapped each other on the back and remarked on the
likelihood of rain. Middlin Buchanon pulled his wizened
granny in a little red wagon, ignoring her squawks. Constant
Squirtty led her blind husband to a picnic table and parked
him so she could continue to mingle. The unsavory crowd
from the poolroom had taken over a picnic table and were
stuffing doughnuts in their mouths. Someone had brought a
radio but turned it off after a withering stare from Mrs. Jim
Bob. I found Darla Jean, who produced a folder with photo-

copied forms that included disclaimers for injuries on the course received from a boggling array of flora and fauna. Rules forbade the use of alcohol, inappropriate attire, obscene language, threats of physical intimidation, weapons, and violence. I could barely make out the last line that required winners to be present at the final ceremony. "They're all signed and dated," Darla Jean said proudly. "I thought I'd wait to see who showed up this morning before I alphabetized them. Mrs. Jim Bob wants everything alphabetized."

"From armadillos to water hemlock," I said, nodding. "Would you and your friends try to figure out who was still here when the meal was served yesterday evening? I'll need their registration information."

"Gee, I dunno. You'd better ask Mrs. Jim Bob."

"I'm the chief of police, Darla Jean. Mrs. Jim Bob can bawl you out. I can arrest you for impeding an investigation."

"I'll get right on it."

I regarded the remaining players. No one appeared to be in mourning for Tommy, but conversations were muted. The husbands and wives of Maggody were again seated on opposite sides of the tent, and hostile looks were flying hard and fast. I wondered how many husbands had slept in tool sheds or pickup trucks for the last three nights. None of them seemed well rested. Jim Bob had sneaked into his kitchen, but only after Mrs. Jim Bob left.

Kevin was sitting by himself, nursing a cup of coffee. "Did you and Dahlia make peace?" I asked him as I joined him.

"Not 'xactly. She packed up the younguns, and they're staying with Ma. I reckon I should have told her about the golf practice, but she cain't keep a secret for ten minutes. She'd have called my ma, and then my pa'd be in boiling water. It jest seemed safer to say I was working late."

"Not your best decision, Kevin."

"Ma said she'll buy us new tires after she makes a hole-in-one. Pa was there to pick up a clean shirt and overheard her. They got into it and she ended up hauling all his clothes out to the driveway and running over 'em with the lawn mower. He's staying with his third cousin Byle in Hasty. Bony's still there, though. I saw him sneakin' sideways looks at Dahlia. If he so much as tries to lay a finger on my wife, I swear I'll knock him clear to the Missouri line. He thinks his poop don't stink jest because he can play golf better than me."

"Then go try to talk to her now," I said, although I hardly qualified as a marriage counselor. When I'd finally caught on to my ex-husband's extracurricular activities in Manhattan, he had frequent flyer miles with an escort service.

"I cain't cross Jim Bob," Kevin bleated. "Yesterday some of my balls landed on the greens. He thinks I have a chance to make a hole-in-one today. Iff'n I do, I wouldn't put it past him to hogtie me and keep me in his truck until the ceremony. He wants that boat so bad he's sweating diesel. He ain't the only one, neither."

I would have pursued this had he not started sniveling. It was more than I could handle on an empty stomach. I filched what proved to be a very stale doughnut, and was forcing it down when Mrs. Jim Bob positioned herself at the front of the tent and clapped her hands until she had our attention.

"I'm pleased to see so many of our citizens have taken an interest in our golf tournament," she said in a voice icy enough to counter global warming for a millennium. "As you know, our goal is to raise money for golf widows. Those of you who are here as spectators will be expected to donate ten dollars each as your contribution to our cause. The high school students will be around to collect money from anyone who's still here in three minutes. Time starts now."

The stampede was reasonably well mannered, although I could hear Middlin's granny carrying on long after they had disappeared. Children bawled as they were hustled into cars and the backs of pickup trucks. Whoever had brought the radio turned it back on in a parting display of bravado.

Mrs. Jim Bob watched with a grim smile until the last of the pickup trucks and cars bounced down the road. "Now, I have an updated list of those who intend to play today, and I've reassigned the foursomes and tee times on the poster behind me. Since we have so few players, everyone will start at the first hole. Leftover sandwiches and barbecue will be available for lunch, for a small fee. We'd like to provide a free lunch, but you have to remember that this tournament is a charity affair to raise money for the less fortunate. Before we begin, I think we should observe a moment of silence for Thomas Ridner, who died in a tragic accident late last night. Had he been a God-fearing Christian, he would have been safely tucked in bed, but he chose to engage in wantonness, vanity, and gluttony. Let this be a lesson for all of us." She clasped her hands and lowered her head.

Her comment evoked guilty grimaces from the local men and pious nods from the women. Dennis took off his sunglasses and looked down, his eyes closed. Amanda frowned at a distant rumble of thunder. Phil Proodle seemed to be offering a prayer, although it could have been of gratitude instead of for the salvation of Tommy's soul. Kathleen Wasson gazed at the table, while the teenaged boy next to her drummed his fingers as if squashing ants. A trio of college boys tried to catch the attention of a girl with ash blond hair (Natalie, I assumed), but she was seated next to Kevin, listening to him with a sympathetic expression. I hoped she had a stronger stomach than I did. At another table, Janna finished a doughnut and licked her fingers.

"Amen," Mrs. Jim Bob said briskly. "The current rankings for those who have chosen to continue are as follows: Bonaparte Buchanon is leading the field at three below par; in second place is Natalie Hotz; in third is Kale Wasson; and in a tie for fourth are Dennis Gilbert and Luke Smithers. The college boys from Farber College turned in respectable scores. Kevin, Jeremiah, Crystal, and Bopeep did nicely. Other players need to improve their technique and concentration. Mayor Jim Bob Buchanon was at the bottom of the list with a miserable score of one hundred and seventy-three.

He also received two warnings for profanity. A third offense will result in expulsion."

From the direction of the men's tables, someone muttered, "Fuck you."

She deigned not to hear it. "As you know, the bass boat is once again available for the first hole-in-one. Mr. Phil Proodle is looking forward to presenting the keys to the proud new owner, should there be one. Let's give him another round of applause for his generosity."

The applause was enthusiastic. Phil stood up and cleared his throat. "Thank you, Mrs. Jim Bob. We at Proodle's Fine Boats are proud to do our part to benefit such a worthwhile charity. And if today ain't your lucky day, come on by and have a look at our incredible inventory and unbelievable prices. We have everything from outboards to party barges." He slapped on a bright orange cap. "Hunt me up and we'll talk turkey."

"More like gobbledy-gook."

"I heard that, Roy Stiver!" Mrs. Jim Bob snapped.

I hurried to the front of the tent. "I am, believe it or not, Chief of Police Arly Hanks. I need to get a statement from everyone who is involved in any capacity in the tournament. Most of them will take only a few minutes. Anyone who doesn't make a statement will be guilty of impeding a police investigation, which can result in a fine and jail time. Subpoenas will be issued. I'll be here for a while, and at the PD the rest of the day. Any questions?"

"You mean us, too?" squeaked one of the high school girls. "All I did was make baloney and cheese sandwiches."

"I put out the cookies," said another. "It's not like that man choked to death on a raisin."

Mrs. Jim Bob edged me aside. "We are not interested in what you did or did not do, Ella Louisa. It's ten o'clock, so I officially declare the beginning of the final round of the Maggody Charity Golf Tournament. Presentation of the awards will be held here at two o'clock sharp. If you are not present, you will be disqualified. Will the first foursome please take their positions at the tee?"

"What if it starts raining?" Bopeep asked timidly.

"The Almighty Lord makes those decisions, and we must adjust accordingly. If any of you miss your tee time, you will be disqualified. It is now two minutes past ten."

The players headed for the poster, jostling each other. High school boys with red bandanas on their arms took off for their assigned holes; the girls giggled and shot me quick glances. Yawning, Amanda Gilbert opened a fashion magazine. Natalie continued to listen to Kevin's whimpers. Kathleen Wasson hovered over her son until he finally went to read the poster. Janna muscled Rip Riley aside to search for Natalie's name. Cora, Bopeep, and Audley approached the tee, each holding a purse, an umbrella, and a few golf clubs. After a minute, a college boy joined them. He did not look pleased.

I went to the buffet table. "All right, girls, let's get your statements out of the way. Heather, Ella Louisa, and Dana Dawn, follow me." We sat down at the end of a vacated table. I ascertained that none of them had seen or heard anything of interest. Yes, they knew Proodle had given beer to some of the caddies, and Tommy had, too. Mrs. Jim Bob had banished the boys for the duration of the tournament, and they'd left cheerfully to go swimming (and drink their own beer). The girls finished serving dinner, cleaned up, and left by seven. They'd heard about the hole-in-one but were more concerned about hooking up with their boyfriends for the evening.

Darla Jean was the only one who aired any grievances. "I worked like a dog all day yesterday," she said. "I kept having to go through the registration cards and pull the names of people who didn't show up, or quit as soon as they learned someone had made a hole-in-one. Most of 'em were too rude to stop by the table and tell me. Mrs. Jim Bob tried to argue with 'em, pointing out they could still win a trophy. Like

they cared. There wasn't but a dozen or so out-of-town players at the supper. I figured they thought that they deserved a
free meal." She gave me the registration forms and a neatly
written list of names. "They're alphabetized."

"Was anyone particularly angry at Tommy?" I asked.

"Was anyone *not* is a better question. Yeah, there were
smiles and congratulations and toasts, but I was glad we didn't
use real knives and forks. There was a lot of drinking going
on. Mrs. Jim Bob was fit to be tied, if you know what I mean.
There was almost a brawl. Billy Dick's pa and Jim Bob started
shoving each other, and then some of the other guys butted in.
Mr. Lambertino called Mr. Cranshaw a nasty name and they
took to rolling around on the ground. Mr. McIlhaney chased
Mr. Whitby down the fairway. Their wives were screeching at
them like crows. Heather and I ducked under the table, and there
was Kevin hunkered up and trembling. It was a hoot."

"Sounds like great fun," I said. "Who was in charge of
the bar?"

"Bony, for the most part. He didn't seem to mind being
stuck in the corner with a bunch of bottles of whiskey. Brother
Verber showed up to say the blessing, but he went into such
a long spiel about salvation and armies and medals that Mrs.
Jim Bob had to tell him to stop. I think he might have been . . .
uh, hanging around the bar too long."

She didn't have anything to add, so I sent her back to her
post. The college boys were grazing at the doughnut table
and flirting with the girls. I herded them to a table. They happily told me that they were there because the whole thing
sounded like a badass joke, and their frat brothers had dared
them. Yeah, they'd stuck around for the barbecue because it
was included in the registration fee. However, they'd headed
for Farberville as soon as they were finished eating.

I wrinkled my nose as I smelled beer, and noted that their
cups were not filled with coffee. "Did you bring a cooler today?"

One of them said, "Didn't need to. That Proodle guy has

four big ones jammed in his backseat. Yesterday he wandered around the course with an insulated bag, passing out free beers to any guy who wanted one. Sort of like roving room service, I guess."

"More like he wanted to get everybody drunk," contributed another of them. "Makes you wonder if he's so all-fired eager to give away his boat."

The last musketeer said, "He didn't reckon on Tommy Ridner's capacity for booze, all day and all night. The princess turned up her nose, naturally. I sliced a ball into the next county when she pranced by me in that prim little skirt. Proodle should have hired her as his secret weapon."

"Why did you come back today?" I asked.

They laughed. "Cold beer and hot chicks," one said. "And whichever of us gets the lowest overall score wins the pool at the frat house—a hundred and twenty-seven bucks."

"And now, maybe the bass boat," said another. "What the hell."

I checked them off my list. I looked around the tent and realized I wasn't in the mood to deal with anyone else before I had a decent breakfast. I decided to stop at Ruby Bee's, then go to my office and wait for Harve to bluster through the door and blame the whole thing on me. I knew damn well I'd get stuck with the case, but I wasn't about to give in until I had my daily dose of carbs and cholesterol.

Tentative raindrops splattered on my windshield as I drove away, and thunder reverberated menacingly. With the exception of a lone figure slumped in the back booth, Ruby Bee and Estelle were the only people in the barroom. Ruby Bee had just gone into the kitchen when I sat down next to Estelle.

"Who's that?" I asked as I gestured at the figure.

"We don't know. He came in shortly after Ruby Bee opened, had a cup of coffee, and dozed off. She said she isn't going to run him off as long as he doesn't bother anybody. How'd Mrs. Jim Bob take the news about poor Tommy?"

"She was more concerned about freeloaders eating all the

doughnuts. The tournament's proceeding as scheduled for those who bothered to show up. As for the rest of them, not even the chance to win the boat was enough to get them to risk their lives on the golf course. I'm surprised I haven't had to put together a search party to find some hapless fool who wandered into the woods to search for a ball. Bony Buchanon's leading the field, in case you're interested."

"Not so's you can tell."

Ruby Bee reappeared. "I suppose you want me to fix you some breakfast? I've already got my hands full getting ready for lunch. Roast chicken and cornbread dressing, mashed potatoes, corn casserole, greens, pole beans, and apple pie." She blotted her forehead with a pot holder. "But I reckon I can hustle up something. You have to eat regular in your condition. Otherwise, you'll get constipated."

"Do you recollect when Eula got so bloated she looked like she'd swallowed a throw pillow?" Estelle said. "Then all those laxatives caught up with her during the Sunday sermon at the Voice of the Almighty. When Joyce told me about it, she laughed so hard she had yellow tears running down her legs. I thought I was gonna have to tie her down so I could finish trimming her hair. I mean Joyce, not Eula."

"A charming story," I said. "I was hoping for breakfast, Ruby Bee, but I'll settle for a grilled cheese sandwich and a glass of milk."

She gave me a look. "I ain't about to let my grandchild come out looking like a toothpick." She went into the kitchen.

"Not that you look like a toothpick," Estelle said, lifting her eyebrows. "Your britches look tighter every time I see you. You might ought to be shopping for maternity clothes."

"Let's talk about last night, okay? What happened?"

Estelle rubbed her temples, careful not to smear her glittery green eye shadow. "It was crowded, and so loud I could barely hear myself think. I don't know how Ruby Bee could even hear what folks ordered, much less keep it straight. I helped out behind the bar, but she was back and forth from the booths to the kitchen fixing burgers, fries, and onion rings. My feet ached just watching her. She was so bone-tired at midnight that she looked like she was about to fall on her face. After last call at eleven forty-five, it took us thirty minutes to finally get everybody out the door. She said she was going straight to bed. Cars and trucks were leaving when I got in my car, and the parking lot was mostly empty."

The Florence Nightingale of the barroom battlefield came out of the kitchen with a plate of fried eggs, bacon, grits, and toast. "If you want biscuits, show up at a decent hour. You figured out who murdered Tommy yet?"

I picked up a fork. "I never solve crimes until after breakfast. It's bad for the digestion." I held up my free hand before Estelle could produce another tale of gastric disaster. "All I know is that you closed up shortly after midnight and went to bed. Did you hear anything from the other units?"

"I wouldn't have woken up if a grizzly bear was fighting a bulldozer," Ruby Bee said. "You heard from Jack?"

"You asked me that yesterday." I spread apple butter on a piece of toast. "The answer's the same."

"I thought he might have called, it being Sunday. Then again, it could be a different day in Brazil. Maybe it's only Saturday there, and he's confused."

"It's Sunday in Brazil," I said, "and only a couple of hours time difference. He doesn't have access to a phone. Even if he did, I've been running around town since dawn. I was at the PD for all of five minutes."

"Maybe you should get your fanny over there now," Estelle said.

I pushed aside my plate. "So I can wait for Jack to call me on his nonexistent phone and we can have a nonexistent conversation?"

"No," said Ruby Bee, "so you can talk to Harve. He's waiting for you."

Eight

The PD reeked of smoke. Harve had made a pot of coffee and was reading my mail. His cigar stub looked like a smoldering pinecone. I wasn't perturbed, since the coffee was stale and the mail consisted of catalogs for hunting and fishing gear. I was used to airing out my office, especially after visits from Raz.

"Where the hell you been?" he asked without looking up.

"Out by Boone Creek, reading the *New York Times*."

He tossed the catalog in the wastebasket and gestured for me to sit down across from him. "What else you been doing in the last three hours?"

I gave him a rundown, then said, "It'll take the rest of the day to get statements, but I'll stay up all night typing them and deliver them to you in the morning."

"You're gonna need 'em more than I do."

"No, I'm not," I said firmly. "The sheriff's department handles homicides. I'm just a backwoods cop without the experience and expertise to investigate a homicide."

"Has it been a whole month since the last one? I have three escaped prisoners to track down, and I don't even have a goddamn office."

I tried to come up with an argument, but the steel jaws of

the trap had already snapped down on my ankle. "I'll poke around, get statements, that sort of thing, but you have to deal with the media and the county prosecutor. Furthermore, you need to loan me a deputy. I don't have enough money in the budget for the gasoline to drive back and forth all day."

"I'll handle the media, but as for a deputy . . ." He dropped the stub in the wastebasket and pushed back the desk chair. "I reckon I better get back to Farberville before Deputy Murtle comes up with a way to burn down the county courthouse as well."

"Hold your horses, Harve. What happened at the crime scene after I left?"

He scratched his head, as though I'd posed a complex, multifaceted question about atomic subparticles. "Well, not all that much. McBeen didn't have anything else to say, except for a whole helluva lot more whining about being rousted outta bed at a gawdawful hour in the morning. He'll do a preliminary autopsy and run some blood tests, but all he's gonna find out is that the victim was clobbered with a three wood. We'll test it for prints. There are hundreds of prints all over the boat, and it'll take a coon's age to sort 'em out. The boat's just now on its way to the lab so we can run all the blood to make sure it came from the victim."

"What if somebody makes a hole-in-one today? Mrs. Jim Bob'll go ballistic if Proodle can't present the winner with the key."

"Proodle can present the key to the city of New Orleans for all I care. The boat's a crime scene, and it's gonna stay impounded until the case is closed." Harve put on his hat and looked around at the office. "This place is a real dump, Chief Hanks. You ought to redecorate one of these days."

I grabbed a catalog and hurled it at him, but he was already out the door. "Bastard," I said loudly as I sat down behind my desk and brushed off the cigar ash, then emptied the remains of his cup of coffee in the wastebasket. I'd been fairly certain that I'd end up with the case dumped in my lap, but I was still annoyed. I threw another magazine at the door, and then another for good measure.

Frederick came into the PD and tactfully stepped over the clutter. "Am I interrupting?"

"Have a seat. I was sulking, that's all. How's it going at the tournament?"

"Mrs. Jim Bob's beginning to crack. When she saw Jim Bob passing a flask, she attacked him with her clipboard and chased him into the woods. It was highly entertaining, at least from a disinterested spectator's viewpoint. Upon her return, she realized that Bonaparte had put out the leftover liquor and was fixing drinks. Proodle's coolers were on the table, too. Drinking on Sunday appears to be a sin comparable only to blasphemy and bestiality. There was a great deal of activity as those with drinks tried to conceal them and those without tried to get one before she closed down the bar."

"So glad I missed it," I said. "What about your boy, Bony? Will he be sober enough to play well?"

"He wouldn't know how to play at all in that condition. I imagine that's something he shared with Tommy Ridner. The only thing, from what I heard. Bonaparte doesn't have—if you'll excuse the phrase—a charitable bone in his body. He's petty-minded, vindictive, and not very bright. If he didn't have a talent for golf, he'd be in prison."

"That's the local consensus." I took a legal pad and a pen out of a desk drawer. "How about I take your statement now? Name, age, et cetera."

"My name is Frederick Cartier, age sixty-two, retired, born in Jackson, Mississippi, with no permanent address. I most recently resided in Las Vegas in a hotel off the Strip. I don't recall the name, but I have the bill somewhere."

"When did you and Bony arrive in Maggody?"

"We checked into a motel in Farberville about twelve days ago. A dreadful place, dirty and noisy, with unsavory types doing business in the parking lot. Bonaparte went to a bar and met a man who agreed to drop him off here the next day. He struck a deal to give golf lessons to the local women until the tournament started, and his aunt invited him to stay at her house. Mrs. Jim Bob insisted that I stay at hers. I was reluctant at first, but the motel became intolerable and there were no other rooms available."

"Why did Mrs. Jim Bob insist? Her sense of hospitality isn't even skin-deep."

"I may have mentioned that I've been involved behind the scenes with charity tournaments in places like Palm Springs and Maui. Jim Bob and I have avoided each other. A certain gentleman called Brother Verber has been a frequent guest. I don't quite know what to make of him. The cleaning woman, referred to as Perkin's eldest for some reason, never says a word but watches me like a sparrow, her head tilted. One afternoon I found her in my room, wearing nothing but my loafers and a silk necktie while she vacuumed. It's been quite an experience."

"Welcome to Maggody," I said. "When I came back, I realized that I'd forgotten how peculiar the people are. For the last forty years Jessibelle Buchanon's been writing threatening letters to former president Hoover because she doesn't find a chicken in every pot. Luciffor Buchanon gets arrested in Farberville every few weeks for standing naked in front of the police department. Abindago Buchanon was caught spray-painting parking meters because they were spying on him. The list never ends. Nothing surprises me anymore. I'm just another patient in the asylum." I picked up my pen. "Let's finish your statement. What did you do yesterday?"

"Mrs. Jim Bob gave me a ride to the tournament site. Due to the high attrition, we reassigned the foursomes as best we could. I instructed the hole monitors, then sent them to their assigned holes. After that, I wandered around."

"I heard there was alcohol consumed."

He smiled wryly. "Oh, yes, to Mrs. Jim Bob's consternation. Tommy ran a bar out of the trunk of his car, serving

Bloody Marys, screwdrivers, tequila shots, and beer. Phil Proodle had cases of beer in his car. Most of the men managed to wet their whistles, and a few of the women. Miss Natalie was carrying a large cup of what she swore was straight orange juice, but it was suspiciously diluted. Mrs. Gilbert did not pretend. Mrs. Wasson, the mother of that annoying boy, accepted a Bloody Mary after her son teed off. Mrs. Jim Bob stormed around, lecturing anybody she could catch. The local boys who'd hoped to caddy were sent away in disgrace."

"Things had calmed down when I got there," I said. "What happened after I left?"

"Which you did rather abruptly, Arly. The sheriff appeared to be distraught when you spoke to him. I was deeply puzzled. I hope it was nothing too serious . . ." He lifted his eyebrows and waited.

It was too dopey to explain. "Depends on your perspective, but it didn't involve a UFO invasion. Let's go back to yesterday afternoon."

"Word of Tommy's hole-in-one spread. A lot of golfers departed immediately. The rest looked as if they'd been sucker-punched. Phil Proodle staggered to his car and stayed there for nearly an hour, his forehead resting on the steering wheel. He was so distressed that I felt a pang of sympathy for him."

"I guess he wasn't all that eager to give away the bass boat. He's a big boy; he should have refused to donate it in the first place."

"I believe it was Mrs. Jim Bob's idea," Frederick said.

I remembered all the times I'd tried to withstand one of Mrs. Jim Bob's dictates. I'd had more success hailing cabs during rush hour in Manhattan—in the rain. I sighed and said, "Everybody ate dinner while the booze continued to flow. After that, the party continued at Ruby Bee's Bar and Grill. Tommy's bragging must have become intolerable, from what I was told. Did you notice anyone who was especially hostile?"

"I wouldn't know, since I wasn't there."

"You weren't?" I said, surprised. "I'd have thought you wanted to celebrate, since Bony was leading the field. You said it wasn't about the boat but about winning the tournament."

Frederick studied the floor. "He did well yesterday and certainly is in contention to win. I'd have gone to the bar to congratulate him and Tommy, but I couldn't face the noise and that twangy music. I had a headache. I get them every now and then."

"Try living here. Did you go to the bar Friday night? Lots of people were there, psyching themselves up."

"No, I thought about it, but I decided that Mrs. Jim Bob deserved all the support I could give her. On Thursday she and Jim Bob had an unpleasant exchange of words, and he was banished to the utility room. He dodged her all day Friday, which infuriated her even more. She threatened to track him down and drag him home by his . . . well, his male anatomy. I insisted that she relax with a glass of wine, and we chatted until ten."

"You voluntarily spent Friday evening with her?" I was perplexed, since I would have preferred to spend the evening locked inside a tiger compound.

"I didn't want her to be alone."

I decided his survival instinct was operating on a forty-watt bulb. "So you were at Mrs. Jim Bob's house both evenings?"

"No," Frederick said hesitantly. "I was there Friday, but not last night." He went into the back room and emerged with a cup of coffee. After a sip, he grimaced and put the cup on the floor. "As I said, last night I had a migraine and couldn't face the thought of Mrs. Jim Bob's tirade about the excessive drinking. I drove to Farberville and ended up at a coffeehouse, having a pleasant conversation with a few academic types. I almost felt guilty about discussing art and literature rather than the weather, golf, and that ridiculous bass boat."

I nodded. "What time did you get back to Maggody?"

"About two. When the coffeehouse closed, an English professor invited everyone to his house. We sat on the deck and talked about Italian cinema—Benigni, Antonioni, Zeffirelli, and the like. I was alone in my opinion that Bertolucci is overrated. What do you think?"

"I think Bertolucci has nothing to do with Tommy's murder. When you drove back to Mrs. Jim Bob's house, did you see any activity in front of Ruby Bee's?"

"Not a thing. If Maggody had sidewalks, they would have been rolled up. I went to the house and straight to bed. I didn't happen to glance at the boat when I drove past the parking lot. I had no idea anything was wrong until you told Jim Bob."

"I need the name of the English professor in case we need to verify your story."

Frederick stiffened. "Am I a suspect?"

"Should you be?"

"I hardly knew Timmy Ridner. Why would I murder him?"

"Same reason as all the golfers—because he'd take possession of the boat if he appeared at the awards presentation this afternoon. You're not a golfer, but you're here to support Bony."

"That's absurd! Bonaparte is no more than a recent acquaintance. We met in Vegas two weeks ago, and when it became prudent for him to leave in the middle of the night, I agreed to drive him here merely out of curiosity. I have no monetary interest in his winnings," he said, his smile noticeably less affable. "As for the name of the professor, I don't recall it at the moment, and I have no idea where he lives. I merely followed his car. I did jot down his name and address on a napkin because I want to send him information about a film festival in San Marino. The napkin is in my car."

A flash of lightning lit up the room, followed almost instantaneously by a boom of thunder that rattled the PD. I looked up, expecting to see a gaping hole in the ceiling. "Whoa," I murmured. "That was close."

Frederick was on his feet. "I'd better get back to the golf course. Mrs. Jim Bob may be reluctant to call a storm delay. We don't need any more tragedies."

As soon as he left, I flipped to a fresh page and started working on a timeline of the previous day. The golfers began to tee off at 10:00 A.M. Tommy made his hole-in-one at about 2:00. Cocktails were served at 5:00, and dinner at 6:00. By 8:00, the party kicked in at Ruby Bee's and lasted until 12:15. The competition to smash the stoplight began shortly thereafter. It ended before 2:00, when Frederick drove through town. Tommy, therefore, had been murdered between 12:30 and 2:00. That fell neatly into McBeen's estimated time of death.

Now all I needed to know was who participated in the friendly little contest to destroy public property, and how Tommy Ridner ended up in the bass boat. Could it have been a group effort, with each loser taking a swing? I'd known the men in the tontine since I was a kid; none of them seemed that coldblooded. Except Bopeep's boyfriend, I amended, although I wasn't ready to cast him as a prime suspect. And why assume the murderer was male? Tommy Ridner could have passed out in the boat. Beating an inert body does not require strength. My thoughts were as moody as the sky as I began to copy information from the registration forms to make a list of names and addresses of the remaining players. In alphabetical order, of course.

Joyce Lambertino was the first golfer to intrude on my haven. Her ponytail drooped down her back like the tail of a coonskin hat and her clothes were so wet that they clung to her. I realized it was raining. I'd been vaguely aware of thunder but had been too engrossed in my list to even glance out the window.

"It'll only take a minute, Joyce," I said. "I pretty much know what happened during the day yesterday. I heard there was a brawl during dinner. Did it have anything to do with Tommy Ridner?"

"He wasn't real popular. It might have been okay if he hadn't kept rubbing it in, but he did. You'd have thought he was the first man to walk on the moon. It was making the menfolk downright surly, along with all the drinking." She shrugged. "It wasn't all that big a deal. As soon as Mrs. Jim Bob ordered Bony to stop serving booze, everybody started leaving."

"And Larry Joe?"

"I wouldn't know. He's been sleeping in the barn, and I don't keep track of his comings and goings. Are we done?"

"Thanks for coming by," I said. I suspected I'd hear similar stories from all the wives. None of them would have dreamed of going to Ruby Bee's barroom to party. Being seen in the presence of a pitcher of beer would lead to lifelong expulsion from the Missionary Society, as well as a lecture from the pulpit. Brother Verber had no hesitancy about naming names. I knew that he took potshots at me from time to time. I could expect a lot more in the future as my belly expanded. Mrs. Jim Bob would crochet me a scarlet letter that didn't stand for Arly.

Elsie McMay called to say that the previous evening she and Lottie had been so appalled by the rowdiness at the dinner that they'd gone to her house to soothe themselves with coffee and pie. Eula and Millicent came in a minute later to say they left as soon as they finished eating. Eula added that Lottie's carrot cake was dry, and Millicent said she had no idea what Jeremiah had done, since he was sleeping on Roy Stiver's couch and could continue to do so until hell froze over, for all she cared.

Crystal Whitby was explaining in great detail what a

narrow-minded, sexist jerk her husband was when the phone rang. I told her to hold the thought and picked up the receiver.

"Arly?" Ruby Bee said.

"This is Deputy Murtle," I said in a husky voice. "Chief Hanks is out investigating a crime. Would you care to leave a message?"

There was a harrumph, followed by, "You just tell Chief Hanks that she better be searching Tommy Ridner's motel room right this minute, 'cause if she ain't, somebody else is."

I put down the receiver, told Crystal to go home, and was out the door before I remembered it was raining. I went back inside to get the car key. I briefly debated whether or not I should take my gun, decided against it, and drove around the side of the bar to the motel.

There were more cars than I'd expected, and several familiar pickup trucks. Phil Proodle's door was open, and I could see a goodly number of men in his room. The whoops and laughter suggested that yet another party was under way. Ruby Bee's was open on Sundays, but she couldn't sell beer. And as far as I knew, none of the husbands could go home to flop in front of the TV and watch the sport of the month.

The yellow police tape on the door of number five dangled from the jamb, and the door was ajar. I parked on the far side of Tommy's Mercedes and approached slowly, regretting my decision not to bring my gun. Before I could bang open the door in a burst of bravado, shouting all sorts of officious threats, Dennis Gilbert stepped out of the room. We were equally startled.

"Chief Hanks," he squawked. He pulled off his sunglasses. "I, uh, wasn't . . ."

"Neither was I." My heart was pounding, but I caught my breath. "What were you doing in there?"

He seemed to be looking at my left ear as he said, "I was hunting for Tommy's car key. We're having a wake for him in Phil's room, and I'm sure he'd want us to drink the liquor in his trunk. The car's locked. I thought his key might be on the dresser."

"Didn't you see the yellow police tape?"

"It was broken, and the door wasn't locked," he said. "I assumed you'd already searched the room. I know the law, and I would never have gone into the room if . . ."

"When did you get back here from the tournament?" I asked.

"Roughly an hour ago. Mrs. Jim Bob finally canceled the day's round after lightning hit a tree less than fifty feet from the first tee. Almost everybody had already come in, but not all of them. It turned into a chaotic scene. She tried to count noses and send some of the high school girls out to round up the strays, but the girls were wailing because of the storm. The tent leaked so badly that we were all soaked."

"Did the rest of the people staying here also come back about that time?"

Dennis put on his sunglasses and looked toward the motel units across the way. "I guess so. Janna Coulter's car was already here, but it's gone now. That white hatchback belongs to Kathleen Wasson. I'm almost certain it was here, too. Jim Bob and his friends were pulling in as we parked. The frat boys decided to stick around for the free booze." He winced as thunder boomed overhead. "Certain areas on the golf course are flooded, and there are a lot of branches down."

"Was the yellow tape broken when you got here an hour ago?"

"I can't say," he said. "It was raining. Amanda was upset and blaming me for bringing her along. No cell phone reception, no sushi, no heated pool and gym, no premium cable channels. She's not handling it well."

I realized that I was going to have to take Amanda Gilbert's statement sooner or later, unless someone confessed. "Did you find Tommy's car key?"

"Yes, sorry. That why we're standing here, isn't it?" He took a key ring out of his pocket. It held enough keys to lock down a prison. "This was on the night table. One of them's the car key. I can't believe he's dead. If I hadn't agreed to"—he swallowed, then moistened his lips—"to sign up, he might have skipped the tournament. We'd be at the club right now, playing gin until the rain stopped. Instead, I'm here, feeling guilty as sin. I know it's not my fault. I just wish I believed it." Oblivious to the rain streaking down his sunglasses, he leaned against the hood of Tommy's car. His shoulders began to shake. "He was my best friend. All I had to do was refuse to let him talk me into it. I don't know how I'll be able to live with myself."

"You don't know that he wouldn't have played in the tournament without you," I said soothingly. "I'm sorry for your loss." I held out my hand for the key ring. "Please remind everybody at the wake that I need statements."

"About the liquor in the trunk. Do you think it would be okay if—"

"No, it wouldn't. Make do with whatever you have, or let the locals contribute their private stashes."

Dennis stumbled into his motel room. I pushed Tommy's door open and peered inside. A suitcase was overturned, its contents scattered on the floor and rumpled bed. Empty bottles, glasses, and plastic cups had been swept into a corner. His golf bag had been dumped. Some of the clubs poked out from under the bed, along with golf balls and colored tees. Cigarette and cigar butts were piled in ashtrays. The bathroom was a disaster, his shaving gear in the sink and his toothbrush on the floor. A leather zipper bag had been opened and thrown into the bathtub.

Either Dennis had tossed the room in his quest for the keys, or he'd found the room in this condition and failed to find it worth mentioning. A third possibility, based on his unfocused eyes and blubbery remorse, was that he was already drunk. He might have started drinking at the tent and resumed in Proodle's room after he and Amanda returned an hour earlier. I made a mental note to have a box of tissues and a pot of strong coffee when he showed up at the PD.

I had a sudden urge to tidy up and refold the clothes. Reminding myself that my apartment looked almost as bad, I moved things around with my foot in case the perp had left a signed confession. From the number of glasses and empty bottles, it was obvious that the party had resumed in this room after Ruby Bee closed the bar. I doubted it would be useful to collect fingerprints, and Harve wouldn't send out a team unless I found graffiti written in blood on the walls.

I locked the door behind me and did my best to stick the yellow tape back up. Tommy's trunk proved to be a well-designed apparatus for dispersing alcohol. It had a wine rack, barred shelves for glasses and bottles, and storage boxes for maraschino cherries, olives, onions, and half-pint bottles of multicolored liqueurs. The space for a spare tire was now an insulated cooler. Tommy hadn't wasted money on appearances; he'd indulged himself with a veritable bar-mobile.

There was nothing of interest inside the car. Paper cups and fast-food wrappers had been tossed into the backseat. Faded newspapers were folded to expose half-done crossword puzzles. Based on the CDs stuffed in the glove compartment and spilled on the passenger's seat, his taste in music leaned toward Willie Nelson, Jimmy Buffett, and the Dixie Chicks. The ashtray was jammed with cigar stubs, and ashes were sprinkled on the console and the floor mats like rampant dandruff.

I made sure the car was securely locked, then went to see who all was attending the so-called wake. Proodle's room was packed with men who smelled of wet dog and pond muck. Kevin was slumped on a corner of the bed, clearly miserable but too cowardly to leave without Jim Bob's permission. I heard the shouts of a crap game in the bathroom. The only female I could see was Amanda, who'd changed into dry, skimpy clothes. Two of the college boys had crowded her into a corner, but she didn't appear to be in need of rescue. The third boy was doing card tricks that seemingly bewildered Larry Joe, Ruddy, Tam, and Earl. It didn't take much.

Nobody invited me in, so I went into the barroom and sat down on a stool. Estelle was still there, as was the unidentified figure in a back booth. Sooner or later, someone was going to have to check him for a pulse.

"Back for lunch already?" she asked tartly. "You're gonna end up bigger'n Dahlia if you keep stuffing your face every two hours."

"Have you talked to her since your adventure?"

"I ain't seen hide nor hair of her, but I don't know why I would. I heard she was staying at Eileen's house, along with Bony. Kevin's lucky she ain't at home, since he'd end up banished to the woodshed like some husbands I could mention. I don't know what's gotten into people these days."

Ruby Bee came out of the kitchen with a peach pie. Once she'd set it on the stand, she glared at me. "I reckon Deputy Murtle gave you my message."

"Did you see someone go into Tommy's room?" I asked, my fingers crossed.

"I just saw that your tape was ripped and the door was open. I'm gonna have to feed that bunch out back afore too long, and I need to start the rolls. You're lucky I took the time to call you, Miss Snippety Britches. Next time I won't bother."

"I'm sorry," I said, trying to sound pathetic. "I'm overwhelmed by all this. I've got to take statements from more than thirty people, and some of them are busy getting pie-eyed drunk as we speak. I'll be lucky if they remember their own names."

Ruby Bee looked skeptical. "I'll overlook it this time, but don't push your luck. I feel like I'm running a henhouse full of foxes. Folks are coming and going half the night, demanding ice or clean towels, tromping the begonias by my unit, whining 'cause they don't like collard greens. I wish every last one of them would go home—and take some of those worthless husbands with 'em. I'm fed up with the lot of them."

"So am I," I said. "At least there's one gentleman in town."

"I hope you ain't referring to Bony Buchanon," Estelle said, her nostrils flared with contempt. "A few days back him and Earl were out in the back pasture shooting beer bottles off a fence. When I went outside and hollered at them to stop, they didn't so much as look at me. Downright rude, if you ask me."

"Roy ain't no gentleman, either," Ruby Bee added. "I heard him singing Frank Sinatra songs in the parking lot last night when I got in bed. I had to hold a pillow over my head until somebody finally hushed him up. Roy sings worse than a coyote in heat."

"That was around twelve thirty?" I asked. "Did you hear anything else?"

"Just the thud when I fell asleep. Do you want a piece of pie to hold you over until lunch?"

"No thanks," I said, lying through my teeth. Estelle's tactless remark held a sliver of truth, although I doubted I could swell to even half of Dahlia's formidable bulk if I lived on nothing but Twinkies and milkshakes for the next seven months. "If you see anything suspicious, give me a call at the PD."

I was halfway across the dance floor when Estelle said, "So who's this gentleman you mentioned?"

I looked back. "Frederick Cartier. He's been staying at Mrs. Jim Bob's house for at least a week. Did the grapevine snap?"

"It did not," Estelle said snootily. "I heard she had a houseguest, but no one said his name. All the ladies have been talking about is the golf tournament and their committee assignments. They're scared to death of Mrs. Jim Bob blaming them if anything goes wrong. Brother Verber's going to get an earful for not persuading God to keep away the storm."

I noticed that Ruby Bee's jaw was slack. "See you later, okay?"

She turned around and went into the kitchen. Estelle and I exchanged shrugs, and then I drove back to the PD in the steady rain. The gray clouds had settled into the valley and showed no signs of moving on anytime soon. Raz's marijuana plants could tolerate temporary flooding, but Earl's greens might be sprouting chickweed by the minute. The fairways might be overrun with displaced snakes and gators (if the rumors were true) and dead branches that carried fire ant colonies and wasp nests.

Who said golf was a game for sissies?

Nine

I needed to find out more about the stoplight scene. All I had was Phil Proodle's version: It didn't happen, but if it did, it wasn't my fault, but I'll pay if there was any damage. Raz Buchanon couldn't have said it better, although he'd never go so far as to offer to pay a plugged nickel. The men were definitely culprits. Natalie Hotz had baited them—and later claimed to be the victim of a sexual assault. I'd hadn't yet met her, much less spoken with her. It was time to correct the situation.

I called Ruby Bee and asked if she'd seen Natalie or Janna, and was huffily informed that she was making a batch of cloverleaf rolls, not running a daycare center. Once she finished griping at me, she said that she hadn't laid eyes on either of them. On that cheery note, she hung up on me.

They had to be somewhere. The SuperSaver offered limited amusement. The Dairee Dee-Lishus did not have inside seating. They could have driven back to Farberville despite my threat to issue subpoenas, but I didn't think Janna would risk a blot on Natalie's precious reputation. And they weren't in their motel room.

That left the leaky tent, abandoned when the tournament was delayed, with bare tables and wet chairs, sodden poster board, crumpled cups lying in the mud. Surely my missing persons hadn't taken refuge in Raz's barn. He'd made it clear he wouldn't tolerate trespassers, and he was capable of violence. Moonshiners are as protective of their stash as mama bears are of their cubs. Bears, however, don't bear arms.

I was on my feet when the phone rang. Hoping it was Ruby Bee reporting that Janna and Natalie had dropped in for lunch, I answered it. "Yes?"

"Thought I'd find out what all's going on out your way," Harve drawled. "Ain't nothing like a rainy Sunday afternoon to sprawl in front of the TV with a cold beer."

"I'm heading out to a wake for Tommy. I'll think about you when we toast him with Glenlivet."

"Some damn fool reporter caught wind of what's going on. The prosecutor called, asking for details. I told him I'd give him an update."

"Have at it," I said. "I need you to run background checks on everybody who's not local. I'd do it myself, but my computer's been down since one of the squirrels died of starvation." I gave him a list of names and addresses.

"You ruled out the locals?"

"No," I said. "I can't believe any of the wives is obsessed with the bass boat, at least not enough to bash in a stranger's head like that. If the victim had been one of their husbands, I'd be taking a harder look at them. As for the local guys, I don't know. A lot of alcohol was served. Stir up a pitcher of greed, frustration, anger, and testosterone, and you get a Molotov cocktail." I told him about the impromptu postmidnight contest. "I doubt it was a good-natured gathering. If Tommy won, someone might have snapped."

"Like Jim Bob?"

"Or any one of them, or maybe all of them. They each took a turn so they'd all be implicated. Agatha Christie's plot comes to mind."

"Have you picked her up for questioning?"

I considering saying yes and suggesting that he break the news to the media. "She's been dead for thirty years, Harve. Found any of your escapees?"

"One of 'em was at his house, sleeping like a baby. Another one turned himself in because he can't stand his wife's cooking. The third one's around here somewhere. Sounds like you better get off your butt and worry about your own case. You ain't gonna get anywhere if all you're doing is drinking whiskey and—"

I went out to my car and drove to the Maggody Municipal Golf Course and Recreation Center. A car was parked on the road, and a solitary figure stood under the tent. I dodged raindrops as I skittered across the muddy stubble. Janna glanced at me, then resumed her vigil.

"What's going on?" I asked.

"Natalie's missing. She must be lying out there in the rain, unable to stand or walk. You need to get together a search party and call for an ambulance. She'll be chilled to the bone and in shock."

"Why didn't you report this earlier?"

"I wanted to make sure she wasn't here, waiting for me to pick her up. When the storm hit, she was on the back nine. Her foursome came in. As soon as that insufferable woman announced that play was canceled, we all headed for our cars. That's when Natalie realized she'd left her wedge in the rough. She said she'd catch a ride. I wasn't happy, but I was drenched and I've been fighting off a chest cold for the last few days. You'd think an old army broad was tougher than that, wouldn't you?" Her expression softened, as if she were remembering her first kiss. "I was the assistant administrator of a field hospital in a Central American jungle, where our worst enemies were malaria and gangrene. I was a top military aide in Indonesia at the time of the Bali bombing. After that, I trained recruits in scorching heat and freezing rain. I worked them until they puked. Now I'm worried about catching a cold. Pathetic."

I had no idea how to respond to her unsolicited résumé. "So Natalie headed out on the course and you drove back to the motel?"

"Frederick Cartier assured me that he'd wait for Natalie. He seems like a gentleman." Her hands curled into fists; if I'd encountered her in an alley, I would have dived into a cardboard box. "It's my fault. Natalie's had no experience with men," she continued. "I've protected her. If the media find any reason to gossip about her, she won't get million-dollar endorsements. She has to be perfect."

"That can't be easy at her age," I said, thinking of some of my less reputable escapades. Maggody had never provided much in the way of wholesome entertainment for teenagers, so we whiled away the time drinking beer on the banks of Boone Creek, tipping cows, skinny-dipping, and studying anatomy in the moonlight. "Perfection's not easy at any age."

Janna regarded me with contempt. "Why aren't you doing something?"

"If Natalie knew where she was going, then she came back at least an hour ago. Frederick dropped her off at the motel, and now she's taking a hot shower and wondering where the hell you are."

She stomped over to her car and drove away, splattering my car with mud. I suppose I should have braved the fallen branches and snakes to search the golf course for Princess Perfection, but I wasn't in the mood. Frederick wouldn't have abandoned her. I drove to the mayoral mansion. Mrs. Jim Bob's pink Cadillac was parked in front. I assumed Frederick's car was tucked safely in the garage. I hoped Natalie Hotz was tucked safely in the kitchen.

Frederick opened the door. "Arly. Won't you come in and dry off?" He did not sound enthusiastic.

"Thanks." I assumed that he was miffed because I'd asked for verification of his alibi. I went down the hall to the kitchen. Mrs. Jim Bob was seated at the dinette, a glass in front of her and a bottle of bourbon within reach. She gave me a bleary look as she filled her glass.

"Come to gloat, haven't you?" she asked me. "Guess you think it's funny that we had to stop the tournament because of the storm." She gulped down her drink without so much as a blink. "I'm sick and tired of your disrespectful attitude and your snide remarks. I hate to think of the grief you've caused your poor mother all these years."

"Wait just a minute," I said, pissed off at her standard litany of my faults. "I didn't lift one finger to interfere with the golf tournament, not even my pinkie. If Ruby Bee is immersed in grief, she does a damn fine job of hiding it. I'm flattered that you think I can control the weather. Shall I hold my breath until the sun comes out?" I clamped my lips together and puffed out my cheeks.

"You can hold your breath 'til you turn blue in the face. That doesn't change things, does it? I've been hearing rumors that you've got a bun in the warmer but no ring on your finger. Like mother, like daughter, I always say. Are you planning to raise your little bushcolt in a motel room, or have you set your sights on a double-wide at the Pot O' Gold?"

I exhaled fiercely. "I thought I'd go to Jim Bob for advice. After all, he has at least one illegitimate child out there somewhere, doesn't he?"

"He got down on his knees and acknowledged his weakness of the flesh, then prayed for divine forgiveness."

"He'd better hope divine forgiveness comes with a lifetime warranty."

"Ladies," Frederick murmured, "let's have a friendly cup of tea together." He began to fill the teakettle at the sink.

Mrs. Jim Bob seemed more in the mood for Long Island tea than Lipton. She replenished her glass and took a deep swig. "As you know, Chief Hanky-Panky, I do not approve of alcohol in any form. I'm drinking strictly to calm my nerves. This last week has not been easy for me." She grabbed a paper napkin and crumpled it in her fist. "The committee chairs failed miserably, so I had to step up and take charge of every last detail. Perkin's eldest decided that she's allergic to electricity. Every time I let her out of my sight, she starts unplugging things. Then I find out that my husband is a greedy, treacherous, conniving liar. How dare he take golf lessons on the sly and enter the tournament!"

"The very idea of him doing all that behind your back," I said.

Her head bobbled emphatically. "All of the husbands—liars and rats! Not one of them volunteered to lift a finger to help us get ready. If Jim Bob or any one of them wins the boat, I swear I'll take it out to the middle of the reservoir and sink it." She raised her glass. "Damn the torpedoes and full storm ahead!"

I pulled Frederick aside. "Do you know where Natalie is?"

"At the motel, I should think."

"Janna said you were going to wait for Natalie while she retrieved a golf club, then give her a ride. Did you take her back to the motel?"

Mrs. Jim Bob banged her glass on the table. "You know what I'm gonna do? I'm gonna sprinkle rat poison on the cot in the utility room. Jim Bob'll get it on his skin and die in agony. When he begs me to pray for him, I'll tell him to call one of his floozies at the trailer park and let her pray for him. Does the Lord Almighty listen to floozies? Ha! He'll burn in hell for all eternity, regretting how he treated me."

"Read the directions on the box," I said to her, then turned back to Frederick. "Well, did you give her a ride or not?"

"No, I didn't. After Janna left, Natalie came over to me and said she'd arranged for someone else to wait for her. There was a sparkle in her eye that hinted of young love. Who am I to interfere? Besides, I'm appalled by the way Janna treats the poor girl, bullying and berating her at every opportunity. What good is success if you sacrifice joy and passion to achieve it?"

"A lovely speech. Why don't you go to the motel and repeat it to Janna?"

Mrs. Jim Bob stood up, clutching the bottle. "I should burn down the SuperSaver, that's what I should do! There's a can of gasoline in the garage. We'll see how Mayor High-and-Mighty likes that. Then I'll start a career in home decorating, and he can find out how hard it is to deal with gardeners and plumbers and Perkin's eldest. Let him try to organize the spring rummage sale!" She sat down and began to sob. "And the potlucks on Wednesday," she said between hiccups. She splashed a goodly amount of bourbon on the table, then raised her empty glass. "If he's in charge, we'll end up with six green bean casseroles and no desserts!"

I looked at Frederick. "Do you have any idea who, or where they are now?"

"None at all," he said distractedly, observing Mrs. Jim Bob as if she were a mutant lab animal. "Shouldn't we do something about her? I'd hate to think she might actually follow through on her threats."

"She'd never risk losing her exalted position in the Missionary Society. Where'd she get the booze?"

"Leftovers from the tournament. After this morning's debacle, she insisted that all of it be put in her trunk. After she finished the vodka, she moved to bourbon. Gin is next."

"Nobody understands me," Mrs. Jim Bob wailed. "I've sacrificed everything for this community, everything! Without moral guidance, people would lie and steal and fornicate with farm animals. It's up to me to maintain the standards of decency laid out in the Bible, even if it means living with ridicule and gossip behind my back. Don't think I'm unaware of it, Arly Hanks!"

She was now drinking straight from the bottle. I gave Frederick a faint smile and left him to deal with her. The storm had rumbled its way out of the valley and the rain was easing up. I stepped in a puddle as I went to my car. My clothes were wet, and my right shoe squished as I drove down the driveway. I thought about Harve, stretched out in a recliner in front of the TV, the remote in one hand and a beer in the other. The kitchen at Ruby Bee's Bar & Grill would be redolent with the heady aroma of parsley, sage, rosemary, and chocolate cream pie. Even my so-called efficiency apartment with its mold and mildew was preferable to my car, which was beginning to smell like manure from my trips to the golf course.

Duty beckoned. I bit down on my lip and drove once again up to the tournament site, wondering if Natalie truly had arranged another ride or simply wanted to get away from Janna for a while. All the likely suspects were at the motel. One of the ladies might have taken Natalie home with her, but I couldn't imagine who. Natalie was the enemy: young and willowly, reputedly an excellent golfer. Frederick had claimed she had a sparkle in her eye. Such descriptions were better suited for romance novels, along with sultry smiles and tingles of lust. It was more likely she'd been slapped in the eye by a wet branch.

The tent looked even bleaker. As I turned around, I saw Raz sitting on his porch. I stopped and put down the car window. "Have you seen anybody around here since the tournament was stopped?" I called.

"Mebbe." He took a sip from a jar and smacked his lips. "Or mebbe not. What's it to you?"

"A young girl's missing. One of the golfers."

"I don't give a shit if all them golfers drownded in the pond. Long about August we'll start seeing their swelled-up bodies in the muck. Won't be a purty sight."

"It won't be a purty sight if I wring your scrawny neck. Have you seen anybody in the last two hours?"

"Saw you prancin' around. I was hopin' you'd fall flat on your ass in the mud."

"Who else?" I said coldly.

"That woman you was talkin' to. She's a mean one, like my half brother Smutter. He was so ornery he used to dump kerosene in the well and toss in a bucket of frogs, just to watch 'em belly up. I reckon that woman would, too."

"What about before that? A blond girl, maybe carrying a golf club?"

Raz grinned complacently at me. "What's it worth to ya?"

"You think I don't know about that stash of 'shine in the root cellar behind Belcher's old cabin? What's *that* worth to you?"

"Ain't no root cellar up there, and iff'n there is, there ain't nuthin' in it." He spat an amber ribbon toward a bucket, then glowered at me like a treed possum. "About ten minutes after ever'body left, the gal walked by. I offered to let her sit a spell on the porch to git out of the rain, but she acted like she din't hear me."

"Did you see anybody else?"

"I had to go inside and change channels on the TV. Marjorie gits right bored watching baseball. If she had her druthers, she'd watch them reality shows all day and half the night." He cackled so hard that moths flew out of his beard. "She likes cooking shows, too. Jest last night we was watching—"

"Thanks, Raz," I said, then returned to my car. Close encounters with Raz always made me itchy, but I didn't have time for a shower and a change of clothes. Natalie had been on foot, heading toward the highway. It was less than a mile, and the chances of being attacked by a buffalo were slim. I would have noticed if she was lying in a ditch. But she had been talking with Kevin earlier in the day, I thought. With almost no encouragement, Kevin would bleat out all his woes—including the fact that Dahlia and the kids were staying at his ma's house. If she'd seen him leave with Jim Bob or one of the tontine members, she'd know his house was unoccupied.

I parked, opened the gate, and went up squeaky steps to the porch. It seemed silly to knock, since I was a cop and she was committing a crime. If this were a scene from a TV drama, the SWAT team would have kicked in the door and stormed the house. This being mundane reality, the door wasn't locked. I went into the living room, which was decorated in yard sale chic. An upturned playpen dominated the middle of the room; mangled toys were scattered among juice boxes and bits of orange peel. The plastic houseplants were near death. A golf club, quite possibly a wedge, was propped in a corner.

"Natalie?" I called. "I know you're here. I'm not in the mood to play hide-and-seek, so don't make me come find you in a closet." I wandered into the kitchen. Jars of peanut butter and grape jelly on the counter tempted me, but I didn't want to humiliate myself in front of my imaginary SWAT team. I squared my shoulders and returned to the living room.

"Hey, Chief Hanks," she said as she came in from the hall-way, a towel in her hand. "I know I'm trespassing, but I had to get out of the rain. I kind of feel like Goldilocks. Thank gawd I didn't find three bowls of porridge on the kitchen table."

Her skin was perfect, I had to admit. Her teeth were white and even. She wasn't as tall as I was, but she probably weighed thirty pounds less. Her ash blond hair was wet but neatly combed and tied back with a pink ribbon, accentuating her high cheekbones and guileless blue eyes. She'd managed not to get mud on her short pleated skirt or bug bites on her ankles.

"Janna's worried about you," I said. "She expected to see you two hours ago."

Natalie sighed. "I know. I keep waiting for her to have a GPS chip implanted under my skin. That way she'll be able to tell when I go to the bathroom in the middle of the night." She pushed aside a plastic truck and sat down on the sofa. "Can you imagine what it's like to have someone spying on you every minute? She keeps a record of everything I eat and drink. I take a handful of vitamins and supplements twice a day. She inspects my fingernails. Sometimes I want to scream."

"Slavery was abolished in the nineteenth century. Why don't you leave?"

"It's hard to explain. It's like I was a scruffy dog at the pound and she rescued me. I'd be a terrible person if I wasn't grateful to her. I was living with my mom and a brood of brothers and sisters in a little town near Fort Sill, over in Oklahoma. My mom's an alcoholic and, well, a slut. She doesn't even know the names of the fathers of most of the kids, including mine. I don't remember her ever keeping a job for more than a couple of weeks. I dropped out of school and started working at a café when I was fourteen. I was terrified I'd end up like her."

"And Janna rescued you." I sat down and gazed steadily at her, trying to get a sense of her sincerity. I've always had a tendency to mistrust beautiful people. "How did she do that?"

"Fort Sill's an army camp. I started dating a corporal, a real nice boy from Iowa, and he taught me how to play golf." She picked up a stuffed animal and squeezed it in her arms. "It wasn't serious or anything. He had a girlfriend back home, and he was crazy about her. He told me he kept all her letters under his pillow so he'd dream about her. I thought that was the sweetest thing I'd ever heard."

"Where does Janna come in?"

"She saw me at the golf course and told me I had a natural talent. I didn't even know you could make money playing golf, but she swore that I'd be able to make millions—with her help. My mother couldn't have cared less what happened to me, so she signed some kind of guardianship paper. Janna resigned from the army, and we moved to an apartment in Farberville so I could play on better courses. I started competing in tournaments at the country club, and then in bigger ones. *Golf Digest* did an article about me. *Sports Illustrated* wanted me to be in their swimsuit issue, but Janna said no. She's as concerned about my reputation as she is about my game. I spend all day practicing, working out at a gym, and running. At night, she makes me study history, grammar, boring old books, and that sort of stuff so I won't sound ignorant. It's not like the interviewers ever ask me about the Battle of Hastings."

It sounded like boot camp, minus the obstacle course and the firing range. Having met Janna, I had no trouble believing Natalie. "How does she afford all this?"

"She never spent a penny of her army pay, and now she gets a pension. She also teaches a couple of fitness classes at the gym. She's so tough that half her clients crawl out to the parking lot after class. She took over a seniors' class, and the manager had to call an ambulance three times in the first month." Natalie giggled as if she were still fourteen and we were having a sleepover. I almost expected her to pass chips and dip, or pull out her yearbook.

I had to remind myself that she wasn't talking about the high school hierarchy. When I lived in Manhattan, I always took whichever fitness class was trendy at the time. We strolled rather than walked. We allowed our husbands to open wine bottles and doormen to open doors. Our most strenuous challenge was wielding credit cards. I was so lost in memories of my previous life that it took me a second to realize that someone was driving past the house. By the time I turned around to look out the window, the road was clear.

"Did you see who that was?" I asked.

Natalie shook her head. "The rain's stopped. Do you think I should leave a note for Kevin's wife, thanking her for letting me hang out here?"

"Definitely not. She's . . . ah, temperamental. Why did you come here, Natalie? Janna offered to wait and give you a ride to the motel, and so did Frederick Cartier. Were you planning to meet someone once the coast was clear?"

"Who would I want to meet—some toothless redneck? One of those piggish local men? I may not have a degree, but I'm not an idiot. I just wanted some time to myself. Janna and I have been crammed in that tiny motel room since Friday."

"You managed to party Friday and Saturday nights," I pointed out.

"It wasn't like there was anything else to do."

Hazy sunlight began to lighten the room. Before she could bolt, I said, "Tell me about the sexual assault. Who, where, when."

"Oh, that." She made a face. "It wasn't a big deal. I'd just as soon forget about it. Janna shouldn't have mentioned it to you."

"Sexual assault's a crime that I take very seriously," I said. "I've been known to ignore shoplifting or running the stoplight, but this needs to be investigated."

"I was dashing across the parking lot when I slipped and tore my shirt. Janna jumped to the conclusion I'd been assaulted, and I was too tired to argue with her. Not that it would have done any good. She never listens to me."

"Why don't you tell me what you did on Friday, beginning with your arrival?"

She began to wander around the room. "I'll try," she said at last, "but I may not remember every little thing. After we checked into the motel, we went to the golf course. As soon as I saw it, I was ready to pack up and go home, but Janna didn't want to hear it. I played eighteen holes with Kale, some guy named Big Dick, and that asshole Bonaparte. If you want to know about Tommy, I met him a couple of years ago at a tournament in Tulsa. He was a fun guy and a real party animal. He'd won his flight and was buying drinks for everybody." She smiled sadly. "Poor guy, getting killed like that. I hope he was so drunk that he didn't suffer. Anyway, after the practice round there was an impromptu party in the bar, like a get-acquainted thing. Beer, burgers, pretzels, popcorn, dancing, whatever. At nine, Janna decided she was tired, so we went to our room. Once she took an antihistamine, she was out like a light. I couldn't see just lying in bed, staring at the ceiling, so I went back to the party and stayed until midnight or so. I guess I had a little too much to drink."

"So there was no assault," I said. "You tripped in the parking lot between the two motel buildings. Instead of telling Janna the truth, you made up the story just so you wouldn't

have to admit to drinking." When she shrugged, I went on.
"Now tell me about yesterday. What did you do after Tommy
made his hole-in-one?"

"I was happy for him 'cause I knew how much he wanted
to win the boat. I was playing with three men from Starley
City. We finished the round and turned in our scorecards, and
then they heard the news and drove off. I drank some champagne with Tommy. Janna glared at me, but I didn't care,
even if it meant running extra laps when I got home. Everybody else was drinking, too. After we ate, we went to the bar.
Tommy was loud and obnoxious, to be honest. Bonaparte
looked like he wanted to pick up the jukebox and drop it on
him. Jim Bob was simmering like a pot of chili. Even Amanda
Gilbert was muttering nasty things under her breath, and she
doesn't give a shit about golf tournaments. The only reason
she tags along with her husband is to flirt with the golf studs."

"Where was Janna?" I asked.

"She said she felt woozy and needed to go to bed. The
next time I looked around for her, she was gone."

"Let's talk about the little contest out on the highway after
Ruby Bee closed the bar." I put my forearms on my knees
and leaned forward. "Don't bother to deny it, Natalie. I've
already got evidence." I did a pretty good job of sounding
confident, even though the golf balls in the ditch across from
the SuperSaver were long gone.

"It was so dumb," she said. "I think it was Bonaparte's idea,
but I'm not sure. Everybody jumped right in. Phil Proodle
said he'd award a bottle of scotch to the winner. Tommy was
bragging how he was going to use the pot to buy fishing
gear. Everybody was really mad at him. I thought the contest was a terrible idea, but I went along with it because I
thought it was better than a lynch mob."

I doubted that she'd been all that reluctant to join in the
fun. "Who ended up participating?"

"Bonaparte, since it was his idea, and Tommy, who'd bet
on the color of his eyes and figure out how to win. Amanda

came along to bitch at Dennis. Jim Bob, that guy called Big Dick, and some other guys whose names I don't remember. The pimply kid, Kale. Bopeep stormed off after her boyfriend said he was in. Proodle was the judge. About a dozen altogether, I'd say. I shouldn't have worried about a hanging. Most of them were too drunk to tie their shoelaces."

"So who won?"

Natalie rolled her eyes. "Take a wild guess. When I left, they were all arguing and Tommy was prancing around with a fistful of money, chortling like he'd won the U.S. Open. It was way after one o'clock, so it was lucky for me that Janna didn't hear me come in. She thinks I should be in my pajamas by nine, reading a biography about a dead president." She put her fingers to her lips. "Oops, I guess I shouldn't say that with Tommy being . . ."

"Dead," I concluded for her. "You have no idea what happened after that?"

"Sorry. If it's okay with you, I should go to the motel and let Janna know that I'm okay."

"I'll give you a ride." I locked the front door when we left, hoping Dahlia never learned that her house had been invaded by a petite blonde who could get lost for a month in one of Dahlia's dresses. As we drove to the Flamingo Motel, I again asked Natalie if she'd planned to meet anyone after the storm hit. She countered with questions about my job and how I got along with the sheriff and men like Jim Bob. Neither of us was satisfied when I dropped her in front of her motel room.

Janna's car was there. I waited for a moment in case I heard shrieking, then abandoned all pretenses of being a professional and headed to my apartment for a hot shower.

Ten

I was feeling new and improved as I went inside Ruby Bee's. I wore my uniform and badge, and my hair was pinned up in a permafrost bun. Ruby Bee gave me a startled look, then ducked into the kitchen; Estelle merely watched me approach. I wasn't sure if my latest sin was of omission or commission, but I didn't really care. Kathleen Wasson was seated in a booth, nibbling a grilled cheese sandwich. I sat down across from her. "You doing all right?" I asked her.

"Oh, Chief Hanks, how kind of you to ask. What a horrible weekend this has been. That nice man was killed, and then the storm, and now we're here for another day. I'll have to call in sick tomorrow. I don't know what we'll do if I lose my job." She put down the remains of the sandwich and pushed aside the plate. "I work for a housecleaning service and get paid by the hour, minimum wage. We barely squeeze by as it is, and it's not like I can work a late shift. People don't want you mopping floors and vacuuming in the evening."

"I'm sorry about all this. I can take your statement now, and then you can go back to Farberville so you won't have to miss work. Ruby Bee will keep an eye on your son."

"I can't leave Kale alone," Kathleen said in a shocked voice. "He may play golf like an adult, but he's not even old enough to vote."

I didn't point out that her baby was currently drinking his

weight with the good ol' boys out back, most of whom thought
a ballot was a sad song. "It's your decision. Why don't you go
ahead and tell me about Friday and Saturday? I'll catch up
with Kale later."

Kathleen picked up a glass of iced tea with an unsteady
hand, took a sip, and then put it down very carefully. At that
rate, I thought, she'd finish it long about midnight. "Kale
didn't want to come on Friday, but I persuaded him. He's done
very well on the junior golf circuit, but it's important that he
makes a name for himself as a serious competitor in the future." Her eyes began to well with tears. "I've raised him on
my own," she continued unsteadily. "His father took up with
a mud wrestler named Betty Boob before Kale's first birthday, and never paid a dime of child support or sent a Christmas present. Kale needed a father, a role model, someone to
admire. I know I spoil him, and there are times when he's
surly. He's still grateful in his own way."

Or might be in twenty years. "You went to the golf course,
right?"

"Kale brightened up when he saw Natalie Hotz. I shouldn't
tell you this, but he has a tiny crush on her. That rude Janna
Coulter wants everybody to believe that her precious Natalie
is as pure as the morning dew, all sweet and modest and
chaste. Well, I know better. I've seen her flirting with men
twice her age—and drinking alcohol, even though she's under twenty-one. She'll end up in a trailer park. As for Janna,
I picture her working as a prison guard or a matron in a
psychiatric hospital. Anywhere she can slap people around
and get away with it."

I cleverly deduced that she and Janna were not friends.
"Did Kale play a practice round on Friday?"

"He played well, considering that sorry excuse for a course.
Afterwards he tried to talk to Natalie, but she was too busy
giggling with those college boys. Janna's face was as purple
as an eggplant. Kale and I came back here, had supper, and
went to our room before things got rowdy. I read while he

watched TV. On Saturday when he heard that Tommy won the boat, he was disappointed, naturally, but determined to win the tournament. You know how boys are. He wanted to impress Natalie." She grimaced at me as if we were compatriots. "I guess age is the only cure for hormones."

I wondered at what age she thought hormones dissolved into an insatiable passion for oatmeal and tapioca. "Did you have dinner at the golf course?"

"Yes," Kathleen said, "but it was dreadful. Not the food, of course. It was very nice. The preacher who gave the blessing rambled on forever about the Salvation Army. There was so much drinking, cursing, and blustering that I was obliged to get Kale out of there before he could be exposed to more of that sordid behavior. These men are not the role models he needs. The only gentleman there was Mr. Cartier. He's always so nice and polite. It's a wonder why some woman hasn't snatched him up. Do you think he could be . . . well, one of those?"

I realized that Ruby Bee and Estelle were apt to be the only two women in town not calculating their chances with Frederick—and not as a role model. "Beats me. Were you and Kale in your room the rest of the evening?"

"I washed some underthings in the sink and hung them to dry on the shower curtain rod. Kale played games on his little computer toy." She began to pick at the sandwich crust, scattering crumbs on the plate. She looked so uncomfortable that I was worried about the possibility of an unpleasant eruption across the table. My backup uniform was stuffed in a pillowcase, along with other clothes destined for the Suds of Fun whenever I got around to it. To my relief, she managed another sip of tea, then said, "I took Kale's clubs out back and hosed them off like I did Friday evening. They were so covered with mud that I could barely tell them apart. I always travel with an old toothbrush so I can get off every bit of dirt. We were both in bed by ten o'clock." She looked out the window with a vague frown, as if the tea had left an unpleasant taste. "The rain's stopped. I told Kale I'd bring him something for lunch. He'd live on canned sodas and ice cream if I let him."

She scurried away before I could suggest that she consult Kale first, since he was liable to be between invincible and invisible—if he hadn't passed out. Even though my thirty-something-year-old hormones were ready for lunch, I walked to the PD.

Les, one of Harve's more capable deputies, was waiting for me. After declining a cup of coffee, he said, "I started running background checks on the names you called in. There're some problems. For one thing, Frederick Cartier doesn't exist."

"Yes, he does. Someone was just asking my opinion about his sexual preferences. He's wearing a dark red cotton sweater, a fetching cravat, white slacks, and is probably holding Mrs. Jim Bob's head over a toilet while she pukes."

"She overdose on piety or something?"

"Something," I said. "Why did you say that he doesn't exist?"

"No Social Security number, no tax returns, no passport application, no voter registration, no rap sheet. You got a driver's license number or car tags?"

I shook my head. "See what you can find out tomorrow from the Mississippi bureaucrats. Maybe the records from that era were destroyed by a fire or are stashed in boxes in the courthouse basement. What else did you dig up?"

"There's an outstanding warrant for Bonaparte Buchanon in California," Les said. "About a year ago, he was accused of drug possession with intent to sell. He agreed to cooperate with the DEA, then vanished. In the past he's been charged for possession of stolen property, assault, statutory rape, and various misdemeanors."

"Do the feds want us to take him into custody?" I asked optimistically.

"He was a minnow in a shark tank, peddling small quan-

tities of coke at golf tournaments. The feds are after his supplier. They'll have to take him if you deliver him to their
doorstep, but they aren't going to expend any manpower or
cash. As long as he stays out of California, he's okay."

"He's not okay in my book. What's the deal with the
statutory rape?"

Les consulted his notes. "He was twenty-one and claimed
she swore that she was seventeen. She was fifteen. In Missouri, nobody gets too riled up about that sort of thing. He
happened to find expensive golf clubs abandoned in the
woods. He had no idea how the stolen wallet ended up in his
hotel room, and he swore that the receptionist had made an
error with the credit card. The assault was reduced to a misdemeanor. There are old rumors in Neosho about joyriding,
underage drinking, vandalism, breaking into empty houses.
Kid stuff."

"Buchanon kid stuff, anyway," I said. "Any more tidbits
to brighten my day?"

"Lucas Smithers is out on parole. He got nailed selling
pot to an undercover cop in Pine Bluff and did time. He's a
veteran, so the judge went easy on him. I'll check with his
parole officer tomorrow. Not everybody works on Sundays,
you know. Sheriff Dorfer canceled my weekend leave. It
wasn't all Murtle's fault. LaBelle should have smelled the
smoke, but she was giving herself a pedicure at her desk.
She had to evacuate barefoot with cotton balls between her
toes."

"Sheriff Dorfer's home, drinking beer in his recliner."

Les growled as he flipped to another page. "Tommy Ridner had a couple of DUIs and citations for disturbing the
peace. He ended up doing a hundred hours of community
service, running golf clinics to raise money for underprivileged kids. The cops liked him because every time he ended
up in the drunk tank, he used his phone call to order a dozen
pizzas. Dennis and Amanda Gilbert are model citizens. Nothing on Kathleen Wasson, but Kale was suspended by the high

school in Tibia last year for fighting. Honorable discharge and various commendations for Janna Coulter. The desk sergeant in Fort Sill told me that Natalie Hotz was picked up for shoplifting, but the charges were dropped." He grinned at me. "It sounds like you're running a weekend therapy session for wayward golfers."

"I'd rather be running away. What about Phil Proodle?"

"A while back he had illegal aliens working for him, washing boats and mowing his yard. He was fined, they were deported, and the judge ended up with a party barge. There have been some civil suits involving repossessions. Proodle's real fond of financing the sale, then tacking on all manner of hidden fees, insurance, escalating payment clauses, late charges, and penalties. The suckers get a month or two behind, and Proodle ends up with their deposits and their boats. He gets away with it because it's all laid out in the fine print. You need a microscope to read it." He stood up and put on his hat. "I'll talk to the Mississippi authorities about Cartier tomorrow, and track down Lucas Smithers's parole officer. Anything else?"

"A week in Hawaii would be nice."

"Buy a pineapple and go visit your boyfriend."

"Yeah." I waited until Les got in his car before I began to sniffle. I could jump in my car and drive to Springfield. I knew where Jack hid a spare house key. I'd find a box of stale cookies and crawl into his bed. If I stayed there long enough, he'd come home and find me under the covers. He wouldn't care that I looked like a sun-bleached manatee.

I forced myself to snap out of it before the sniffling turned teary. After sorting through the computer printouts Les had left, I made notes about Kathleen's and Natalie's statements. I was pondering my next move when a category five pain in the ass burst into the PD.

"What happened to the goddamn boat?" Jim Bob roared. "I sent Kevin over to the SuperSaver to get bags of ice, and when he got back, he said the boat was gone."

I rocked back to avoid intoxication by proximity. "The sheriff impounded it."

"What the hell does that mean? How am I supposed to win the fuckin' boat if it's impounded? You get off your ass and go fetch it! That's an order, Chief of Police Whatever-your-name is. And don't give me any shit about how you can't. Get that goddamn boat back here or you're fired!"

"Cool it," I said irritably. "Sheriff Dorfer had the bass boat hauled to the crime lab. The boat will be released when the case is closed."

"To hell with that! You want to keep your job, you make sure the boat's in the SuperSaver parking lot tomorrow afternoon. I don't aim to twiddle my thumbs while the boat's in Farberville all summer."

"Why are you so sure you're going to win it? From what I heard this morning, you're not exactly tearing up the course. Even Bopeep scored better than you did."

His jaw began to quiver so violently that he was in danger of biting off his tongue. If he did, I suspected he'd spit it at me. "I don't give a rat's ass about scores! All it takes is one lucky shot." He abruptly stopped. His eyes slitted, he backed off and sat down in the visitor's chair. "Sure, them others have a better chance, but I ain't giving up. There's no way I can ever afford a boat like that, what with Mrs. Jim Bob redecorating the living room every other week. My overhead's rising at the SuperSaver 'cause folks are cutting back to basics like beans and potatoes. I'm barely meeting expenses. If I had the boat, I could git away and relax. Otherwise, I'm gonna go plumb crazy like Diesel and take to living in a cave. You understand that, doncha?"

I couldn't remember when he'd ever attempted to explain himself to me. "If you cooperate, I can close the case and put in the paperwork to get the boat released. If you don't, all I can do is keep plugging away until I run out of leads. The boat could remain impounded for months, maybe years. Got that?"

"Yeah," Jim Bob muttered. "What do you want from me? It ain't like I killed anybody, fercrissake. I barely knew the fat sumbitch."

"Let's start with this tontine nonsense," I said, relieved that he was back to normal. The idea of being on amiable terms with him made my teeth ache.

"Who told you about that?"

"It's all over town, for pity's sake. Men are worse gossips than women. For the record, give me the names."

He said each name as he counted on his fingers. "Ten of us."

"Tontines are illegal."

"We signed a contract written up by a lawyer. It's notarized and everything. Besides, you think anybody's stupid enough to claim the boat for hisself? This is a small town."

"How could I ever forget it? I lie awake at night just to count my blessings. Let's get back to the tournament. You met Tommy on Friday?"

"He showed up in the afternoon with that newscaster fellow and his wife. She had her nose stuck up so high she could've stumbled over a ladybug. Soon as she got out of the car, she was bitchin' about the motel, the humidity, how her cell phone didn't work. Anything you name, she thought it was there to make her miserable."

Obviously, Jim Bob would sell his soul to get into her panties. "What about that evening?"

"Everybody ended up at Ruby Bee's. Most of us in the tontine got booted out of our houses on Thursday, so it wasn't like we had anyplace else to go. After last call, the party moved out back to Ridner's room. He had the fanciest damn bar in his trunk and could mix up most any drink. A couple of hours later, the party broke up."

"Was Natalie Hotz a participant?"

His forehead wrinkled like a bloodhound's. "Yeah, some of the time, anyway. She and that butch lady had supper and stayed for a while. They left, but then Natalie came back on her own later. I wasn't paying any attention to her, since she made it clear before the practice round that I'd be wasting my time. She ain't my type, anyway. No hips, no tits. I saw her cuddling up to Ridner." He scratched his chin. "She talked to Proodle and a few other fellows. I dunno."

"Did you see her leave with anybody?" I asked. When he shook his head, I gave up and moved on. "Tell me about yesterday."

"Everybody showed up at nine thirty or thereabouts. Ridner was making screwdrivers and Bloody Marys, and Proodle was slipping beers to everybody when Mrs. Jim Bob wasn't watching. Folks began to relax a little bit." To demonstrate, Jim Bob stretched out his legs and crossed his feet. He looked annoyed when he realized that he couldn't plop his muddy shoes on the edge of my desk.

"Until Tommy made his hole-in-one," I prompted him.

"Lucky bastard hollered like he'd taken a piss on a pot of gold. A lot of players quit, but others kept on playing just in case Ridner's hole-in-one didn't count for some reason. Mrs. Jim Bob has so many damn rules that nobody was sure."

"Did you know Tommy had to be present Sunday afternoon to officially win?"

"I didn't bother to read the crap, I just filled it out and wrote a check. I didn't much care when Mrs. Jim Bob announced it at supper. Ridner didn't look like he was gonna fall over dead from a heart attack." Jim Bob got up to pour himself a cup of coffee. He took a taste and spat it out. "You ought to take a hard look at Proodle. He was whimpering like a baby when he found out. Just don't go thinking I had anything to do with Ridner's murder. Maybe I ain't grieving over it, since it means I have another chance to win the boat. Can you get on with this? I'm getting a bellyache from all your dumb-ass questions."

I was getting a bellyache, too. It had been more than an hour since breakfast, after all. "But you boys were up to partying afterward, weren't you?"

"It sure as hell wasn't a celebration," Jim Bob said sourly. "Yeah, everybody went to Ruby Bee's. This time Ridner was buying pitchers, like he damn well should have. Nobody was feeling real kindly toward him. Natalie finally had to drag him off to a corner and talk to him before he got his ass whupped. After that and a lot more beer, things got friendlier. When Ruby Bee announced last call, everybody left. I didn't know about Ridner 'til you showed up this morning. Is that all?"

"I wish it were," I said with a sigh, "but you seemed to have forgotten about the bet. The stoplight's city property, Mr. Mayor. What if a shot had gone crooked and broken a window? And standing in the middle of the road in the dark? You all could have been flattened by a chicken truck."

He pursed his lips as he tried to concoct a story that I might buy (if I had the IQ of a rock). "It wasn't nothing but a friendly little bet. I didn't believe for a minute that anyone would actually be able to hit the stoplight. Hell, I wasn't sure anyone could hit a golf ball. We were just blowing off a little steam, that's all. Getting some fresh air before we got in our trucks. Come to think of it, I was protecting Maggody from drunken drivers. That's one of my responsibilities as mayor."

This from a man who'd once driven his riding mower into Boone Creek while wearing nothing but a red bra around his neck. "Names," I said.

"Hell, I dunno. Pretty much everybody that was in the bar."

"Did Kale Wasson participate?"

"Yeah, but that kid can't hold his liquor. Ridner had to help him grip the club, and we all stood way back when he swung. Took him three tries to even hit the ball." Jim Bob sniggered. "It rolled about twenty yards and then stopped in the middle of the road. It looked like an RV had laid an egg."

"Tommy Ridner won, right?"

"Yeah, the dickhead got lucky again. I'd had enough, so I went on home and snuck in through the garage. I started thinking of Cartier up in the guest room, sleeping on clean sheets and soft pillows, while I was stuck in the utility room on a wobbly cot, with an old army blanket and the stink of ammonia. The bastard's lucky I was too drunk to go upstairs and throw him out the window."

"Was his car in the garage when you got there?"

Jim Bob shook his head. "I'd have fallen over it if it was. Look, I got to get back to the guys and tell 'em about the boat."

He ducked out the door and swaggered away in the direction of Ruby Bee's Bar & Grill. I went outside and looked at the stoplight. When it switched from green to red, the yellow light remained unlit. I doubted that would cause havoc during rush hour. The only time we had an increase in traffic was when a rare funeral procession was headed toward a cemetery. Most Buchanons preferred to be buried in one of the small family plots scattered over Cotter's Ridge. At least I hoped they were buried.

I walked over to the parking lot. The competitors had chosen a spot about fifty feet from the target. Eventually Tommy had been declared the winner and collected the pot from Proodle. The pot may have been the last straw.

Tommy must have decided to stumble down the road to examine his prize. He had his driver with him (he would have done better with a chauffeur along). Gloating, he'd climbed into the boat so he could snuggle in the padded leather seat and caress the dashboard. Someone had followed him, or guessed where he might go.

"Thinkin' of taking up the game?" Roy said from the porch of his antiques store.

I went across the highway and sat down on the pew. "The wake must be over. Did you run out of booze?"

"Yep. I was just now sitting here, trying to recollect when I last raised your rent. Been a good while."

"It's been a while since I read up on the statutes about

gambling. It's illegal in Arkansas. Running a gambling house is a felony, and the sentence can run up to three years." I paused. "You really gonna raise my rent, Roy?"

"I ain't decided as of yet. The booze was running low, and when Jim Bob showed up and told everybody about the boat being impounded, that was it. Some of them went to get something to eat. Earl's asleep on my sofa, snoring like a tuba. I came out here to get away from it. I don't know how Eileen puts up with that racket, night after night."

"I can hear you from upstairs," I said. "At your finest, you sound like a dump truck bouncing down a cliff."

He harrumphed under his breath. "You ain't so quiet yourself when that fellow spends the night in your apartment."

It was time to change the subject. "Tell me about last night."

"The menfolk went to Ruby Bee's to cry in their beers. There wasn't any shortage of that, what with Tommy buying pitchers and keeping everybody's glass filled." He picked up a jelly jar of iced tea and took a drink. "After Ruby Bee announced last call, I came on back here. Tam was passed out where you're sitting, and Rip was in the bathtub. I fixed myself a sandwich and a glass of milk."

"You didn't hear any ruckus in front of the bar?" I asked.

"I had the radio on in the kitchen. When I looked out the window, all I saw was Tommy and his friends from Farberville. They were in the middle of the highway, jabbering. When I took a blanket out to throw on Tam, I saw Tommy weaving down the center line toward the SuperSaver." Roy rocked back and forth for a moment, then added, "There might have been somebody behind the Flamingo sign. I thought it was just a branch moving in the breeze."

I peered at the sign. Next to it was a large bush that Ruby Bee insisted was an azalea. She knew this to be true because she paid $9.79 for it at a nursery several years ago. I'd long since given up pointing out that it had never bloomed.

"You seen Brother Verber lately?" I asked, thinking of

the most likely suspect to lurk behind a bush. He'd been caught peeping through a window once, and accused of it several times a year.

"Yesterday evening, when he said grace before supper. He carried on so long the brisket was stone cold. You don't think he has anything to do with this, do you?"

"No, of course not. He might have seen something, though. I guess I'd better hunt him up sooner or later." I envisioned myself listening to one of his interminable diatribes about my wicked ways. "Later would be better."

"Like in a month?" Roy said, amused at my expression.

"More like in a year." I gazed at the puddles alongside the road while I thought. There was one screeching discrepancy in the versions I'd heard of the Saturday night festivities. "What do you make of Kale Wasson?"

"He's a pain in the ass, like most boys his age. He slobbers over Natalie Hotz, but she's so far out of his league that he'd need a passport to get within a mile of her. The boy's also a sore loser, from what I heard. The women he played with said he was snide and nasty, laughing at 'em when they made a bad shot."

"His mother would disagree with that."

"Kathleen reminds me of a sickly mole I found in my tomato bed. I had to put the poor critter out of its misery, but I felt like shit afterwards. Moles are blind, in case you've forgotten. The only thing Kathleen can make out is the halo above Kale's head. He was so rude to her this morning that I was ready to slap him upside the head. At supper he was giving her hell because she hadn't packed his lucky blue shirt, so it was going to be her fault if he lost today."

"Well, he didn't lose today," I said. "There's always tomorrow, I suppose."

"Gonna be interesting," Roy drawled. He tipped his hat down to cover his face and entwined his fingers over his belly. "Mighty interesting . . ."

I left him snuffling contentedly and returned to the PD. I called Harve and, when he answered, said, "What about Tommy Ridner's wallet?"

"I'm fine, thank you. How about yourself?"

"This is important, Harve. Unless you want to skip the rest of the ball game and come out here, answer the question."

"The wallet was in the boat, down by where his feet were. There were bloody smudges on it, but no usable prints. Half-dozen credit cards, along with about two hundred bucks. It's the bottom of the eighth, with the bases loaded and one out. Can you make do without the details until tomorrow?"

I promised to try, then hung up. Robbery was not the motive, which ruled out the local miscreants and random hitchhikers. The golf tournament was the catalyst. I was considering my next victim for interrogation when Janna came into the PD. I willed myself not to groan.

"I want to thank you for finding Natalie," she said.

"Just doing my job." And wishing she would go away.

"She told me what really happened on Friday night. I should have suspected as much. The only thing that would keep her out of trouble is an ankle bracelet."

I didn't mention that Natalie was more worried about a microchip implant. "Well, she's back and safe for the time being," I said.

To my dismay, she sat down. "I wish I believed it. I see the way men leer at her. Tommy Ridner was one of the worst. Twice her age, loudmouthed and fat. He's been after her for two years. When she won the state championship, he sent her flowers. He was whispering with her after the practice round, and I was afraid they were making plans to meet later."

"Were they?"

"She says not. I was determined to stay by her side that night until we were both in bed, but I could barely keep my eyes open. It must have been the combination of a couple of beers and the antihistamine. It happened again last night, even though I was drinking club soda."

"Do you think Natalie and Tommy found a way to have some private time last night?" I asked cautiously.

"Oh, I think he had other plans last night," Janna said with a smug smile. "A couple of weeks ago at the country club bar, I overheard an interesting exchange."

I was appalled when Janna described the conversation involving Tommy, Dennis, and Amanda. "Are you sure you didn't misunderstand them? The room was loud, and you were at another table. It could have been a joke."

"It wasn't a joke. Amanda was furious, and when she's furious, she makes sure everybody knows it. After she stormed out the door, Tommy and Dennis kept on talking about it. I couldn't hear much of anything, but I did see Tommy call over the waitress and have her sign her name on a napkin. He gave her a twenty, so I assumed she was acting as a witness."

"Dennis dotes on his wife. Why on earth would he agree that she'd have sex with Tommy in any case? The idea is"—I grappled for a word—"*medieval*. Disgusting, too."

"Men's brains aren't located between their ears."

She had a point. "I'd better talk to the Gilberts and clear this up," I said.

After she left, I rocked back to think. If Janna was telling the truth, then Amanda and Dennis had a motive, individually or as a couple. The fact that Roy had seen Tommy walking alone toward the SuperSaver didn't mean that he couldn't have been followed minutes later. On the other hand, Janna had been eager to tell me about the bet that conveniently produced the motive. Janna had been unaware of Natalie's whereabouts. Natalie had no alibi—but neither did Janna.

I was halfway to the door when the phone rang. I debated for a moment, then went to my desk. "PD," I said.

"Oh my God, Arly! You got to get here fast! Somebody's gonna get killed!"

Eleven

I recognized Eileen's voice. "Killed? What's going on?"

"It's an emergency! Please, you got to stop this!"

I drove to her house and parked. Eileen came running out the front door, her hands flapping. "If she doesn't kill him, he's gonna kill her!" She grabbed my arm and dragged me to the porch. "Be careful, Arly," she added as she shoved me inside the house.

I crept down the hall and peered into the living room. Dahlia was sitting on the floor in the middle of the room, placidly eating a cookie. Her dark green tent dress made her look like a tropical mountain rising out of a hardwood ocean. She licked her lips and nodded at me, as if we were at the SuperSaver.

I stayed in the doorway, totally baffled. Nobody appeared to be attempting to kill anything, except for the box of sandwich cookies. The silence made the scene all the more surreal. "Is everything okay?"

Dahlia took out another cookie as a male voice said, "Get this goddamn cow off of me! I cain't barely breathe."

I ventured a few steps into the room. There was a foot sticking out from under Dahlia's dress. I looked harder and saw a hand clutching the edge of the area rug.

"Who are you sitting on, Dahlia?" I asked.

"She's sitting on me, moron," the voice said. "I'm liable to suffocate any second."

I looked at her. "Who's that?" When she ignored me, I went around the couch and poked her shoulder. "Dahlia, get up!"

"Ain't no point in trying to reason with her. She's crazy as a hoot owl on Halloween," croaked the voice. "Shoot her or something."

"Dahlia," I said, "you have to let him up. If you don't, I'll have to arrest you for . . . causing grievous bodily harm. Either get up or put your hands behind your back so I can handcuff you." As if my bargain bin handcuffs would fit around her wrists.

Grunting, Dahlia struggled to her feet. Her victim moved just as slowly, wheezing and coughing as he sat up. Bony's face was cherry red. I looked him over carefully, since I'd only caught glimpses of him at the tournament. He had not bounced far from the Buchanon family tree. His sly squint reminded me of Jim Bob. His hair, on the other hand, reminded me of a discarded towel at a lube shop.

"Well, Dahlia?" I said, bemused.

"He got fresh with me."

Bony groaned piteously. "I was sitting there, minding my own business. Dahlia sat down next to me, so I felt obliged to visit with her. I was in the middle of telling her about my putt on fourteen yesterday when out of the blue she pushed me on the floor. Before I could get up, she sat on me. I yelled and kicked, but she wouldn't budge."

"I am a married woman," Dahlia said, her chins quivering. "You had no call to get fresh with me."

"You are a disgrace, Bonaparte Buchanon," Eileen said from the doorway. "You wait outside while I get your things together. You'd better pray that I don't tell your Uncle Earl what you did."

"Or Kevin," Dahlia added grimly.

I hurried him out to the front yard. "Are you as stupid as you look?"

He took a comb out of his pocket to restore his hair, then looked up with a smirk. "Dahlia's been mooning at me ever since I came back to town. She panicked when she heard Aunt Eileen come home. She's just coverin' her butt."

I wanted to mash in his face. "You should be more worried about your own butt. Earl can be real ornery. Tell me about yesterday and last night."

"Aunt Eileen drove me to the tournament. I played damn good, even after that asshole made a hole-in-one. Since I couldn't win the bass boat, I sure as hell was gonna win the tournament. I mean, what would I do with a boat? Haul it from tournament to tournament? Later, I got fed up with Ridner's bragging and was ready to take it outside when Natalie finally got him to shut the hell up. Then he came up with this dumb-ass bet. I figured he was drunker than me, so I got in. Some of the other fellows jumped on the chance to get revenge. I guess you heard the bastard got off a lucky shot. I lost my temper and was going for his throat when Uncle Earl grabbed me. He and some other guys drove me here and left me in the yard. After a while, I went inside and slept on this very couch."

"How long did you stay outside?" I asked.

"I wasn't wearing a watch."

"Long enough to walk to the SuperSaver to say a eulogy over the bass boat?"

"Hell, no. I could barely make it inside without falling on my butt, and I wasn't in no mood to say whatever you said over a boat in a parking lot. I ain't a nutcase like Dahlia. I ain't a killer, neither."

I realized that he was sounding more and more like a backwoods Buchanon. "While you were lying in the yard, didn't you start brooding about this injustice? Maggody's your home turf. In comes this guy with money falling out of his pockets, and he snatches the boat from under your nose. Didn't that make you angry?"

"I already said I was pissed off," Bony said, "but this sure as hell ain't my home turf. Frederick insisted on coming. If

I'd known about all the drugs, I might have showed up sooner."

I gaped at him. "What are you talking about?"

"Go spend some time in the pool hall or the barbershop. Some guys over in Spittel County got themselves a meth lab, and they come round ever so often. Cocaine from Mexico comes through here on its way east. Raz had forty acres of pot afore it was plowed up for the golf course. Some of those mousy housewives gulp down antidepressants by the handful. You think Amanda doesn't pop diet pills every day? Even Ridner brought a stash. When we was hanging out in his motel room Friday, I saw a bottle of Dilaudid in the medicine cabinet. It came from a pharmacy in Mexico."

I felt as if I'd just emerged from a cocoon, my eyes blinking in the harsh light. Frederick may have been right about having the water tested, starting with the tap in my kitchen. The pot was old hat, but meth and cocaine and pharmaceuticals? Oh my.

"I don't know what Dilaudid is," I admitted.

Bony gave me a condescending smile. "It's a narcotic, stronger than morphine. Legal here, as long as you have a prescription. Ridner mentioned there was something wrong with his lower back. I guess he could control it with the pills, 'cause he sure as hell wasn't feeling any pain last night."

I couldn't see any relevance to the crime, but I made a note of it. "You said you came here because Frederick insisted. Why did he do that?"

He shrugged, momentarily forgetting that he was supposedly in agony. "You'll have to ask him. I cain't figure him out. From the way he carries on sometimes, you'd think he was from a wealthy family, the president of a big-ass corporation or a senator or an ambassador. I'll bet he's never farted in his whole life."

"Married?"

"He never said anything about it, but why would he? It's

none of my damn business. I was married once myself. I don't know where she is these days. Probably back to stripping in a sleazy bar on the outskirts of Reno."

It was my business, though. "Frederick told me that he was from Mississippi."

"So?" Bony took a tentative step. "Dahlia must have did something awful to my spine. She's lucky I can still walk, since otherwise I'd sue her for every penny she and Kevin have tucked away in a cookie jar. I want to file charges for assault and battery."

"Whatever you want to do," I said, "but you'd better keep in mind what happens to men who try something with local women in this neck of the woods. You won't be safe in the general population at the jail. On a brighter note, you may end up in a federal prison. I hear it's a great place to make new friends, especially in the shower."

"I gotta find some aspirin. If you want to trot over to Ridner's room and get me a handful of Dilaudids, I'll owe you big-time." He tried to wiggle his eyebrows suggestively, but they wouldn't cooperate.

Leaving him to face Eileen's fury, I returned to my car. I was just down the road from the mayoral mansion. Frederick Cartier's elusive answers were gnawing on me like termites. I didn't think he was involved in Tommy's murder, but I wasn't buying his story, either. I couldn't cross him off the list until I found out why he was in Maggody. People don't slow down as they drive through town; if anything, they speed up out of instinct. My radar gun keeps the town from going bankrupt.

I knocked on Mrs. Jim Bob's front door, hoping she wouldn't yank it open and accuse me of consorting with pornographers or playing footsies with sex fiends. When I'd left earlier, gin was next on the list. She could be well into scotch by now.

Frederick opened the door. "Yes?"

I waited to be invited in, then said, "I need to talk to you. Is Mrs. Jim Bob still in the kitchen?"

"She's upstairs, resting. I've had a difficult time this afternoon, and I'm looking forward to solitude." He started to shut the door.

I elbowed my way past him. "Would you prefer to talk in the living room or the kitchen? You know, I'd really like a glass of water." By this time I was in the kitchen. I sat down at the dinette and folded my hands in front of me. "You might as well make yourself comfortable. I'm sitting here until you tell me the truth."

"The truth . . ." he murmured. "Truth is defined by perception and perspective. You say the sky is blue, and I say the sky is blue. How can we know if we're seeing the same color? Which of us is telling the truth? Is the glass half empty or half full?"

"You told me you were born in Mississippi. Is that half true or all bullshit?"

Frederick's lips twitched. "It's true."

"There's no record of your birth certificate."

"How curious," he said. "If my mother was alive, she'd be very distressed to hear this. Are you disputing my corporeal presence? Am I a figment of my imagination, as well as yours?"

I ordered myself to keep my temper and play his game. "I'm fairly sure you have a corporeal presence of some sort. What you don't have is a birth certificate, a driver's license, a Social Security number, or a passport."

"I don't have malaria, either."

"Why are you in Maggody? Bony said it was your idea. You said it was his. Problem is, Bony's too dim-witted to lie about it. He needed to get out of Vegas, and you offered him a ride here. This is the last place he'd choose as a safe haven. The golf tournament's a joke. I don't know anything about the PGA, but I can't imagine that a win would affect his ranking or his reputation."

"I enjoy traveling into uncharted territory," he said. "I've been to every continent except Antarctica, and I'll find a way to get there before I die. In a past life, I must have been a wandering albatross."

"You have a knack for wandering around the truth. Please save this philosophical crap for your cabernet crowd. That reminds me—I need the napkin with the professor's name and address. You said you have it in your car."

"It'll take me some time to find it. I don't want to make you wait while I sort through the contents of the glove compartment. I'll drop it off at your police station in a day or two."

"I don't mind waiting," I said. "In fact, this will give me a chance to see this classic car I've been hearing about." I headed for the door that led through the utility room to the garage. "Are you coming?"

The black car was dauntingly large and shiny. It had a peculiar bump on the top of the trunk, the size and shape of a tire. Even in minimal light, chrome glistened. It fit into the garage with only inches to spare. "Wow," I murmured as I squeezed between the bumper and the garage door. "Go ahead and find the napkin, Frederick. I promise not to leave any smudges or fingerprints." I glanced across the top of the car at Frederick, who was in the doorway, his arms crossed. He did not look like a proud owner, graciously accepting compliments. "I wish I had leather seats. The upholstery in my car is so dirty and faded that I don't know what color it was originally. One of these days the car's going to up and die on me."

"We need to talk," Frederick said, then went back into the house.

Rather than squeeze my way back around, I got in the backseat and slid across the gray leather. It was wide and comfy, a lovely spot to take a nap. I rested for a minute, then went into the kitchen to find out what his next fabrication would be.

He was seated at the dinette with bottles of gin and tonic water, a sliced lime, and two glasses. "Mrs. Jim Bob was unable to finish the gin. I hauled her upstairs and put her to bed. Oh dear, you're on duty. I promise I won't tell Mayor Jim Bob."

"Tell him anything you want, including the fact that his wife passed out in broad daylight—and on Sunday, to boot." I sat down across from him. "Are you changing your story about your whereabouts last night?"

"I have an old friend who lives in Farberville. We spent the evening together. She's married, and her husband is on a business trip. Although all we did was talk, I don't want to put her in a compromising situation."

"How considerate of you," I said coldly, "but I need her to confirm it."

"I don't see why. Her husband will arrive home this afternoon."

"And you're too much of a gentleman to endanger her reputation." I shook my head. "You're nowhere near the top of my list of suspects, but I'd like to cross you off so I can turn my attention elsewhere. I can't do that until your alibi is confirmed. For all I know, you could have parked your car in a dark corner of the SuperSaver lot and waited for Tommy. Furthermore, you're going to have to tell me who you really are."

He wasn't squirming in his seat, or allowing any trace of nervousness to be reflected in his eyes, but I could almost smell his adrenaline pumping. "I will not divulge the lady's name unless you have strong cause to suspect me," he said at last. "I had no motive to murder Tommy Ridner. I am Frederick Cartier, and I'm from Mississippi. I have no paper trail because I choose not to. My income is nontaxable and I don't have a job. My pocket was picked in a Vegas casino, so I can't show you a driver's license. If you will be so kind as to excuse me, I'd like to rest now." He took his glass and left the kitchen; seconds later I heard his footsteps on the staircase.

If I'd thought I was going to bell the cat, I had underestimated its wiliness. I hadn't gotten within arm's length. Frederick had produced another alibi, equally flimsy. He was aware that I had no particular reason to suspect him. But he didn't know, I thought smugly as I went out to my car, that I had memorized his license plate number.

I stopped at the PD and called Les to ask him to run the number, then went to Ruby Bee's for lunch. The local men were sitting in booths by the jukebox, glumly eating burgers and onion rings. The lone man in the corner appeared to be asleep. The proprietress and her partner in crime were conversing across the bar. As I approached, they broke it off as if I were an undercover agent sent by the state ABC to make sure no beer trickled out of the tap.

"How are you feeling?" asked Ruby Bee. "Have you talked to Jack?"

"Since you last asked a couple of hours ago?" I sat on a stool next to Estelle. "Any chicken left?"

"I'll see." Ruby Bee picked up some dirty dishes and went into the kitchen.

Estelle tilted her head so she could peer down her nose at me. "You're making your mother sick with worry. I can tell just by looking at her that she's not getting enough sleep. She's liable to break out in hives if you don't set her mind at ease."

"I can't call Jack," I said patiently, "and he can't call me until he returns to civilization. The National Geographic Society can contact them in case of an emergency. Getting knocked up doesn't qualify."

"You could let Ruby Bee go with you to your next appointment with the obstetrician."

"That's a good idea. Maybe it'll calm her down a little bit to know I'm not having quintuplets. I'm not even having twins, in case that was your next question. One baby, gender unknown. If you're planning to knit booties, avoid blue and pink."

Estelle nibbled her lip as she gazed at her reflection in the mirror behind the bar. "My third cousin's stepdaughter's entire layette was in camouflage, right down to the diapers.

They were counting on a boy, but they got a girl. You never know, do you?"

"I guess not." I paused when Ruby Bee emerged with a plate piled high with chicken, dressing, mashed potatoes, and gravy. "Thanks. I was going to eat earlier, but I ended up talking to Kathleen Wasson. Her version doesn't jibe with my information. I don't suppose you ran across anything of interest while you cleaned their room?"

"This ain't the Hilton," Ruby Bee said. "I made the beds and left fresh towels. I didn't set foot in Tommy's room yesterday, and I ain't about to clean Phil Proodle's room tomorrow morning until he checks out. I'll have to fumigate it and shampoo the carpet. It'll stink worse than a derelict outhouse."

"You haven't fallen for his charm?" I asked as I ate.

Estelle snorted. "There's nothing charming about a maudlin drunk. He was in here last night, darn near blubbering about that boat. I don't know what got into him. Since Tommy was killed, it can go back to his lot."

"The boat's been impounded," I said. "Even if the case is solved soon, it'll take time to get it released. All sorts of judges, clerks, and officials have to sign paperwork, and since it's low priority, nobody will be in a hurry."

"Well, he deserves it," Ruby Bee said. "I disliked him the minute he marched in here and demanded a room. He's as sneaky and mean as a muskrat. The next time one of his commercials comes on, I'm gonna change channels!"

"That'll show him a thing or two," I said. "Better yet, buy your next party barge online. Just watch out for 'Some Assembly Required' or 'Batteries Not Included.'"

"You making any progress?"

I put down my fork. "I'm not going to tell you anything until both of you promise not to meddle. Your intentions may be good, but your efforts lead to disaster."

"We promise," they said in unison, like angelic members of the choir.

I didn't believe them, but I needed to talk things out, and Harve was glued to his recliner for the duration. "There was a little problem at Eileen's house earlier," I said, then described the scene. "My best guess is that Bony made crude advances. Unfortunately, he isn't permanently disabled."

"If Earl hears of it, Bony will end up on crutches just the same," Ruby Bee said. "I never trusted him when he came summers. He spied on folks staying out back."

Estelle sniffed. "I knew right away there was something wrong with him. He stomped all over my marigolds and stole a pot of begonias off my porch. Elsie nearly caught him red-handed throwing eggs at her house."

"I heard it was Sacramenta Buchanon's youngest," Ruby Bee said. "Bony had been sent home the week before on account of getting drunk out by the creek."

"So now you're making up an alibi for him?" Estelle said disdainfully.

Ruby Bee gasped. "How dare you accuse me of making up anything!"

I jumped in before Estelle could respond. "After I left Eileen's, I went to talk to Mrs. Jim Bob's houseguest. He's harder to grasp than an eel. I couldn't get a straight answer out of him. He told me he's sixty-two and was born in Mississippi. I don't know if either of those is true. I don't know why he's in town. Bony says it was Frederick's idea, and Frederick says it was Bony's. This isn't a Top Ten vacation destination."

Estelle wasn't about to be nudged aside. "Bony has kin here, so most likely it was his idea. This fellow just came along out of curiosity. You have to admit Maggody has a unique culture, if you take incest and moonshine into consideration. I'm surprised someone hasn't written a book about all the nonsense that goes on in this little town. It'd have to be sold as fiction, though, since nobody would ever believe it."

"Stranger than fiction," I said. "See y'all later."

It occurred to me as I went out the back door that I hadn't

had dessert. I wavered briefly, then went to the Gilberts' room to find out about the purported bet. No one answered the door when I knocked, but their car was there. I knocked again, then waited. I wasn't about to barge in on them if they were in the midst of an afternoon delight. Cursing under my breath, I was trying to figure out what to do when Luke came out of Proodle's room.

He nodded at me. "Afternoon, Chief Hanks."

"Is Proodle in his room?"

"In bed, sucking on an empty bourbon bottle. He got all teary when he heard the news about the boat being impounded."

"I need to ask you a few questions." I took out the master key and unlocked the door of the unoccupied motel room, opened the curtains, and sat down on one of the twin beds. He sat down on the other, watching me as if I might be a vampire.

"I heard you're staying with Bopeep at the trailer park," I began. "How long?"

"A few weeks. I didn't have a job, and she said I might be able to find day work around here."

He was a lot more handsome than Bopeep's typical boyfriends, most of whom were covered with tattoos and scars. His eyes were brown and ringed with lashes, his face slightly round, his hair curly; he would still be carded at bars when he was thirty. Or forty.

"You did some time at the state prison," I said.

"Yeah, I sold a little pot to the wrong person. My bad."

He obviously wasn't going to spill his life story without prodding. I'd once interrogated a suspect in a murder for nineteen hours. By the time the guy shut his mouth, I knew everything about his parents, teachers, disappointing birthdays, phobias, pets—and where he buried the body. I wasn't sure it was worth it.

"You're a veteran, right?" I asked.

"I enlisted in the army after I graduated from high school.

Damn stupid thing to do, but I was all pumped up with the idea of going into battle. I did four years and quit. My last lady friend kicked me out, so I accepted Bopeep's invitation." He took a pack of cigarettes out of his pocket but put it away when I shook my head.

"Have you ever played golf before?"

"I used to fool around some, but there aren't any putting greens at the prison farm. Do you reckon that's cruel and unusual punishment?"

"Right up there with torture. Write your congressman. Did you play a practice round on Friday?"

"No, I was too busy trying to find a place to sleep. Bopeep dumped all my clothes and stuff outside the trailer and told me to stick a golf club someplace that sounds damn uncomfortable. I'd played the course a couple of times after Earl mowed. Snakes all over the place. I didn't see any reason to risk my life until it mattered."

"Did you notice the marijuana plants in the rough?" I asked.

"I can't say I did, but I believe you. Raz is a real nature lover, roaming all over Cotter's Ridge, enjoying the fresh air and sunshine. 'Shine, anyway."

The pot was the least of my woes. "You were at the party Friday night, I'm assuming, and again last night. Lots of anger aimed at Tommy, and lots of beer. Tell me about the shoot-out at the stoplight."

He lay across the bed and propped his head on his bent arm. "Everybody tried to keep their voices low, so they were hissing at each other like geese. The redhead was griping about how childish it was and on and on. Jim Bob came damn close to making a divot in the pavement. It may have been on purpose, since it was Ridner's driver. Jeremiah was bent over double behind the motel sign. There was so much confusion that it took an hour for everybody to take a shot. After Ridner hit the stoplight, it got real nasty. I decided to go sleep in a shack on Cotter's Ridge."

"What about Natalie Hotz?"

"She was a little unsteady on her feet, so I walked her to the door of her room. My mama taught me to look after ladies in distress." He grinned at me. "You feeling any distress, Chief Hanks?"

"Then you headed for the shack?"

"Took me half the night to find it in the dark. This morning I took a shower at Roy's, and then he drove me to the golf course. Do you think it'll be okay if I take a nap here? I don't want to get on Ruby Bee's bad side."

"Neither do I," I said as I left.

Twelve

I knocked again on the Gilberts' door, and this time Amanda opened it. She was wearing a T-shirt and had a towel wrapped around her head. Her face was damp. My rigorous training at the police academy led me to theorize that she'd been in the shower.

"May I come in?" I said. "I'd like to ask you and your husband some questions."

"Sure, but Dennis isn't here. He went for a walk, although I have no idea where. He's been brooding about Tommy's death. They were friends for a long time, all the way back to elementary school. Like brothers, I guess."

I sat down on the corner of the bed. "Did that put a strain on your marriage?"

"It bothered Tommy when Dennis and I got married two years ago. He sulked for months because Dennis wasn't as eager to play poker in the locker room half the night, or drink beer and watch football. Tommy ran a business during the day, but at five o'clock he turned into a frat boy. I thought he was crude and boorish, but I put up with him for Dennis's sake."

"How did you and Dennis meet?"

"At a media conference in Dallas. His station sent him. At the time, I produced a local morning talk show about fashion and wardrobe tips. Dennis and I ended up at the hotel bar, having drinks. Our relationship took off from there. Three months later I cheerfully quit my job and moved to Farberville." She studied my light blue shirt. "Let's go shopping the next time you're in town. You'll look much better in earth tones. Sage green, cranberry, pumpkin, colors like that."

"Someone might nibble on me," I said, smiling. If she was willing to feign friendliness, I was willing to reciprocate—as long as she didn't pull out a suitcase filled with Barbie dolls and tiny accessories. "Are you a golfer?"

"Good heavens, no. I find it incredibly boring, but occasionally I force myself to ride around the course in a cart when Dennis can't find a partner. I try my best to stay awake when he tells me about every single shot on all eighteen holes. I have no idea why golfers find that so fascinating. Most of the time I don't even know what he's talking about. I mean, mulligans and doglegs and birdies?" She rolled her eyes for my benefit. "They sound like soup ingredients."

"But not very good soup. Do you accompany Dennis to all the golf tournaments?"

"I enjoy them, as long as there's a decent bar in the clubhouse and parties in the evening." She wrinkled her nose. "This place isn't at all what I anticipated, and now we're stuck here another day. Dennis feels like he should be doing something about Tommy, but he's helpless until we get back to Farberville. I'm already planning a tasteful memorial service at the club. What do we do about the body?"

"I'll give you the medical examiner's number," I said, "but he'll have to tell you the procedure. It probably depends on locating Tommy's next of kin."

Amanda took a carry-on bag out of the closet. I held my breath until she pulled out a silver flask. "This is my emergency stash, and now's definitely the time. I can't think straight. Want a drink? It's a cognac."

"No thanks." I waited until she'd poured herself several inches. "I need to ask you about a bet between Dennis and Tommy. It concerns the tournament."

"That silly thing?" She laughed as she sat in a chair and crossed her legs. "How on earth did you hear about it? No, let me think. We were at the club . . ." Her eyes narrowed as she took a sip of cognac. "Janna Coulter. Tommy said something about seeing Natalie at the first tee, and Janna never lets her stray too far. She told you, right? Janna has absolutely no sense of humor. The kindest thing I can say about her is that she's single-minded, in every sense."

"The source doesn't matter. It's my understanding that the bet was based on whether or not Tommy made a hole-in-one. If he lost, he had to pay Dennis a sum of money. If he won, then your, uh, sexual cooperation was the payoff." I felt myself blushing, but Amanda didn't so much as blink.

"Tommy was trying to needle me, that's all. I pretended to be outraged and stomped out of the room like a diva. Dennis admitted later that they'd joked about it a little longer, but that was the end of it. I accepted his apology and bought myself a pair of Manolo Blahnik stiletto heels in Tulsa the next day. I have no idea why you think it was anything more than juvenile blustering."

"Maybe," I said, "but it does give either you or Dennis a motive to kill Tommy."

Amanda put down the cup and began to towel-dry her hair. "Give me a break. I just explained that this so-called bet was a farce. Dennis totally forgot about it until he saw the credit card statement. The shoes were expensive." She peered at me through auburn straggles. "Even if there was a bet, I can assure you that they knew I had no intention of honoring it. I love my husband, Chief Hanks, but not enough to debase myself. I survived an ugly divorce in my twenties. I worked days and went to night classes to get a degree in communications, and I did it without anyone's help. Do

I sound like the sort of woman who'd allow herself to be sold to the highest bidder?"

I thought this over while she poured herself another shot of cognac. From what I'd been told, she'd been drinking since ten o'clock in the morning, first at the golf course, then in Proodle's room, and now in her motel room. She appeared to be sober and articulate, but practiced drinkers could be sly.

"After Tommy won the stoplight pool," I said, "you and your husband lingered behind with him. What happened?"

"Nothing," she said as she shook her tangled mass of hair. "Tommy asked Dennis if he knew anything about hooking up a boat trailer. They talked about it for a few minutes, then Tommy invited us to go sit in his stupid boat. It's like he was the center of his own universe, so whatever made him happy was supposed to make everybody else happy, too. He was walking down the road when Dennis and I left."

"Did you see anyone lurking, maybe behind the motel sign or next to the bar?"

"It was dark and we were exhausted," she began, then hesitated. "You ought to ask Natalie Hotz. She and Tommy were awfully cozy this weekend, like sweet peas in a pod. I've been wondering about the two of them since a tournament last year at Hilton Head. I heard rumors they played nine holes in the moonlight."

I tucked the gossip in the back of my mind for further consideration. "Do you have any idea when Dennis will be back?"

"I don't even know where he went. Some of us were having a drink in Phil's room when Dennis just got up and left. I came here to wash the stench of smoke out of my hair. I was getting ready to take a nap when you knocked."

"You're not worried about him?"

"Not at all. He was this way after his mother died last year. Depressed, but not suicidal or anything like that. There was one thing. He wasn't talking much, but he kept glancing around the room at people's faces. All of a sudden he got this weird expression, like he'd come up with an idea. I tried to follow him, but I had to fend off Jim Bob. By the time I got outside, Dennis was gone."

"Do you think he suspected someone?" I asked.

"You'll have to ask him yourself. I'll tell him to call you. Is there anything else, Chief Hanks? I have a splitting headache, and I need to lie down."

I couldn't think of anything, so I went out to the parking lot between the two buildings. Janna's car was parked in front of number three, and the Wassons' car in front of number four. Tommy's car, the Gilberts' car, and Phil Proodle's car were in their respective places. Dennis's whereabouts were unknown, but I could sympathize with his need to be alone to deal with his grief.

I left my car in front of Ruby Bee's and walked to the PD, zigzagging between puddles. Roy had gone inside, I noted. Since the husbands were still outcasts, they could be in his back room plotting how to win the bass boat. They couldn't write the test answers on their palms or hide crib sheets under their shirt cuffs. No one was playing by himself, and each hole had a monitor as well. Mrs. Jim Bob was a pain in the ass, but she wasn't stupid.

I, on the other hand, was feeling stupider than a flour beetle. What could have occurred to Dennis in Proodle's room? I hadn't really seen who all had been there. Even if Dennis had an epiphany, it could have been provoked by an absence as easily as a presence. If Amanda had told me the truth. There was no reason to assume she had, since no one else had bothered to.

I was doodling on my pad and dreaming about pineapple upside-down cake when Les called.

"Got a good one for you," he said. "The license plate number you gave me indicates the car belongs to Rosalie Wicket. Mrs. Wicket lives in a nursing home in Yazoo City,

Mississippi. I called over there, and whoever I talked to said that Mrs. Wicket is in her mid-nineties, has outlived three husbands, wanders the halls wearing nothing but pearls, and lusts after Mr. Abelmeister, who resides across the hall and still has his teeth. She swears she doesn't own a car."

"But she does," I said, perplexed. "It's parked in Mrs. Jim Bob's garage. I sat in it, for pity's sake. Mrs. Wicket may be senile, but I'm not." Or so I hoped. "It was a Mississippi plate. Maybe I got the number mixed up."

"Chrysler Imperial Crown Coupe, right? That's Mrs. Wicket's car, whether or not she knows it. I couldn't get much more out of the nurse's aide, except that Mrs. Wicket hasn't had a visitor in the ten years the aide's been working at the Sunset Valley Retirement Home. If you want to call Yazoo City, have at it. I'm going home."

I found the page with my notes from the interviews with Frederick and added the information about Mrs. Wicket. The car had not been reported stolen or totaled in an accident, so I had to presume that Mrs. Wicket had simply forgotten about it. If there was an explanation, Frederick hadn't volunteered it.

I reread my notes on Kale and Kathleen Wasson. I had a fairly good idea about what Kale had been doing, which was partying like a deranged debutante. His mother was oddly unaware of this, either because she was delusional or because she was profoundly unintelligent. The previous night he'd been in the bar, and afterward in front of Ruby Bee's trying to shatter the stoplight. Hadn't she noticed the empty bed?

As for Kale, I had yet to take his statement. I wondered if there might be something between him and Natalie. In public, she snubbed him, but it could be a ruse. They might have been alone Friday night, which would explain her disarray when she got back to the motel room. Kathleen would have lied to give him an alibi. And then lied about the previous

night—even though she knew there were witnesses? Amanda
had implied that Natalie and Tommy were overly familiar. If
Kale was besotted with Natalie, he had a motive to kill
Tommy. Chivalry and/or jealousy, for starters. So did Janna.
So did everybody in Maggody. Everybody in the county, for
all I knew.

I couldn't revisit the scene of the crime, since it was behind locked doors in Farberville. I wasn't in the mood to
scramble all over Cotter's Ridge to find Dennis. The only
thing that I wanted to do was settle back and take a nap.

It proved to be an excellent choice.

Estelle had her elbows on the bar, her cupped hands holding
her chin. She idly watched Ruby Bee, who was washing
glasses in the sink and setting them on a towel to dry. The
lunch crowd had gone except for the fellow in the back. She
wondered if there was any reason to go find out about him,
then decided that it wasn't worth her while. She stirred her
coffee. "You're gonna have to tell her, Rubella Belinda
Hanks," she said for the umpteenth time.

"Mind your own business." Ruby Bee set down the last
glass and let the water drain out of the sink. "She's better off
not knowing."

"She has a right to know," Estelle persevered. "What if
she decides to get a copy of her birth certificate? All you
have to do is fill out a request form and send a check to Little
Rock." She waggled her finger at Ruby Bee. "Don't pretend
it couldn't happen. She might want a passport so she can take
a vacation in Mexico or Hawaii. Mark my words, sooner or
later she'll find out the truth."

Ruby Bee began to wipe the surface of the bar as she
mulled it over. "Now's not the time," she said at last. "She's
up to her neck with this murder investigation."

"That's exactly why it *is* the time."

"I wouldn't know how to begin."

"At the beginning, that's how," Estelle said mercilessly.

"You were nineteen, and it was your first time away from home . . ."

I was lost in a dream about hail-sized golf balls when the phone rang. I rubbed my eyes as I picked up the receiver. "PD," I said, glancing at the ceiling in case I needed to take shelter under my desk. I knew the drill, having practiced once a month throughout elementary school. It was always disappointing when nothing happened.

"Chief Hanks?" said Amanda. "Am I disturbing you?"

"What's the matter? Has Dennis come back?"

"No, and I'm worried. He's been gone for more than four hours. I went to the bar, but nobody's seen him." Her voice thickened. "What if he went up that mountain and broke his leg or sprained his ankle?"

Déjà vu all over again. First Natalie, and now Dennis. Clearly golfers had more difficulty than ducks when it came to keeping in a row. Then again, I'd never dealt with drunken ducks.

I looked out the window. The sky was once again steel gray, and the light had an eerie green tinge. A second storm was moving in. If there was more rain, the golf tournament would be delayed yet another day, and I'd be doomed to listening to lies and evasions until my brain trickled out my ears. "It's too early to get alarmed, Amanda. Dennis may have been taken in by a church lady and is currently being subjected to tea and cookies. Sit tight and I'll make some calls."

"How can I when Dennis might be lost? He's all I have. I don't have any family, and I don't have any close friends. Well, there is Jame, but I can't get hold of him."

"Jame?" I echoed.

"My hairstylist. He's on a cruise with his partner. He's very good, by the way. Remind me to give you his number. He could do miracles with your hair."

"My hair doesn't want to walk on water," I said. "Give

me fifteen minutes to see if I can locate Dennis. I'll either call you back or come over there."

I called all the wives and dowagers, with the exception of Mrs. Jim Bob, who was liable to be comatose. None of them claimed to have seen Dennis, although there was a remote possibility that one of them had locked him in her basement. (Grendal Buchanon had kept her sister in the root cellar for six months before anyone noticed, and another three months before the family called the sheriff's department.)

I walked across the road to Roy's antiques shop. In the back room, the tontine was having an official meeting that involved cards, poker and potato chips, beer, and overflowing ashtrays. Larry Joe was asleep on a sofa, and Big Dick was snoring in a recliner. "Has anyone seen Dennis Gilbert?" I asked from the doorway, unwilling to fight through the pungent haze.

My presence was not met with cordial smiles. Roy slapped down his cards and said, "In Proodle's room, a while back. Not since then."

Jim Bob raked in a mound of chips. "Does it look like we're running a fuckin' babysitting service?"

"Has anyone seen him since Proodle's party?" I demanded more loudly.

"He took off like a bat outta hell," Tam said as he popped open a beer. "You aimin' to deal anytime soon, Jeremiah? The cards are starting to grow moss."

I went into the room and snatched the deck out of Jeremiah's hand. "I want everybody's attention. Did Dennis say anything before he left?"

"Don't reckon he could have if he tried," said Ruddy. "He was damn close to mewling like a baby. His eyes was full of tears. I figured he went outside to puke, which was fine with me. Whenever my dog pukes in the house, Cora makes me get on my hands and knees and clean it up."

"Anyone else notice him when he left?"

Earl looked up at me. "He was real upset. He was mumbling to himself, mouthing the word 'Tommy' over and over again."

Roy took out his pipe and a tobacco pouch. "I was surprised he could stand up, much less make it out the door. He damn near knocked over one of those college boys fawning all over Amanda. Didn't act like he'd even seen him."

"Drunk as a skunk," said Jim Bob, remembering that he was supposed to be helping me solve the case.

I put down the deck and went outside. Lightning flickered beyond the crest of Cotter's Ridge. Surely Dennis wasn't so intoxicated that he was unaware of the approaching storm. I continued to Ruby Bee's Bar & Grill. A trio of good ol' boys nodded politely at me as I walked by the booth. I pretended not to notice the bottle in a brown bag. Estelle gave me an unusually hard look as I sat down next to her.

"Has Dennis Gilbert been in here this afternoon?" I asked.

Ruby Bee came out of the kitchen, then froze. "What do you want?"

"I'm hunting for Dennis Gilbert," I said, momentarily unnerved by her show of hostility. "His wife's worried."

Estelle put her hand on my shoulder as if I were the one behaving like a startled cat. "Amanda came in a few minutes ago and asked the same thing." Her grip tightened until I could feel her fingernails dig into my flesh. "You should go talk to her right away."

Wondering if Dennis was a prisoner in the kitchen, I glanced at Ruby Bee, who was more deeply rooted than a stump and about as friendly. "Yeah, I'll do that. See you later." I gave her a chance to respond, then went out back and walked slowly along the gravel lot toward the door of number six. It was not unthinkable that Ruby Bee and Estelle were responsible for my latest missing person; on one occasion they had participated in a conspiracy to hold a bureaucrat hostage. Anything was possible. I noticed the tape on the door of Tommy's room had again come loose and was puddled like a bright yellow rattlesnake. As I gathered it up, I saw a smear on the step. A dark brown smear, as in dried blood.

I opened the door cautiously, listening for a gasp or a telltale creak. I took a step inside, then shrank back as I saw Dennis Gilbert's body on the bed. Blood had soaked the pillow and splattered on the bedspread, the carpet, and the wall next to the bed. The back of his head looked as gruesome as Tommy's had.

I clamped a hand over my mouth, closed my eyes, and concentrated on breathing slowly until I could trust myself. I inched around the bed to get a better look at Dennis's slack face and filmy eyes. There was no point in checking for a pulse, but I forced myself to lift his wrist. His skin was still warm, his hand flaccid.

I made sure no one was hiding in the bathroom or the closet, then called Harve. I told him what I'd discovered and then, after he finished sputtering, said, "I don't care if the score's tied. You're the Stump County sheriff, not the referee. Call McBeen on your way out the door."

"Umpire," he growled.

"Is that German?"

"Baseball has umpires. Football has referees."

"That is so good to know, Harve. I've been sending my résumé to the wrong people all these years. I'll expect you and McBeen in half an hour, at the Flamingo Motel behind Ruby Bee's."

I went outside and leaned against Tommy's car. Amanda came to the door of her room and said, "Chief Hanks? Have you found out something about Dennis? Is he having tea and cookies somewhere? If he is, he's in big trouble when he gets back. I've been crawling the walls. I could just kill him!"

I wanted to tell her she was a tad too late for that. "I'm afraid I have some bad news," I said gently as I herded her back into the room. I tried to glide over the gory details, but she seemed able to visualize the scene on her own. Her face turned chalky white as she sank to the bed and began to whimper like a wounded animal. I fluttered over her for a minute, then gave up and called the barroom. Ruby Bee's chilliness melted when I told her where I was and why. In the background, I heard Estelle volunteer to administer first aid. I suggested that a bottle of sherry might serve better than a tourniquet.

As soon as I saw Estelle march out the back door, I returned to Tommy's room. I was not surprised to see a bloodied golf club in one corner. The carpet was scuffed from all the guests on Friday night. I doubted footprints could even be differentiated. Dennis's face looked serene, as though he'd dozed off. There were no defensive marks on his arms or knuckles. I wondered if he, like Tommy, had been too drunk to fight back.

I could hear Estelle chattering in the next room, which meant Amanda would have heard raised voices or sounds of violence. She couldn't have slept through it, but she had taken a shower earlier. It was impossible to tell if anything had been taken. I continued into the bathroom. I flipped the mirror back and studied the contents of the medicine cabinet: a grungy tube of toothpaste, bottles of mouthwash and Pepto-Bismol, a box of condoms, a razor, and an aspirin tin. Tommy had been well prepared for hangovers and sex. Sex with whom? Tommy had won the bet with Dennis, but it was hard to believe that Amanda hadn't made her objections known. The same Amanda who'd implied that Natalie and Tommy had something going on the side that did not include tees and golf balls. Neither Janna nor Kathleen Wasson was a likely candidate. It made more sense to assume that Tommy never left home without condoms.

As I closed the mirror, I spotted a white pill on the floor under the sink. Since the sheriff's department lacked a skilled CSI team, I picked up the pill. It was shaped like a triangle with softened corners, and the numeral 8 was stamped on it. It was apt to be Dilaudid, I thought as I put it down next to the faucet. McBeen would either recognize it or have it analyzed. There was no bottle, however. I looked in the medicine cabinet again, just to be sure, and then searched the bathroom. I went back into the bedroom and carefully picked through the clothing on the floor, the contents of the wastebaskets, the closet, and finally the golf bag. Had someone been so desperate to get the pills that he'd killed Tommy merely to gain access to his motel room? Dennis had found the door unlocked before noon, and the room appeared to already have been searched. Why had the perp returned?

The distressing presence of the body sent me outside to wait for Harve and his vigilant deputies. Estelle was still in Amanda's room. Since I couldn't hear anything, it was likely that they were making inroads on the sherry, along with whatever emergency rations Amanda had stashed in her bag. I wasn't about to poke my head in the door.

Kale Wasson came around the back corner of the building, carrying a misshapen pillowcase in his hand. His shoes and pants were covered with mud. He slouched toward the door of number four, presumably hoping I wouldn't notice him. Alas, he'd forgotten to wear a cloak of invisibility.

"Kale!" I called, beckoning to him. "I want to talk to you."

He stumbled as he veered in my direction, then caught himself before he fell. "Yeah, what?" he said in that churlish tone that teenagers perfect in middle school.

"What's in the pillowcase?"

He glowered at me. "Aluminum cans. I'm into recycling."

"Oh, really? Did you have any luck on the ridge? I love crumpled aluminum cans more than chocolate-covered cherries. Let me see."

"So it's pot." He dropped the pillowcase. "Is that all, Miss Cop?"

"It's Ms. Chief of Police to you, Kale. Do you want to do this here, or would you prefer for us to have this conversation in the motel room—with your mother present?"

"Like I care?"

I reminded myself there was no legal justification for spankings. "I'm not going to charge you with possession, since I know for a fact that the marijuana in Raz's pasture is about as potent as crabgrass. Lose the attitude or I'll change my mind. Got it?"

"Yes, ma'am," Kale said, smirking.

"Your mother thinks you were asleep at ten o'clock last night, but I know better. It must have been almost two before you staggered in. Care to explain?"

"She's crazy. Hell, she thinks the sun rises from my ass every morning. It doesn't get dark 'til I take a crap."

"Try again," I said, "and this time show some respect for your mother. The big bad sheriff's on his way here now. If I turn you over to him for questioning, you won't be playing golf in the morning—or anytime soon. What's it going to be?"

"I don't know where she went last night. I got tired of sitting by myself, so I went over to the bar to see what was happening. I drank some beer. Later, Ridner came up with this idea about the stoplight. The mayor was in on it, so I didn't see any harm. After it was over, I came back and went to bed."

"Your mother went somewhere last night and didn't get back until two? Didn't you ask her where she went?"

"Why should I care? When she's around, she won't stop yammering about golf and tournaments and scholarships and all that shit. It gets real old."

I turned around as Harve parked his car. His expression looked as if he'd run over dozens of skunks on the way from Farberville. A couple of deputies got out of the backseat. Seconds later, McBeen drove up in his death wagonette. I turned back to Kale. "We're not finished. Wait for me in your room. If your mother yammers at you, all the better. I'll expect full cooperation when I get there."

He stalked away toward number four. I went over to Harve and told him what I'd found. He ordered his deputies to search the immediate area and then went inside. McBeen glowered at me. I pointed out the dried blood to the deputies, then walked across the gravel to continue the conversation with Kale.

Janna came outside. "What's going on?" she demanded, gesturing at the official vehicles. Natalie stood behind her, her eyes round.

"There's been another incident," I said. "Please stay in your room until further notice." Ignoring their questions, I knocked on Kale and Kathleen's door.

Kathleen promptly opened it. "Chief Hanks, what on earth is going on? The sheriff and all those uniformed men. I don't know what to think. Did something happen?"

"Yes, something happened. Did you see anyone go in or out of Tommy's room this afternoon?"

"I brought Kale his lunch, but he wasn't here. He left a note that said he was going on a hike. The woods always smell so fresh after a storm, don't they? I took a nap and woke up only a few minutes ago. I'm so sorry. Is there something else I can do to help you?"

"For starters, you could tell the truth." I could hear water running in the bathroom. Kale may have believed he'd found a safe haven, but I was in no rush to go back to Tommy's room until Dennis's body was removed. Kathleen stiffened as I came into the room. "Where were you last night?"

"Right here with Kale. You have no right to treat him like a criminal. He's a minor, and I won't give my permission for you to question him. I am aware of my legal rights, Chief Hanks. Neither of us will speak to you without a lawyer present. Kale needs to concentrate on his game tomorrow."

"You've been watching too much TV," I said. "All I want to know is where you were last night after eight o'clock. If you want to call a lawyer, that's up to you. There aren't any local ones, so you'll have to persuade one from Farberville to drive out here. Keep in mind it's Sunday afternoon. It may cost a bundle."

Kathleen clamped her lips together like a peevish garden gnome. I sat down and said, "You don't have to say a word. I'll just wait for Kale to finish his shower or whatever he's doing in the bathroom. He and I have some issues to resolve. He picked half a pillowcase of marijuana at the golf course."

"I'm sure Kale had no idea what it was. He'll be taking biology in the fall, so he was most likely collecting local specimens to identify. His grades are very good, but he can do better if he applies himself. He almost made the honor roll this spring."

"It must be hard for him to keep up his grades while he's going to golf tournaments."

"Goodness, yes. He's so dedicated that he practices every single day when weather permits. I drive him to Farberville on weekends so he can play the municipal course. I can barely afford the greens fee at the better courses. You wouldn't believe how expensive the tournaments can be. Even the price of a sandwich in the clubhouse restaurant—outrageous!"

Kale came out of the bathroom, a towel wrapped around his waist. "You still here?" he said to me.

"As far as I can tell," I said. "I asked your mother where she was last night, but she doesn't want to discuss it. I hear you're taking biology this fall."

"It was pot, okay? I dumped it behind the building before I came in here." He snorted at his mother. "Just tell her where you were last night. I don't need an alibi because I didn't kill the guy. I wanted to, but so did everybody else."

"Because of the boat?" I asked.

"No." Kale stared at the worn shag carpet. "Because of Natalie, if you really want to know. He kept brushing up against her and fondling her butt. She had to put up with it on account of his connections. He was buddies with golf magazine columnists. He invited her to play at a tournament this summer in Palm Springs."

"You were jealous," I pointed out. "That's a strong motive." Kathleen cleared her throat. "Kale couldn't have done anything wrong because we were both here all night. There's a Gideon Bible in the dresser drawer. Get it out and I'll swear on it."

"Gimme a break," Kale said. "She already knows I was in the bar last night."

Her jaw twitched irresolutely as she struggled not to throw him under the bus (as if Maggody had any buses). "Kale might have slipped out for a few minutes," she said at last. "Perhaps even an hour."

I shook my head. "More like six hours, give or take."

She stared at her son. "You told me you came back at ten."

"Time flies when you're drunk."

I was fed up with both of them, but if I went outside, I'd feel obliged to talk to Harve—or even worse, McBeen. "Kathleen, I know you weren't here. Your car was missing." I hoped it was, anyway.

"I drove to Tibia," she said numbly. "I was so sure that I packed Kale's blue shirt, but it wasn't in his bag when we got here. It does wonders for his confidence. I couldn't bear the idea of him losing tomorrow because of my stupidity. It's nearly a two-hour drive each way, and it took me forever to find the shirt. I don't know how it could have ended up in the hamper. I ironed it Thursday night."

"Okay, you drove home to fetch the magical blue shirt. Where is it?"

"In the closet," she said. "It got damp this morning, but I brought my traveling iron so I could touch it up." When I said nothing, she went to the closet and took out a rather ordinary blue knit shirt. "Are you satisfied?"

"For the moment. You've told me your story, Kale, but you don't seem especially fond of telling the truth." I shushed Kathleen before she could lunge to his defense. "Do you and Natalie have a relationship?"

"Not really," he said sullenly. "She acts like I'm just a kid. When I graduate from college, the age difference won't matter. I'll be winning tournaments left and right, so she'll have to notice me."

Although they were only a couple of years apart, the chasm between them would always be as gaping as the Grand Canyon, I thought with a flicker of sympathy. Once he shed his teenage scales, he would meet a nice young thing who baked pies and made her own clothes. Kathleen would not go quietly into the night.

"Tell me what you remember about the stoplight shoot-out," I said.

"Tommy won, so I came back here and went to bed."

"Did you see Natalie and Luke?"

"Luke? Why the hell would she hang out with a redneck like that? Natalie likes old guys with money."

"I saw the two of them whispering yesterday," Kathleen said. "He's the one who was jealous enough to kill Tommy."

I shrugged. "He said he walked her to her door."

"And you bought it?" Kale snorted. "Why would he dump her at the door and go back to that pig from the trailer park? Bopeep looks like a cafeteria lady who can't get enough mystery meat and peanut butter cookies."

There was a knock on the door. It proved to be a deputy with an adolescent face and the physique of a dedicated couch potato. "Sheriff Dorfer's waiting for you, ma'am," he muttered.

"Stay inside until further notice," I said to Kale and Kathleen, then allowed the deputy to escort me into the bowels of hell.

Thirteen

Harve was waiting for me in the parking lot, his fists on his hip like a sumo wrestler. He yanked the cigar butt out of his mouth and said, "God damn it, Arly! Can't you keep folks from murdering each other for more than one blessed day? You got more corpses out here than I got termites in my basement. Is this some kind of ploy to give me ulcers? If it is, you're doing a mighty fine job."

"This is hardly my fault," I retorted. "Homicides belong to the sheriff's department. I told you I didn't want this case, but you insisted. And where were you when that man was killed? Sprawled in front of your TV. Why don't you retire and let someone who cares run the department? Surely after your innumerable decades as sheriff, you'll get a comfortable pension."

"You threatening to run against me?"

I crossed my arms. "No, but somebody should." I realized that Janna and Natalie were peeking out the window. Kale and Kathleen were in their doorway, as was Proodle in his. Even Estelle opened the door of number six to stare. All we were missing was a marching band with majorettes twirling batons. "Shall we continue this somewhere else?" I said to Harve. "Like under a bridge or in a cave?"

"We ain't done," he muttered. He grabbed my arm and took me inside Tommy's room. Dennis's body had been removed, but the sickly sweet odor of blood lingered. "So you found the body about an hour ago. Any idea what he was doing here?"

I repeated what I'd been told about Dennis's abrupt departure from the wake and the general opinion that he was drunk and upset. "He might have come here to mourn Tommy in private," I continued. "No one else seemed to care, not even his wife. Either the perp followed him or stumbled into him by surprise. The rest of it is obvious."

"Can you account for everybody's whereabouts?" Harve asked.

I leaned against the wall and thought. "Not really, since we don't have a precise time of death. When Proodle ran out of booze, the party broke up. Some of the local guys may be able to alibi each other. I can't see why any of them would have a motive. Dennis didn't snatch the bass boat from under their noses. He might have remembered something about last night, though."

"Like what?" Harve said skeptically.

"If I knew, I wouldn't be standing here, would I? Tommy supposedly had a bottle of Dilaudid, but all I found was the one pill on the bathroom floor. Can you have your men search the pasture and the trash bin?"

Harve issued the order, then went to his car to catch the baseball game on his radio. I decided to check on Amanda, steeling myself to offer the standard banalities. I was surprised to see Estelle in the midst of giving Amanda a manicure.

"It was my idea," Estelle said. "It's helping her deal with her pain."

Amanda's eyes were red and puffy, but she managed a weak smile. "Estelle was kind enough to volunteer, and it's a distraction. Every time I think about Dennis, my throat gets so tight I can barely breathe. Have you found the monster who did this? Is it the same person who killed Tommy?"

"I don't know," I said. "There are similarities. Did you

hear anything from the room after you came back from the wake? Voices, noises, the sound of a scuffle?"

"Are you asking me if I heard my husband being beaten to death?"

"Goodness, Arly," Estelle murmured, "can't this wait? Amanda's in shock, as well she should be, considering what happened. This ain't the time to interrogate her."

I really, really wanted to drive to Springfield and take refuge in Jack's bed. "This is hardly an interrogation. If you heard anything whatsoever from Tommy's room, it'll help pinpoint the time of the attack."

"No," Amanda said, pushing her hair off her forehead. "At least I don't think I did. I heard car doors slam, doors close, some talk as the men headed for the barroom. I was so tired that I wasn't paying any attention."

"There you go." Estelle beamed at Amanda. "I just got in a shipment of nail polish last week, all the new summer shades. I think Candied Apricot Swirl would go nicely with your coloring."

"Before you debate this delicate issue," I said, "I'd like to ask if you knew anything about Tommy's use of a pain pill called Dilaudid."

"I didn't realize he was still taking them." Amanda studied her fingernails with great intensity. "He got some in Mexico after he strained his back. He claimed it happened while he was fishing, but I doubt it. I believe the word is *puta* in Spanish. His rich friends knew how to get him a prescription, so it was legal. He hadn't mentioned being in pain for a couple of months. Is it important?"

"According to a witness, Tommy brought a bottle with him. It's disappeared."

"So he took the last few and tossed the bottle," Amanda said. "I don't see why it matters. Shouldn't you be looking for the person who killed Tommy and Dennis? I don't know what I'm supposed to do. Now I'm on my own, and I've never . . ." Tears dripped down her face. She took a tissue out of her pocket and blew her nose, then looked up like a child lost in a mall. "I guess I should call Dennis's brother in California. He's a curator or archivist in some museum. I don't know what to do about the funeral and all the details. Then there's the TV station, our lawyer, the insurance company, the bank, and whoever else needs to be informed. I feel so confused and alone—and frightened. What if I'm next?"

Estelle squeezed her hand. "I'm here for you, and so is Ruby Bee. If you're scared to stay here tonight, I can put you up in my guest room. It's right cheerful, if I do say so myself. Why don't you pack your pajamas and toothbrush? I can trim your hair and add some more highlights. It'll make you feel more confident to know you're looking your best."

Amanda nodded. "If it's all right with Chief Hanks . . ."

"No problem," I said. Amanda went into the bathroom to collect her toiletries. I turned my attention to Estelle, who was fidgeting with the bottle of nail polish. "What's the deal with Ruby Bee?"

"I have no idea. Shouldn't you be out hunting this maniac before he kills somebody else?"

"It's on my list," I said. "Right now, I'd like to know why Ruby Bee is behaving the way she was back in the bar. I felt like a redheaded stepchild."

"It's none of my business. Take it up with her."

"Don't give me that bullshit. There's nothing in Maggody that you consider to be none of your business. We're talking everything from hiccups to infidelity. Ruby Bee's not going to tell me. That leaves you."

"Hush," she said. "Amanda's liable to come out any second. If nothing else, it's none of *her* business. You don't want folks to gossip behind your back, do you?"

"Folks have been gossiping behind my back since the day I returned," I said coldly. "There are already rumors about my pregnancy, and there's nothing I can do about that. Is Ruby Bee trying to defend me?"

"In a way," Estelle said. "Now run along and investigate while I help Amanda pack her bag. She's so devastated that she's apt to confuse her mascara with her toothbrush." She raised her voice. "Amanda, is everything okay? Do you want me to find your slippers and bathrobe?"

I screwed up my face while I tried to recall a tidbit that had been tossed at me. Fired at me, not from an air rifle but from a Winchester .30-06 rifle. And Mrs. Jim Bob had me in the crosshairs. I gave Estelle a hard look. "Was Ruby Bee married when I was born?"

She blinked.

I was headed for the bar with the single-mindedness of a Scud missile when Harve yelled at me. I increased my speed, but his subsequent yell would have shocked Mrs. Dorfer. "What?" I said over my shoulder.

"Git over here and see for yourself!"

It was a hard call, but after thirty-odd years of living with a lie, ten more minutes couldn't do much harm. His car radio was blaring as I went back to the doorway of number four. "Did your team make a touchdown?"

"There's a fine line between ignorance and stupidity, and you're wandering toward the far side." Harve showed me a bottle in a plastic evidence bag. "One of the boys found this in the weeds behind the building. It's Dilaudid. Ridner's name is on the prescription label, along with a bunch of other crap in Spanish."

I took the bag and shook it. "The bottle's not empty. It's from a Mexican pharmacy and originally held a hundred pills. Sounds like about a dozen now. Were there any pills on the ground?"

"Not after the boys trampled all over the place. It plays hell with your theory, you know. There ain't no point in killing two people to get the pills, then throwing them away. Whoever killed Ridner and that Gilbert fellow had a whole 'nuther motive."

"That looks like blood," I said as I continued to examine

the bottle, unwilling to defend my theory, my honor, my country, or anything else. If extraterrestrials had landed ten feet away, I would have given them directions to the Pentagon in a nanosecond. "Somebody tried to wipe it off but couldn't get it clean. Tommy bled out in the boat, not in this room. It has to be Dennis's blood." I thrust the bag at Harve. "Maybe we'll get lucky and find a fingerprint. Not that we'll be able to match it. These people aren't likely to volunteer to get their fingers dirty—especially without a court order, which we can't get without reasonable cause, which we don't have."

"Like you said, somebody wiped it off. We found blood on a hand towel in the bushes. I agree that it's likely to be Dennis Gilbert's blood, but all McBeen can do is run the standard test to find out the type. The DNA comparison has to be done at the state crime lab. It may be months afore they get around to it."

"Ask McBeen to determine the alcohol level and test for traces of Dilaudid in blood samples from both Tommy and Dennis," I said. "He should be able to do that at the county lab."

"Ask him yourself." Harve got back in his car and turned up the radio so loud the hula girl on his dashboard began to shimmy.

I found an idle deputy and asked him to show me where the bottle was found. It was a lot easier than asking McBeen anything, including the time of day. The spot was no more than twenty feet beyond the building. Whoever had thrown it had been in a hurry, I thought. If Kale had taken it, it would be in the bottom of one of Raz's ponds, undiscovered until the annual August drought. I moved him a little lower on my list, but not to the bottom. No one had made it there yet.

The deputy wandered back to the crime scene. I found a stump nearby and sat down. As much as I wanted to confront Ruby Bee about the particulars of my birth, I set it aside and concentrated on the case. The perp who'd murdered Tommy

sixteen hours earlier was still on the prowl. He'd searched
Tommy's room sometime between the death and the time I
ran into Dennis, circa noon. Assuming he was looking for
the bottle of Dilaudid, he hadn't found it the first time, possibly because he was unaware of the old-fashioned medicine
cabinet behind the mirror. On his second attempt, he'd run
into Dennis, beaten him to death, and left with the bottle.
Why didn't he empty it into his pocket before he threw it in the
pasture? It would have taken a matter of seconds. If he wasn't
after the Dilaudid, then what in hell's name *was* he after?

He or she, that is. I've always believed in equal opportunity.

Mrs. Jim Bob groaned as she filled the kettle with water.
Her tongue felt like a bloated caterpillar. Her head throbbed,
her eyes stung, and her hair hurt. She'd already taken two
aspirin tablets in her bathroom, but she decided to forgo pru-
dence and take two more. If it killed her, she wouldn't care.
If she was lucky, it'd kill Jim Bob as well. They could say
their farewells at the Pearly Gate; she would sweep into
heaven while he took the elevator to Satan's boiler room.

The kitchen counters were clean and there were no dirty
dishes in the sink. At least Jim Bob hadn't been sneaking
around while she was upstairs. It took her a minute to remember that she had a houseguest. A murky swirl of memories came back. Frederick, solicitously keeping her glass
full. What she'd said to Arly. Not that Arly didn't deserve to
hear it, Mrs. Jim Bob thought primly. "And you shall know
the truth, and the truth shall make you free," the Bible ad-
monished. Why, in April Brother Verber had preached a sermon on that very verse, although he'd been referring to
income tax deductions.

She recalled having a dizzy spell right at the dinette,
most likely caused by stress. The minutiae of running the
golf tournament were more insidious than flesh-eating bac-
teria. Frederick had helped her upstairs to her bedroom,

eventually carrying her over his shoulder like a laundry bag. She'd giggled whenever her nose pecked his back. He'd closed the drapes and plumped the pillows. He'd knelt by the bed and slipped off her shoes, then massaged her feet to help her relax. His voice had been as gentle as a spring breeze. And then . . .

Her memory crashed into a blank wall. Tea spewed out of her mouth and dribbled down her chin. He must have put her in bed—and she'd woken up in her undergarments! Not once in her entire life had she gone to bed without a proper nightgown. She wished she could swivel her eyeballs backwards so they could search her brain more intently. Surely she hadn't . . . One of the Ten Commandments, tucked in between murder and stealing, forbade adultery. She knew it well, since she often quoted it to Jim Bob before she made him drop to his knees to beg for forgiveness from the Almighty Lord. Women had been stoned for lesser offenses. Up until now, she'd been without sin and always ready to cast the first stone.

She wanted a fresh cup of tea, but she couldn't trust her legs enough to stand up. It wasn't her fault, if it had happened. But could lust be lurking within her heart? Frederick was everything that Jim Bob wasn't. He was tall, handsome, polite, well dressed, wealthy, and agreeable—the very essence of a true Southern gentleman. Jim Bob wore baggy jeans and a gimme cap, kept a pint of whiskey in his truck, and visited floozies at the Pot O' Gold.

If she had—which she hadn't—at least she had good taste.

Brother Verber was not the one to turn to for spiritual advice. He swore that any confessions he heard were protected by religious privilege, but she herself was kept informed almost daily of all minor lapses within the congregation. There was no one else she could ask about this possible sin, since there were no witnesses other than Frederick and herself. No one else knew—and no one else would ever know.

Mrs. Jim Bob fixed herself another cup of tea. All she needed to do was drop a few hints to Frederick and gauge his response: either a conspiratorial smile or a bewildered stare. She was feeling rather complacent until she realized that the Missionary Society was meeting at her house shortly.

"Good heavens!" Eileen said as she passed the plate of oatmeal cookies to Elsie McMay. "That nice Dennis Gilbert was murdered? The same person that murdered Tommy? How truly dreadful." She wondered if she had it in her to snatch up a golf club and attack an intruder. Probably not, she concluded. She was more likely to offer to make him a ham sandwich.

"Don't get yourself in a dither. There's no proof it was the same person." Lottie Estes took a cookie and peered at it. "It would be a real coincidence if it wasn't, though. This isn't New York City."

Eileen winced at the very idea. "What else did you hear, Elsie?"

"According to Parsnip Buchanon, who happened to be in the garbage bin behind Ruby Bee's, Arly went into the last unit on the right. She came out looking pale as a blob of mayonnaise. Parsnip was just finishing lunch when the sheriff's department showed up. They took a corpse out in a body bag and put it in the medical examiner's van. He overheard a deputy say it was Dennis Gilbert. When the police informed her, Amanda Gilbert fainted dead away on the doorstep of the next room."

"What about the weapon?" Lottie demanded.

Elsie made them wait while she finished the cookie. "A bloody golf club, just like before. Parsnip saw it clear as day."

"Does Mrs. Jim Bob know about this?" asked Eileen. "Even if the tournament's not canceled, I'm not about to go roaming around Raz's pasture with a killer on the loose."

"I don't know. I called her as soon as I heard the news, but no one answered. I tried again a few minutes later, and

Frederick answered the phone. I asked to speak to Mrs. Jim Bob, but he hemmed and hawed and said she'd call me back later."

"Peculiar." Eileen nibbled a cookie while she tried to come up with a sensible explanation. "You don't think the two of them were . . . doing something, do you?"

"Unthinkable," Lottie said firmly.

"It's not unthinkable if I'm thinking about it," Eileen pointed out. "Frederick Cartier is not an unattractive man, particularly when you compare him to Jim Bob."

"Such nice manners," murmured Elsie.

More murmuring ensued.

I told Janna and Natalie about Dennis and asked them to be in the barroom in an hour. Kathleen Wesson was told likewise. I knew where Amanda was, and decided to leave her there for the time being. That left Phil Proodle, our celebrity-in-residence for the infamous Maggody Charity Golf Tournament. He'd last been reported to be asleep with a bottle. I refused to picture it as I knocked on his door.

"What?" he said, clad in a terrycloth robe as he yanked the door open.

"Are you aware of what's been going on outside?"

"I heard voices and car doors slam."

"Dennis's body was found in Tommy's room," I said, watching him carefully. "He was beaten to death with a golf club, too."

"What a shame." Proodle's eyes shifted. I wasn't sure how to read it, in that he was a salesman and therefore shifty-eyed by profession. "He was here a couple of hours ago, him and his Amanda. What happened to him? How's she taking it? Should I go offer my condolences?"

"She's staying elsewhere. Did you see anyone going in the direction of Tommy's room earlier this afternoon?"

"After the party broke up, I took a nap. Selling boats is a high-pressure business, and most of the time I handle it

without a hitch. But these last three days have been gawdawful. Now, I just want to get through it with my skin intact.
Can I still leave tomorrow? My sales guys are a bunch of
lazy apes. All they've been doing is playing poker in the
break room, while the receptionist runs up my long distance
bill talking to her mother. I'm having a big sale the week
before the Fourth of July." He pointed at me. "Uncle Sam
wants you to own a boat!"

"Are you married?" I asked.

"My wife and I are staunch supporters of our church, our
community, and this great nation. Patty organizes fashion
shows to raise money for charities. I'm a member of the
school board. What does my personal life have to do with
this sordid turn of events? Am I under suspicion?"

"Everyone is under suspicion, Mr. Proodle. You appeared
to regret offering the bass boat as a prize. It would have gone
to Tommy, had he not been murdered. Very convenient for
you, isn't it? No winner, no prize awarded."

"Come inside." He tapped his foot until I sat down on a
chair. "You listen up, young lady. I have important friends at
the state capitol. If you so much as leak one word to the media, you'll be slapped with a lawsuit for slander. You shouldn't
even be wearing that police uniform. You self-righteous
feminists would be better off with husbands and children.
Patty keeps a clean house and makes sure dinner's on the
table when I get home. I let her deal with the trivial matters
while I provide her with food, shelter, and a comfortable
life. What's more, she's grateful for it."

I counted to ten and, when that didn't help, continued to a
hundred before I said, "Tell me what you did last night after
the stoplight nonsense was over. Who left, and who lingered? Did you duck behind the motel sign to relieve yourself and were too embarrassed to risk exposure? Did you
pee, Mr. Proodle?"

His jaw dropped, emphasizing his neck wattle. "How

dare you speak to me that way! Give me the telephone number of your superior."

"Drop by the PD and I'll write down the number for you. Sheriff Dorfer will be thrilled to hear from you. What happened after Tommy hit the stoplight?"

Proodle seemed to realize that I wasn't going to melt like Patty. "You'll have to excuse my outburst, Chief Hanks. I've never been accused of anything more serious than speeding. Why don't you run along and try to find this murderer?"

"The stoplight."

"Yes, the stoplight." He tried an avuncular approach. "You look tuckered out, Chief Hanks. Would you care for something to drink? Water, a soda?" When I didn't respond, he sank down on the edge of the bed. "As soon as Tommy won, I handed him the money and came straight back here. I didn't notice what the others did. They could have stuffed him in a burlap bag and left him under the stoplight for all I cared." He held up his hand. "Wait, I didn't mean that. He won the boat fair and square. I wasn't happy about it, but I figured he might send me some referrals. I have a fine inventory of Jet Skis and WaveRunners. If you're ever in the market, you call the lot and ask to speak to me personally. We can work something out so your payments aren't a worry. I always give city and county employees a special discount on top of our everyday low prices."

"When you came back here, did you see anyone going into another room?"

"Are you sure you won't have a drink?" He pulled a pint bottle out of his suitcase and took a gulp. "Not going into another room, no. Natalie and that young man were disappearing around the far end of the building. I was puzzled 'cause there's nothing out there but an overgrown pasture."

"Kale Wasson?" I said, sitting up.

"No, a local fellow. I don't recollect his name. He was here a couple of hours ago, drinking whiskey and putting the make on Amanda. She wasn't crawling all over him, but she didn't object when he patted her fanny."

I ran through the cast. A tidbit of a conversation popped up like a prairie dog. "Luke, right? Dark curly hair, muscles, wearing a T-shirt and jeans."

"Yeah, that's his name."

"Did Dennis object?"

"Poor fellow. I don't think he noticed. He was sprawled in the chair you're sitting in, sucking down scotch like he'd found a water fountain in the desert. He looked more likely to burst into tears than throw a punch. After a while, he staggered out of the room. That was the last I saw of him. What happened to him?"

"Go back to last night," I said. "You saw Luke with Natalie?"

"He had his arm around her, like she was too plastered to walk on her own. It's lucky for her that Janna wasn't standing outside with a strap. That woman reminds me of my great-aunt Sapphire. She had a sharp tongue, and we were terrified of her. After she died, the police discovered four corpses in trunks in her attic. She had a thing about meter readers."

"Did you see Kale on his way to his room?" I asked.

"No," Proodle said, "but I wasn't paying much attention. All I wanted to do was go to bed. If you're finished, I need to call Patty. She's going to an organ recital at the church this evening. How long do you intend to detain us?"

"Not one minute longer than necessary. I can promise you that."

"What about the tournament? It should be called off before somebody else is killed."

"Or before somebody else makes a hole-in-one?" I suggested brightly.

He looked away. "That's not what I meant, although it would be easier if I just had the damn boat towed back to my lot. When will it be released?"

"Beats me. I'm going to talk to Mrs. Jim Bob, then meet

with all of you in the barroom. Be there in forty-five minutes."

I drove once again to the mayoral abode. Thus far, the tournament had been on, off, on, off, and set to be switched back on in the morning. My reading light got less action in a week. I parked and went up to the porch.

Mrs. Jim Bob threw open the door. She had a smudge of flour on her cheek, but she lacked Betty Crocker's warm smile and twinkly eyes. "I didn't expect to see you so soon, Arly. The Missionary Society is going to arrive in less than an hour, and I've got a cake in the oven. I need to set out the china and silverware. State your business."

I obliged. "There's been another murder."

Her face turned as white as the flour. She wobbled so wildly that I caught her arm and steered her into the living room. Once she was settled on the sofa, I said, "Shall I get you a glass of water?"

"No, I'm fine. It's just that—that on top of everything else, I don't know what to do. I always know what to do. The tournament was supposed to be a modest fund-raiser for the needy golf widows. It wasn't supposed to be—to be a bloodbath! Tell them to take their corpses and leave town!"

Mrs. Jim Bob was still drunk, I realized. She may have been able to bake a cake on instinct, but she was in no condition to think straight. Lucky me. I sat down next to her, and in a soothing voice, said, "I can't let them leave town. Don't you want to know who was murdered?"

"I don't care," she whimpered. "It doesn't matter. I'd just as soon they all kill each other, then drive home. I'll be at the side of the road to wave good-bye." She wiped her eyes with a tissue. I was prepared to let her linger in her blissful, inebriated universe when she abruptly threw the wadded tissue on the floor and snapped, "Yes, of course I want to know who was murdered! I'm waiting, missy. Are you going to sit there like a petrified frog or are you going to croak it out?"

Jekyll and Hyde had found room on the sofa. "Dennis

Gilbert was the victim," I began. "His body was discovered in Tommy Ridner's motel room earlier this afternoon. Same cause of death. I'm working on a motive." She gazed blankly at me. "You have to decide about the golf tournament, Mrs. Jim Bob. I think it's time to cancel it once and for all. The perp's out there. Nobody should be on the golf course tomorrow."

"What about the bass boat? That's why they came, you know. They pretend to care about golf widows, but I see right through them. They don't give a whit about faith, hope, and charity. They're here out of greed. As it says in the daily devotional book in the guest bathroom, 'who being past feeling have given themselves over unto lasciviousness, to work all uncleanness with greediness.' I think that sums it up nicely."

I was having trouble following her logic. "What do you want to do about the golf tournament?"

"We'll cross that fairway when we come to it."

"Okay," I said. "Then the tournament continues?"

"People who live in glass houses shouldn't play golf."

"The tournament is canceled?"

"A fool and his golf ball are soon parted," she said. "You must excuse me. I have to de-ice the cake before the ladies arrive." She wafted out of the room.

After a few seconds to pull myself together, I wafted out of the house and sat in my car, my forehead on the steering wheel. Every last soul in Maggody was a liar and/or an idiot. There was not one person I could trust. Jack was five thousand miles away, photographing cockatoos. I felt as if I were in a rain forest as well, although mine was of my own making. If he weren't incommunicado, I would have arranged to meet him on the beach in Rio de Janeiro. And never come back. Our child would be bilingual and tan. I would contribute to the household budget by carving coconuts to resemble Buchanons, right down to the squinty eyes and sneers.

When I had exhausted my store of self-pity, I drove back

to the highway and ran the stoplight out of spite. I parked between a couple of familiar pickups and went into Ruby Bee's. The proprietress promptly went into the kitchen. The suspects from the motel (sans Amanda) were seated in several booths, apparently having failed to bond. Bony and Earl were eating burgers at the bar. The lone figure in the corner was seeping into the faux leather upholstery. The rest of them stared at me. I was thinking of how to begin when Jim Bob, Jeremiah, Kevin, and other members of the tontine came in.

"What about the tournament?" Jim Bob demanded.

A sticky question. "I'm not sure," I said. "Mrs. Jim Bob is mulling it over. I think it's a bad idea to continue, but I won't interfere. Thing is, nobody is to leave town for the time being. That includes all the locals who are involved in the tournament in any capacity. Nobody drives to the co-op for layer grit without my consent. Nobody runs into Farberville to shop." I stopped for a minute. "Does everyone know about Dennis Gilbert's murder?"

I wasn't surprised when they all nodded, since the grapevine was more efficient than the Internet in the dissemination of information. The CIA could take lessons from the Missionary Society. "All right," I continued, "are all of you clear about what I said? No exceptions. If you leave town without a hall pass, I'll issue an APB and have you taken into custody."

"For what?" Proodle said. "This is not a police state. We're American citizens and you're violating our constitutional rights."

"Absolutely," I said. "Any more questions?"

Everyone who was standing sat down, and those who were seated resumed whatever they had been doing. I assumed Ruby Bee would reappear to take orders and dish out soup made from the noon special. Chicken noodle soup sounded like an excellent idea, but not in an environment chillier than arctic water.

I stopped at the PD to make a couple of calls, then at the Dairee Dee-Lishus to fuel myself with a cherry limeade. The drive to Farberville gave me time to think.

Once Ruby Bee got everybody served, she took a quarter out of the cash register drawer and went down to the pay phone at the end of the bar. She'd looked up the number in her address book. The jukebox was playing a sentimental ballad. Nobody was so much as looking in her direction. All she had to do was pick up the receiver and dial the number.

She glanced around as she squeezed the quarter in her sweaty palm. It wasn't like she was calling Buckingham Palace to chat with the queen, or the Vatican to speak to the pope. If someone else answered, she figured she could disguise her voice. Why, she could make herself sound exactly like a Mexican, having learned a few words in Spanish a while back. "Buenas nachos," she whispered. "My llama Rosita."

It was a stupid idea. She put the quarter back in the drawer and wiped down the bar with a dishrag. Luke asked for a refill, but she gave him a dark look. He had enough sense not to repeat his request. The song on the jukebox was now an oldie from the 1970s, painfully familiar. She continued making wide shiny circles on the black surface, her lips barely moving as she sang, "You're so vain . . ." She pictured herself singing it to him, since he'd thought everything was about him.

She took the quarter out of the drawer and returned to stand in front of the pay phone. This time it *was* about him, but also about her and a whole lot more. She'd almost rallied the courage to pick up the receiver when the phone rang. It was so startling that she ducked into the ladies' room and locked the door.

Fourteen

I parked in front of the Farberville PD and went to the front desk. A middle-aged woman with streaky blond hair and dark roots gazed at me without interest. I was charmed, since I was accustomed to LaBelle's snoopiness. It often took ten minutes of feints and lunges to get past her to Harve's office.

"Arly Hanks," I said briskly. "Sheriff Dorfer called about me."

"Yeah, I got it somewhere." She pawed through the clutter on her desk until she found a memo. "Okay, yeah, an officer to get you inside a residence. You're supposed to fill out a form, which means I have to dig one out of the filing cabinet. We're always short-handed on weekends. Can't this wait 'til tomorrow?"

"I'm working a double homicide," I said less briskly.

"Good for you. I'm working a double shift to pay my medical bills. I was diagnosed with bursitis in both knees six weeks ago. Last year it was gallstones, and the year before that I had an emergency appendectomy. I spent my birthday on an operating table. I can hardly wait for next year."

"Do I need to talk to the chief?" I said.

"Chief Turbutt's lucky to be able to work. He practically lives on antacids and milk. His doctor blames it on smoking and stress. My sister-in-law had the same thing, bloody stools and all, but she finally said to hell with it and had the surgery. You should have seen the staples on her belly. I told her next time the surgeon could just unzip her." She chuckled. "Get it? The staples looked like a zipper."

"Is there an officer waiting for me?"

"You should have asked me that right off the bat, instead of prying into personal medical problems." The woman scowled as she picked up the receiver, punched a few buttons, and told Officer Davies to report to the desk.

Officer L. Davies strutted in, his thin lips so tightly pursed that he resembled a bloated badger. "Chief Hanks?" he barked. "Officer Davies here. I've been assigned to assist you." It was clear that he would have preferred to beat me senseless with a nightstick.

I told him what I needed him to do. He seemed disappointed that he would not have the opportunity to bully little old ladies or arrest teenagers for skateboarding in the park. We did not make amiable conversation as he drove to a neighborhood in the historic district. The houses were old, the yards immaculate, the sidewalks swept. I wondered why Tommy had chosen a neighborhood where parties revolved around cupcakes and balloons.

I followed Officer Davies onto the porch of a gray-shingled house with white gingerbread trim. The porch swing had a fresh coat of paint. He fiddled with a set of lock picks, then opened the door. "Wait here while I search the premises," he said, fondling his handgun in a leather holster. "Once I'm sure it's safe, I'll allow you in while I stand guard on the porch."

"I think not," I said. "I'll call the PD when I'm finished. They can track you down."

"I advise against that, ma'am."

"Maybe I should speak to Chief Turbutt and let him deal with you, Officer Davies. I understand he's in a bad mood these days."

Officer Davies's eyebrows merged like a slather of mud. "If you insist on disregarding my advice, the Farberville

Police Department will not take responsibility for whatever may happen to you."

"Run along." I fluttered my fingers in dismissal. "This shouldn't take more than an hour. You have plenty of time to bust senior citizens whose dogs poop on the sidewalk."

I closed the door to emphasize my point, then turned around to survey the territory. Tommy's living room contained a leather couch, a matching recliner, and a flat-screen TV the size of a twin mattress. There were a couple of beer cans on the coffee table, but otherwise it was surprisingly tidy. The kitchen was unremarkable except for a wineglass rack and cabinets crowded with bottles of top-label liquor. The refrigerator contained standard bachelor fare: a jar of mayonnaise, a package of baloney, a carton of milk, and a case of beer. An adjoining room served as an office. It was crammed with a metal desk, filing cabinets, computer equipment, cardboard storage boxes, and piles of folders and disks. It had a semblance of organization, however, and I decided it hadn't been searched in recent days. Or dusted in recent years.

Upstairs, I took a quick look inside a guest room, then went into the master bedroom. The bed was neatly made, and clothes hung in the closet. A biography of Cardinal Woolsey lay on the bedside table. The bookshelf held more biographies, classic literature, and a couple of gardening books. One should never judge a golfer by the cut of his shorts, I told myself.

The bathroom counter was a pharmacy of vitamins, supplements, antacid remedies, heating pads, ankle and knee supporters, and amber prescription vials. It took me a while to spot a bottle that matched the one found behind the Flamingo Motel. It had the same label, but its seal was intact. Tommy was clearly a fan of Dilaudid, or quite possibly addicted to it. According to my little golden book of narcotics, Dilaudid had a high potential for abuse and posed a risk for respiratory failure. Taken with alcohol, it could be deadly. But it hadn't killed Tommy.

I was looking through dresser drawers when I heard the front door open. I thought I'd locked it, but Officer Davies could pick the lock in seconds. It was time for a game of hide-and-seek, to be concluded when I snuck up behind his sanctimonious backside and scared the holy shit out of him.

Footsteps moved toward the back of the house. I eased down the stairs and peered along the hall that led to the kitchen. The refrigerator door opened. I had no idea what Officer Davies was up to, unless he was hoping that I'd been stuffed inside it. The refrigerator door closed and a floorboard squeaked. Maybe he thought he'd frighten me into a display of maidenly distress. Well, he was in for a shock that rivaled the San Francisco earthquake of 1906.

The kitchen was unoccupied, leaving the office as my ground zero. I crept across the kitchen, took a deep breath, and burst into the room. "Kaboom!" I screeched.

Amanda Gilbert fainted.

This was not my desired scenario. I stood over her for a few minutes, my arms crossed, as I waited for her eyelids to flutter. They did not. Eventually I lugged her into the living room and dumped her on the sofa. I sat down until my heart stopped pumping like a wildcat strike, and then got up to fetch a damp washcloth. She saved me the bother by opening her eyes.

"Chief Hanks?"

"So it seems," I said.

"What are you doing here?"

"Getting ready to ask you the same question," I said. "You're supposed to be at Estelle's house."

Amanda took several deep breaths. "She's very kind, I guess, but she insisted on treating me like a helpless infant. She kept trying to persuade me that I needed a trim. My last haircut cost ninety dollars. I wasn't about to let her come after me with a pair of scissors from Wal-Mart." She wiggled into a more upright position and touched the back of her head. "Sheesh, I have a lump the size of a golf ball. Why on earth did you come up on me like that? Is that some kind of police procedure?"

As good an excuse as any. "You haven't explained what you're doing here in Tommy's house," I said.

"I stopped by to see if the houseplants need to be watered."

"There aren't any houseplants, Amanda. Besides that minor problem, you were in the office. The only thing growing there is mold. What were you looking for?"

"It's going to sound screwy," she said. I did not disagree. After a lengthy moment to make up a story, she gave me a rueful look. "Tommy's address book. I want to notify his family as soon as possible. Dennis was going to handle it, but now it's up to me, I guess. Except for Dennis, Tommy didn't have any close friends. He had golf partners, drinking buddies, and old frat brothers. He must have relatives somewhere, but I have no idea how to get in touch with them."

"A touching story, but with a low credibility factor. The address book is on the desk, hard to miss. You were searching the top drawer."

"I must not have seen it."

"Your husband was murdered this afternoon, Amanda. Shouldn't you be overwhelmed with grief, or at least trying to get in touch with *his* family?"

She lowered her eyes. "I warned you it would sound screwy. I just couldn't sit there at Estelle's house and gush over her display of fingernail polish bottles any longer. When she went to the bathroom, I grabbed her car key and left. I couldn't bear the idea of going home and seeing all of Dennis's things scattered around. The newspaper on the table, the dry cleaner's receipt under a magnet on the refrigerator, the photograph of him accepting a trophy at a tournament in Palm Beach." She squeezed out a few tears. "The funeral, the reception. Is there somebody I can hire to do all this?"

"Try the yellow pages. You're claiming you came here to escape Estelle, which I admit is plausible. Then it occurred to you to find Tommy's address book. Why did you think it was in his office?"

"I wasn't thinking," Amanda said sulkily. "I was in shock—and it's a helluva lot worse now, thanks to you."

I studied her for a moment. "You're welcome. Were you looking for Tommy's stash of Dilaudid? It's in the bathroom upstairs."

"Does this drug have something to do with his murder? Whoever it was could have broken into this house over the weekend. Everybody knew Tommy would be out of town for the tournament. He's been chortling about it for weeks. But if the bottle was in plain sight, why didn't the addict take it? I mean, why go all the way to Maggody to murder Tommy—and Dennis? I don't get it."

Neither did I. Rather than continue the pointless dialogue, I said, "You'd better get Estelle's car back before she reports it stolen to the state police."

She slunk out of the house. I returned to Tommy's office and flipped through the address book. Most of the entries were women, but I found the name of a Ridner in Florida and copied down the information. I set the book aside and poked around for whatever Amanda wanted so badly. All I came up with was utility and credit card bills, bank statements, appraisals, bids from contractors, and other fancy things. Tommy had been in decent financial shape, especially if he overlooked income from his golf bets. After I completed my search upstairs, I called the Farberville PD and went out to the porch to wait for Officer L. Davies.

"I call the meeting to order," Mrs. Jim Bob said, lightly tapping the gavel on the dinette table. She felt much better, having had a glass of gin to settle her nerves. "I have to decide whether or not to cancel the tournament. I will entertain your opinions before I make the call."

The members of the Missionary Society were oddly quiet. Most of them were watching Mrs. Jim Bob's face for any lingering signs of remorse. She wasn't glowing—or glowering, for that matter. She was darn near placid, Eileen thought from a corner. Millicent opted for the word "mellow." Elsie and Eula exchanged uneasy looks. Even Bopeep, who was usually too busy thinking about her own problems to pay attention, was unsettled.

"No point in canceling it," Audley said bravely.

"Unless it looks like another storm is coming in," Crystal said. "I jumped out of my skin when lightning hit that dead oak tree this morning."

Lucille raised her hand. "What about the killer? I don't aim to be on the golf course if he's on the loose, especially since I'll be providing the weapon."

"He'd better not try anything with me," said Joyce. "When Larry Joe got the flu last winter, I split a rick of wood and stacked it in the carport by myself. Nobody's gonna sneak up on me. I got three wily children."

Eileen stepped forward. "If I don't win the bass boat, Earl's going to sleep in the barn 'til hell freezes over. I say we finish the round in the morning."

"If it's not overcast," amended Crystal.

Mrs. Jim Bob smiled benignly at them. "Shall we have some coconut cake after we have a show of hands?"

Officer Davies kept his lips pursed as he drove me to the PD. His chin stuck out, and his fingers on the steering wheel were bloodless. I pitied the next jaywalker he spotted. Said pedestrian could end up in prison, or as flat as a paper doll in the middle of the street. His mother must have been worried when he began pulling wings off flies in his playpen.

I went inside the PD. The blond woman sniffed as I approached her desk. "Excuse me," I said. "Can I see the arrest log from last night?"

"I'm too busy to track it down. Come by in a couple of days."

"Too busy reading a romance novel? Gee, that's a new one. Where's Chief Turbutt's office?"

"He ain't here today. He ate pizza last night and it didn't agree with him. He knows better than to eat pepperoni and jalapeños." She turned a page and resumed reading.

"Shall I track it down myself?" I asked. "I'd hate to make a mess of your . . . mess."

"Hold your damn horses," she grumbled as she ripped off a corner of a form and used it as a bookmark. "You want anything in particular?"

"Traffic violations," I said. "Cars towed, parking tickets."

"Based on what I've heard about Maggody, people should roll up their car windows and lock their doors before they drive through town. I wouldn't live out there if my life depended on it, which I guess it would. Must be all that inbreeding." Her lower lip extended, she pecked on the keyboard until the printer began to hum. "Saturday is prime time. There was a street fair yesterday. Thurber Street was blocked off, and vendors sold beer on the sidewalks. Lots of drunk-and-disorderlies, property damage, fights in alleys. A good two dozen cars were towed. You don't want to know how many traffic and parking tickets were issued."

"I'm interested in a Chrysler Imperial Crown," I said.

She rolled her eyes and turned back to the computer. "You should have said so, instead of letting me print out all the citations. How do you spell the kind of car?"

I spelled the kind of car very slowly. When a page slithered out of the printer, I picked it up. I felt a tingle as I spotted the pertinent words. Same make, same license plate number. Frederick Cartier had not lied when he said he was in Farberville the previous evening. His only crime was parking too close to a fire hydrant. I wrote down the location, thanked the woman, and left.

The street turned out to be in a neighborhood that was

the opposite of Tommy's. Houses were small and unloved. Screen doors were torn, windows cracked. The lawns were no better than the fairways at the Maggody golf course. Frederick's tryst had taken place in a dingy white house. Even the fire hydrant, streaked with spray paint, looked depressed.

I kept an eye on the children in the next yard, who might have been Fagin's latest recruits, as I went to the front door and knocked. I was taken aback when it was opened by a man clad only in faded plaid boxers and flip-flops. His chest looked like a bear pelt, but his head was shiny. As was a prominent gold tooth.

"You looking for me, little lady?" he said. "You're in luck, 'cause I'm ready and willing. Come right on in and make yourself at home."

"No thank you," I said. "Does anyone else live here?"

He stuck out his lower lip. "Nah, just me and Oliver."

"Oliver Twist?"

"Oliver, my shih tzu." He noticed my badge. "You really a cop, or are you a spy for the American Kennel Club?"

"I'm really a cop. I'm looking into the whereabouts of Frederick Cartier last night. Was he here?"

"Never heard of him."

His credibility rating was lower than Amanda's; she'd at least attempted to come up with a story. "Maybe you know him by another name," I suggested tactfully. "I know he was here. He was issued a parking ticket at eleven o'clock. His car was parked in front of this house, a teeny bit too near the fire hydrant."

"Frederick Cartier." He screwed up his face, pretending to think. "There were some fellows over last night. One of 'em could have been this Cartier you're asking about. It was a poker game, not a tea party, and I didn't check IDs at the door. No name tags or introductions, just cards, booze, and dollar bills. I hear Oliver stirring in the kitchen, so if we're done here . . . ?"

"Not yet. Cartier is six feet tall, with silver hair. Expensively dressed, driving a vintage Chrysler Imperial Crown, black."

"He could have been here. Like I said, I didn't pay attention to names. I was down on Thurber Street all afternoon, drinking beer. I was feeling no pain when I got home. All I remember about the poker game is that I lost seventy dollars to fuckin' trip nines. I had kings and fours." He shut the door in my face.

"I'm very sorry for your loss," I said to the rusty door knocker, then returned to my car and flipped through my pad of notes. Frederick had three alibis thus far: the professor, the anonymous paramour, and the poker game. He could have skipped the first two, if he'd been playing poker. There would be witnesses to verify his story, albeit reluctant ones. The man in the boxers, for starters. He had failed to ask why I was tracking down Frederick. Disinterested people could still be interested; it was almost instinctive. The man had shown no curiosity. If he'd said that Frederick was there, I would have accepted it as an inelegant alibi. It didn't explain why Frederick hadn't simply said so to begin with.

I pulled out a street map and located the Gilberts' address. They lived in what must have been one of Farberville's first subdivisions. The houses were small, with carports instead of garages. Some had partial brick veneers. I drove around for a few minutes until I spotted their house. It could have belonged to a retiree on a pension, a police officer, a teacher, a firefighter, or a midlevel factory worker. Or, I amended, a newscaster in a small town who spent his salary on a country club membership, golf tournaments, and a Mercedes. Since Amanda had intended to search Tommy's house, I assumed whatever she sought was not in her own house.

I had one more stop before I headed home. I drove up a winding road to the country club. The mini-mansions on the hilltop were disturbingly similar, right down to the spindly trees that would provide shade in the next decade. I parked between a Hummer and a Porsche and went inside the clubhouse. The bar was nearly deserted. Two couples shared a table, and another couple was bickering with a different one. I sat on a stool and waited until a waitress emerged from a back room.

"Sorry, honey," she said as she put a cocktail napkin in front of me. It was beige, with a green border that matched the immaculate course. "What would you like?"

"Just information. Have you heard about Tommy Ridner's death?"

Her smile faded. "Such a nice man. He pinched my butt whenever he had a chance, but he was generous with tips. Most of these rich people leave a dollar or two, then drive their expensive cars home to their six-bedroom houses so they can swim in their heated pools. The only pool I have is under the kitchen sink. The roaches swim laps in it."

"Mine put in a diving board last summer. So Tommy was a favorite of yours?"

"I cried when the manager told everybody this morning. I wanted to take the rest of the day off, but I can't afford it. My kid got braces, and I'll be making monthly payments on his wedding day. You sure you don't want a drink? It's on the house."

I agreed to a glass of orange juice. I sipped while she went to see if any of the patrons were in need of refills and then came back around the bar. "Tommy and the Gilberts were close friends, weren't they?" I asked her.

"I wouldn't put it that way. Tommy and Dennis were tight. Used to be they were out here most afternoons and all weekend long, talking, playing gin, cracking jokes. After Dennis married D'Amanda—uh, Mrs. Gilbert, he and Tommy stopped hanging around together so much. Everybody slithers down in their seats when she marches in. I keep waiting for her to drag Dennis out by his ear."

She was doomed to disappointment, but I decided to let the manager break the news. "Mrs. Gilbert didn't like Tommy?"

"She'd just as soon spit on him as say hello. That's what made it so darn funny when—" The waitress put out her hand across her mouth.

"When . . . ?" I said softly, leaning forward.

"Nothing. If I get caught gossiping about the members, I'll be fired in a split second. No excuses, no exceptions. They're free to talk all they want about each other, but the staff isn't supposed to hear one word of it."

I slid a five-dollar bill under the napkin. "I swear I won't tell anyone."

The bill vanished. "I guess I can trust you. It was a week ago or so. Tommy and Dennis were at their table, talking about an upcoming golf tournament. They got to arguing about who could make a hole-in-one. I perked up my ears, since when somebody makes one at this club, he or she has to stand a round of drinks in the bar, and I get to add the gratuity to the tab. Anyway, in comes Mrs. Gilbert and sits with them. They make a bet right under her nose. She goes ballistic and jumps down their throats. After she's gone, they keep laughing and raising the stakes. Half the room was snickering, since Mrs. Gilbert's not real popular. Too old for the soccer moms and too trashy for the society ladies. Later Tommy scribbled on a napkin and had me witness it." Her expression sobered. "He was a real kidder. It's like his ghost is sitting at his table. No wonder there's hardly anybody here today."

"What did Tommy do with the napkin?" I asked.

"Tucked it in his shirt pocket. Hey, if Tommy has any family, be sure and give them my condolences. I'm gonna miss him."

I couldn't come up with any more reasons to linger in Farberville, so I headed for Maggody. When I saw a familiar roadside rest area, I pulled in. A short walk along a path strewn with paper cups and aluminum cans led me to a trickle of a creek. I sat down and watched the water flow over mossy rocks, leaving swirls of brownish foam. I became oblivious to trucks on the highway as I considered what I'd heard from the witnesses. Despite their best efforts, a few had slipped up and told the truth. Fragments began to fall into place. Tommy's death had closed Act I, and Dennis's death was the focus of Act II. That left Act III for the grand denouement, as soon as I came up with it. I was more in the mood for *Our Town* than *Hamlet*. I'd played Emily in our high school performance, and memorizing my lines had almost killed me. So had falling off the ladder.

It began to rain. I drove to Maggody and parked at the PD. The evil red light on the phone was blinking. For once, I was pretty sure it wasn't Ruby Bee. I should have called Estelle to find out if Amanda had reappeared, but that would have given her the chance to sputter about car theft and ingratitude, along with whatever else occurred to her. I was running low on sympathy.

The first message was from Harve. I dialed his home number. "Chief of Police Ariel Hanks," I said. "What's up?"

"Did you get in Ridner's house without a hitch?"

I told him about the bottle of pills and Amanda's ill-fated intrusion. I then described Frederick's purported poker buddy and the information I'd picked up at the country club. "I don't think Amanda killed Tommy," I continued. "She relished their encounters, when she could taunt him. Tommy must have, too. It was a game for them. That left Dennis as the spectator, his head swiveling back and forth while the two took cheap shots at each other."

"You don't think they had something on the side, do you? Pretending to be enemies makes a good cover."

I leaned back in my chair. "No," I said slowly. "Amanda's been around the block a couple of times. She knew that if they had sex, she'd lose her power. No fun in that."

"It'd give her a motive to kill him. She might have thought Tommy was making a move on Natalie. Women in their forties don't take kindly to being replaced by sweet young things."

"You speaking from experience, Harve?"

He mumbled a phrase that made me glad I wasn't within reach. "I talked to McBeen earlier. He said he'll do the blood test tomorrow. We found a few prints in Ridner's room that were in the system, but Les already told you about Lucas Smithers and Bony Buchanon. It's hardly worth mentioning, since Ridner's party included half the town. I guess you didn't make the cut, eh?"

"As in haircut?" I asked blankly.

"For someone who lived in New York City, you don't know shit. At a big golf tournament, there's a qualifying round. The cut is what decides who all gets to play the next round."

"They don't play much golf on Fifth Avenue. No, I didn't go to the party. I had better things to do, like scrub my toilet. Life's exciting out here, Harve. A regular roller coaster of thrills and spills." I was getting bored, so I hung up.

The next message was from Estelle. As soon as I heard her shrill voice, I erased the rest of it. If Amanda hadn't returned the car by now, there was nothing I could do about it. Well, there was nothing I was willing to do about it, anyway. The final message was from Janna Coulter, who sounded frantic in an incoherent way. I listened to her message again, then gave up and drove over to the Flamingo Motel.

Janna yanked open the door. Her eyes were embedded in swollen flesh, and her face was mottled. "It's about time! I called you almost two hours ago. I even asked Ruby Bee where you were, but she claimed she didn't have a clue. Is there an Elm Street in this horrid town? A black hole?"

"Calm down. I was following a lead, but here I am. What's wrong?" I said to be polite, since I was fairly certain what her response would be. The police academy stressed the need for diplomacy with the public.

Wobbling, she backed into the room until she bumped

into a bed, then sat down. "Something's wrong with me. I'm so sleepy I can barely see straight. It's like an out-of-body experience. Could it be a stroke?"

"Stay awake and tell me what's going on," I said sharply.

She tried to focus on me. "After you left, Natalie and I came back here. She suggested that I take another antihistamine and lie down. All of a sudden I felt like I'd been hit by a truck. One minute I was talking, the next I was passed out on the bed. A noise from the next room woke me up. Natalie was gone. I went to the barroom, but she wasn't there. Phil Proodle said he hadn't seen her. There's no place to go in this town—no café, no gym, no shops."

"Did she take anything with her?"

"Nothing's missing except her purse." She rubbed her eyes. "Her suitcase and clothes are in the closet. She refused to tell me where she went this morning after the tournament was stopped. You have to tell me so I can go find her."

"You're in no condition to drive. You didn't have a stroke; you had a reaction to the medication. The best thing you can do is sleep it off. With luck, Natalie will be here when you wake up."

"What if she's not?" Janna whimpered.

I was thoroughly exasperated. "What if pigs had wings? For starters, we'd be dodging pig shit. But we're not, are we?"

I got back in my car and went to fetch Natalie. Again.

Fifteen

I parked by the tent and walked back to Kevin and Dahlia's house. The good news was that the rain had driven Raz inside; the bad news was that it had one less target. I was so annoyed that I wanted to stomp through the puddles, leaving a muddy path of destruction in my wake. Could these people not stay put for fifteen seconds?

I barged through the front door. It would be very awkward if Kevin and Dahlia were cuddled around a lemon meringue pie in front of the TV. They were not. "Natalie Hotz, haul your sorry butt in here right now!" I shouted as I detoured into the kitchen to dry my face with a dish towel. "You, too, Luke Smithers!" I sat down on the couch and squeezed a stuffed sheep. "I'm waiting!"

Natalie came into the room. She was in no way perfect, with mussy hair and smeared mascara. She looked more like a petulant convenience store clerk, doomed to chomping gum and selling cigarettes to underaged kids. "Why can't you leave me alone?" she said fiercely. "I'm an adult, free to go where I want to go."

"And do what you want to do." Luke grinned at me as he posed in the doorway, dressed only in frayed jeans. His abs rippled like corrugated iron, and his biceps bulged. The state prison didn't invest much in rehab, but the weight room had all the trappings of a pricey athletic club (except, perhaps, a smoothie machine). "What brings you out in the rain, Chief Hanks?" he drawled.

"You noticed it was raining?" I said.

Natalie flopped into a chair. "I cannot believe this. Did Janna send you? Are you like a bounty hunter in your free time?" She wiggled her fingers at Luke. "Would you be a sweetie and get me my purse? I feel absolutely naked without lipstick."

"Sit," I said to Luke. "No, Natalie, I am not working for Janna, but I am doing her a favor. If I'd told her where you are, she'd be crawling through the door in a couple of hours. She can barely walk, thanks to your tender loving care. Tommy had been using Dilaudid for a long time and built up a tolerance. Janna, on the other hand, keeled right over, didn't she? Is this the first time you've switched it with her antihistamine?"

"At a tournament in Houston I put half a pill in her beer. It worked pretty good, but I was afraid she might build up a—whatever you called it. There's no way to explain my absence in this town. It's not like I could say I'd gone to the spa for a massage or to the pro shop to sign autographs."

"Did you steal the pills from Tommy's room?" I asked.

Her face flushed. "I am not a common thief. He gave them to me."

"You were arrested for shoplifting, Natalie. That's common around here." I glanced at Luke, who was warily observing the exchange as his biceps deflated. "Did you go through basic training at Fort Sill? Don't bother to lie about it. The army has records." Somewhere.

"Yeah, and it's a hellhole. Flat, windy, dusty, hotter'n blazes in summer. I did officer training there, too. After ten months, I was begging to be deployed to Iraq." He turned his liquid eyes on Natalie. "I wouldn't have made it without you, honey."

"It was exciting," Natalie added. "There's a dumb rule about army guys messing with civilians. Luke would go to the golf course, and I'd hide in the woods until we were sure it was safe. Sometimes I'd fix sandwiches and we'd have a picnic."

He nodded. "If Janna had caught us, I would have been court-martialed in no time flat. Ironic, isn't it? If I hadn't taught Natalie to play golf, Janna wouldn't have her precious protégé. None of us would be here now."

"Right out of O. Henry," I said, untouched by the travails of young love. "I assume you did more than play golf."

"So what?" Natalie said.

I did not point out that by my calculations, she was no more than fifteen at the time. My jurisdiction didn't extend into Oklahoma, but I'd make sure to mention it in the official report. The army's jurisdiction extended past Andromeda. My job was to uphold the law, not to enforce Mrs. Jim Bob's misbegotten version of morality. "You kept in touch?"

Luke cut her off before she could gush. "After I got back from overseas, I saw an article about Natalie in a golf magazine. It mentioned that Tommy Ridner lived in the same town, so I took a chance and enclosed a note for him in an envelope with my letter to Natalie. He turned out to be a nice guy."

"It was incredibly romantic," Natalie confided in the husky voice of a cabaret singer. "I mean, I saw Tommy almost every weekend at the club. I'd pass him my letters to Luke, and he'd slip Luke's letters into my locker. My hand would shake so hard I could barely open the lock. When Luke moved so close, I thought I'd go out of my mind. Janna won't let me have a cell phone, so there was no way Luke could call me. The tournament was like a miracle. I pretended I didn't want to go so Janna wouldn't get suspicious." She glanced over her shoulder as if international spies were hiding behind the play-pen. "I burned all his letters, just in case."

Such a loss to posterity. "You found some opportunities to meet this weekend," I said. "Is that what was going on Friday night?"

"Luke and I, uh, went for a walk. I tripped in the weeds

and got all dirty and scratched. I was sneaking into the bathroom to use a washrag when Janna sat up in bed like a
mummy in one of those scary movies. I had to tell her something." She narrowed her eyes at me. "Then I had to tell you
something. I couldn't tell you the truth because I was afraid
you'd tattle to Janna."

"You can't trust cops," Luke said.

"No argument from me. Tommy gave you the Dilaudid to
knock out Janna?"

Natalie nodded smugly. "Three pills on Friday afternoon.
It was his idea, mostly. He suggested that we should act all
cozy so Janna would be distracted. There were a couple of
times when I thought she was ready to kill him." She put her
fingertips on her lips. "I didn't mean it that way."

"Weren't you worried that she might recognize you?" I
asked Luke.

"She didn't pay any mind to recruits. I had a different
drill sergeant. We all stayed out of her way on account of her
reputation. She almost bit one of my buddies' head off—and
I mean literally."

A gory image flashed across my mind. "What are your
plans for the future?"

Luke cut Natalie off again, and most likely not for the
last time. "Natalie's going to be a good girl and keep her
nose clean until she starts making serious money. Then Janna's history and I'll manage Natalie's career. I see us getting
married at St. Andrews, surrounded by dudes in kilts playing bagpipes. We're talking the cover of *People* magazine."

"And we live happily ever after," Natalie concluded.

I stood up. "Natalie, you need to go deal with Janna. She's
in bad shape. I'm not going to do anything about the breaking and entering, but this is the last time. Don't come here
anymore, okay?" I went outside and walked to my car, wondering how long Luke would hang around after the sports
media found a photogenic newcomer.

I wasn't about to hunt up Janna and tell her the big news.

She might be lingering in Ruby Bee's, so that was out. I didn't want to go by Mrs. Jim Bob's house and find out about the future of the golf tournament. The Dairee Dee-Lishus was closed because of the rain, since this was not the day for dining al fresco. Estelle's house was out; I'd either have to listen to a tirade about Amanda's treachery and ingratitude or be assailed with fingernail polish. I didn't need to go looking for a headache. On that note, I went upstairs to my apartment. It was gloomy enough that a light might show in my window, so I grabbed a box of crackers, a notebook, and a candle and took refuge in the bathroom. After making a nest of damp towels, I settled in to write a letter to Jack.

Mrs. Jim Bob put the used plates and forks in the sink and ran water on them. The meeting had gone well. She'd had no intention of canceling the tournament, but she'd held her peace until the ladies agreed of their own accord. No one had asked about Frederick's whereabouts. It was just as well, since she had no idea where he was. His car was gone, but his clothes were in the closet, his toiletries stored neatly in the guest bathroom. Which meant he'd be coming back.

She poured herself a medicinal glass of gin and went out to the patio. She had to do something about dinner, but she wasn't sure how best to do it. If she set the table in the dining room, he might interpret it as a sign of gratitude for his lecherous behavior. Or worse, as a romantic gesture. On the other hand, if they had a casual meal in the kitchen, he might think that she was feeling cozy and tender. Who knew what he might make of the stuffed pork chop casserole she'd taken out of the freezer?

It would almost be easier if Jim Bob was there, she thought with a shudder. He'd tuck his napkin under his chin and eat the pork chops with his hands, like the barbarian he was. There was nothing romantic about greasy fingers. However mortified she was, Frederick would not get any outrageous thoughts about future intimacy.

Lust was a sin. She'd been reared to believe that a proper Christian wife was modest and efficient. In matters of conjugal duties, she was cooperative. Her grandmother had told her to think of England. Mrs. Jim Bob hadn't known what England had to do with it, but she'd kept her eyes closed and concentrated on pictures from her eleventh-grade history book.

In less than twenty-four hours, the tournament would be over. When Bony left, Frederick would have no excuse to stay in Maggody. Good riddance, she told herself. The bass boat would be hers. She'd sell it and put the money in her private account until she had time to go shopping in Tulsa. Better yet, she might just take a trip to Europe and Italy to see the Gothic cathedrals. The Lord Almighty would approve of a first-class pilgrimage. Why, she'd visit the pope and tell him all about the charity golf tournament and how she'd sacrificed to provide for the poor golf widows. She'd have her picture taken with him. She made a note to find out what his name was before she got there. She hoped it was Pope Pious.

"I got some business to see to," Jim Bob said as he slid out of the booth. "I'll catch you boys later."

"What business might that be?" asked Roy.

Big Dick leaned forward. "On a rainy Sunday afternoon?"

"Tontine business?" Tam passed the bottle to Jeremiah. "You aimin' to tell that lawyer to burn the paper we all signed?"

Jeremiah wiped his mouth on his shirt cuff. "I don't like the sound of this, Mr. Mayor. You'd better not be screwing with us."

Jim Bob managed to look wounded. "All I was fixin' to do was to go over to Starley City and buy some beer, fercrissake."

"I'll go with you," Big Dick said as he struggled to his feet. "You got a tarp to cover the beer? I ain't in the mood to get hassled by a state trooper."

"He ain't gonna sell me anything stronger than soda pop if you come along," Jim Bob said quickly. "He's already been busted twice by the ATF. Soon as I get back, we'll play some more poker over at Roy's. Big Dick, you run down to the SuperSaver and get some chips and that spicy beef jerky. Tell the checker I said not to ring it up."

When Jim Bob got in his truck, he bounced his forehead on the steering wheel. How could he have been so friggin' stupid as to say he was gonna go buy beer? Now he'd have to follow through so the boys wouldn't suspect anything. He didn't know for sure the guy in Starley City was still selling Sunday beer. Now he was gonna have to drive all the way there, scrounge up a couple of cases, and drive back— and then see to some business. At least, he thought as he started the engine, it would give him time to find a pay phone to call the lawyer and tell him to fire up his grill.

Bonaparte Buchanon was not lacking relatives in Maggody, but he figured he wasn't real popular with most of them. Aunt Eileen sure as hell wasn't going to take him back and feed him rhubarb pie in her kitchen. Dahlia might well decide to sit on him until blood squirted out his nose. Uncle Earl wouldn't feel kindly once he heard about the unfortunate incident, and Kevin would come after him like a rabid possum.

He ran through all of his kin, crossing them off for one reason or another. It was getting chilly in the abandoned New Age hardware store. He was afraid to hang out at the poker game, since the story of his minor transgression might surface on the grapevine. Kin or not, the menfolk of Maggody didn't take kindly to anyone messing with their women.

One last name came to mind. Bopeep had been a little brat when he'd been sent to Maggody in the summers. An ugly little brat with big ears and crooked teeth, he recollected. She'd winked at him during the lessons, and made him put his arms around her to correct her swing. He decided to wander over to the Pot O' Gold and see if she was hanging around. Luke had been kicked out of her trailer;

maybe he wouldn't be able to get back into her good graces until after the golf tournament was over. Which might never happen if it kept raining. Another day or two, and the Fouke Monster might come stumbling out of Boggy Creek, just like in the movie.

Rust made the arched sign hard to read. Most of the trailers in the Pot O' Gold looked like they were vacant, but Bony knew he was being watched from behind makeshift curtains. He caught a glimpse of Eula Lemoy before she ducked out of sight. He circled behind her double-wide and tapped on Bopeep's door.

She appeared in a floral housecoat, her hair in foam rollers, a can of soda in one hand and a baseball bat in the other. "Oh, it's you," she said, lowering the bat. "I was afraid you might be the crazy man that's been killing everybody. I'm as twitchy as a nun in a bikini. C'mon in."

"If I'm not intruding . . ." Bony looked past her to make sure Luke wasn't there. His ribs were sore, and he didn't want to get pummeled by a jealous boyfriend. They tended to do that, he'd learned a long time ago. "Are you by yourself?"

She caught his arm and pulled him inside. "Not anymore. You want a sandwich or something to drink? I got a bottle of vodka hidden in the back of the closet. You sit right here and I'll fetch it."

Bony moved magazines, a pizza box, an empty ice cream carton, and a dozen aluminum cans off the sofa, then sat down. The walls were covered with framed prints of cottages in gardens, forests, and sand dunes. Crocheted doilies were strewn on every surface. Wildflowers withered in jelly jars. There were so many ruffles that the furniture seemed to hover above the shag carpet.

Bopeep returned with the bottle. Her hair was now pulled back in a tight ponytail, and she wore high heels decorated with pom-poms. "You want this with Dr Pepper, Diet Pepsi, or apple juice?"

"Just ice," he said weakly. He watched her while she wobbled into the kitchenette and fixed the drinks. When she sat down, he scooted close to her. "Who'd have thought my cousin would look like a Vegas showgirl? You were a cute kid, but you sure have grown up, Bopeep."

She giggled. "I disremember if we're fourth cousins twice removed, or fifth cousins."

"We're kissin' cousins," Bony purred in her ear. "That's all that matters."

"Sez who?" She put a throw pillow between them. "I already got a boyfriend. For all you know, him and me are getting married next month."

"Where's your engagement ring?"

"I took it off before I got in the shower," she said. "It's on the counter in the bathroom, Mr. Know-It-All."

Bony licked the corners of his mouth. "Just like you took it off before every golf lesson? I think you're teasing me, Cousin Bopeep. You've got too much class to get hitched to a backwoods loser like Luke." He nudged the throw pillow off the couch. "He'll expect you to go camping with him. Do you want to spend the rest of your days scratching mosquito bites and cooking over a campfire?"

"Nothing wrong with that."

He risked a few more inches. "Of course there ain't. If that's what you want, you can have it—but you can have more, too. For instance, after you're married, you could tell Luke that you want to visit your mother, then meet me in Las Vegas. I'm a celebrity out there, so they always give me a fancy suite with champagne, baskets of fruit and chocolates, and a Jacuzzi big enough for two. Free movies, room service, plush bathrobes. Doesn't that sound better than a leaky tent and a sleeping bag?"

"I s'pose so," Bopeep said, pretending to be doubtful. "But if Luke found out . . ."

Bony clutched her thigh. "I'd never let that happen in a million years. You don't think I'd be so low down as to bust up someone's marriage, do you? How long have we known each other, Cousin Bopeep? Would I ever do anything to hurt you?"

She told herself he was like a magnet, drawing her to him. There was no way she could resist his smoldering eyes and sophisticated talk. Besides, it was mostly Luke's fault for not being there to protect her. "I wouldn't want anyone to get hurt."

He slipped an arm around her shoulder and squeezed. "You gotta trust me," he murmured as his fingers fiddled with the top button of her housecoat.

"Okay, I'll trust you." She slapped away his hand and took a swallow of vodka. "But you'll have to be satisfied with a quarter share. I came up with the plan and I've taken all the risks. I hope you can follow orders better than you can teach golf."

I ripped all fourteen pages of my letter into tiny pieces and flushed them down the toilet. Once the last flake disappeared in an eddy, I repaired my hair and tossed the empty cracker box in a wastebasket. Somehow, I'd missed lunch, and it was time to rectify the error by appeasing the munchies in my stomach. To my surprise, Ruby Bee's Bar & Grill was closed. I felt betrayed by my very own mother, who'd nursed me through chicken pox and puppy love, who'd taken me back into the fold after my disastrous marriage, who made me angel food cakes for my birthdays. Who'd lied to me for three decades.

Roy was not sitting in front of the antiques shop. I went inside and wound my way through a labyrinth of chairs, coffee tables, floor lamps, and shelves cluttered with oddments of dishes and ancient appliances. Larry Joe was draped across an easy chair, snoring like a backhoe on a hillside. Nearby on a pile of blankets, Jeremiah snored in atonal harmony.

Roy was seated at his kitchen table, working on a crossword puzzle. "What's a nine-letter word for mean-spirited?" he asked without looking up.

"Maggody."

"It's only seven letters, but I have to admit it came to mind."

"Where is everybody?" I asked as I opened his refrigerator.

"If you mean every last person on the planet, I can't help you. After Ruby Bee up and closed the bar, some of the guys went to the Dew Drop Inn for supper. There was a fair amount of discussion about how you'd react, but they finally agreed they didn't give a shit. Jim Bob drove to Starley City to pick up some beer."

Roy's refrigerator was down to condiments, shriveled carrots, and a carton of onion dip. "Did Ruby Bee say where she was going?"

"She just handed out sandwiches to the folks staying at the motel and skedaddled. You heard about the golf tournament?"

"Yeah, Roy, I understand they're having one in this very town. What now?"

"Mrs. Jim Bob called a meeting. The final round starts tomorrow morning at ten, come hell or high water. They're equal possibilities."

"Malicious."

He chuckled. "I already wrote it in. I was just testing you."

I walked over to the PD to find out if anyone was waiting to confess. I was greeted only by the blinking red light on the answering machine. I hit the replay button and began to search through desk drawers for a stale cinnamon bun or a candy bar. The first message was from Estelle, shrieking about her car and the ingratitude of some people. I fast-forwarded through the tirade. Audley wanted to know where Rip was because the dishwasher was leaking. The next was from Estelle, still ticked off and wanting to file charges for car theft. Eula Lemoy had seen a prowler in the Pot O' Gold. Boswana Buchanon had fascists in her attic again. Joyce wondered if it was legal for her to take Larry Joe's shotgun on the golf course. The tape ended without a message from Ruby Bee.

Bracing myself, I dialed the number of the medical examiner's office in the basement of the hospital. McBeen must have been giving himself bile transfusions from his corpses, because he flew into a verbal rage when I identified myself. I let him carry on for a few minutes, then said, "Let's stop before you accuse me of causing the fall of the Roman Empire. What did the autopsy on Tommy Ridner turn up?"

"Do you know how tedious it is to do an autopsy on two hundred and forty pounds of blubber? It took three of my boys to lift him onto the table. Let me get my notes." I listened to elevator music until he came back. "Ridner had liver problems, gallstones, and a herniated disk. Thick calluses on his hands, typical for obsessive golfers. You want the details of his abscessed tooth?"

"The cause of death would be more helpful."

"Blunt force trauma to the head, as any fool could see. Multiple fractures of the skull. Whoever attacked him continued to wield the weapon after the victim was dead. All the blood was Ridner's. We found a tiny sliver of what appears to be silicone in the wound. It'll have to go to the state lab for further analysis." Papers shuffled for a moment. "Blood alcohol level was four times the legal limit, and there were minute traces of Dilaudid."

"Any defensive wounds?" I asked optimistically.

"You got a hearing impairment, Chief Hanks? His blood alcohol level was four times the legal limit. He couldn't have defended himself against a flyswatter. Speaking of which, we've begun to see maggots. That confirms my estimated time of death."

I swallowed. "What about the autopsy on Dennis Gilbert?"

"This is not an auto factory, and we don't produce an autopsy every fifteen minutes. Thanks to you, I've been up since six this morning. I'm going to go to the cafeteria to have a sandwich and a slice of day-old pie. If and when I'm ready, I'll tackle the second body."

I replaced the receiver and leaned back to regard the ceiling. Chemistry classes had bored me. The only use of silicone that came to mind was breast implants. The obvious candidate was Amanda, but McBeen had mentioned a sliver rather than a smear, and she wasn't noticeably lopsided. I wondered if she could be addicted to Dilaudid. Even if she was, she had no motive to murder Tommy. All she needed to do was sneak into his house while he was at the country club, which presented frequent opportunities. Earlier, she'd let herself in. I hadn't thought to ask her if she had a house key, but I wouldn't be surprised if Dennis did. And she hadn't gone straight to the most likely room to find another bottle of pills.

The telephone rang. I promptly answered it, hoping it was Ruby Bee with a dinner invitation. It was Estelle. I gritted my teeth as I waited for a lecture, but she said, "It's about time you got back from wherever you went. Where's Ruby Bee?"

"I don't know," I said. "I thought she might be at your house."

"Not unless she's hiding in the cellar. I've been calling her unit and the barroom for more than an hour. This ain't like her, Arly."

I would have preferred the lecture. "No, it isn't. Is Amanda there?"

"She's upstairs in the tub. When she got back, I gave her a piece of my mind, and she apologized. Not so much as a word about why she took my car, mind you, but I let it go on account of her being a widow. Grief can make you do crazy things. I knew a fellow back when I was living in Little Rock whose wife died. He wore her clothes every day for a year, right down to her pantyhose and pumps. He got fired from his job at a bank and took up grooming dogs."

"I guess I'll go try to find Ruby Bee."

The most logical place to start was Ruby Bee's Bar &

Grill, illuminated only by neon beer signs in the front window. Her car was not parked in front of her unit, and it was dark inside. I went to the back door of the barroom, took a key from above the sill, and let myself in. There was enough light to make my way to the kitchen. I opened the refrigerator and fixed myself a plate of leftovers, then went to the back booth and sat down. "How'd you get in here?" I asked.

"Same way you did. Not much of a challenge."

"You the escaped prisoner?" I asked.

"Sorry."

"It'd be a lot simpler if you were," I said as I picked up a drumstick.

He took out his wallet and showed me his ID. "I thought this case would be a lot simpler," he said wryly. "This is one crazy place, Chief Hanks. I'm just going to hang around another day and see what happens next."

"Can you share any information?"

"Sure, if I want to be reassigned to border duty in Texas for the rest of my life."

"Suit yourself." I took the plate into the kitchen and left it in the sink, and made sure the door was locked when I left. It was time to talk to Phil Proodle. The light in his motel room was on, the curtains drawn. I could make out shadowy movement inside.

I knocked on his door. "Mr. Proodle, it's Arly Hanks. Open the door, please."

He was either very slow or very drunk, but he finally yanked open the door and did his best to loom. "This is getting tiresome, Chief Hanks. You have violated my civil liberties by detaining me without any evidence that suggests I'm guilty of some infraction."

I scooted past him and sat down. "The infraction happens to be two cold-blooded murders, but you're such delightful company that I'd detain you for parking in a handicapped space."

"That seems to be the level of your competence," he said,

scowling. "I shall call my lawyer tomorrow and file a law-suit against the town, the golf tournament, and you person-ally for false imprisonment, mental anguish, loss of income, and anything else I can think of. You'll be sorry you ever messed with me, missy."

"I already am. Let's talk about this boat you reluctantly offered as a prize."

He stayed near the door, his arms crossed. "I am a good citizen, and always eager to assist charity fund-raising events. My business buys ads in the high school yearbook every year, and allows the band to hold car washes on the lot. We sponsor fishing tournaments for disadvantaged youth. Last summer we provided free hot dogs at an outing for nursing home residents."

"You were upset when Tommy won the boat. I have sev-eral witnesses who can verify this." Or one.

"They were mistaken," Proodle said.

"They said you were sobbing in your car."

"Are you implying that I killed Tommy Ridner because he won the boat? That's absurd. My loss was minimal. I sold the boat once and made a profit. It depreciated when it was towed off the lot. As it is, I get a hefty deduction for the charitable donation, as well as free publicity. I didn't really care that he won the boat." He stepped in front of me so he could peer down from his pedestal. "Why don't you run along and play somewhere else? I don't have time for this silliness."

"Too busy packing?" I said innocently, gesturing at the open suitcase on the bed.

"I intend to leave tomorrow as soon as possible. I've al-ready had to reschedule the weekly sales meeting because of your petty dictate. Is it your time of the month, Chief Hanks? Are you depressed because of PMS? That's the reason why women should stay home and work off their frustration in the laundry room."

If there'd been a clothes dryer nearby, he'd have found

himself permanently depressed. "I feel the same way about chubby old men with bad toupees," I said with admirable control. I stood up, forcing him to retreat. "There's something special about this particular boat, isn't there? As you said, it's not a serious financial loss. You must have some perverted attachment to it. Heifers and goats rouse all manner of manly passion around here. It's rumored that Raz's sow shares his bed. Oh, and let's not forget Dawson Deever. He tried to marry his Mr. Coffee machine. He was run out of town for being a homosexual. You like to sit in the bass boat at night, Mr. Proodle? Drink a little wine, stroke the leather—"

"How dare you!" he sputtered. "I ought to put you over my knee and paddle you, you hussy! This is slander. I'll see to it that you pay for this!"

"I was just asking." I warned myself that I was giving him an excuse to avoid the question. "Does it have something to do with the boat's original owner? What's his name?"

Proodle yanked a handkerchief out of his pocket and wiped his forehead. "I don't even remember the guy, much less his name. He made the down payment but fell behind on his monthly payments. He was sent a certified letter warning him that he had to catch up or lose the boat. It was perfectly legal. I'm sure he wasn't happy when the boat was repossessed, but it was his own damn fault."

"If you say so. First thing in the morning, the sheriff will get a warrant to paw through your paperwork and find out the owner's name and address. I hope he backs up your story so you won't be charged with impeding an investigation. Judges take a dim view of that."

His forehead was glistening as sweat coated it. "The guy went to prison, okay? He has nothing to do with any of this. You're chasing your tail, Chief Hanks. Why don't you take a harder look at those pissant golfers in your hometown? They're the ones who were so outraged when Ridner won the boat."

"Dennis Gilbert didn't win the boat."

"Maybe they thought he was the most likely candidate to make a hole-in-one tomorrow. Bunch of dumb rednecks. Bony and Natalie better watch their backs, too."

"Nobody's going to waltz off tomorrow with anything more than a recycled trophy," I said. "The boat's been impounded. It'll be covered with cobwebs and mouse droppings before it gets anywhere near a lake."

"You think I don't know that?" he whimpered as he sank down on a corner of the bed. "Go away and leave me alone. I've got more important things to worry about than those murders."

I didn't, but I left anyway. Ruby Bee's car was back in its normal place, and her bedroom light was on. I considered banging on her door, but the idea of listening to even more lies was too much of a burden. As far as I knew, everybody was where he or she was supposed to be, at least for the evening. Natalie was out of Dilaudid, so presumably Janna was safe. Kale was standing at the far end of the building, smoking a cigarette (or something else). His mother was apt to be inside, darning his socks.

I headed for the PD to work on my theory.

Sixteen

The next morning I opened my eyes cautiously. My alarm clock had not yet startled me out of a dream. The sun shone through my dusty window, and sparrows chattered at Roy's bird feeder. Not a blessed soul was standing over my bed, griping, whining, or demanding answers—or reporting yet another missing person. I could hear the faint drone of an airplane in the great blue yonder, carrying the more fortunate to sanctuaries free of rednecks, mutants, and murderous golfers.

After the standard morning rituals, I walked over to Ruby Bee's and sat down at the bar. The only occupants were truckers, strays, and the man in the back booth. I was eating a warm blueberry muffin when the proprietress emerged from the kitchen with plates in each hand. She pretended not to notice me as she went over to a booth.

When she came back, I smiled and said, "Oatmeal and milk, please."

Ruby Bee was unnerved, no doubt having prepared herself to be peppered with questions about her AWOL status the previous evening. "Is that all? Doncha want scrambled eggs and ham with redeye gravy? Are you feeling sickly?"

I held up a hand before she could whip out a thermometer. "I need to get over to the PD. I assume you heard that the golf tournament's final round starts at ten. There is a light at the end of the tunnel, but there are a couple of corpses on the tracks."

"That Coulter woman told me when she came in for coffee as soon as I opened. I haven't seen any of the others yet. I expect all of them to drag in pretty soon. Oatmeal, coming up. You want a couple of muffins to take with you?"

I shook my head and turned around to gaze at the scattered customers. No one bothered to gaze back. After I finished eating, I gave Ruby Bee a little wave and went to the PD. I looked over my notes, sighed, and called Harve at home.

"Hope you got some good news for a change," he said.

"Maybe," I said. "Is Les at the Farberville PD?"

"No, he's back at the office, and I'm on my way there. The fire didn't damage the front rooms. The quorum court has an emergency fund, and they coughed up enough to clean up the foam and spray air freshener. The inmates have been dispersed to other jails."

"You find the third inmate?"

"Not yet, but we will. The dumb shit'll be wearing the orange jumpsuit. The only rehabilitation for some of these fellows is a brain transplant."

"Your job's safe," I said. I brought him up to date on what I'd learned (and what I'd hadn't), my theories, and my conspicuous lack of proof. He failed to sympathize or offer any advice, so I hung up.

Les was more helpful. He agreed to send a team to the warehouse where the bass boat rested on its trailer, and promised to call the Jackson courthouse at nine. After some searching, he came up with the telephone number of the Yazoo City nursing home where Mrs. Rosalie Wicket, purported owner of a Chrysler Imperial Crown Coupe, resided.

I dialed the number and rocked back, bracing myself to deal with a frigid bureaucrat armed with government rules and regulations concerning privacy.

"Good morning, Sunset Valley Manor. May I be of help to

you?" The woman's voice dripped with molasses, although considering the locale, it might have been Spanish moss.

I explained who I was and asked for information concerning Mrs. Wicket. "Whatever you're allowed to tell me," I added.

"Why, honey, I'm just glad to know somebody still cares about that sweet lady. Miss Rosalie's been here since God made little green apples. Her kinfolk used to come visit, but they died or moved away."

"Could I speak to her?"

"All you want, but she won't have a clue who you are or what you're asking. She's in her happy place, cuddling her pillow like it was a baby. Yesterday she thought I was her sister and we were getting ready for cotillion. Better than last week, when she thought I was her mother. I ain't near that old." The woman laughed.

"Do you know anything about these kinfolk who moved away?" I asked.

"Lemme think. One of her brothers died in World War I, and the other one moved north during the Depression. Her sister married a preacher man. After he died, she came back with her children and lived with Miss Rosalie. Miss Lucy died a good thirty years ago. Miss Rosalie's babies died as infants, so she was real partial to her nieces and her nephew. The nieces never married and are buried side by side in the family plot. I don't recollect what happened to the nephew. There were some cousins from Hattiesburg, but we ain't seen them in a coon's age. When you get to be Miss Rosalie's age, you discover that you've outlived your generation."

"How long have you worked at Sunset Valley Manor?"

"Thirty years, give or take. My family lived across the street from the Wickets. Miss Rosalie was always good for a cookie and a glass of cold lemonade on a hot afternoon. Hold on a minute." She muffled her receiver and spoke to someone. When she came back on the line, she said, "It's been real nice talking with you. Yesterday during visiting hours, someone snuck a bottle of scotch to Epiphany T. Jones. He's hollering at the top of his lungs. You have a nice day, honey."

I'd hoped to ask her more about the nephew, but I didn't need to. My theory about how Frederick acquired the Imperial Crown Coupe made sense, although I didn't know if Miss Rosalie had given it to him or he had simply taken it. He could renew the license plate every year on a Web site. He'd mentioned that his family had moved around a lot while he was a child. He could have been born in a different state, I supposed, but that meant he'd lied. It was challenging to come up with an explanation, especially when the truth was liable to be innocuous, as was his alibi for Saturday night.

I couldn't construct a motive for him to have killed Tommy. No one seemed to have a motive to kill Dennis—unless he had seen someone attack Tommy. If he had, then why hadn't he told me? And according to Amanda, she and Dennis had returned to their motel room after the stoplight shoot-out.

Kathleen Wasson had been on her own at the significant time, I realized. I had no idea how long it actually took to drive to Tibia and back, or if she'd really gone there. Maybe Kale's sacred blue shirt had been in the bottom of her suitcase. She'd lied to him because she wanted to spy on him. If she was pretending to be meek and drab, she was doing a damn fine job of it. I tried to imagine her face contorted by rage, her teeth bared, her arms wielding the golf club without mercy. She would have had to climb into the boat to attack Tommy, which meant she was packing a stepladder in her trunk. She'd hadn't been at the wake when Dennis staggered out of the room, but she could have seen him go into Tommy's. It was a hard sell, even for me.

I called Les again. Ignoring his groan, I said, "Can you get in touch with the police in Tibia and ask them to check with the Wassons' neighbors? I need to know if anyone saw signs of activity at the house between nine and midnight on Saturday night."

"You sure you don't want me to rustle up a herd of singing cows?"

"Oooh, that'd be cool."

"You were right about the bass boat, by the way. The original buyer was a scumbag who insists on being called 'Da King.' He's doing time at the state prison for drug trafficking. He should be out on parole, but he tried to kill a guard with a broomstick last month. Da King isn't going to regain his throne any time soon."

I rewarded myself with a small smile. "Also, see if anyone knows how long it takes to drive between Tibia and Farberville."

"Did young Kale rush home for a quickie with his girlfriend?"

"You think young Kale has a girlfriend?"

"I'll get right on those singing cows," Les said. "Do you want me to keep on Cartier's birth certificate? The courthouse staff should be arriving soon."

"This is more important. Let me know what you find out." I fiddled with my notes until I could no longer put off the call to McBeen. My stomach began to roil as I dialed the number.

"What?" McBeen barked with his typical charm. "I told you not to call me, Chief Hanks."

"And good morning to you, too," I said. "Did you complete the autopsy on Dennis Gilbert?"

"Don't you think I'd call you if I had?"

"No. You wouldn't call me to tell me my hair was on fire. What about the autopsy on Dennis Gilbert?"

"I've got the preliminary report here somewhere. There were two car wrecks and a suicide over the weekend. Your guy died of blunt force trauma. Low priority, since I'm trying to establish the identity of the passenger in one of the wrecks. Dental records don't help when the guy had no teeth. What's more, he was fried to such a crisp that we can't get a usable print and—"

"The blood work on Dennis Gilbert is all I need. I

certainly wouldn't want to distract you from more important cases."

"Hold your horses. Here it is." He cleared his throat to annoy me. "Blood alcohol was two point one. The Dilaudid . . . hmmm . . . quite impressive. I rarely see a level like this. Occasionally the police bring in a DOA, usually a filthy addict that smells to high heavens."

"Please don't make me drive over there and shake it out of you."

"His level was extremely high, enough to kill him even without the alcohol. He was alive when he was beaten, but most likely comatose. I'd estimate he ingested a dozen pills."

"He was beaten to death while he was unconscious?" I said.

"Definitely a waste of time and energy. Just like this conversation."

I was appalled, but not surprised. Both victims were unable to defend themselves, Tommy because of his alcohol consumption and Dennis because of the overdose of Dilaudid. I was beginning to see the link between their deaths. Seeing, however, was not the same thing as proving. I returned to the issue of the bass boat, which was at the core of everything that had happened. Proodle produced the bomb; Tommy's hole-in-one lit the fuse. The explosion had been fatal.

Estelle dragged Amanda into the barroom and settled her on a stool. "Order whatever you want. Ruby Bee won't charge you on account of you being a widow and all. What's more, I won't say one word about all the long distance calls you made on my telephone last night and this morning. I don't mind living on beans for the rest of the month. Just don't start thinking everybody in the world is as charitable as I am."

"I'm really, really sorry if I ran up your bill," Amanda said meekly. "I couldn't use my cell because there's no signal out here. Once I get settled, I swear that I'll reimburse you."

"Don't forget you used up a tank of gas." Estelle folded her arms on the bar and stared in the mirror. Tendrils of hair were already falling loose from her beehive, and her lipstick was smudged. There'd been no time for her to see to her own personal grooming, not with Amanda sending her to the motel room three times for different outfits and certain cosmetics she'd overlooked the day before. She herself had made less of a fuss on her high school prom night.

"Morning," Ruby Bee said as she came behind the bar. "What do y'all want? I made blueberry muffins earlier, and they're downright tasty."

"Dry toast and black coffee," Amanda said. "I don't want to look like a black blimp at the funeral."

"You've made the arrangements?"

"As best I can. Nothing can be finalized until Dennis's body is released." She grabbed a napkin from the dispenser and held it to the corner of one eye. "I'm thinking I'll host a memorial reception at the club for him and Tommy at the same time. I hope the committee will let me scatter their ashes on the course, or at least in a water hazard." She buried her face in her hands and began to sob.

Estelle snorted. "You didn't sound all broken up when you talked to that lawyer this morning. For a minute, I thought you were applying for a loan to buy a new car."

Amanda looked up. "This was so unexpected that I'm in a financial pickle until the will is probated. There's not much in the checking account, and I can't cash Dennis's paycheck without the station's approval. My credit cards are maxed out. The lawyer's going to call the bank and arrange for a short-term loan until the insurance company comes through. That could take months. In the meantime, I've got utility bills, club membership dues, my personal trainer . . ."

"You might need to get a job," Ruby Bee said ruthlessly.

Amanda grabbed a fistful of napkins. "What would my friends think? I'd rather die than be caught behind a counter selling perfume. I have no secretarial skills, no computer training. I can't expect the TV station to hire me out of pity. I'm not about to end up in a menial pink-collar job."

Estelle glanced at her, then said, "I'll have sausage and eggs, grits, hash browns, and one of your blueberry muffins."

"Coming right up," Ruby Bee said.

I needed a script that might provoke my suspects into indiscreet admissions. The golf tournament tent would have to serve as my drawing room. Frederick would be offended if I asked him to play the butler, and Mrs. Jim Bob would throw a hissy fit if I suggested that we sip brandy during my grand denouement. I practiced arching an eyebrow as I pointed an accusatory finger, but my eyebrow refused to participate and my finger quivered. My denouement was doomed to be second-rate.

At ten o'clock, I called the sheriff's office. LaBelle answered crisply, as if she were sitting at the reception desk of a powerful corporation, coordinating calls between foreign dignitaries and high-ranking government officials.

"I thought you were in the throes of post-traumatic stress syndrome," I said. "Bedridden, on oxygen, sipping broth with a compress on your fevered brow."

"State your business."

"For Harve's ears only," I said.

"In regard to what?"

"I'm going to be his secret Santa this Christmas. I want to ask him about his tie collection."

LaBelle paused. "Why doncha call back when you have something significant to report. If you hadn't staged your little golf tournament, Harve would have been here when the fire broke out. I can still feel the terror when the smoke billowed out the door like an evil demon. It's a miracle I didn't faint on the spot. Why, I had the most horrible nightmare Saturday—"

"Please let me speak to Harve before I lose my mind and

stuff cotton balls between my toes," I said. "That would be worse than a nightmare."

She abruptly put me through to Harve. I told him what I intended to do. He guffawed at first, but quieted down as I went into detail. "Bring a couple of deputies with you," I concluded. "The doughnuts will be stale, but the fireworks will not be a disappointment."

"Unless they fizzle out," he said. "Oh, and Les has been doing your busywork. He said to tell you that a neighbor saw Mrs. Wasson arrive at her house around ten o'clock Saturday night. Tibia's about an hour and a half from Farberville. There was something else, but I disremember . . ." A match scritched, followed by a contented sigh. "Now it's coming to me. There ain't no birth certificates for anyone named Cartier in Mississippi. Les said to tell you that you owe him a mai tai, whatever the hell that is."

With two umbrellas and an extra maraschino cherry. I made a necessary notation, stashed my thick pile of yellow papers, and went over to Ruby Bee's Bar & Grill. When I got there, I detoured behind the building and noted that Tommy's battered Mercedes and Amanda's glistening Jaguar were the only two cars parked in front of the units. Everyone else was at the golf tournament, trudging through the untamed rough or trying to fish golf balls out of bottomless puddles. The snakes and mosquitoes would be invigorated from the heavy rain. Homeless hornets would be buzzing angrily. I hoped Mrs. Jim Bob had designated a first aid committee.

I sat in a booth to avoid the necessity of conversation with my mother. The idea of another muffin made me queasy, and my presence seemed to make her queasy as well. The dance floor looked larger than a basketball court. The neon beer signs reflected red and yellow hues on it, as if it were a desert at sunrise. The trucker Bedouins, exhausted after their trek to the oasis, slurped coffee. It was more challenging to cast Estelle in the role of a scrawny belly dancer. One of these days, I reminded myself, my belly would be dancing a jig of its own accord.

I finally forced myself to go up to the bar and sit on a stool near Estelle's roost. "Where's Amanda?" I asked.

"I'm not her babysitter," Estelle answered tartly. "You'd think I was her servant from the way she's been acting. She didn't want coffee, and then she didn't want tea. Her split ends looked like straw. She had to try three different shades of fingernail polish before she was satisfied. She'd just die on the spot if she had to drink tap water. Was she getting a blackhead on the side of her nose? Her white skirt was too white, her blue skirt was too short. Did her shorts make her butt look fat? Yammer, yammer, yammer. She spent more time on the phone than I do in a month of Sundays, and then some. I was ready to—"

"She's at the tournament," Ruby Bee cut in. "She caught a ride with Kathleen Wasson and Kale. She said she might as well work on her tan as hang around Estelle's all day."

"Eating ice cream," the beleaguered hostess said with a snort. "She had me go to the SuperSaver and buy her some with exotic names like Mucho Mocha and Creme de Menthe Parfait. Four dollars for a little bitty carton that ain't more than a couple of spoonfuls."

I wished I had a gallon of each. It was too early for the final round to be anywhere near completed, but I drove up the road and parked behind Mrs. Jim Bob's pink Cadillac. The tables beneath the tent were sparsely occupied. None of the previous day's moochers and spectators had dared to risk another dose of Mrs. Jim Bob's venom. The buffet table was down to an aluminum coffee urn, a stack of cups, and an empty doughnut box. Roy was reading the *Stump County Courier*, a treasure trove of inane articles and photographs of Little League teams. Darla Jean had stacked her shoe boxes and was sitting with a few of the involuntary volunteers from the high school. Proodle was slumped at one table, his hands clasped as if he were lost in prayer. Lottie Estes was armed with a clipboard, but she didn't seem to have anything to do. There were fewer than thirty competitors left, and most of them were already on the course. Joyce, Bopeep, Audley, and one of the college boys were on the first tee.

"How's it going?" I asked Lottie.

"Just fine, thank you. This is the last foursome. Mrs. Jim Bob decided she ought to get an early start so she could be back in time to get ready for the presentation ceremony. I assured her that I was quite capable, since I've taught home ec for more than forty years. When I began, the girls were so polite and eager to learn how to become homemakers, but these days they think that all they have to do is operate a microwave. They don't even know how to make popcorn on a stove."

"Where are the trophies?"

"Brother Verber has them for safekeeping." She glanced at her clipboard. "We changed the time because most of the golfers didn't show up this morning. He'll be here at two o'clock sharp, prepared to say a few words about our worthy cause and the responsibility of good Christians to help the needy."

"No lunch?"

"We are trying to raise money, not squander it. Our budget was not planned to accommodate another free meal. To celebrate the finale, Eula is bringing a sheet cake, and my girls will serve punch made from cranberry juice and ginger ale. One could easily mistake it for pink champagne."

One in a million, maybe. I wandered over to Janna, who was scribbling in a notebook. "Feeling better?" I asked her.

"Yes, thank you. I simply needed to rest. When Natalie returned from her visit with Cora, she was most solicitous. She went to the supermarket and bought a brand of antihistamines guaranteed not to make you drowsy." She added a notation. "I'm revising Natalie's workout schedule. She let her game slip this weekend. I think an additional session in the weight room every day will help. There'll be no more beer or pretzels when we get back."

I left her to it. Amanda was seated in an aluminum lounge chair upwind from the pigsty. In a display of mourning, she wore modest pink shorts and a blouse that covered her midriff. She put down a magazine when I approached.

"Thanks for not getting me in trouble yesterday," she said. "I feel like such an idiot. I guess I just snapped from the stress. If you hadn't been at Tommy's house, I would have watered the furniture and vacuumed the ceilings. I'm not the sort of person who can sit and wait. Please don't think badly of me, Arly."

"Why would I do that? By the way, I'm going to lift the ban on leaving town after the ceremony. I'm sure you're all sick of Maggody by now."

"Well . . . it might be nice to go home. I have so many details to attend to. I have an appointment with my lawyer tomorrow. He's promised to make it all as easy as possible for me."

"I hope he does." I moved on to Darla Jean and her group. "Ready for this to be over with?" I asked them.

"I'm counting down the seconds," Heather said. "At least we had something to do the first day, what with lunch and the supper. Yesterday we got positively drenched hauling everything to car trunks."

"Now we're watching the weeds grow," Billy Dick said with a yawn.

"Mrs. McMay says we have to stay here so we can load the tables and chairs," Darla Jean said morosely.

"And take down the tent," said a boy with blinding braces.

I looked sternly at Billy Dick. "You'd better stick to *watching* the weeds grow. If I catch you in possession of a particular weed, there'll be hell to pay."

He gave me an innocent smile. "I'm in training for football. We take up practice in August, you know. Coach would bench me if I got caught smoking or drinking."

"Billy Dick's been building up his arm muscles by bending his elbow," Heather said, giggling.

"Have not!"

"I saw you Saturday morning," she retorted.

"Have you seen Frederick Cartier this morning?" I asked before the spat escalated. They all shook their heads.

I returned to Lottie's table in time to see Eileen drive a ball in the direction of Humper County. Her ensuing remark might have been enough to get her booted out of the Missionary Society.

"She's determined to win," Lottie said blithely. "They all are. It was so tense around here earlier that I felt as though I should have worn a combat helmet. I'm not sure some of these marriages will survive."

"Because of a boat?"

"It's much more complicated than that, Arly. This town is still living in the era when women didn't have the right to vote. The Nineteenth Amendment was passed almost a hundred years ago."

She was about to continue when we heard a whoop from somewhere on the golf course. Lottie dropped the clipboard and clutched my arm. "Is someone hurt? Has that madman come back? Do something, Arly!"

Janna joined us as a second whoop came from beyond the sprawling brush and oak trees. Birds were frightened into flight. I froze, straining to hear more noise. Elsie McMay hurried to the edge of the tent, the teenagers on her heels.

"Do you think somebody made a hole-in-one?" gasped Darla Jean.

"No shit, Sherlock," Billy Dick said. "That, or they found a nest of rattlesnakes."

Proodle groaned so loudly that we all turned around. "Please, God, let it be rattlesnakes," he said, his eyes turned upward. "Or copperheads, or a wild boar. Maybe a bear. A bear would be good."

"It's unlikely," I said, "that two foursomes simultaneously ran into bears, boars, and snakes." I glanced at Lottie's watch. "At precisely noon."

"What about the killer?" Proodle said as if pleading with me to buy an upscale party barge instead of a used canoe. "You should have caught him, Chief Hanks! He's out there with an ax, slaughtering people hand over foot. What if he comes this way?" When I failed to respond, he bolted for his car and dove across the front seat. His anguished cry lingered in the air.

Everybody else started jabbering at me to do something, anything, save the golfers, protect them from certain death, find the bodies, call for help, organize a posse, etc. When they ran out of suggestions, I said, "Let's wait here, okay? As Lottie told me earlier, these golfers are determined to win. Some of them seem to have gone to extremes."

"Like killing each other?" asked Elsie, her voice trembling.

"Could be," I said, although I didn't believe it.

Not very much, anyway.

Seventeen

Jim Bob was the first to come stumbling down the fairway, swinging a golf club like a sword. "I did it! I did it! I god-damn did it!" He tripped over a rough spot, scrabbled to his feet, and resumed his triumphant charge with a clump of mud on his chin.

"Did what?" Billy Dick said.

Heather punched his arm. "Made a hole-in-one, you mo-ron!"

"Him?" Janna said. "Is this for real?"

He stumbled into a table and sprawled in front of us. "I made a hole-in-one!" he gasped. He grabbed Lottie's ankle. "Write it down!"

"Wait just a minute!" yelled Mrs. Jim Bob, approaching briskly with a driver in one hand and her purse in the other. She saw Jim Bob, who was bent over, gasping. "Did I hear him a few minutes ago? Is he in need of medical assistance?"

"I made a hole-in-one," he grunted.

"Don't be ridiculous." Her hand tightened around the club. "I made a hole-in-one at precisely noon. He's drunk. You may record it, Lottie."

"I made mine first—at eleven fifty-nine!" Jim Bob said. He was so agitated that his face resembled a puffer fish. Not an appetizing sight.

"I made mine at eleven fifty-eight!" Mrs. Jim Bob countered. "Mine was first, so I win the bass boat!" She looked more like a great white shark.

"No way!" he snarled. "I win the bass boat!"

"Nobody wins the blasted boat!" Proodle said as he pushed his way through the crowd. "Don't you morons know the boat's impounded? Do I need to define the word for you? It's in a pound surrounded by a chain-link fence and barb wire."

The remainder of the golfers picked their way through various botanical entanglements and approached. The college boys were joking and shoving each other, apparently handling their disappointment well. Natalie kept her face lowered as she joined the increasingly rowdy group. Jim Bob and Mrs. Jim Bob continued to shout at each other, and at Lottie, who was hanging on to the clipboard for dear life. Proodle tried to drown them out by shouting the word "impounded" at them as if it were his mantra. The men had dark expressions as they came out from behind a line of scrub oaks. Audley, Eileen, Cora, and the other wives looked as though their soufflés had sunk. They all felt the need to voice their opinions at the top of their lungs.

I watched at a safe distance. As long as the violence kept to bloody noses and black eyes, I wasn't about to jump in. It was getting tedious when Lottie climbed onto a table and blew a whistle loudly enough to set dogs howling in Tibia.

"Your attention, please!" she said. "We are not going to get this settled by behaving in an uncivilized manner. We will allow each claimant to make his or her case. Arly and I will then consult with the hole monitors to verify the details."

"Why her?" demanded Jim Bob.

Lottie regarded him through her bifocals. "Because she is an unbiased party."

"Unbiased, my ass."

"That's a violation of the obscenity rule!" Mrs. Jim Bob said as she shoved him aside. "He received two warnings on

Saturday. The rules on the registration form make it clear that a third violation results in expulsion. He cannot win the boat."

He stuck his face in hers. "I already won the boat when I made the hole-in-one fifteen minutes ago. Whatever happens now don't count for squat."

"The boat's been impounded," Proodle added for good measure. "Nobody can win the boat!"

"Stuff it!" Earl roared at him. "The boat ain't gonna be impounded forever. Jim Bob won fair and square." His tontine cohorts all nodded.

"The Missionary Society claims title to the boat," Crystal said. "It's going to pay for a memorial park to benefit the community."

Mrs. Jim Bob moistened her lips. "A generous share of the profit from the sale, that is. This tournament is meant to raise money for golf widows, not to give certain parties an excuse to loll about in the middle of a lake. We cannot have menfolk missing Sunday morning services out of sloth. Sloth is a deadly sin, as we all know."

"A sloth is also a mammal that hangs upside-down in trees," Roy said. "I don't reckon it's deadly, though. Just slow and lazy."

"Precisely!" Mrs. Jim Bob said.

Lottie blew her whistle again. "I want everyone to sit down right this minute and be quiet. We will mind our manners and watch our language." They must have feared after-school detention, because they did as ordered. "Now then, we shall wait for the hole monitors to return. No talking, understood?"

I held up my hand. When she nodded at me, I said, "As long as we're waiting, there are a few things I'd like to clear up. Let's begin with the bass boat. Not only is it a fancy and very expensive toy, it's also responsible for two deaths."

"Boats don't kill people," one of the college boys said. "Golf clubs do."

I glared at him. "Take your buddies and leave before I think of something to charge you with. Public drunkenness comes to mind."

He gave me a look of disbelief. Rather than mention that public drunkenness was epidemic, he and the other two boys trudged up the slope. Seconds later, they drove off. I spotted Raz on his porch, cradling a shotgun. Just what I needed.

"No," I continued, "boats don't kill people, as a rule. This boat is different. This boat is very, very valuable. It's a whole lot more valuable than it was the day Proodle sold it to a man who calls himself Da King, who's currently serving time at the state prison."

"No, he's not," Proodle said, then stopped.

"Did you think he was threatening you on the phone?" I asked. "He wasn't, unless you were accepting collect calls from the Cummins Unit. Whoever it was really had you scared. What was it: broken kneecaps, pulverized organs, decapitation?"

"Worse," Proodle said. "But it had to be this King man. He spoke in a hoarse whisper, like a knife scraping sandpaper. He called two weeks ago and demanded that I return his boat. He knew I'd repossessed it and put it on the lot for sale."

I held up my finger. "Or he told someone about it. A fellow inmate, for instance. The only person here who's done prison time in this state is Luke. Did you happen to run across Da King while you were chopping cotton?"

Luke shrugged. "Yeah. Everybody there knew he was furious about losing the boat. It's all he ever talked about. I was damn glad I had nothing to do with it. He's one mean dude."

"Do you know why he cared so much?" I asked.

"Not really. It was expensive, but he was a heavy-duty drug trafficker. Before he got caught, he was pulling in several grand a week. He had a real thing about it, though. I finally got sick of listening to him and pointed out he could afford to replace it. He damn near scalped me with his teeth."

"He must have named the boat for his sweetheart," Elsie contributed brightly.

"I don't think so," I said. "He bought the boat not only for status, but also as a safe deposit box. The crime squad found a box welded under the deck, way at the front end of the boat. The box contained twenty kilos of cocaine, estimated street value of more than half a million dollars."

"Half a million dollars?" Jim Bob gurgled.

"It doesn't come with the boat," I said.

Proodle's mouth fell open and his eyes bulged like marbles. "In the Ranger? I can't believe it. Don't go thinking I knew anything about that, missy. The boys cleaned it up and put it back on the lot. I never touched it." He stood up and began to back away. "Luke knew. That's why he pretended to be King and made the calls. Last night he said he was gonna feed my liver to the geese in the park!"

"Wait just a friggin' minute!" Luke sputtered. "I've never called you. It must have been somebody in Da King's organization. I wouldn't know what to do with a kilo of cocaine if it fell on my head. And I'm afraid of geese, on account of being attacked when I was a kid."

I gestured at Proodle to sit down. "I don't think Luke made the calls. It would have been in his best interest to lie low and wait. He didn't come to Maggody for the boat. You want to elaborate, Luke?"

"I heard about the golf tournament." His attempted smirk was unconvincing, but I gave him points for quick thinking. "I haven't played in years, and I thought it sounded fun. It wasn't like I had anything else to do."

"What about me?" Bopeep squeaked. "You told me that you wanted to move in because I excited you and made you feel like a real man." Her forehead crinkled as she worked on it for a moment. "Reckon that was the day after the local newspaper mentioned the golf tournament. You were using me, weren't you? You slime bag! You want to know the truth? I felt sorry for you 'cause you're a loser. You and your itsy-bitsy prick."

"An itsy-bitsy teeny weenie?" Bony said with exaggerated innocence.

"It is not!" Natalie said, then inhaled sharply. "I mean, that's a cruel thing to say. You shouldn't talk about anybody like that. The Hollywood studs aren't pounding on your trailer door, Bopeep Buchanon or whatever your name is."

"They're the only ones who aren't," Eula said out of the corner of her mouth.

Bopeep curled her fingers. I decided it was time to return to the topic at hand. "Did you tell anybody about Da King's boat, Luke?"

"Her," he muttered, tilting his head in Bopeep's direction.

Proodle's jowls quivered. "You made those threatening calls, you common hussy? You deserve time at a prison. Chief Hanks, arrest her for terrorist threatening!"

"Not yet." I saw Harve and his deputies park behind my car. At least they'd save me from having to transport the perp to Farberville and locate an available cell. Boys with red bandanas on their arms had gathered behind my audience. It was going to be interesting to hear what they had to say about the purported holes-in-one, but it could wait. "I did consider the possibility that Bopeep might have killed Tommy Ridner to make sure Proodle got the boat back. He could then be coerced into handing it over or paying twenty or thirty thousand."

"*She* demanded fifty," Proodle said. "I was supposed to get it tomorrow and wait for instructions. Small, unmarked bills and that nonsense. Why haven't you arrested her?"

"Kiss my ass," Bopeep said in her own defense.

"We're getting there," I said, irritated at all of them. No one had so much as mentioned the two murders that had taken place in the last thirty-six hours. I would never again look at any boat without being repulsed. I made a mental note to tell Jack that a honeymoon cruise was out.

Mrs. Jim Bob had regained her authoritarian demeanor, although she was somewhat stymied. Lottie had the ultimate symbol of power—the clipboard. I watched her assess the potential loss of dignity if she hitched up her skirt to climb onto the table. She opted to stand on the bench. "This is all very interesting, I'm sure. However, the awards presentation is scheduled for two o'clock sharp. Since no one bothered to finish the round, the first place trophy will be awarded to yesterday's winner—Bonaparte Buchanon."

"And the bass boat?" demanded Jim Bob.

"Well, I did make the *first* hole-in-one. Filbert Buchanon was the hole monitor on the twelfth hole and will certify the time of my shot."

Jim Bob growled. "Axle Hammerjack'll certify my time at one minute earlier than your time. Ain't that right, Axle?"

"He most certainly will not," Mrs. Jim Bob said firmly. "Go ahead, Filbert—tell them I made the first hole-in-one. You *do* remember, don't you?"

"Axle," Jim Bob said, "speak up afore I choke it out of you."

Axle was too busy looking for an escape hatch to reply. Filbert was twitching like a palsied frog. Everyone stared at them, and a lot of eyebrows were rising. The average IQ in Maggody doesn't approach triple digits, but most everybody comes in out of the rain eventually. Even Kevin was getting suspicious. Filbert broke first. Howling, he took off down the road past Raz's shack. Axle caught up with him before they disappeared from view.

Lottie handed me her whistle, and I blew it until I had center stage. "No one is going anywhere or doing anything until these murders are cleared up. The boat is just a . . . well, just a boat with half a million dollars' worth of cocaine in its bow. Two men died yesterday, one after midnight and the other early in the afternoon. And on my watch." I took a

deep breath as I looked them over. Did I want to raise a child
in this environment? I'd endured it only because Ruby Bee
wasn't a bigot, a drunk, or a fool. Decidedly in the minority.

"Uh, Arly," Kevin said, "you ain't wearing a watch."

I gave the whistle back to Lottie so I could put my hands
on my hips. "All right, we now know why Proodle was so
upset when Tommy made the hole-in-one. He may have
wanted to kill him, but he's all bluster, no guts. If he'd known
about the cocaine, it wouldn't have been in the boat. The
same goes for Luke, who had plenty of opportunities to re-
move the cocaine the last few nights."

Bopeep wiggled her finger at Luke. "What if he tried last
night, and Tommy caught him in the act?"

"Tommy was too drunk to do anything," I said. "Whoever wanted to get to the cocaine might have had to wait for
a few minutes, until Tommy staggered away or passed out.
There was no reason to kill him. I believe nobody in town
knew about the cocaine, with the exception of the gentleman
from the DEA." I gestured at the man who'd been haunting
Ruby Bee's. "He wanted to see if Da King had tipped off a
supplier."

"Then no one here had anything to do with it," Mrs. Jim
Bob said. "Now that we've settled that, I think it's time to—"

"It's time to consider other motives for the two murders,"
I continued. "Kathleen Wasson, for example, wanted the
boat because it was worth a lot of money. Kale had a reasonable chance of winning it, once Tommy was out of the picture. Money, bragging rights, publicity—one step closer to a
golf scholarship."

"I can understand why you thought that, Chief Hanks,"
she said in a mild voice. "It crossed my mind while I was
driving to Tibia. It was only when I got home that I realized
Kale had taken his blue shirt out of his suitcase intentionally. He is still my son, and I will defend him, but I'll be
damned if I'm going to put up with his shit any longer." She
spun around and looked him in the eye. "You'd better get a

job if you want to go to college, because I'm not paying for any more golf tournaments. That nice Mr. Thigpen who lives on the corner wants me to go line dancing with him. I need a new wardrobe."

Kale retreated a few inches. "You got it all wrong, Ma. I never touched my shirt. You're the one who screwed up. I had to have it so I could have a second chance to win the boat for you. I swear it."

"Stuff it," she said.

I waited a moment in case she wanted to bawl him out for a while longer. When she looked away, I said, "Since you're in the limelight, Kale, let's discuss your motive. You didn't care all that much about the boat, did you? You cared about Natalie, and well beyond infatuation. Not only couldn't you have her, you had to watch Tommy hugging and caressing her Friday and Saturday night in the barroom. An old guy with a belly, groping her in front of your face. That must have made you angry."

"He didn't deserve her," Kale said, his expression surly. "So what if I was angry? I didn't kill the guy."

"But did you break into his room and trash it?" I asked.

"The door wasn't locked. Anybody could have done it."

"How do you know the door wasn't locked?"

Kale ducked his face, but his ears resembled red rose petals. "Okay, so maybe I went in his room. I only had a couple of minutes before I had to get to my room. I figured my mother could be back anytime after midnight. I kept an eye out for her while we were taking shots at the stoplight, just in case she drove back into town."

"That's why Proodle didn't see you in the back parking lot," I said. "You were already in Tommy's room." I did not mention whom Proodle *had* seen. It would surface at some point, and the ensuing melee would make the Battle of Manassas look like a Labor Day picnic. Janna, Natalie, Luke, Kale, and Bopeep; none of them would back down, and none of them would take prisoners.

"He was a jerk," Kale muttered. "I thought maybe he left his wallet in there."

"It was in the boat," I said. "There was cash in it, so I had to rule out scavengers. I had great hope I could still pin the murders on one of our local citizens, but it wouldn't fly. The wives had flounced home in their petticoats, so they couldn't have known about the stoplight nonsense. As for husbands, they were too drunk to scratch their balls. From what I heard, none of them was capable of crawling to the SuperSaver parking lot. Forget climbing in the boat. They're all wearing the clothes they had on Saturday morning, and nobody's sporting bloodstains. Grease and ketchup stains, yes. The stench of whiskey and beer, sweat, and muck could kill a skunk. Let's hope PETA doesn't hear about this."

Mrs. Jim Bob tapped on her wristwatch. "It's five minutes 'til two."

I gave her enough of a nudge to force her off the bench. "So we come to Natalie and Janna. Janna didn't need money, and she had no idle time to go fishing. She wanted Natalie to win the tournament. Bony was leading the field, but she wasn't worried about him."

"I'm a professional golfer!" Bony said, outraged. "She damn well should have worried about me. I won the Rapid City invitational three years ago, and came in second at the Florida Hideaway Homes tournament. I made the cut in Tucson last summer. I can't remember the number of times I made the cut in Augusta."

"Zero," Janna said.

"Moving right along," I said, "Janna did have a motive. She thought Tommy was fooling around with Natalie, whose reputation was as important as her golf game. Tommy may have been a good guy, but he was the classic loose cannon when he was drinking. Which was often, and in the presence of the media and the inner-circle golfers. Janna thought it was vital to keep Natalie away from Tommy."

"So I killed him to keep his mouth shut?" she countered

skeptically. "And Dennis saw me, right? That's why I killed him." She held out her fists. "Go ahead and handcuff me, Chief Hanks. The sheriff's here. He can take me in, book me, fingerprint me, interrogate me, and throw me in the dungeon. I'll plead not guilty, but the jury will convict me and I'll end up on death row."

"Janna," Natalie said, "don't say anything else. I'll get you a lawyer, and it'll be okay. I know you didn't do it. I'll swear to it on the witness stand."

"You'll make a fine witness," I said, "because you really do know Janna couldn't have killed Tommy. Thanks to you, she was too doped up to walk to the bathroom, much less the SuperSaver."

"I was *what*?" Janna yelped as she grabbed Natalie's wrist. "You doped me up? How dare you, you backwoods slut? After all I've done for you, the sacrifices I've made, the years spent turning you into a semblance of a young lady— you doped me up so you could sneak off and behave like trailer trash?"

"I resent that," Bopeep said.

Eula cackled. "You *resemble* that. How many so-called boyfriends have you had since you moved in? What about the red-bearded guy who used to root through my garbage can at night? Or the fellow who liked to come outside nekkid as the day he was born? Or the one who wore your panties on his head?"

Lottie blew her whistle. I gave her a grateful smile, then stared at Bopeep until she faded into the group. "Although she may have wanted to, Janna didn't kill Tommy. Nor did Luke and Natalie, who were otherwise occupied. We're running out of suspects, aren't we? At this rate, I'll have to confess just for closure."

Amanda came over and perched on the end of the table. "I know where you're going, Arly, so let's get it over. Tommy was Dennis's best friend. He damn near worshipped him for more than thirty years. They were good-natured rivals, not enemies. Dennis was proud when Tommy won a tournament. I'm shocked that you'd accuse a dead man of this horrible crime. Dennis can't defend himself, but I can. If you spout off any more of this, I'll have my lawyer sue you."

I sat down near her. "Dennis killed him. I know it, and so do you." I heard murmurs and grumbles behind me, but I didn't turn my head. "The medical examiner found part of a broken contact lens in the wound. When I talked to him yesterday morning, he had trouble focusing on my face. He must not have brought a spare, because he had to wear sunglasses despite the cloudiness." I had no idea if the sliver of silicone was from a contact lens, but it made as much sense as anything else that had happened in the last few days. If backed into a corner, I could come up with an explanation for a herd of unicorns in Raz's barn.

Amanda bit down on her lip while she considered this. "Dennis did tell me he lost a contact lens on Saturday. He said Tommy tackled him on the thirteenth green. The lens must have gotten tangled in Tommy's hair."

"His crewcut? No, he killed him because of you. The bet wasn't a joke. Tommy took it seriously, didn't he?"

She slipped off the table and blinked indignantly at me. "Of course it was a joke. How could it not be? I'm not a slave."

"If it was a joke, why did Tommy save the napkin that spelled out the details? Why was his wallet searched and then discarded? Why were you in his house yesterday?" I took a folded napkin out of my shirt pocket and held it up so she could see the green border. "Details and signatures, including that of a witness."

She tried to snatch it out of my hand, but I'd anticipated it and moved my hand out of her reach. "Tommy was determined to get his payoff," I said. "Maybe he swore he'd be discreet if you went along with it. Even if he had, Dennis couldn't bear the idea. You were the one thing that he could lord over Tommy. If he couldn't have a tournament trophy, he could have a trophy wife. The idea of Tommy's hands on you, his breath on your face, his sweat on your skin—too much."

"I told them no," Amanda said, "and they knew I meant it."

"Which meant that Dennis would welch on a bet. How long do you think Tommy would have kept that to himself? He was more likely to have the napkin framed so he could hang it in the country club bar. Dennis could say whatever he wanted, but it was the kind of joke that Tommy would keep alive for years. Everyone at the country club would know. So tawdry, so vulgar."

"Tommy started making smart-ass remarks as soon as he made the hole-in-one. Dennis had to endure it all the way to the eighteenth green. And Tommy didn't stop after that. He kept it secret from the others, but he went out of his way to remind Dennis and me every chance he got. When he hit the stoplight, he said it was better than winning the Triple Crown."

"So you went back to the motel room, and Dennis followed Tommy up the road," I prompted her.

"Dennis was beside himself when he finally returned. He felt so horribly guilty about what he'd done, but Tommy refused to back down on the bet. When Tommy started to describe what he planned to do to me, Dennis lost it. He couldn't face telling you. He was going to turn himself in as soon as we got back to Farberville. I tried to talk him out of it, but he was determined. I finally agreed that it was the right thing to do. He was going to plead guilty because of temporary insanity. I'd sell the house and move into an apartment until he was released. After that, we'd move away and make a fresh start."

"And live happily ever after."

"We would have, if someone hadn't killed him," she said, her voice shrill. "Whoever it was ruined everything. I loved my husband, and I was willing to wait for him however long I had to. The judge would have sympathized and sent him to a psychiatric unit. Dennis thought he could write a book about his experience."

I could now hear sniffles behind me. Eula was probably holding a hankie to her nose, while Joyce and Millicent shook their heads sadly. Even the untouchables were likely to be touched by her story. I would have been, too, if it were true.

"You may have discussed all those things," I said. "I'm sure Dennis was tempted to accept the blame. But it kept gnawing at him yesterday. He could barely keep his balance on a very taut tightrope. If he made it across, he faced humiliation and unending guilt. He'd killed his best friend. He couldn't justify it to himself and take the easy way out. No, he had to suffer the consequences. He went into Tommy's room, took a handful of Dilaudid, and lay on the bed. It took you a while to realize where he'd gone, didn't it? If you'd caught up with him after he left the wake, you might have been able to talk him out of suicide. Instead, you went into your room, expecting to find him there. You waited, you paced, you tried to figure out where he could be. It wouldn't have mattered if you'd gone to Tommy's room immediately. Dennis only needed a minute to take the pills. No one could have saved him."

"He looked so goddamn smug!" she said bitterly. "Maybe he thought he'd made peace with his conscience, but what about me? I was going to be the widow of a murderer. Can you imagine how that would look? What's more, I'd be broke. I gave up my job when we got married. The house is mortgaged, and the bank account's empty. Was I supposed to go on welfare and live in a roach-infested tenement? Those places don't have pools and hot tubs, you know. People get shot all the time. I sure as hell wasn't going to live happily ever after in a place like that."

I had a feeling she wasn't going to be booking massages at her future residence. "All you had to do was dispose of the bottle of Dilaudid to make it look like a copycat murder. You'd be the widow of a victim killed by a psychotic killer. And a wealthy widow, as well. Dennis's employer provided life insurance, and I think we'll find a policy signed shortly after your marriage. Is there a suicide clause?"

"I didn't kill him, though," she insisted. "He was already dead. There's probably some tiresome law about mutilating a corpse, but it's a misdemeanor."

"I hate to break it to you, Amanda, but he wasn't dead. All that blood on the wall, the bedspread . . . not postmortem."

"He was dead!" she screamed, lunging at me. "You didn't see him. I jabbed him and slapped him, but he was gone. He was dead. I swear he was already dead."

I shook my head as Harve put a hand on her shoulder and escorted her up to the road. By the time she went to trial, her lawyer would have a forensics expert to testify about the possibility that Dennis was within seconds of death. The jury might take pity on her. The insurance companies would not, however.

"Well, then," Mrs. Jim Bob said, "instead of waiting for Brother Verber, let's get on with the awards ceremony. Girls, fetch the cake and paper plates from my car. Darla Jean, there's a paper tablecloth in that box with the cups. Have Billy Dick help you unfold it and put it on the table. Mr. Proodle, I assume you have the title to the boat."

"No one is getting the boat," I said.

"I told you so," Proodle said. "It's been impounded."

I shook my head. "To be accurate, it's been taken by forfeiture because it contains contraband. It is now the property of the state. This man is an agent from the DEA. They've been after Da King's organization for years. They just had a little trouble locating the cocaine, but once they did, they decided to sit back and see where it went."

He had enough sense not to smile. Jim Bob and Mrs. Jim Bob went at him like buzzards, flapping and cackling. The rest of the husbands and wives eyed each other, aware of how they'd blundered into the criminal world.

I drifted out of the tent area and went to the edge of the woods, still thinking about Tommy, Dennis, and Amanda.

Did everyone have a small demon inside that fed on greed, envy, and lust? I took the green-bordered napkin out of my pocket and unfolded it. The orange juice stain resembled Brazil, sort of. Now that the case was nearly over, I'd have time to drive to Springfield. Suddenly I felt a chill, as if the breeze had turned icy for a brief moment. Dumbfounded, I looked up as a cloud passed in front of the sun.

I finally realized there was shrieking behind me. I turned around, prepared to pry Mrs. Jim Bob's hands off Jim Bob's neck. Or try, anyway. To my bewilderment, a lone figure was riding up on a mule, his face hidden by a ghoulish Halloween mask. He sported a vest made out of aluminum foil, and he peered out from under an upturned saucepan. His weapon of choice appeared to be a bent trophy.

"I am the Horseman of the Apocalypse!" he roared, thumping his chest with the trophy. He started to topple over but caught himself. "I come to fight against Satan's army! Christians, you have nuthin' to fear but fear myself!"

Mrs. Jim Bob froze. "Brother Verber? What in heaven's name are you doing dressed up like that?"

"The devil has casted his net of greed upon y'all, and I am your salvation army!"

"He's drunker'n Cooter Brown," Jim Bob said, sniggering. "Attaboy, Brother Verber. Save us from eternal damnation!"

Brother Verber turned the pot handle to get a better view. "I ain't so sure anybody can save your soul, Jim Bob. Many's the time I told you to drop to your knees and pray for forgiveness!"

"Fuck you!" Jim Bob spat.

"You and the mule you rode in on," called Bony, saluting him with a beer. "Remember how you tried to tan my hide when I stole your wine? You chased me all over hell and high water, but you was too damn drunk to catch me! Wanna try again, preacher?" He put his thumbs in his ears and waggled his fingers.

I had no intention of interfering. Maggody wasn't on the

Broadway touring companies' itinerary, but this promised to provide plenty of entertainment. All I needed was a *Playbill*.

"Just a goddamn minute!" Raz hollered from the porch. "Now I recognize you, Bony Buchanon. You may be kin, but we don't put up with anybody attacking our wimmen. I heard how you tried to put your filthy hands on Dahlia. I reckon I'm gonna chop you into bait afore I throw your sorry ass in the pond!"

"You had the balls to get fresh with my daughter-in-law?" roared Earl, his hands balled into fists. "You ain't a real Buchanon. Your great-grandpappy stole my great-grandpappy's prize mule and hauled him off to Missouri. You're descended from a mule thief, you sorry piece of shit."

Bony backed toward the tee. "I ain't responsible for my great-grandpappy. I'm still a Buchanon, same as you. I din't try anything with Dahlia. She was the one who was flirting with me." He stumbled but managed to stay upright. "What's more, I'm a member of the PGA! Don't that count for anything?"

"Not to me," Jim Bob said as he sidled around the tent. "You got nowhere to run, Bony. Ain't nobody gonna lift a finger to save you."

Kevin came out of shock. "I'm fixin' to break your fingers, one by one. Then I'm gonna start on your ribs." He scrambled over a table, knocking over coffee cups and almost landing in Heather's lap. "How could you do such a horrible thing to my little flower bud? Did you touch her? Did you grab her and hold her down, put your hand across her mouth?"

"Nothing happened," Bony said as he made it to the tee. "Well, she sat on me, but you can ask her if I so much as touched her. She was the one who wanted to—"

"Shut your lyin' mouth," Raz snarled, "and git ready to kiss your ass good-bye." He raised his shotgun and fired into the sky.

Behind us, the side of the barn burst open, flinging slivers of wood like shrapnel. I ducked, then scrambled under a table as a red golf cart came careening across the pigsty. The driver's head was shiny, and his beard streamed over his shoulder like a ratty gray scarf. His orange jumpsuit added a splash of color. "Let's git that sumbitch, Cousin Raz! All the time I was in jail I kept missing the good ol' days when we tarred and feathered peckerheads like him!"

Raz jumped on the back of the cart. "Yahoo, Cousin Fez! We'll skin him alive afore we tar and feather him!"

Bony turned and ran as if his life depended on it, which it did. Raz, Kevin, Jim Bob, Earl, and the other men took off after him. The obscenities were highly creative. I'd underestimated the local vernacular.

Mrs. Jim Bob glared at Brother Verber, whose mouth was hanging open as he tried to figure out what had happened. "Now look what you've done," she said. "I'd planned on a nice, civilized ceremony, with refreshments served afterwards. We can hardly proceed with so many participants scattered all over the golf course."

"Satan's army!" Brother Verber kicked his mule hard enough to propel it into a shambling gallop. "Don't you worry, ladies. General Willard Verber will save you!" He promptly slid off the mule into the mud.

Darla Jean and Heather collapsed in laughter.

So did I.

Eighteen

I was sitting on the bank of Boone Creek, pitching rocks into the water, when Ruby Bee sat down next to me. I acknowledged her presence with a nod.

"You've got every right to be riled at me," she said.

On the far bank, a turtle slid off a log. The recent rain had left the water sluggish and muddy. The sunshine tried to sparkle, but the water seemed to suck it down. "I'm not mad," I said softly. "Not very, anyway."

"I was gonna tell you when you were younger, but I decided there wasn't any reason to burden you with my past." Ruby Bee tentatively patted my knee. "Would it have really made a difference? You turned out just fine, didn't you? Now you're gonna get married and have a baby." She peeked at me. "You *are* gonna get married, aren't you? I mean, you don't have to. Estelle and me will be here to help out. One of us can babysit so you can keep your job."

"Frederick Cartier was arrested this morning outside of Amarillo. He had Mrs. Jim Bob's silver in his trunk and the contents of the tournament bank account in his pocket. The state troopers were frustrated because he didn't have any valid identification. They found a tournament flyer in his car and called me. I told them what I knew, but it wasn't much."

"Fred Carter's his name," Ruby Bee said. "Or that's what he was calling himself thirty-odd years ago."

"When you met him," I said flatly.

"I was nineteen, and it was my first time away from home. I took the bus to Hot Springs to stay with my aunt and uncle, and my cousin Annabel. I'd never seen such a fine city before. All these big, fancy bathhouses, the hot springs bubbling out of the ground, restaurants and cafés on every corner—and the racetrack. Annabel took me one afternoon. The only horses I'd ever seen were sad old things pulling wagons of hay. The racehorses were sleek and high-spirited. Annabel knew how to sneak into the fancy club, and that's where I met Fred. He was with some of his friends, drinking cocktails and betting on the races. I felt like I was in a movie." She sighed. "Annabel told her parents we were helping with a church bazaar, so we could meet Fred and his friends almost every day at the racetrack."

"You obviously met elsewhere, too."

Her shoulders sagged as I looked at her, and her voice tightened. "Only one time. Fred won a lot of money that afternoon and insisted on taking all of us out to dinner at a snooty restaurant. He ordered bottle after bottle of French wine. We lingered for a long time, thinking we were the wittiest people in the whole world. When the waiters shooed us out, we went to a nightclub and danced. Somehow, we ended up parked by a lake. The stars were as bright as I'd ever seen them."

"You had sex in the backseat," I said, trying to hide a small shiver as I remembered the feel of the leather. There are some details that offspring never need to hear. "And you got pregnant. Did you tell him?"

"I didn't find out until I was back home. He'd given me an address, but the letters I sent him were returned. Annabel confronted him at the racetrack, and he told her that he was already married. She said he felt real bad about not having told me and promised to write. He never did. Annabel found out later that he wasn't married after all, but by then he was long gone."

"You told everybody you were married to a man named Hanks."

"It's a family name on my paternal side. My mother made me change my name to back up the story. She even convinced herself it was true. Right up until she died, she'd ask how my husband was getting along out in Texas."

"You recognized him right off the bat, didn't you?" I leaned back against the hickory tree and looked up at the leaves, struggling not to judge her. "You could have told me then."

"He was real careful not to come into the bar. His car looked familiar, but I figured I was crazy. Lord knows I hadn't thought about him for years, up until you were in the same situation I'd been. Not that you'd been abandoned by a scoundrel or anything like that. I mean single and pregnant."

"You didn't mention his car."

"Well, I wasn't sure it was his until you mentioned the name. Fred was a right slick liar from the day I met him. He and I had a long talk Sunday night, parked by the low-water bridge. He had all sorts of excuses for acting the way he did. I'd be surprised if there was more than a grain of truth in any of them. He finally admitted that he came to Maggody in hopes of meeting you. He wanted to tell you that he's your father. I told him that was his decision, not mine."

"He met me," I said. "I kind of liked him, even though I knew he was lying to me all along. He couldn't offer his alibi for Friday night because he was with some old friends. One of them might have blurted out his name."

She wiggled into a more comfortable position. "I have to say I'm glad he didn't murder Tommy or Dennis. At the worst, he's a con man and a liar."

"Dear old Dad," I murmured. I remembered thinking there was something familiar about him. There was; I saw it in the mirror every day.

We sat in silence for a long while. I figured Ruby Bee was thinking about those giddy times in Hot Springs. I decided to send the information about Fred Carter, alias Frederick Cartier, to the Amarillo authorities and then let it go. As Ruby Bee said, I'd turned out okay. So had she.

"I had a call from Jack's sister last night," I said.

Ruby Bee beamed as she grabbed my hand. "Is she planning the wedding? I'm not one to meddle, but you deserve the wedding I never had. His children will make right cute attendants. His daughter can sprinkle flower petals on the path, and his son can be the ring bearer. Did you choose your colors? I always fancied blue and white. As the mother of the bride, I can wear lavender. It goes right nice with blue. If you don't get going soon, it's gonna have to be baby blue."

"He'll be home in plenty of time," I went on, aware that she wasn't listening. "She talked to an assistant director who was in Belém to pick up supplies. Everybody's fine."

"Estelle says she can rent a gazebo, so you can get married in her backyard, but I don't want to be distracted by mosquitoes when you say your vows. I wish the bar and grill was fancier . . ."

I gave her a hug. "It'll be perfect."